DreamStorm

DreamStorm
Book 4 of The Dreamhealers Saga

M. C. A. Hogarth

mcahogarth.org

DreamStorm
Book 4 of The Dreamhealers Saga
First edition, copyright 2018 by M.C.A. Hogarth

M. Hogarth
PMB 109
4522 West Village Dr.
Tampa, FL 33624

ISBN-13: 978-1987677867
ISBN-10: 1987677862

Cover art by MCA Hogarth

Designed & typeset by Catspaw DTP Services
http://www.catspawdtp.com/

Be careful how you interpret the world: It is like that.
—Erich Heller

By the grace of God above
I'll shine the light 'cause I am loved
—Adam Young, "My Everything"

TABLE OF CONTENTS

CHAPTER 1

SAY AGAIN?" JAHIR SAID, but the spring that bloomed in the mindline made it clear he'd heard Vasiht'h clearly. It was that flush of happiness that inspired Vasiht'h to repeat himself, for the pleasure it gave them both.

"Luci would like to know if we'd be willing to attend her wedding." Vasiht'h spread the invitation. "She's having it on Seersana, in the university's religious row, believe it or not."

Jahir set aside his own tablet, cupping his mug in long fingers. "Is she? I wonder why. Did she say?"

"No, so we'll have to ask when we get there." Vasiht'h glanced at him. "We are going, aren't we?"

"Oh, we must."

Vasiht'h grinned down at the invitation. It was spare, completely in keeping with Lucrezia's personality . . . which had been atypical for homeworld Harat-Shariin, but perfectly suitable for a colony-bred pard who'd had non-standard desires. "We've got a month before we have to show. That gives us plenty of time to move our schedule around."

"And find a gift?" The mindline carried a flavor, like that anise liqueur they'd tried once and found so puzzling. "Is that customary?"

"I . . . don't know, actually." Vasiht'h thumbed down, looking for details. "I think the homeworld ceremony involves the family giving the guests gifts, but Luci might be doing something differently. Let's see . . . ah, here we go. 'Gifts welcome but not necessary,' it says. And 'Donations to genetic research foundations suggested.' Maybe that means she's marrying a non-Harat-Shar?"

"Or perhaps it is a cause her work brought her into contact with."

"Or that." Vasiht'h laughed. "Goddess, I can't wait to ask her."

"And to see the university again?"

"And that." Vasiht'h set the tablet down. "Do you want to, too?"

The Eldritch considered, looking down at the steam rising off the mug. "It was a good place for us both."

Was that humility? Reserve? Or something else? Vasiht'h could appreciate the Eldritch's pauses, but they were never simple. Nothing about an Eldritch was simple. "It was."

"Why then would I not wish to?"

The mindline wasn't suggesting anything; it remained washed with Jahir's sunlit gladness at the news of Luci's forthcoming nuptials. Probing was probably a bad idea, but Vasiht'h couldn't help trying, just a little. "I don't know. Going backwards maybe? It's been five years. Longer than that, a little. We've moved on." He paused, trying not to wince as he really listened to that. Saying that five years was long for a Glaseah would only compound the error. Or hastening to say that time was relative, and five years could be a long time? Goddess, there was no fixing this particular blunder . . .

Gently, Jahir said, "We never leave behind those things that form us. And as I am grateful for the events that shaped my life on Seersana, I would be pleased to return."

Vasiht'h sighed, smiled. "You always know just what to say."

"Not always," the Eldritch said, "But sometimes. Sometimes."

⸙

Five years *was* a long time, though. Vasiht'h reflected on it later as he shopped for the wedding, jogging through the Commons of Starbase Veta. The two of them had arrived on the starbase straight into a probationary period, during which they'd been forced to prove their worth to the community . . . or rather, Vasiht'h had, because the starbase's administrators had been more than willing to extend their hospitality to a member of the Alliance's most mysterious allied species. It was that Eldritch's mundane partner they'd had problems with. They hadn't been the only ones either, because at least two of the therapists who oversaw Veta's populace had been skeptical of their method- ologies. Six months hadn't been long enough to convince those two of the merits of esper dream therapy, but it had been long enough to make the most strident of their detractors decide to give them a chance.

And that had been five years ago. Now Vasiht'h couldn't imagine living anywhere else. Their practice was so busy that they had to turn away patients, and their ties to the medical com- munity were robust enough that they had a network of special- ists and peers they could refer cases to when they couldn't handle them. They had friends, too—people they could have dinner with, meet for coffee, turn to for help—though they didn't need to socialize nearly as much as Vasiht'h had assumed.

Having a mindline was . . . better than any partnership Vasiht'h had ever dreamed. More satisfying, in the same way his relationship with the Goddess was. To know there was someone who'd always be there for him, who would always love him. . . .

Vasiht'h caught his expression in one of the windows and made a face. His sister would have teased him endlessly about his syrupy eyes if she'd seen it. But he couldn't help it, for the same reason he now had a virtual bookshelf with several handfuls of romances by an immensely effervescent author who'd driven him crazy with her first book.

He loved an Eldritch, who loved him back. It was the most wonderful thing in the world.

Which wasn't to say they didn't have their troubles, because all relationships did. But that was all right. They would manage.

Vasiht'h stopped outside a shop specializing in local produce and wrinkled his nose. Maybe Luci would like wine from one of the starbase vineyards? Some of it was good, though he could tell through the mindline, sampling it across his partner's palate, that it wasn't superlative wine. Maybe unavoidably, given the closed ecosystem. But Luci would probably cut fruit into it anyway, so did it have to be perfect? He tried to remember if the pard liked chocolate, and if so, what color, and kept walking.

Five years. Did Jahir love their life as much as he did? Was uncertainty behind that tiny pause? Regret? Or was he reading too much into it?

Thinking of what he knew of the Eldritch, Vasiht'h sighed ruefully. No, more likely he wasn't reading *enough*.

—————∽∾∽—————

Jahir found it entirely appropriate that the day brought correspondence from mother, who was currently in the Seni Galare apartments in the capital for the Summer Court. Like all her letters, it had been handwritten and then digitized for its journey across the Alliance, because sending the physical object would have been expensive and ill-advised, given the Eldritch dedication to the Veil. Jahir himself couldn't have navigated back, had he been pressed to: the Queen's dedicated courier service handled all the passengers going to and from the Eldritch homeworld, none of whom were permitted onto the bridges of their specialized ships. What few passengers there were. Jahir was probably the most recent of those emigrants, and he could have named only two or three others who'd gone before him in his lifetime, that he knew of.

The Eldritch went to the summer court to negotiate alliances and ensure allegiances between families, so his mother's observations of those activities formed the bulk of her letter.

. . . your brother, of course, is not interested in marrying. My refusal to betroth either of you in the cradle remains a subject of gossip, but pay it no mind, my love. I know you will choose wisely when you do,

and your brother with you. In the mean, it does no harm and a great deal of good to be here, even without children to settle. The Queen is strengthened by every partisan who arrives to the court. Her enemies remain committed to cutting off what little congress we maintain with the Alliance . . . as if we have so much already! Any less contact and we will be well and truly isolated, and what good will that do any of us, I ask you?

You know yourself, my son, how much we have to learn from the other and the alien. Your letters have been a delight to me. I am so pleased to hear that you are spending your time away profitably, and look forward to the day I might make the acquaintance of your off-world associates, particularly your partner. Do you take good care of him, for such gems come infrequently into a life.

Jahir smiled fondly at the words. Few, seeing his mother, would think her such an iconoclast, but under the demure demeanor and perfect mask she was as fiercely devoted to the stars as the sons she'd reared. How had she done it, he wondered? How had she imparted that love? Or had it been solely that she had refused to stand in the way of it?

The events on his world concerned him, but they always had. Given the glacial speed at which the Eldritch initiated change, he doubted anything would disturb the status quo for the decades he planned to be away. He would return before anything erupted, surely, and help his mother and the Queen who'd been so generous in funding his visit to the Alliance.

He set to his response to her letter, and unlike her wrote it on the data tablet directly, though it recorded his handwriting faithfully. Sealing it and sending it left him free to sort through the remainder of his mail, but none of it required an immediate response. Strange to have so much of it; leaving a public tag out had required a great deal of work, given how assiduously the censors installed by the treaty erased all evidence of his existence online. He'd had to prevail on a client for help, writing a tag he could access without inspiring an alert that he'd touched it. Once she'd managed that feat, he'd asked her to begin on more delicate tasks; her acquiescence was responsible for what little ability he had to maintain records in the Alliance.

Now that he thought of it, that former client had been one of their patients from their practicum on Seersana.

Jahir set the tablet down and went to the kitchen to start on a simple soup. Vasiht'h was shopping—only partially out of agitation, he judged, but it would harm nothing for his partner to return to a meal. He loved Vasiht'h, more than he could adequately describe, with a quiet certitude that he would never have imagined possible for a mortal relationship. Vasiht'h was family. But of the two of them, the Glaseah was far more apt to find anxieties in everyday circumstances. It was clear to Jahir that Vasiht'h was worried about whether Jahir was . . . contented? With what they had? And that this had come to mind because their return to Seersana would recall the circumstances that saw them graduate there, and Jahir's choice to go clinical rather than medical.

Jahir suspected his partner still worried that the Eldritch regretted that choice. But no amount of protestation on his part would convince Vasiht'h otherwise. Perhaps because some part of him did regret it. Not actively, in a way that would corrode his contentment with what he had. Regrets could be that way: something that gave contrast to the present and its excellences. It was the regrets that demanded action, that bled like wounds, that cut up one's peace.

These kinds of regret should have separate names, he thought as he set to slicing mushrooms. It would make the situation easier to explain, because the mindline would reveal those shadows, as certainly as breathing. That it would also reveal Jahir's acceptance of them wouldn't matter, because Vasiht'h would have opinions about those regrets, opinions that would be more real to him than Jahir's. No mindline, no matter how storied, changed that part of humanoid nature. Jahir smiled, thinking of his early experiences with Vasiht'h, and his naïve belief that being able to hear another's thoughts, sense each other's feelings, would make communication easier. What it did was make it more complex.

He would have it no other way. Life complicated people, gave them a texture, endowed their souls with a richness. That he could experience this directly with his partner was, he believed, a blessing.

Clear soup, he thought. It would inspire the Glaseah to make something to accompany it . . . and a Glaseah in a kitchen was, he had learned, a calmer Glaseah.

The mindline warned him of his partner's approach long before Vasiht'h reached the door. By the time the Glaseah peered inside their apartment, the soup was simmering and Jahir was looking through their spice cabinet. Before Vasiht'h could speak, the Eldritch said, "Why do we have nine varieties of peppercorn?"

"Instead of sixteen or seventeen or forty?" Vasiht'h put his bags on the counter, the mindline surging with a champagne-foam amusement. "Because I haven't had the chance to buy them all yet."

"Which of these embarrassment of riches do I want for this application?" Jahir asked.

Vasiht'h padded into the kitchen behind him and leaned over the pot, sniffing. "Winter soup? Mmm. Um. The gold ones, from Asanao."

Jahir brushed the vials aside until he found the correct one. It still amazed him, the technology in even the most innocuous of the Alliance's devices. These vials that maintained an internal environment so that the spices in them never lost their freshness . . . how had they been manufactured? He couldn't even imagine their price. No doubt here they cost almost nothing because of the economic infrastructure that backed their creation. But it still felt like magic. "Here."

Vasiht'h picked up the vial from the counter, absent. "This needs . . . bread? Rice? Hmm. Something solid to chew."

"There is duck in the soup?"

The Glaseah wrinkled his nose, sniffing. "So there is. Good choice. You haven't gotten too far with it . . . let's thicken it up and pour it over rice. It'll make a nice base for a sauce."

"Very good. Shall I prepare anything else?"

"More vegetables. There's some in the grocery bag."

Obediently Jahir went into it. "Did you find something for Lucrezia?"

"Not yet, but you know. We have time."

"So we do," Jahir said, and ignored the suspicious tickle in the mindline. He concentrated on his belief in it, willing the Glaseah to accept it.

Vasiht'h chuckled a little. "All right. Message received."

For now, anyway. Jahir wondered how this particular anxiety would develop, if it would. And he would not have wagered on it remaining quiescent. He suppressed his sigh, tempered it with fondness, and ignored the glance the Glaseah threw at him. "Shall we go early?"

"Hmm?"

"To Seersana," Jahir said. "We have many friends there. It would be pleasing to have time to visit."

Vasiht'h tapped the ladle on the pot. "It would, yes. How long?"

"Is a week too little?"

"It's longer than I was thinking!" The Glaseah chuckled. "But yes. I'd like that."

"Then we have work to do after dinner, with our client schedules."

"And I'll have to shop faster," Vasiht'h said.

"Woe," Jahir said, smiling. "Such hardship."

"We do have it good, don't we."

Chopping the broccoli, Jahir said, "Do you not forget it, arii."

CHAPTER 2

V ASIHT'H COULDN'T DESCRIBE how weird it was to walk through campus in the middle of spring, watching the bustle of students, and not be part of it. He didn't feel old enough or different enough to be looking down on them from some rarified height of experience, so it seemed unnatural not to be joining the stream of people on their way to classes. But then . . . he'd spent almost ten years here, between his undergraduate and graduate years. Maybe this disorientation was normal?

Consulting Jahir would probably not be useful. For either of them. You didn't ask the alien friend with ten times your lifespan if it was strange to feel out of place in a place you shouldn't because you hadn't marked the time passing.

And yet: "I feel it also."

Vasiht'h glanced up at the Eldritch. The weather was cool enough that his friend was wearing a high collar and a light scarf, but the sunlight invested Jahir's face with a warm glow that worked well with his honey-yellow eyes. He looked happy, which in an Eldritch meant a slight curve of the mouth and a faint upward bow of his lower eyelids. It was only under that, in the mindline, that Vasiht'h sensed the faint bittersweet taste of nostalgia, like hibiscus tea. Not bad, just . . . yes. Whatever that was.

"I should have known you would," Vasiht'h said, smiling. "So where first? We're early. No one's expecting us for an hour. Gelato?"

Jahir did smile then, more obviously, and a twinkling merriment scattered the mindline with glitter. "Tea and Cinnamon. There will be time enough for gelato."

That's where they had lunch, then, and it was a good choice: Tea and Cinnamon was a café in the middle of campus, next to the student center, and from their table by the window they had a fine vantage. It was the middle of up-week a month after midterms, and there were a gratifying number of people going about the business of learning.

"Strange that it looks less cosmopolitan now that we've been living on Veta so long," Vasiht'h observed. "Back when I first moved here, it felt really urban."

"It is urban," Jahir answered over his cup of coffee. "There are more people in this one university than in some cities on this planet, much less on other, less populous ones. But we have been residing in a port city, which is another level again more diverse than this."

"I love it," Vasiht'h said. "Not that all these Seersa aren't great, but . . . I like the variety we see every day." He listened to bits of conversation as they passed, focused on exams, school, new romances, parent problems. "Also it's a little odd that they're all so young."

Jahir, who'd been holding his mug near his lips, hid a smile at his wrist.

"No, really!"

Kindly, his Eldritch friend didn't observe that Vasiht'h was only five years past his own college career. "It is a university."

"I know," Vasiht'h said. He laughed. "Can you imagine if we'd stayed here? We'd have a practice like Minette's."

"I would not want Minette's practice," Jahir murmured.

"Me neither. Not that it doesn't have its moments, I'm sure, but . . ."

"You like a medley," Jahir said.

"Don't we both?"

His Eldritch partner looked out the window for a long moment, his eyes focused here, there, watching the people go by. What was it like, Vasiht'h wondered? To go from the homogeneity of the cloistered Eldritch homeworld to the Alliance Core? Even Seersana, homeworld to the Seersa and so leaning toward a higher number of them in any crowd, had diversity to surfeit even the most jaded palates. Phoenixae with their shining feathers; centauroid Ciracaana gliding past, their heads hovering far over their classmates'; every Pelted race of the Alliance in all their varied coats and colors . . .

"Yes," Jahir said. "This is sacred."

Why that made Vasiht'h blush, he couldn't have explained. He didn't try, just resumed work on the hazelnut pastry. There were scones in Tea and Cinnamon's baked goods case, but he'd known better than to order one. They were probably good, but it would have been hard not to compare them with the café's on Veta, where the recipes changed daily and were as creative as they were unexpected, and delicious.

"I remember," Jahir said, surprising him, "when I first went to the student clinic, Healer KindlesFlame thanked me for incrementing the clinic's total alien count by its penultimate statistic. They had only failed to see one alien race, once they'd added Eldritch to their tally."

Vasiht'h canted his head, thinking. "Naysha? No, there's a water tank here. Platies, maybe? Or . . .Faulfenza?"

"Chatcaava," Jahir said.

"Oh!" Vasiht'h grimaced. "Yes. Probably an empty day in the Goddess's mind before one of those pops up here. Unless someone pulls a full-blown peace treaty out of nowhere, and that doesn't seem likely to me."

"What a thing it would be, though."

Vasiht'h tried to imagine being better friends with the draconic shapeshifters on their border. Nothing he'd ever heard suggested they'd be peaceful neighbors, much less anything more positive. "Or maybe we'll find more alien species? Faulfenza were the last that I know of, and that was a while ago. . . ."

"The universe is infinite, and its glories beyond our experience."

"Amen," Vasiht'h murmured. And smiled. "Our little universe is enough for me."

Armin Palland's office hadn't changed in the time Vasiht'h had been away. At all. It was still the lived-in office of an overworked but contented professor, with precarious stacks of books and papers, and more books in bookshelves, and a desk that had seen better days and floors that were scuffed by the footwear—or claws, nails, talons—of thousands of students. Palland himself looked nearly identical, too: still a graying Seersa with ruddy pelt and paler champagne points, and bright, far too perspicacious eyes. On one hand, Vasiht'h was glad his former major professor hadn't aged precipitously—wasn't that the cliché? That when you spent time away from people older than you, when you finally saw them again you were shocked at how much older they'd gotten? But on the other, it was disturbing how little had changed. Five years was a long time. Or it wasn't. Which was it?

"Still working on things, are you?" Palland said, amused. "Come in, Vasiht'h-arii. It's good to see you again."

Vasiht'h padded into the office and flopped on the cushions scattered in the seating area in front of Palland's desk. "It's good to see you too, alet." He glanced at the office. "Not even a new poster?"

"I like the ones I have." Palland grinned. "You get used to things."

You get into ruts, is how that finished, Vasiht'h thought ruefully. Was that it? What was the difference between contentment and a rut?

"Ground control to Vasiht'h . . . come in, please." When Vasiht'h looked up sharply, the Seersa chuckled. "Really working on something, I see. Biscuit?"

"As long as it's a light one. I just came from lunch."

"Out of luck, it's shortbread. But at least it's good shortbread. Mantaiya brings it back from the dairy bowl on the opposite side of the world, when she visits her parents." Palland set out a small plate and leaned back to fetch the pot beside the window. That hadn't changed either: that the least cluttered part of the office was the surface where he kept his teapot and mugs, and that the mugs didn't match. "So, my former student, what brings you back? Are you angling for a new degree?"

"Goddess," Vasiht'h exclaimed. "One was hard enough!"

Palland's eyes twinkled as he poured for them both. "Sure about that, are you?"

"Yes," Vasiht'h said firmly. "A friend of ours is getting married at the shrine hills. We decided to come early and visit everyone."

The Seersa chuckled. "Well, it's great to see you in the flesh. I've heard good things about your career. You're enjoying yourself?"

"It's marvelous," Vasiht'h said, eyeing him. "And are you serious? You've actually heard things about my career? Have you been checking up on me?"

"Yes, but that's not the only reason I know. You do get write-ups in newsletters and journals."

"I . . . we . . . do?" Vasiht'h stammered.

"Surprised?" Palland was enjoying this. Far too much. "You pioneered a new treatment method in therapy. You know how often that happens?"

"A treatment method people still aren't sure about," Vasiht'h muttered, turning his mug. He'd gotten the chipped Seersana U one, white with the university emblem. "We were more notorious than famous for a while there."

Palland snorted. "Looking on the dim side of the cloud, I see."

"Do I even want to see these write-ups?" Vasiht'h asked.

"Depends on how thick your pelt is." Palland grinned. "It's the usual response to anything new. Some people are fascinated, some are horrified. Everyone wants to poke it with a stick."

Vasiht'h covered his face with his hand.

"Sure I can't interest you in another degree?" When Vasiht'h looked up, Palland said, "What is clear is that everyone really wants more data on how your methods work, and for that, you need more practitioners. You were interested in teaching . . ."

Vasiht'h suppressed a groan. "I do not want a research degree. I hated research."

"So, don't get one? Pursue a doctorate in clinical or medical." Palland spread his hands. "There's more than one path to a classroom."

"How did I come here to catch up with my major professor from college and end in a conversation about going back to school?" Vasiht'h eyed him. "What are you trying to talk me into?"

"That depends on what you're working on." Palland put his cheek in a hand and lifted his brows. "Most of my alumni waltz in here and tell me all about their wonderful careers, their successes, and how much their lives are working for them. You slink in here—"

"I don't slink!"

"—and wonder why things haven't changed. Which suggests to me that you feel like something hasn't. On the inside."

"I had to go into psychology," Vasiht'h complained. "Which means I get psychologists for mentors."

Palland grinned. "So what's really on your mind, arii?"

"Goddess alone knows." Vasiht'h sighed, grumbled. "I don't think I know how to be happy."

"Obviously you need more shortbread." Palland pushed the plate over with the tip of a finger. "I disbelieve this assertion, however. It lacks nuance."

"Our practice is doing well," Vasiht'h said. "We help a lot of people. We have a great place to live, and peers who respect us— some of whom had to be brought around, even—and everything is . . . well, it's exactly what I wanted. And I love it!"

". . . but?" Palland prompted.

"But . . . am I supposed to? Am I stagnating? Shouldn't I be learning something? Trying new things? Growing as a person?"

"Worrying about whether your partner is bored?" Palland suggested.

Vasiht'h covered his face with a hand again. "Ughn. Is it so obvious? Because if it's obvious to you, it's probably really obvious to him."

"Probably," Palland agreed, affable. He nudged the mug. "Drink."

The tea was a strong, clear, black varietal, something more like what Jahir would have drunk. But Vasiht'h was grateful for it after the heavy shortbread. Which . . . he'd eaten one of without noticing. "Professor?"

"Armin."

Vasiht'h looked up, ears sagging.

"You're not my student anymore, but my colleague," Palland pointed out, leaning back with his mug. "If a junior one."

"Armin-alet," Vasiht'h said, torn between flattery and alarm. He didn't feel old enough to be colleagues with a man who'd overseen his flailings as a fresh new student. "Would you ever give up your job?"

"Teaching and advising?" Palland smiled. "No, never. I love what I do." He folded his arms, pursed his lips. "I might move, maybe . . . I'm not married to Seersana, and the wife's been making noises about seeing other worlds at some point. But I'm good at this, and I love it. And even if I never left Seersana, it would still be a good life." He grinned. "I'm planning to keel over in the traces."

"You want to be one of those doddering ancients that can't be fired because of tenure, but who no one can make heads or tails out of because he rambles all the way through two hours of lecture?" Vasiht'h asked, amused.

"Sounds like every Heaven," Palland agreed, laughing.

"How . . . how did you know?" Vasiht'h asked. "That this was where you belonged?"

"You want me to say 'oh, you'll know?'" Palland smiled at some internal memory, eyes lowered. He huffed, leaned forward, put down his mug. "You do know. But not always immediately.

Sometimes it takes years of doing something before you think 'oh wait. I like this.'" He cocked his head. "What I want to know is why you don't believe yourself, since you already know you like what you're doing. Is it your partner's fault? Or is there something else going on? Maybe you feel like you're failing your family?"

"My family would insist I'm not failing them," Vasiht'h said, thinking of Sehvi and his mother. And then remembering Bret, he wrinkled his nose. "Most of them."

"So that's not it," Palland said. "Or at least, not mostly it." He lifted a brow. "You fretting over your partner's future for him?"

"I don't want him to get bored," Vasiht'h muttered.

"Because . . . he's showing signs of boredom?"

Vasiht'h played with the handle of the mug, turned it on the desk. "He almost graduated off the medical track. I sometimes think he wants to go back to it. Or maybe become a healer from the ground up."

"Has he said anything about wanting to do so?"

Vasiht'h snorted. "Eldritch don't tell you what they want. You're supposed to guess."

"Oh, I see." Palland nodded. "That's why you're a mess."

The Glaseah looked up.

"You're trying to anticipate his needs because you think he won't express them to you, or if he does, you might miss them. Or misinterpret them. And in the absence of actual data—because I'm betting you haven't asked him directly—you are coming up with every single possible scenario and fixating on the awful ones."

"It's unfair to assume I don't ask him what he wants just because I can't tell you!" Vasiht'h exclaimed. "Because when you do ask him, he says something but it's not always an answer. Or it's an answer, but not to the question you asked. Besides, direct questions are like backing him into a corner."

"Probably popped out of a face-saving culture, then," Palland said. "My poor beleaguered student."

"I thought you said I wasn't a student anymore."

The professor chuckled. "Not formally. But the nice thing about our profession, arii, is that you never stop learning. Which is how it should be: none of us should, or we die before we're in the ground." He waved a hand. "Seriously. Stop thinking about your partner and your quest for perfection as his soulmate, and tell me about *you*. About Vasiht'h. What is Vasiht'h's dream?"

"Vasiht'h's dream is to have a happy life doing xenotherapy with his Eldritch partner," Vasiht'h said. When Palland eyed him, he blushed and rubbed his cheek, hoping it would obscure the flushed skin near his eyes. "I mean that. I love what we do. I want to do it until we're old. Maybe have some kits at some point to tumble around our feet. When I feel wise enough to raise them."

"No one's ever wise enough to be a parent," Palland said. "That's why having kits makes us so much wiser so fast. For some things, the only possible training is on-the-job training." He frowned. "I'm a little concerned, though, that you can't really see a life goal for yourself, apart from what you're doing with your Eldritch, arii."

"I thought that was the point of partnerships," Vasiht'h said. "You go through life together."

"You do, yes, but you don't suddenly decide your own needs don't exist."

"I know my needs haven't stopped existing! That's why I'm so worried about trampling his!"

Palland's ears sagged and he shook his head. "Would you be offended if I suggested you might want . . . oh, a therapist?"

Vasiht'h chuckled, rueful. "Only if you won't laugh if I tell you I already have one."

"Good. Then I'll leave handling this to them and go back to selfishly enjoying your company, without the psychoanalysis." Palland refreshed his tea. "But I'd like you to think about it, arii. What you would do, if you were alone. It's important for us to know who we are by ourselves, because otherwise we don't value what we have to give to others. And it sounds a lot to me like you don't understand just how much you bring to your relationship—right now, as it exists, not in some future perfect world where you've seen to your Eldritch's every need."

Vasiht'h blushed again. "Do we ever know that, really? I mean . . . isn't that why we need other people so much?"

The Seersa's brows rose. Then he pointed at Vasiht'h. "There, now. That's a glimmer of wisdom right there."

"So I'm right," Vasiht'h said, sighing in relief.

"I said 'a glimmer,'" Palland replied, plucking up a shortbread. "That's not enough to excuse you from doing the work. Because no matter how useful it is to compare our perceptions to an external perspective, we still have to commit to trying to sort it out on our own."

Vasiht'h thought that sounded lonely. And exhausting. And . . . probably useful. At least partially. He tried to imagine a world without the mindline telling him, as it was right now, that Jahir existed and was nearby, a mindline that implied he wouldn't ever be alone again, and clamped down on his flinch. "I guess that's the problem," he said, thinking of the years of clients they'd helped. "Life is too complicated for 'it's always this' or 'it's always that.' It's usually 'it's this, unless it's that, and some-times it's not even any of those things, and by the way this part explodes.'"

Palland laughed. "Yes. Keeps it interesting, I think."

"You'd think so!"

"I would, yes. So, tell me about these skeptics with whom you were so notorious for a time. That sounds like a good story."

"Well," Vasiht'h began, "It involves a dog . . ."

"I admit," Jahir said, "I never thought I would find you here, alet."

KindlesFlame rose from his chair, laughing, and waved to the opposite seat. "Sit, Jahir. It's a pleasure to see you, and even more of one to surprise you."

"I'm not sure why," Jahir offered, "as when I first arrived, everything was new to me, and you witnessed much of my strug-gle with it." He crossed the airy room, finding the cleanliness of its lines both lovely and unlikely. Such high ceilings should have combined with the hardwood floors and the minimal ornamentation to create echoes and problematic temperature control, and yet the apartment was so comfortable he imagined most people wouldn't even notice how odd it was that it wasn't. The magic of the Alliance could be subtle as well as overt.

The chairs were set on a balcony overlooking a wooded ravine, and beyond them: mountains. The view was glorious; Jahir paused at the rail to stare at the vista, inhale the coolth of the morning, still damp from the mist burned off by the sun. The scent of pine was so strong it was almost as if he'd bruised the needles in his hands. "Oh, but this is beautiful."

"Isn't it?" KindlesFlame had moved back toward the kitchen, but his voice carried clearly. "Can I get you anything? Coffee? Tea? Something stronger?"

"I cannot know how you need the latter, with such surroundings." Jahir looked for the bird he heard whistling but couldn't spot it. "Coffee would be good, thank you. It's cool out."

"More so here than in the middle of the capital," KindlesFlame agreed. "One of the things I like about it. I'm not much of a city boy."

Jahir looked over his shoulder. "I beg your pardon? Says the man who was dean of a major college?"

The Tam-illee laughed. "Yes, I know. I love the bustle. But when the day's done, I want to put it to bed. Get some quiet in."

"And that is how I find you here. On sabbatical."

"You say that like it's some rare disease." KindlesFlame sounded amused. "Don't tell me, Healer . . . is it terminal?"

"Is it?" Jahir asked, turning inward.

"Iley Everlaughing!" The Tam-illee brought two mugs with him and set them on the table before dropping again into his chair. "Dire, alet. Very dire. I'm not dead yet, you'll note."

"But you are not working either. I didn't think you would be ready to retire."

"I'm technically not retired," KindlesFlame said over the rim of his mug.

"Ah."

". . . just considering it."

Jahir stared at him, then took up his own mug and had a seat across from his mentor. "I feel this requires explanation, and yet I would not ask."

"Which is nearly as obvious as you ever get about personal questions, so you must be concerned." The todfox grinned. "It's not serious, I promise. But I've been at the university for three decades now. I'm allowed to want a change of pace."

"I see now," Jahir said, warming his fingers. "As when you went from the dean of the medical school to the head of its clinic."

"Yes. Chasing a new perspective on things. You calcify, staying in one place. We're not meant to be sessile." Another smile. "You understand that better than most of the people I know, I imagine."

"Yes," Jahir agreed. "So does this sabbatical constitute a sufficient change of venue? Or will you move on, do you suppose?"

"Depends on if anything comes up," KindlesFlame said. "I've got some offers to investigate before I make any decisions. Until then, I'll probably do some lecture tours. I get enough invitations to talk at conferences to stay on the road all year if I wanted, and in the past I've had to turn most of them down. I enjoy being out, and it'll be good for my curriculum vitae."

"And . . . your family?" Jahir asked, delicately. "You have never mentioned them."

"And this looks like a bachelor pad, is what you're suggesting." The Tam-illee chuckled. "That would be because I've been single again for a good two decades. Maybe I'll meet someone while I'm out on the circuit. No, I have nothing to tie me down, alet, and a great deal left to learn and experience. The clinic's been wonderful, but it's time to hand it off to someone else for a while."

Jahir exhaled, settling himself. "Rather a large change."

"It is, isn't it? But I'm excited. Which is as good a sign as any that it was time to shake things up a bit. Which brings me to you, ah? What are you planning to do with all those continuing education credits you've been accruing like some kind of dragon on a hoard of gold?"

The mental image was striking, and amusing. "I had no idea you were tracking my progress. Or even that my progress was trackable."

"It's hard not to keep your hand in," KindlesFlame said. "I looked after you mentioned one too many esoteric topics in our correspondence. And while it wasn't exactly easy to tie the data down, they have to keep it somewhere to know whether you've requalified for your license." He cocked a brow. "You are going somewhere with all that extra education, aren't you?"

"Is it so obvious . . ."

The Tam-illee laughed. "Yes? To you too, I assume. You're doing it on purpose, aren't you?"

Was he? When he and Vasiht'h had settled into their permanent location on Veta, he'd begun taking extra classes for the pleasure of learning, and because their licenses did require some amount of continuing education. At the time he'd pulled up the course list for a generalist healer-assist degree as inspiration, but he had long since ceased to notice, when consulting it for what he should take next, that his actions would inevitably result in him having completed the theory portion of the degree.

. . . which he had. "It was not my intention. I was merely pursuing my interests."

"And your interests have landed you with all the credits necessary for *another* degree," KindlesFlame said, mouth curving. "So is it that you intend to work your way through every degree in the known worlds, because you love learning? Or is this a more specific obsession?"

Jahir tried not to wince. "Calling it an obsession seems . . ."

"Accurate?"

"Prejudicial," Jahir chose, ignoring his mentor's amusement and his own chagrin. "But it's a moot point, as without the practicum I cannot receive the license."

"True. But you can sit for the written exam and then arrange to do the practicum at your local hospital." KindlesFlame leaned over and set his mug on the table. "They'll log your time for the licensing board and as long as you get in the requisite within five years, you'll be fine."

"I . . . I beg your pardon?" Jahir asked, startled. "They would permit me to go about it backwards?"

The Tam-illee chuckled. "There are multiple routes into the license. You've been working on the educational institution model, because that's what you know, and how most people do it. But there are apprenticeship programs as well, plus the on-the-job training model, which is where they take people who've either had experience and need the theory or vice versa and arrange for them to get what they need. You'd be going in under that model, and for that you take the theory exams to prove you've got the book learning down. Then you have five years to get in the practicals." KindlesFlame laced his fingers over his abdomen, slumped in his chair. "Assuming you have to do much of that. They might apply your Selnor experience toward it. It won't get you all the way there—psychiatric residency isn't the same—but the fact that you worked a medical track in a critical care unit will weigh in your favor."

"God and Lady," Jahir said, startled. "You mean to tell me I might be credentialed as a healer-assist within five years?"

"Two, probably. It takes most people less than that but they work at it full-time." Studying him, KindlesFlame nodded. "You're going to do it. Good for you."

"I have not said—"

The other man snorted. "What's stopping you? Having that in your back pocket's a good thing, and it's not like the continuing education for both is going to break your stride if you've managed to accrue one and a half times the credits you need for the degree in your downtime. It would be a handy thing if one of your clients starts having a seizure, or you discover one of them has a medical issue that might be interfering with their ability to make the most of your therapy."

What good he could do on his homeworld as a modern healer! Some part of him had been cherishing that future, the one where he returned with the fruits of the Alliance's many excellencies. And how badly did the Eldritch need medicine. The faltering birthrate, the appalling number of deaths in childbed, the avoidable deaths from accident and the more mysterious ones from illnesses no one could name or explain . . . his world needed researchers, doctors, specialists in pharmacology, midwives, and hospitals. . . .

But he wasn't planning to go home to stay, not for many many years. And he had no idea what Vasiht'h would say if he discovered his partner had been secretly pursuing an alternate degree. No amount of protestation on Jahir's part that it hadn't been an entirely conscious decision would offset his partner's anxiety about the wherefores of the situation. Jahir sighed.

"Now that's a long face for what sounded to me like good news." KindlesFlame's brow went up. "What's inspiring it?"

"I like the life I have now," Jahir said slowly. "I do not relish the prospect of disturbing it."

"No reason this should," KindlesFlame said, unconcerned. "They offer the exams quarterly in all the Core sectors. Find the closest, take it, leave. Then volunteer at your local hospital— which you've already been doing—and eventually you end up with a license. What needs to change?"

"That sounds . . . minor enough."

"The exams take three days," KindlesFlame said, folding his legs. "And inevitably the licensing boards schedule them in the prettiest places they can find. They can afford to, since most people get their licenses through school; the only people left to go for it sideways are usually older and can afford the trip. It's ideal for vacationing." He grinned. "I almost envy you."

"Perhaps you can become a proctor as one of your 'changes of perspective'?"

The other man laughed. "Not a bad idea. But speaking of which . . . I've noticed you eyeing the view. Would you like to take a hike through the backyard?"

"Oh, absolutely!"

As Jahir rose, KindlesFlame said, "Seriously, my student. You've done the work, and the credits are good . . . for now. But they're going to expire if you don't use them for something, so decide soon whether you want the paper to go with the knowledge, mmm?"

"I promise to consider it," Jahir said.

CHAPTER 3

T HAT THE GIRLS HAD GROWN should have come as no surprise, and yet the sight of them surprised Jahir . . . for he
and Vasiht'h had left them as children, and returned to find
poised young ladies, sitting at one of the high tables in the coffee
shop attached to the hospital's garden. Or at least, mostly poised,
because their approach caused all four to jump from their chairs,
eyes alight. Kuriel and Meekie descended on Vasiht'h with glad
squeals, and Jahir hung back to watch his partner disappear
beneath their enthusiastic embraces before he turned to the
human teenagers waiting behind them. Amaranth was gowned
in the hospital patient's uniform, soft top and bottoms, and slip-
pers, but she had her chin lifted and her cropped auburn hair
stubbornly styled with pins that cast a veil of moving sparkles.
Persy was standing beside her in street clothes, her arm hooked
through her friend's. They now had adult faces, and if Amaranth's
bones were more prominent than one expected in a girl of her
age, she still looked healthier than she had as a child.

Which she wasn't any longer, so he gathered Amaranth's
hands and bowed over them, as he might have a family member's, and then did the same with Persy's. Through their fingers
he felt their effervescent delight at the gesture, savoring it. Only

when they'd made their best attempts at maintaining what they felt was a properly adult dignity, did they give up and hug him, together. With that touch he gathered their changes in: the grief, the strength, Amaranth's continuing fight . . . Persy's dedication to her. Their love of the other girls. Their sense of *purpose.* The latter was overwhelming, enough that when he parted from them they could see his comprehension in his face, somehow. Here again were people who knew him well enough to read him.

"You feel it," Amaranth said. She had a young woman's voice now, the melody line a touch lower than before. "Don't you? You can tell."

"I can tell," he answered. "And I hope you will explain everything to us. We can't wait to listen."

Kuriel and Meekie by then had come for their hugs, leaving the humans to Vasiht'h's embrace. The flush of health on the latter made it clear the treatment she'd received on Selnor had allowed her to make a full recovery, and she looked every inch the cheerful Tam-illee teenager, complete with painted swirls on the insides of her ears to match her colorful glass jewelry. The former was no longer in the hospital's gown, but her fingers, tail-tip, and ear-tips were still dyed bright purple, as they had been when she'd been seeking a way to manage her symptoms, and her gaze . . . at some point, Kuriel had lost the tinge of pessimism that had darkened her hazel eyes.

"Let's sit!" Kuriel said, tail swishing. "We can have coffee!"

"But at a different table," Meekie said, frowning. "This one's too tall for Manylegs."

Vasiht'h laughed. "Yes, absolutely. Let's find a table I don't have to climb onto."

They repaired to a cozier corner that suited them all, and Persy excused herself to get drinks. She insisted on buying some for Jahir and Vasiht'h, too.

/Let them,/ Jahir murmured before Vasiht'h could protest. / *They are claiming their autonomy.*/

/I know. I just wanted to be the one to buy the snacks!/

Jahir hid his smile at the amusement in the Glaseah's voice.

/Next time, perhaps./

"So we find you outside the hospital," Jahir said, when they were all together again.

"Except for me," Amaranth said. "But . . . that's all right. I'm getting better."

"She is," Persy agreed. "She's doing great on the same treatment they tried on me."

"And the rest of you?"

"We're done with the hospital!" Kuriel exclaimed. "Even me! Though I have to go back every week for treatments." She flexed her purple fingers. "They think this is something I'm going to have to manage all my life. But that's okay? Because it means I have a rest of my life, you know?"

"You weren't the last one out after all," Amaranth teased.

Kuriel's ears sagged, but she smiled sheepishly. "No." More steadily, "But you'll get out too."

"We're helping Amaranth with school," Meekie told them. "So when she's done, she can jump right into classes with us."

"We're all going to school for the same thing," Persy agreed. "And we're planning to do college together."

"Here!" Meekie exclaimed.

"Stop, stop!" Amaranth said, laughing. "You're overwhelming them! Start from the beginning."

"Okay, the beginning," Meekie said, ears flipping outward. Then she rallied. "It started with you leaving, Vasiht'h-alet."

"What?" Vasiht'h asked, bemused.

"When you left to get Pri—" Kuriel stopped herself, the insides of her ears pinking. "Um, to go get Jahir-alet. You remember we decided then that we were going to stay and help other people like us. Kids like us."

The faint embarrassment easing through the mindline felt like an itch. Jahir glanced at Vasiht'h with interest.

/I'll explain later?/ Aloud, Vasiht'h said, "Right. So . . . you meant it!"

Persy snorted. "Of course we meant it! Anyway, Jill-alet told us there are lots of jobs that we could do relating to kids who have to stay in the hospital. Most of us are going with some form of therapy, but—"

"I want to be a doctor," Meekie said.

"Yeah. So. We've set up a volunteer group."

"A what?" Vasiht'h asked, ears sagging.

"I know," Kuriel said, rueful. "We wanted to do nothing but leave, and once some of us do, we turn right around and go back in!"

Meekie took the conversational floor back. "We go see other kids and we tell them our stories—"

"Not just in the hospital," Persy added. "Outside it too. We talk at other schools and stuff."

"And we tell them not to give up," Meekie finished.

"Or why we need money," Kuriel said. "So we can use it to buy things to give to kids. Or to travel."

"Travel!" Vasiht'h exclaimed.

"Kayla's still on Selnor," Meekie said. "Her dami found a good job there and didn't want to move. But her tapa's really good at fundraising? So he's been helping us set up. Kayla's got two other girls on Selnor with her, that's our Selnor branch. We have branches!"

"We call ourselves Nieve's Girls," Amaranth said. "Because we are."

That struck so hard Jahir flinched, and immediately all of their attention fastened on him and all of them reacted, wide-eyed, staring, reaching across the table or the mindline. Vasiht'h most intimately: /Arii?/ But the girls too, in various expressions of dismay.

"No," he said. "No, it's well. It's a perfect name."

"Until you get some boys in there. Then what?" Vasiht'h wanted to know, which made all the girls erupt into giggles. 'Nieve's Kids' was rejected immediately, but all the other alternatives inspired a great deal of humor, from Nieve's Posse to Nieve's Honor Guard.

"We'll figure it out when we need to," Persy said finally.

"Yes," Vasiht'h said. "Yes, you will. So tell us all about school."

"Oh yes," Jill said to them when they walked upstairs to see her. "They are on fire with this plan of theirs—oh, for me?" She accepted the bag, peeked in it and laughed. "Coffee, of course. You remembered."

"Of course we did," Vasiht'h said. */You more than me. . . ./*

/You remembered too, arii./

/Thank the Goddess she didn't give up caffeine while we were gone!/

"Anyway, they're doing great in school," the human said, sitting back down at her station. "I have no doubts at all they're going to accomplish what they say they will. They don't just talk to kids . . . they go to General, too, and sing songs to the elderly, and comfort the non-natives, and bring donuts to the staff."

"They've found a calling," Vasiht'h guessed.

The human smiled at him, eyes bright. "They certainly have."

Quietly, Jahir asked, "Alet? What is Amaranth's prognosis?"

Jill glanced at him with a smile that didn't reach her eyes. How remarkable smiles were, that they could contain such nuance. One need not be an esper to understand the emotions that had prompted the complexity of her expression. "You picked up on that, did you."

"Persy said something about the treatment that worked on her working for Amaranth?" Vasiht'h said, his unease thickening the mindline with a cold fog.

"Persy *wants* the treatment that worked on her to work on Amaranth, but it doesn't seem to be," Jill said. "But to be honest, aletsen, Amaranth's still alive after years of this thing chewing on her. Cancers as virulent as hers—and Persy's—usually kill people within a handful of years, and both of them made it from childhood to a point where Amaranth is worried about make-up and dating. I'm not happy that Persy made it into remission and Amaranth didn't despite their having the same diagnosis, but . . . I'm cautiously hopeful that if Amaranth made it this far, she'll make it to remission."

Which was all they could ask of medicine. Jahir said, "Thank you. For telling us."

"You two are on her list of people allowed to know. Which should make you both feel pretty good, because you know human privacy restrictions are more stringent than Pelted ones." She smiled at them both. "So . . . what about the two of you? What have you been up to?"

/We're going to be telling this story a lot,/ Vasiht'h murmured.

/You will be. I will simply smile and add a word here and there./

Vasiht'h snorted aloud and said, "I hope you have some time free . . ."

"Depends. Do I get a free dream therapy session?" At Vasiht'h's expression, she started laughing. "Joking! Mostly. Go ahead, I'm on break."

They spent an enjoyable half hour there, speaking with Jill. All the girls had left her care save Amaranth, who'd been joined by a new set of residents, and she mentioned their tribulations in passing before continuing on to general news about the hospital, the staff, even her life.

"Engaged!" Vasiht'h said as they head back toward the center of campus, where a Pad station was the only obstacle between them and gelato on the art side of the university. "She wasn't even dating when we left!"

"It doesn't take long, sometimes," Jahir murmured, thinking of his own life. When Vasiht'h glanced at him sharply, he added, "You and I needed only an afternoon."

That softened the edges in the mindline. Vasiht'h smiled, jogging alongside him. "More like a moment. When you met my eyes . . . you remember?"

His first sight of Vasiht'h, tangled up in children's jump ropes, so mysterious and so non-threatening, and that twinkle in the Glaseah's brown eye when the Eldritch had noticed his complicity in that entanglement . . . "How could I forget?"

Vasiht'h beamed up at him.

"Seersana will always be special," Jahir said, feeling the shape of it in his heart, and his life. "No matter how far we go. Because of that."

"Yes," Vasiht'h said, the softness of that in the mindline gentle as a new spring. "I feel the same way."

Jahir glanced at him with another small smile, and they walked together beneath the new leaves, down old paths that were as familiar as a childhood blanket.

It wasn't until they were most of the way to the gelateria that Vasiht'h sorted through the implications of that statement. That places could be special even after they were left behind. Before he could let that fester, he blurted, "I worry too much about things, don't I?"

His partner said, "It is part of your strength."

That made Vasiht'h stumble to a stop. Jahir paused a few strides away, waiting, so Vasiht'h hurried to rejoin him, and once again they resumed walking side-by-side. How many beats of his paws went by for every one of his taller friend's strides? He wasn't the musician, to know instinctively. But there was a rhythm, one natural to them now, and resuming it calmed the Glaseah. Mostly. Enough to keep talking. "Part of my strength!"

The feel through the mindline . . . it was like trying to balance on a beam. His friend's eyes were narrowed, slightly. Thinking. "The shadow side of your strength. There is no strength without casting one. You care, arii. So you worry."

That was such a kindness, and so embarrassing, that Vasiht'h didn't answer. It wasn't the words—well, it was the words. The words made it clear that Jahir had put thought into what made Vasiht'h special, enough to have a ready answer when asked. But the sensation in the mindline overwhelmed all possible speech: effusive as an embrace, welcome as sunrise, endless as the days in the mind of a goddess.

His worries mattered to him. Vasiht'h knew that in a day, an hour, maybe a minute they'd come back to gnaw at him some more. But for one glorious heartbeat, he understood those worries as clouds in a clear sky, subject to wind and temperature changes, but ephemeral. There would always be weather, but the weather wasn't the sky. That one glorious heartbeat lasted forever because time was just as arbitrary, and Vasiht'h believed from the pads of his paws to the tip of his nose that one day the Goddess would show him what it was like to live without counting seconds like beads on a string, one after another.

It also ended when he took his next breath. And as expected, his anxieties were still there, tagging along at his heels like homeless puppies. That mental image was so strong that Jahir glanced at him and said, "Arii? You are not hoping to adopt a dog?"

Vasiht'h laughed. "No. Dogs I'll leave to Allen. We have enough on our plate without adding more."

"Like gelato," Jahir said. "And here we have arrived at the station."

"Just in time." Vasiht'h glanced up at his friend as he walked past him, through the door. The room was empty, so they choose one of the Pads and set it to their destination. "Do you know what flavor you want?"

"Not yet," Jahir said, preceding him over the Pad. "I shall see what there is to see first."

Vasiht'h followed him into the university's art district, out of the building used as the receiving station and into the clear gold light. Impulsively, he said, "That's one of *your* strengths, you know."

Jahir laughed. "That I love novelty?"

"That you're willing to adapt to things. I mean, the core things about you, those you hold to hard. But everything else . . . you just . . . move with. Like water. That's one of the ways I know when you're stuck, actually. Because you stop that. Like water dammed up behind branches." Startlement felt like static electricity discharging on the fingers, this time. Vasiht'h laughed and pushed down his fur. "Okay, that's strange when you don't have a pelt."

"I . . . imagine so. I had never considered it thus."

Thinking of Palland, Vasiht'h said, "We don't always know ourselves very well, without someone to tell us."

"Context," Jahir said after one of those infinitesimal pauses anyone else might have missed, but Vasiht'h was proud not to. "Context allows you to place yourself within an environment, and understand how you fit there."

"You're really good at fitting yourself into new ones," Vasiht'h said.

"And you," Jahir said, "Are good at making your existing ones feel like home." He opened the door to the gelateria. "After you, arii."

Vasiht'h trotted inside, pleased. Blushing too, but that was all right. He'd take it. "Those girls . . . I can't believe how together they are, and so young."

A pulse of sorrow, gray like rain and cold. "Their situation did not lend itself to remaining children long."

"I guess I was lucky," Vasiht'h mused. "I got to ease into adulthood. No tragedies, no crises. Nothing to age me too quickly."

"Is that luck?" Jahir asked. When the Glaseah frowned, his friend said, "There are advantages to growing up quickly that you will never have." He smiled a little. "Perhaps you would worry less if your perspective had been broadened by hardship."

"Maybe," Vasiht'h said slowly. "But . . . I'm selfishly glad it hasn't been." He stopped in front of the refrigerated case, felt the shadow of his friend over his back as Jahir came to a halt behind him.

"That they've found a path so quickly doesn't make your journey any less valid," Jahir said. "Because you took a gentler route."

"I know," Vasiht'h said, and was even sure—fairly sure—that he meant it. But he ordered the mandarin orange anyway, in the hopes that it would chase away the taste of what he feared might be envy.

The university had several on-site hotels, but Vasiht'h had booked them into lodging in Kavakell, the world capital. Jahir had asked him about it at the time, and the Glaseah had said it would be

'fun to see the city' and 'besides, it's only a Pad away.' On seeing
their destination, Jahir had felt a pulse of astonishment, and
through the mindline sensed his partner's smug satisfaction. /
You like doing this to me,/ he observed, smiling at the Glaseah.

/*You make it worthwhile,*/ Vasiht'h replied, beaming.

Their hotel took up a whole floor of a building that curved
like an amphitheater around a plaza with a park sculpted around
shops and nooks for outdoor performances. Offices, residences,
and shops shared their building, and its roof was another garden
space, complete with a pool that poured a waterfall down a series
of guided curves, accumulating on various balconies before finally
gushing down a slide to the plaza at ground level, where it filled a
lake stocked with freshwater fish and lilies. The plaza led out into
the city's shopping district, and it was busy: full of people shopping, talking, lounging and watching singers or dancers or poets.
When the two of them arrived at sundown, the evening illumi-
nation was just beginning to glow, and not only was the building
strung with lights, they danced in subtle patterns.

"It's strange to think that Veta's city is more pastoral than
most Core cities," Vasiht'h said as they took a glass lift to the
hotel floor. "But it was built to feel like a small pedestrian city
with Pad access. Not too tall, not too obvious with the high
technology."

Because his friend took for granted that things like smart-
glass windows—windows at all, of sufficient quality—were
not obvious high technology. Jahir felt a flush of affection for
Vasiht'h, and through him, the Alliance with its careless acceptance of the impossible and wondrous.

"So this is . . . kind of different from what we're used to."

"The starbase at the Wall is more like this," Jahir said. "But
you're correct. This is . . ."

"Flagrant?" Vasiht'h asked, amused.

"Extravagant," Jahir said. "As only the Alliance might be."

Their room featured a wall of windows looking down on the
plaza where it intersected the shopping corridor, and by the time
they reached it, the lights had begun to smolder in the lowering

cobalt blue of the evening sky.

"This place has a spa that fits even me!" Vasiht'h said. "I think I might try that. Do you want to come? There are plenty of privacy options, and it looks like their pool is beautiful."

"Perhaps later," Jahir said. "I would like to walk."

"We can meet for dinner later?"

Jahir smiled. "I will let you see to my feeding, yes."

Vasiht'h laughed. "Good. This place *also* has a great restaurant. They specialize in tiny portions, but you order a lot of them."

That made him laugh too. "How well you know me, arii."

"Well, it's been seven years or so."

"So it has."

They parted, and Jahir went down into the city, and there . . . he walked. Past the sculpted park and into the shopping district, crowded with walkers searching for novelty, for entertainment, for amusement, for the chance to spend time with friends and family. He walked in a sphere of his own space, for everyone knew his requirements as one of the Alliance's most recognizable alien species, but it was no hardship for them to cede that space to him. The district's thoroughfares had been designed for pleasure and throughput—how many engineers had that required, and where was that specialty taught in the university, he wondered?

Jahir took an espresso at a café, at one of its high outdoor tables, leaning on its surface and watching the Pelted and their allies go past: speaking here not just in Universal, but in the vast and exotic native tongue the Seersa were constantly evolving in their quest to understand language. Afterward, he walked until he found himself again in the park, seeking shadows and finding none, for even the emptiest spaces were lit as if for a holiday. Looking up into the boughs of a tree, he found it hung with tiny white lights, soft as fireflies, restless in the breeze.

Nieve's Girls.

Oh, Nieve.

Jahir leaned against the tree, folding his arms and letting his eyes close. This near to the bark he could smell the sap of it, the spiced living scent of something growing . . . as she would never grow, save now, through the quietly heroic acts of her friends. What would she have been like, had she not died in his arms? He cracked his eyes, imagined her drifting through the park, the wind sifting her gown and the dove gray hair she'd missed so much. He couldn't picture what she would be like healthy. Could only barely imagine her as a teenager, with an adult's face but a child's soft padding. Was it a failure in him that he could not see her as a grown woman? That he couldn't imagine her grappling with the mundane responsibilities of that life? She'd seemed so ethereal. Angels did not pay taxes.

Smiling a little at himself, Jahir straightened and resumed his wanders. KindlesFlame's advice echoed in his mind, mixing with the resolve of the maidens, and all the knowledge he'd acquired by what appeared to be accident to the naïve observer. Had it been too painful for him to admit that unresolved traumas were motivating his actions? How much of his fascination with medicine remained a commitment to Nieve's memory?

Was that necessarily a bad thing?

What he was doing with Vasiht'h brought him contentment, and he believed in its importance. He felt no great impetus to drop everything and dedicate himself to becoming a healer. As KindlesFlame would have been the first to point out, barring accident he had time. Nor did he feel he was done learning what he needed to learn from being a therapist.

But if it would cost him very little in time and focus to acquire a second license . . . would it not be prudent? Or was that yet another justification, and, if so, what was he lying to himself about this time?

He had approved of Vasiht'h's visits to Allen for therapy. He wondered if he could ever make so brave a choice for himself, and knew it impossible. Even had the Veil not mandated his silence about so much of what shaped him, he simply could not be comfortable revealing himself to anyone here. Anyone, save one, and even that required delicacy, as all relationships did. And this issue in particular was perfectly positioned to aggravate all his partner's insecurities.

Of course, if he had time, he could retake the classes for a license at some later date. That might be the kindest path. And it would cost him nothing—he could afford both the wait and the expense.

Nieve's Girls. How she would laugh, and delight at the acts of her friends. Smiling, Jahir headed back toward the hotel, and the promise of a restaurant with tiny courses.

CHAPTER 4

L UCI'S WEDDING DID NOT take place in the Harat-Shariin
shrine on campus, and not, Vasiht'h observed, because she'd
decided to wed a different race. Her fiancée was an imposing
Harat-Shariin leonine, broad-shouldered with the dense build of
a deadlifter, and he wore his stunning black mane in multiple
braids that fell in heavy ropes past his shoulders. He was affable
in the way that enormous people often were . . . he obviously had
nothing to prove, and was also head-over-tail for Luci. The way
they looked at each other made Vasiht'h wonder if they didn't
belong in a romance novel of their own. Was this how sexually-
attracted people normally looked when they were happy?

Come to think of it, did he have that kind of hopelessly sweet
look on his face when he thought of Jahir?

The two of them stood in the grassy bowl between the shrine
hills with the rest of the guests and the wedding party, enjoying the sunshine and the cool breeze. Someone had built a dais
shrouded with cream and gold flowers and swathes of butter-
yellow fabric before scattering the field with more flower petals.
Rows of chairs had been set up for those who wanted to sit, and
there was a table with refreshments, waiting for the ceremony's
completion. They needed only the Angels' priest and priestess to

begin, and it was no hardship, waiting.

"How splendid they are!" Jahir observed, standing alongside him.

"They really are, aren't they?" Vasiht'h said, pleased. "I can't remember the last time she looked so happy. We'll have to ask them how they met."

"Or you could ask us," a voice behind them drawled. All three of their former quadmates were standing behind them. The two Seersa shoulder to shoulder, Brett smirking and Leina with her hands on her hips, and the tawny Ciracaana looming behind them.

"I can't believe they showed up and didn't tell us they were coming!" Leina agreed."Mera, you should step on them."

"One too tall," the Ciracaana said, unperturbed. "Other, too broad. No use." His mouth gaped in a long-muzzled grin, all teeth. "Good to see you both again."

Vasiht'h laughed. "Brett! Mera! Leina!" He hugged them, one by one. "We couldn't not come."

"Luci will be glad. When she notices you." Brett grinned. "She's kind of obsessed right now."

Leina swatted him. "He's talking as if they just met. They've known one another a year, though."

"Met at work," Mera said, shaking his head. "Never know when it will come for you. Like a predator, springing from the grasses. Love, with all its fangs."

Leina covered her face with her hands. "Your metaphors, Mera. Whyyyyyy."

"Because they are true," the Ciracaana replied, still grinning. "Best love has fangs. Anything else is too weak to last."

"That's right," Brett said. "You've got to be able to drag it back to your lair, after all."

Vasiht'h eyed him. "I'm going to pretend I can't hear any of this."

"Good luck!" Brett laughed, cuffed him lightly on the shoulder. "So the two of you are still together, too, I see? What have you been up to?"

"Working, what else?" Vasiht'h said. "We have a practice over on Starbase Veta."

"Ooooh, fancy," Leina said. "A *starbase* practice."

"They needed good encore from schooling on a Core world," Mera said.

"We have to hear all about it after the ceremony," Brett agreed. "Speaking of which, looks like the priest got here. You all want to sit?"

"Fellow four-legged can sit with me at the end of the row," Mera said. "Come, Vasiht'h-arii."

So they did sit together, in one of the rows near the dais with a fine view of Luci and her man, whose name was Antonin. The ceremony wasn't anything like the traditional Harat-Shariin weddings Vasiht'h had researched, much to his relief, because he wasn't sure how he would have told Jahir that they were required to show up naked. In fact, Vasiht'h couldn't tell what kind of ceremony it was, once it started. The priest and priestess were both Harat-Shariin and called on the Angels and Kajentarel equally, which was already unusual. The emphasis on monogamy was also rare for mainstream Harat-Shariin culture, and the solemnity even more so. But the ritual was simple and shorter than most Pelted editions. The ring exchange was common to too many pledging ceremonies to suggest where it had taken its inspiration, and the kiss was as well. The latter was more chaste than Vasiht'h had expected, but so heartfelt he blushed anyway.

So he couldn't tell where she'd gotten the template for her pledging ritual, but it was perfectly Luci. The way she glowed and her new husband's shyly tender looks were enough to melt even a calcified heart. When the pair of priests announced them wed, the entire congregation erupted into cheers, and then dissolved at the couple's behest into mingling and enjoying the refreshments.

Leina sighed as they rose. "That was so romantic."

"And this is so ridiculous!" Luci interrupted, joining them. "Look at the lot of you, so serious. I didn't know you *could* be serious." But there was a smile fighting with her mouth and winning, and she laughed. "You all came!"

"Of course we did." Brett patted his hip suggestively. "And we expect invitations to the baby presentations too, so when you get with the kit-making, don't forget us."

"Brett!" Leina exclaimed. "Ignore him, Luci. Healers are crass."

"Also, apparently, failures at anatomy. Not the right place for babymaking, you are grabbing, Brett."

"Ugnh, not you too, Mera." Leina covered her face.

Luci snickered and hugged them all, save Jahir, before indicating her husband with a flourish. "This is Antonin! He's also a healer, so he's fine with the crass jokes."

"So long as they're anatomically correct," Antonin said, his voice an amused basso rumble. "But I know some remedial classes that might help with that . . . ?"

Brett laughed. "You would have fit right into our student dinners!"

"I'm sorry I missed them." The leonine grinned. "Maybe we can make a go at it? Dinner tomorrow?"

"Since we have the reception now, and I'm planning on being busy tonight," Luci said.

Leina pressed a finger to Brett's mouth. "Don't even."

Mera chortled. "You see what you have been missing, Antonin-alet."

"And I don't have to miss it any longer." The leonine chuckled. "Good to meet you all. Any friend of Luci's is welcome with me."

"Now go drink the sangria!" Luci said. "I had enough of it made to get even you drunk, Mera."

"By all means. Show me to the table."

Luci had to make herself available to all her guests, of course . . . that left Vasiht'h and Jahir to enjoy the company of their college friends, which was no hardship. Leina and Brett had graduated and gone on to careers in medicine, with the former working on the orbital station and the latter still on Seersana, if on the other side of the world. ("Just getting cold there . . . was nice to get away!") Mera had completed his graduate studies, decamped to his homeworld on a two-year grant to study his own people, and returned to work on a doctorate in what was still called anthropology. The Ciracaana did not live on campus, though: "Have graduated from being poor student, to being poor student with delusions of grandeur. Far too highbrow now for mere on-campus apartments."

The camaraderie was as easy as it had been when they'd been in school together. From Luci's reception, they all wandered to lunch in the city, where Jahir had a diffident suggestion that naturally turned out to be a delicious find.

/How do you always know these things?/ Vasiht'h asked over the second course while Brett and Leina debated the merits of the local wines they were sampling from the flight one of them had ordered.

/I listen,/ Jahir answered after a moment. /And I smell./ A strong impression then, walking through the crowds at night: snatches of conversation, a woman exclaiming about cheeses, her friend about the service; the yeast-and-grape aroma wafting between groups of people, clear despite the musk of the Pelted and the perfume of the surrounding flowers in the planters lining the street.

/Of course you do,/ Vasiht'h said, fond. /While the rest of us are distracting ourselves with talk and our own thoughts, you're doing something useful./

A gentle softness, like the pleasure of a warm blanket in the cold. /Communion with other people is never useless./

Vasiht'h began to reply and stopped himself. How often had Tiber chided him for negative self-talk? He didn't even know where he'd learned the habit. His sister's voice, suddenly: 'From your brother, of course.' He ignored the memory of her. Some answers were too easy. Weren't they?

"Oh ho!" Brett said, interrupting Vasiht'h's thoughts. "What's this? Someone's been sneaking into our textbooks! And by 'our' I mean mine and Leina's!"

Over his glass, Jahir murmured, "I was enjoying your story until the point where the details made no sense."

Leina whooped. "That was the most genteel take-down I've *ever* heard."

"I'm *wounded*," Brett said theatrically, pressing a hand to his breast with a mournful expression. "Absolutely *wounded*."

"What did I miss?" Vasiht'h asked, bewildered.

"Only Brett telling one of his tall tales, which would have held up for everyone except, apparently, a closet pharmachemist," Leina said, reaching for the bread.

"Your partner called him on the science," Mera told Vasiht'h, amused. "Never good when your audience knows the jargon. If you don't."

"I do know the jargon, thank you very much," Brett said, laughing with a hand pressed to his ribcage. "Speaker-singer! It's just if I use all the actual, correct words it doesn't sound right to laymen, so it's not as funny."

"I'm not a layman!" Leina protested.

"Yeah, but you've heard all my stories already!"

Leina smeared her bread with herb butter. "Truth."

"So if you must know," Brett told Jahir, "It was delivered by patch, not AAP, because the absorption rate was better. And to the inside of the ear, if you're about to twig me about whether we shaved some poor patient's arm."

"I didn't think the coral-derivative aggregation inhibitors were small enough to pass through the skin?"

"They didn't used to be," Brett answered. "But they found a way to cut the molecular weight by twenty percent, and that makes them good targets for transdermal—what the many hells, though, arii, when did you get this hardcore and can we sit down and shoot the breeze about this separately?" The Seersa was grinning, but his bafflement was obvious. "Vasiht'h? Help me out here. What has your partner been up to?"

Vasiht'h, distracted by the sense of the Eldritch's mind during this recitation, looked up. "Um . . . what? Oh. Continuing education?" He glanced at Jahir, who inclined his head. And left it that way, the way he did only when he was feeling particularly sheepish about something.

"That's one hell of a con-ed path there," Leina said, laughing. "You'd better be careful, Vasiht'h, or you'll end up married to a doctor."

"Doctors. Notoriously crass," Mera said. "But fortunately not so good at anatomy, as relating to breeding." He patted Vasiht'h's shoulder. "You are safe."

The painful itch in the mindline was definitely embarrassment. Bordering on mortification. None of which mattered when weighed against the pleasure Vasiht'h had sensed from his partner, working at the medical details of Brett's story. Though 'pleasure' wasn't quite right. Satisfaction, maybe. A stretching feeling, like being able to run when you were restless, and the relief of that motion. Despite it purportedly connecting their minds, Vasiht'h rarely got any sense of his partner's intelligence through the mindline, but this once . . . yes. He touched, just a little, that understanding of the quickness of his friend's mind, and the ease with which it made and explored connections. Enough to find it breathtaking, and beautiful, too beautiful to find it intimidating.

The Eldritch wasn't looking at him. That was fine, because it gave Vasiht'h time to sort through his reactions, through love and awe, along with confusion and curiosity and a host of other things besides.

"I love my work," Jahir was saying in response to their friends' teasing, and from the mindline that was true, so true Vasiht'h couldn't question it.

"And I'm not looking to marry," Vasiht'h finished, rejoining the conversation. "At least, not yet."

"That's too bad," Leina said. "Glaseahn kits are *adorable*. Ask me how I know."

"No, really, ask her," Brett said. "Or she'll die. She wants to tell this story so badly."

Vasiht'h laughed. "All right, all right. Tell me the adorable Glaseahn kits story. Just don't expect it to make me leap for the nearest temple."

"Gods and spirits forfend," Mera said. "More baby

presentations to attend. We must wait for Luci's before we complicate our schedules further."

After lunch they spent an enjoyable hour wandering the shopping district, recalling the many amusing expeditions they'd undertaken to furnish Vasiht'h and Jahir's first flat off-campus. They debated the merits of the fashions of the day, coveted various hand-crafted items from wind-chimes tuned to different modes to furniture designed for the comfort of multiple species, and wound up in a ridiculous disquisition about what kinds of entertainment were best for offsetting what kind of situation ("Near-future espionage thrillers, good for when you've had the sixtieth boring request at work and know you're looking at a future of nothing but stupid boring requests. But if you've just had to suffer through a family member's repeated 'I haven't learned anything so this keeps happening' drama, then you want a contemporary meet-cute romance. Preferably same-species for minimal cultural misunderstandings.")

Heading back to the hotel after a very pleasurable afternoon, Vasiht'h said, "I'm so glad we came."

"As am I," Jahir said.

Vasiht'h knew that wouldn't be the end of it, but for now it was perfect.

The following day they met Luci for brunch at a sunny café on the medical side of campus. Jahir was aware of Vasiht'h's attention and pretended not to notice. Even if the Veil permitted casual explication of his feelings, he would have been hard-pressed to put them into words. There was too much yet in his heart, and he had not spent enough time deriving right action from any of it; when he thought he knew, he found his plan disrupted . . . as Brett's story had disrupted his decision to put the test off.

The exploration of emotion for its own sake felt selfish and counter-productive. This belief almost certainly constituted a betrayal of the tenets of their profession, and yet Jahir knew no other way to be. There were too many ways to regret, to sink into misery and never escape. One needed some code by which one could order one's actions.

His preoccupation left him prey to Luci's ambush. "So . . . back during your residency. The hero of the wet outbreak on Selnor. That was you, wasn't it?"

"I . . . beg your pardon?"

Vasiht'h's unease felt like a friction burn across the mindline, making the pull and shift of it uncomfortable.

"You never said," Luci continued, casual. She dunked a rolled up pancake in her syrup. "But it was obvious, so you might as well admit to it."

"If it's so obvious, why are you bringing it up?" Vasiht'h asked, ears sagging.

"That's my fault," Antonin said, abashed. "I was on Selnor for that, if on the other hemisphere, volunteering at the Fleet hospital in Terracentrus. My area of research is community intersection with acute and trauma care, and that was a high profile example of law enforcement becoming involved with a hospital."

"Oh," Vasiht'h said, startled. "That actually sounds fascinating?"

"It is!" Antonin rumbled, eyes lighting.

"You're getting him started," Luci murmured affectionately, and her husband's ears drooped a little. He grinned at her, abashed. "Anyway, when he mentioned it, I told him you were involved. At least, that's my assumption. You were, yes? Both of you, I'm betting." She lifted a brow.

/I guess there's no hiding it,/ Vasiht'h muttered.

/Given that the entirety is probably public record . . ./ Inasmuch as anything involving an Eldritch could remain so, with the censors at their work.

"Just a guess," Luci said. "Since you went that way, Vasiht'h, and the reports mentioned a Glaseah and his residency partner."

"How they failed to state the residency partner's species is baffling," Antonin agreed. "You'd think 'One of them was an Eldritch' would be newsworthy."

Jahir suppressed his resignation, sensed Vasiht'h's as well. It soured the raspberry jam he'd been using on his toast.

/*Should we?*/

Should they indeed. /*It harms nothing at this point.*/

/*Your privacy?*/ Vasiht'h pointed out, and Jahir flushed, turning his face down to hide whatever evidence made it to his cheeks. /*You think I wouldn't care about that?*/

/*I know you do, arii. I am merely aware that my standards of privacy are . . . unusual. In the Alliance.*/

/*Doesn't make them invalid,*/ Vasiht'h said sternly. /*I'll tell her—*/

"What on the battlefields are you two doing?" Luci asked, fascinated. She had her chin in her palm and a puzzled expression on her face.

"They are joined espers, so they are probably discussing their united front," Antonin said, unperturbed. "You shouldn't call attention to it, darling. It's rude."

Luci's ears drooped. "Oh, sorry, ariisen. Ignore me."

/*It harms nothing,*/ Jahir said, pitying her. Accidental trespass on cultural taboos he wasn't even allowed to warn people of . . . it felt arbitrary and cruel. /*It is far enough in the past.*/

"Fine." Vasiht'h looked at Luci and Antonin, ears flat. "You can ask, but don't make a big thing about it. There's no point in asking you to keep secrets because the moment you tell anyone anything, you should be comfortable with everyone knowing it. But don't head straight to a news outlet or anything."

Antonin brightened. "You really don't have to discuss it, if you don't want to?"

"But he'd love to know," Luci murmured.

Vasiht'h sighed. Chuckled. "Obviously. Go on, then, arii. We'll talk."

Antonin's questions were circumspect . . . for a Harat-Shar, positively understated. Listening, Jahir wondered where he'd been reared, and what microsociety had created his fascinating blend of courtesy and discretion. No wonder Luci had loved him: she'd had her own issues with her mother culture. Antonin never asked why Vasiht'h answered most of the questions, nor pressed

Jahir for his perspectives.

Listening to their misadventure in Heliocentrus through the lens of Vasiht'h's experience, mediated by years of safety, was its own revelation. While it was obvious his partner no longer felt the immediacy of the situation, time hadn't filed the sharp edges off Vasiht'h's emotions either. Through the mindline, Jahir experienced the tug of his grief, his indignation, his despair and frustration. And his fear—that above all—his fear, and the anger it inspired. His partner was still defending Jahir from the ghosts of those past cruelties, from the people who'd taken advantage of him, from the Eldritch himself and his tendency toward self-immolation. It took Jahir's breath away. Not that Vasiht'h should feel those things on his behalf, for he'd realized long before the Glaseah had that Vasiht'h could and did feel grand passions. But that years later, Vasiht'h's love for him kept those emotions, and the crusades they inspired, alive . . . that was humbling.

"You're a lucky man, you know," Luci said to him as they watched their partners talk.

"I do know," Jahir replied. "And I am. Very much so." He glanced at her, smiled. "As are you."

"After so much waiting . . . yes, I really am." She sighed, smiling at Antonin. "I hope it never gets old for me, the way it hasn't for you."

"It won't," Jahir murmured. "When it's real, it never does."

Luci gave a purring chuckle and tilted her glass at him. "To happy endings, arii."

"And what they begin," Jahir replied.

"An amazing experience," Antonin was saying, concluding his discussion with Vasiht'h. "I am grateful that you were both there and that you survived with so few complications." The leonine looked at Jahir. "I have one question for you, alet, if I am allowed."

"Continue," Jahir said.

"Do you have any insight on why this pivotal crisis brought you closer together, rather than straining or sundering your relationship?" The leonine folded his hands together on the table. "I have seen a great number of relationships collapse under stress. Since the two of you did so well, I would value any advice."

"Not that we're planning on undergoing any pivotal crises anytime soon," Luci said lazily.

"No." Antonin flashed her a radiant smile. "But I like to learn from people who are farther along the path. You never know when the notes you took will save a life. Or a soul."

The mindline sank under the pressure of Vasiht'h's discomfort. "That's . . . putting a lot on us that I'm not sure we deserve? I mean, we're not all that much older than you! Or at least, I'm not."

"You might be our age," Luci said. "But you've been doing the 'living together' thing a lot longer than us. Plus helping people having problems with it in your work." She cocked a brow. "Yes? Should I ask why the therapist wants to crawl under a rock when someone suggests he might be competent at something?"

Jahir said nothing, sipping from his glass.

/I heard that,/ Vasiht'h muttered.

Jahir pushed his complete innocence back through the mindline, which made the corners of his partner's mouth twitch upward.

"You know what? I'll let you answer that," Vasiht'h said, and turned to Jahir with an expectant look and a merriment in the mindline.

"Now he's done it," Luci murmured to Antonin.

Jahir set his glass back down and placed his napkin on the table, folded. "I love him."

"Is that all?" Antonin chuckled, his ears sagging. "We've got that part down, I think."

"I also trust him with my weakness," Jahir said. "When I am aware of it, which is perhaps less often than is healthy." He glanced at Vasiht'h. "Much harm is done—accidental and tragic—by those who are afraid to reveal their vulnerabilities to those they claim to trust."

"And you?" Luci asked Vasiht'h. "You trust him with your tender underbelly?"

"No question," Vasiht'h said firmly.

"You sure about that?" The pard sounded amused. "The whole 'aware of your weaknesses' part seems like a great place to trip. And you have four feet to do it with."

"We can only work with what we know," Vasiht'h said. "For everything else, we have therapists."

Luci laughed. "All right, then. To therapists!"

"That's the sixth toast you've done this brunch," Vasiht'h said.

"What can I say . . . the champagne here's good."

This being their last full day on Seersana, they parted ways once more: Vasiht'h wanted to see some of the staff from the general hospital where he'd done his second research study, and Jahir wanted to drift. Which he did, with all the ease of a long willow leaf on the surface of the creek on the Seni Galare lands, allowing the crowds to take him where they would. This might have been his life had he not met Vasiht'h: always observing but never partaking in the shorter lives of the Pelted. How well he recalled his nightmares on the topic, of tending gardens of dying flowers. His partner had rescued him, and evidently considered himself still on duty. Jahir found it charming, that Vasiht'h could overlook so entirely this protective streak that made him as ferocious as a more violent person. To defend, Jahir thought—that demanded as much of a soul as any aggressive act. More, because one had to give everything to the attack while remaining gentle enough at core to care for the objects of it. But such metaphors would never find a comfortable home in his partner . . . not because he lacked the emotional capability, but because the Alliance had not prepared him for it, experientially.

How kind a place it was, the Alliance. How grateful he was to live here. And yet, he had a heritage he could not extirpate, and duties he refused to shirk, no matter how long he would be in their fulfillment. Being Eldritch had given him the perspective that allowed him to love the Pelted's busy society, and to marvel at its vitality. Dwelling among them—fully, not as an observer—would give him, in turn, the tools he would need to go home without shame, with gifts.

Which returned his thoughts to where they'd begun when he'd awoken this morning. It was time to address them. In a café gilt by the slanting rays of the afternoon sun, Jahir sipped an affogato gone liquescent and looked up Nieve's Girls. They had a node in the u-banks, unsurprisingly, with information about both the "founding chapter" and the Selnor chapter, which as yet had only one more member, a tigraine Harat-Shar with an intense blue stare and 'a love of rebel knitting.' He paused to study her portrait, wondering how her addition to the group would shape it, and smiled at the thought of a rebelliously knitting Harat-Shar. Only in the Alliance would something as basic and necessary as making clothes be considered an act of artistic deviancy.

Abandoning the public nets for the ones he suspected he had access to only because of his membership in an allied alien race's royal House, Jahir looked up the group's financial information: as the girls had reported, Kayla's father was their financial officer, and in charge of handling charitable donations.

Jahir checked his funds. When they'd begun accruing at a rate even he found extravagant he'd split a tranche of it off and consulted his mother, who'd sent him a name of an investment agency. He hadn't questioned that they had an investment agency; the Queen did not lack for money, and it had to come from somewhere. He'd made sure he never received statements, since he could think of nothing more likely to cause a nervous explosion from his partner, but he checked the balances quarterly. Until now, he'd donated to causes when they'd struck him, in one-time gifts. This, though . . . he wrote instructions for the fund manager. A recurring donation would not go amiss, and he wanted to know where the girls would take their group if they remained committed to it and had the resources.

And that left him with naught to do but contemplate his own situation, and how less simple it was to resolve than the girls'.

He put his tablet away and wrapped his fingers around his cup, resting his lower lip against the ceramic. He had time. Barring tragedy, he had time.

CHAPTER 5

ETOURING TO PALLAND'S office after his visit to the hospital took almost no time. It took even less thought, which was for the best because Vasiht'h's head was too busy with the thoughts he had to have room for anything else. He arrived to find his professor in conference with a student, so he sat in the waiting area and pressed his paws onto the carpet to keep from rubbing them against one another. As it was, he found himself kneading the fibers and guiltily pulled his claws in.

Jahir would have been watching people, stuck in this situation. Once upon a time, Vasiht'h would have done that too, so he tried again. Unfortunately staring at all the students coming and going only increased his disorientation. He really, really didn't feel old enough to have moved on from this environment, and yet the people entering the advising office were young enough they still looked glossy, like the polish hadn't worn off.

Strange to think he wasn't *upset*, exactly. Restless, but not anxious. Impatient. That was the word he wanted. Impatient.

He was still pondering that when Palland stuck his head out his office and raised his brows. "Ready to re-enroll?"

"No!" Vasiht'h exclaimed. And laughed. "You're incorrigible."

"I do try. What brings you by?"

Vasiht'h stood. "I actually have a question about school."

"You have magically arrived at the right place to ask such questions!" Palland smirked and waved him in. "Should I get more cookies?"

Vasiht'h followed him in. "What does it take to become a healer-assist?"

One of his advisor's ears sagged. "I beg your pardon? I didn't think that was your thing, arii."

"It's not," Vasiht'h said. "But it might be my partner's."

"This again . . ."

"No, no." Vasiht'h waved his hands and dropped onto his haunches. "I'm not saying that to have a panic attack about him leaving me. I want to know if he could almost have a degree without me knowing about it!"

"That . . . almost sounds worse, doesn't it?" Palland opined, brows still up.

Vasiht'h sniffed. "Only if he was doing it to leave me. Which he isn't." He wrinkled his nose. "The worst it could be is 'he did it without telling me because he was afraid of upsetting me', which is also bad, but not as likely as 'he was doing it without really thinking about it.' Which is the situation I think we might actually be in. Maybe. So . . . what does it take?"

Palland was pouring himself a fresh mug of coffee, and the studious way he was doing so. . . .

"You already know!" Vasiht'h bent close enough to look into the Seersa's face. "You do, don't you?"

Palland scratched his cheek. "Well, Lafeyette and I still talk." He brightened. "Getting to know him better was one of the benefits of the two of you working together. Fantastic man, Lafeyette. I'm terribly fond of him."

". . . and?"

"You know if I knew something, I couldn't tell you without violating the confidences of a healer who might have been discussing an infamously private species's plans. Hypothetically speaking."

"A healer who was apparently discussing them with you,

already in violation of that species's privacy needs?" Vasiht'h pointed out, ears flattening.

Palland flinched, dramatically. "Ouch. I can neither confirm nor deny that we might have been talking about our favorite students, who happen to work together. Hypothetical, remember?"

Vasiht'h leaned closer. "But?"

"But nothing," Palland answered, crossing his arms.

Vasiht'h grimaced. "I'd argue with you but it won't accomplish anything, will it."

"Not at all." Palland relaxed, reached for his mug and had a sip. "But as a completely unrelated point of interest, you might research licensing board exams. You know. Just to see how people come to them via multiple educational paths. Don't bother with the ones related to the university. You'll find the post-educational institution paths more . . . mmm . . . intriguing. Since they apply to so many fewer people, you understand. It would be relevant to your practice. In terms of . . . ah . . . you having a general sense for how the medical ecosystem works in the Alliance. You being part of it."

Vasiht'h beamed. "Thanks, alet."

"Any time," Palland says. "And you know, if you ever wanted to finish that research degree . . ."

The Glaseah snorted. "Not likely. And before you say anything else . . . no I'm not against teaching. I might even like it. But not until I'm older."

"I hate to tell you this, Vasiht'h-arii, but a person's perception of whether they're old enough for any given activity is largely unrelated to reality."

Vasiht'h laughed. "I believe you. But until I convince me I belong in front of a classroom, I'll stick with what I've got."

"Mmm," Palland said. "Well, when you change your mind, I'll be around. With cookies."

"When I change my mind, I'll bring the milk."

———❄———

From there, Vasiht'h detoured to the medical school's library, where an entire section on career management walked him through the steps of various paths to a healers-assist license. A little more research, this time using his data tablet, netted him a selection of dates and worlds. One of the choices leaped out at him immediately, and he doublechecked the date and pricing. Sitting back, he rubbed his eyes and watched the students drifting through the room. The library still had stacks of books, for people who had an easier time absorbing information off paper, and the building had been designed with multiple alcoves with nooks and tall windows. Vasiht'h was sitting in one of those nooks, basking not just in the natural light, but in the feeling that, for once, he wasn't making a stupid mistake because he'd failed to analyze his own reactions to something.

He also thought, briefly, of being a Palland to someone else's Vasiht'h one day. It didn't seem like a bad thing. He could almost imagine it. Almost, because . . . where was Jahir in that picture?

Vasiht'h sighed a little, smiled. He checked one more thing, then left the library for the open air, where he could have a conversation without disturbing anyone. He selected the proper commtag and waited while it rang, trotting down a sidewalk dampened by a brief spring shower.

"Vasiht'h? Why can't I see you?"

"Sorry," Vasiht'h said. "I'm walking. I didn't expect you to answer . . . aren't you at work?"

Sehvi's sigh was gusty. "Your nephew is sick again. I took him to the doctor this morning, now we're home watching viseos. Or we were until he fell asleep about an hour ago. I'm hoping—desperately and futilely—that he isn't going to give this bug to his sib. Or his father. Or me."

"You're always the last one standing," Vasiht'h said, amused.

"Mom always is. So where are you walking? The least you could do is point the tablet so I can see."

"So bossy," Vasiht'h said, laughing. "I'm on Seersana with Jahir for a classmate's wedding."

"Oooh, weddings! I love weddings. So romantic."

Vasiht'h snorted. "You can't fool me, ariishir. I know what

you consider romantic now."

"Says the Glaseah with at least nine Rexina Regina novels of his own. . . ."

"She grew on me," Vasiht'h said firmly. "You took the healer licensing exams, didn't you?"

"I . . . wouldn't be working if I hadn't." Sehvi sounded suspicious. "Whyyyyy?"

Vasiht'h found a nice bench and sat next to it so he could look at her. "Where did you take yours?"

His sister looked like a mother with a sick kit: that odd combination of bleariness and hyper-focus that characterized someone who hadn't gotten enough sleep but wasn't letting that get in her way. "On Tam-ley. The big teaching hospitals always have licensing exams going for students wanting to graduate. I didn't particularly want to travel, since I was a little distracted at the time."

"By Kovihs?" Vasiht'h teased.

"Yes," his sister said, unapologetic. She grinned wearily. "I wanted to stay close. But I hear I missed out by not choosing to sit post-degree. There are some really fine destinations if you're switching careers and feel like traveling. Or if you have to, if you live someplace that doesn't offer them." She cocked her head. "And now . . . I ask . . . why are you scheming on your partner's behalf?"

"I'm not!" Vasiht'h exclaimed. "I'm just trying to make things easier for him?"

Sehvi put her chin in her palm and groped for the cup of coffee just off screen, pulling it over with a rattle. "This should be good."

"Unless I've missed my guess," Vasiht'h said slowly, "He's either gotten all of, or at least enough of, the educational credits to get a healer-assist's degree. And from what I've read, that means if he passes the exam, he can get the license as soon as he puts in enough hours in an apprenticeship program or interns at the local hospital. He can do that part-time while still working with me."

"Uh-huh," Sehvi says. "And you want him to get this degree because. . . ."

"He wants it?"

"Are you sure?" she asked. "I mean, wasn't all the drama five years ago about him learning that he *didn't* want that?"

Vasiht'h held up a finger. "And *yet*. He still took all the credits. Or I think he has."

Sehvi eyed him.

"I am almost completely sure. And you don't see him when he talks about it. He lights up."

Sehvi looked in her empty cup. "I need more of this for this conversation."

Vasiht'h laughed. "I can't believe I'm getting it that wrong!"

"On two hours of sleep everyone gets everything wrong and needs to be corrected." She rose and padded into her just visible kitchen, pouring her cup full and returning with a cookie. Pointing at him with it, she said, "You can study something without wanting to do it."

"True," Vasiht'h said. "I don't think that's the case with him."

"But why do you think he likes this more than what he's doing with you? Doesn't he 'light up' about therapy?"

"Yes?" Vasiht'h said, thinking of it and smiling. "Yes. He does. But you can love more than one thing, ariishir. Seriously? Why does it have to be chocolate or raspberry?"

"When it could be chocolate *and* raspberry?" Sehvi snorted, took a bite of her cookie, which looked like oatmeal. "Because you only have so much stomach. If you're already full, you have to choose."

Vasiht'h suppressed a laugh. "This metaphor is ridiculous."

"On the contrary, this metaphor is useful, because it demonstrates the problem with your reasoning. Which is that despite having unlimited time in a linear progression if you're immortal—" Sehvi walked her fingers across her kitchen counter, dislodging a crumb. "—you still don't have unlimited hours within a daily context."

"He's not immortal," Vasiht'h said, rueful.

Sehvi waved a hand. "Details. The fact remains—" Again, with the cookie pointing, and with it bitten now Vasiht'h could tell it had Tam-leyan pecans and apple? Date? Some kind of fruit in it. "He's only got so much time in a day. If he's filling it up with being a healer-assist, he's not filling it up with you."

"Assuming he wants to practice medicine," Vasiht'h said. "Which he might not."

Sehvi snorted. "So he goes through the trouble of getting the license and doesn't do anything with it? He'd still have to do the continuing ed to keep the license active."

"Better a couple of classes a year than redoing the entire college education?" Vasiht'h shook his head. "No, I still think it's a good idea for him to do it."

"And . . . you've decided that for him."

"No!" Vasiht'h flushed, touching the side of his muzzle and feeling the heat radiating off it. "It's not about me deciding what he should do. It's me deciding how *I* feel about what he's going to do. In advance. So that I don't react badly to it when he springs it on me."

"Just as long as it's that and not you, say, arranging the whole thing for him and springing *that* on him instead."

"Would that be so bad?" Vasiht'h asked wistfully. "It would be an amazing anniversary present. We're going to be five years in practice next month. . . ."

"Because that would be choosing for him," Sehvi said. "Maybe he wants to do this thing, maybe he doesn't. But you don't get to decide what he does with his life. Even if . . . no, *especially* if you feel like it would make an amazing anniversary present. Because nothing says 'happy anniversary' like 'I'm going to make your life choices for you from now on'? No, ew. Bad."

"A Rexina Regina hero would make it work," Vasiht'h observed, just to watch her reaction. "And the heroine would melt into goo at his strong and controlling personality!"

"Fortunately for all of us, romance novels are fake," Sehvi said, unconcerned, finishing off her cookie. "Leaving us the luxury of enjoying them without having to pass judgment on their unrealistic depictions of relationships."

"Is this the part where I remind you that you gave me HEALED BY HER IMMORTAL HEART to help me with my relationship problems?"

"Of course I did," Sehvi answered. "It was the contrast between their completely unbelievable relationship and your real one that gave you the necessary perspective." She beamed over her coffee mug. "There is a *method* to your sister's madness."

"Is that what you're calling it now . . ."

She laughed. "Ariihir, I love you and you're a dear but I need to take a nap. You won't do anything drastic and stupid while I'm sleeping?"

"Like book my partner an anniversary trip with me to the white sands of Tsera Nova?"

His sister perked up, eyes wide. "Wait, are you serious?"

"Mmm-hmm. I looked it up. Next quarter's is in two months, coinciding with summer on Tsera Nova." Vasiht'h grinned. "The test's given on the orbital station. No doubt to keep the people taking it from being distracted by the views."

Sehvi smacked her hand on the counter. "I was totally wrong. You should book those tickets immediately. Have you seen that place? It's gorgeous!"

"I don't know," Vasiht'h said, looking up at Seersana's gray sky. "All that sand in my fur . . . sounds kind of irritating . . ."

"That's what fur blowers are for! Ahhhhhh, you have got to go and tell me all about it, call me the moment you get there I want *details*."

Vasiht'h laughed. "I'll take your very good advice on not making my partner's decisions for him under advisement, ariishir." He nodded, affecting a look of sage wisdom. "I can't help but think that you might be right. I'd hate to be in any way coercive. You know."

"You are awful," Sehvi said, laughing. "I'm going to sleep. Tell me how it goes, all right?"

"My life as a romance novel hero," Vasiht'h answered, grinning at her. "I can't imagine what'll happen next."

"Your partner will bake you cookies and tweak your nose and tell you how adorable you are . . . no, wait, that's my line." She thought. "His too." She leaned forward and kissed the screen. "Smooch, big brother. Love you."

"Love you too, ariishir."

Smiling, Vasiht'h tucked his tablet back into one of his saddlebags and squinted as a droplet of water smacked his nose. There was a Pad station in the center of the medical campus; as he rose and headed that way, the droplet became a drizzle. At least it wasn't cold, which made it merely annoying, not uncomfortable. Vasiht'h's pawpads squelched as he took a shortcut across a field, which made him think inevitably of those white sands he'd seen in the viseos of Tsera Nova. Even a relative shutaway like him had heard about it as one of the Alliance's premiere vacation spots: a colony just close enough to the Core's major homeworlds to make the trip feel like a jaunt without being painfully distant, and with an idyllic climate maintained by a complex weather system that had been pioneered for it specifically after the colony charter members had completed the terraforming. Not that it had needed much of that, but they'd further sculpted its already dazzling beaches and dotted the resulting paradise with verdant plants to nod pacifically in its breezes.

Vasiht'h wasn't sure what it was about the sea, but every sapient species so far seemed to respond to it viscerally. Tsera Nova had a single small continent framed by a succession of largish islands and archipelagos that afforded multiple opportunities to enjoy the ocean vistas. And if the natural beauty wasn't enough—if it could be called natural, given how much of it was contrived mechanically—it also had a reputation for the finest resorts and the most amazing food and entertainments suitable for everyone from parents with new children to the wildest of party animals.

It wasn't a cheap place to visit. Vasiht'h was counting on that to work in his favor. Grinning, he ducked under cover to wait out the rain as it intensified. He might not be the hero of a romance novel, but he had a few tricks worthy of the cleverest of protagonists. *I love you,* he thought, *that's why I know you so well.* And then he smiled, chagrined. *Now if only I knew myself half as well as I do you . . . !*

CHAPTER 6

IT HAD BEEN JAHIR'S INTENTION to make a graceful escape from Seersana. He had no reason to believe he wouldn't; even had he been inclined to attach his name to any of his charitable activities, the u-bank censors would sweep up the evidence. He preferred it thus: he derived his pleasure from the act of giving, not from the reactions of the recipients, and in fact the contemplation of being forced to witness other people's gratitude discomfited him in the extreme. He had money—well and again, he had done nothing to earn it, save be fortunately born. To be thanked for letting it pass out of his hands into the coffers of those using it for worthy causes . . . it was difficult to support. He had spent some time studying the economics of the Alliance after his discussion with KindlesFlame when first he moved to Starbase Veta; overwhelmingly, his impression of it was as a confused tangle of consent and the usual injustices of physical reality and the social systems that sprang up to address them. As much as possible, he embraced the ideal, preferring to allow people to work with his gifts without any of the emotional burdens incurred by associating with him as their benefactor.

It was not always appropriate to pass silently through the lives of others. This, he judged, was one of those few exceptions.

He was therefore unnerved to exit the hotel lobby with Vasiht'h to find Kuriel, Meekie, and Persy waiting in ambush. The hiccup in his step must have communicated through the mind-line, because Vasiht'h threw a glance at him, brows lifted, before greeting the girls with open arms. "This is a nice surprise! We're on our way out, but we're glad we got to see you one more time? We have a few hours before we make our shuttle . . ."

"We know," Persy said.

"You know!" Vasiht'h exclaimed.

"You told Jill when you were leaving, Manylegs," Kuriel said, dyed tail waving.

"And us where you were staying, while we were talking," Meekie added.

"We did not!"

"Sure you did," Persy said, hands in her pockets. "You mentioned taking a Pad to the hospital and being able to walk through the shopping district for meals, and this is the best hotel in this area that meets both those criteria."

"And only the best would do for our princes," Meekie finished.

"After that, it was just a matter of asking if anyone had seen an Eldritch in the area," Kuriel finished, ears perked. "Since we knew the hotel wouldn't tell us if you were staying, if we asked. And of course, you're highly noticeable, especially as a couple. Lots of people said they'd seen you coming in and out of this plaza, so . . . here we are!"

/They're a little terrifying, aren't they??/ Vasiht'h asked.

/Rather a great deal./

Vasiht'h eyed him. */Why does that sound ominous?/*

Jahir suppressed a sigh he knew would feel like a vacuum between them, accepted there would be no escaping this situation without discomfort. */Ask them why they've come./*

"I don't know how I got elevated to princedom," Vasiht'h began. "And I'm almost scared to ask if there's some reason for all the work you did figuring out where and when we'd be . . ."

"Don't worry, it's not a fancy kind of princyness," Meekie said, comforting. "You're obviously the prince of cookies."

Kuriel grinned. "Cookies need royal representation too."

"And we're here because we want to say thank you." Persy folded her arms and looked at Jahir. "Because . . . it was you, wasn't it?"

"Dare I ask how you derived the conclusion," Jahir said, resigned.

"Princes also have lots of money, and you never really denied the whole 'dragon on a treasure hoard' thing," Persy said.

"And also, Persy and Kuriel are scary with computers," Meekie said. "Kayla's tapa was pretty aghast." She grinned, tail swishing. "We got *such* a lecture."

"Did you," Jahir murmured.

Kuriel's ears sagged. She looked up at the sky and said, "Um, yeah, something about . . . ah . . . respecting the wishes of our donors, particularly in regards to privacy. . . ."

"Oh, I see now," Vasiht'h said. "He tried to give you secret money and you found him out?"

"We guessed," Persy said, stressing the last word.

"Yeah, 'who would have a lot of money' and 'who would have been sending it from a location near this hotel the week they came to visit us after five years away'," Kuriel said, voice trailing off. She folded her arms behind her back, rocking on her painted toes—eye-piercing cyan today. "Locational data isn't tied to people, but, you know, if you can unearth it, then you can use common sense to figure that out. Sometimes."

"I think you're oversharing," Meekie said to her.

"No, it's all right," Persy said. "In this case, anyway, because we owe it to Prince Jahir. So that he knows that we didn't do anything illegal and we weren't *snooping* on purpose. It's just that it was a big donation and we were suspicious."

"In a good way," Meek assured them.

Vasiht'h chuckled. "We've got time before the shuttle leaves. Let's get ice cream."

Kuriel brightened. "Really?"

"Your princes need it if this discussion is going to go any further. Particularly the taller of the two. Me only being the prince of cookies." Vasiht'h canted his head. "Can I expand my . . . uh . . ."

"Aegis," Jahir murmured.

"My that to include all baked goods?"

"Oh, sure," Meekie hastened to assure him. "It's the least we can do."

"It really is," Vasiht'h said. "And since you girls are apparently so good at snooping, you can tell us where the best ice cream place is."

"I know!" Kuriel exclaimed.

"Lemme just tell Dami we're going to be a little later than we planned," Meekie said. "She worries."

As Persy and Kuriel discussed the best possible site for their dessert and Meekie called her mother, Jahir braced himself for the inevitable. When it didn't come, he chanced a look at his partner and found the Glaseah smiling up at him crookedly, sitting on his haunches with his tail wrapped around his feet.

/I'm not going to bite, you know./

/I know?/ Jahir answered, sheepish.

Vasiht'h looked at the girls. /You gave them money for their project?/

/I . . . wanted to see what they would do, if they didn't have to fret themselves with . . . unnecessary concerns?/

Vasiht'h wrinkled his nose, his pensiveness a warm weight in the mindline. /They have to learn how to budget. That's important./

/They have already been at the work for over two years. Surely that is a good enough grounding in fiscal management, particularly with Kayla's father at the helm./ Jahir watched them, his fondness for them and his pride at their ambitions pushing away his ambivalence. /Only look at them, arii. Would you not help them if you could?/

Vasiht'h followed his gaze and sighed, and it felt like contentment. /Yes. Of course./ He folded his arms. /I don't guess they'll run out of your donation anytime soon./

Thinking of the recurring schedule his manager had set up, Jahir answered, /Not if they're careful./ Aloud, he asked, "So?"

"We've decided," Persy said. "And Meekie's done with her mom, so . . . that way?"

"Lead, then," Jahir said, "And we follow."

On the way, they talked . . . mostly about the girls' families, and how nice it was to be autonomous after so long in the hospital. Jahir couldn't decide whether he was astonished at how much freedom the girls had, or chagrined at how much more he'd had at their relative age. Even coddled as the heir to the estate, he'd spent long days on his own exploring the grounds, and when he wasn't in more sedentary lessons, he'd been learning to ride—a dangerous pastime on a world without modern medicine—or handle livestock. And unlike these girls, there would have been no way for him to call for help, had he found himself injured and alone.

But they had access to wonders he had only been capable of imagining after his mother granted him access to the Queen's Wellstream. To wander abroad in such a city with friends and enough money in pocket to enjoy themselves. . . .

/How fortunate we are,/ Jahir said, wonder tinting his voice.

Vasiht'h glanced at him and smiled. */Yes./*

When Persy stopped in front of the restaurant, Jahir sighed.

/Let me guess . . . this is the place you did it from./ Vasiht'h chuckled. "Don't you think this is rubbing it in a little bit, girls?"

"We thought we'd make right by buying you both your drinks?" Persy said, her cheeks pink.

"And not with your money!" Meekie added. "With our money. We don't use the charity's money for ourselves."

Kuriel said, "At least, we don't now. Kayla's tapa says eventually we need to pay ourselves."

"But we don't yet," Persy said. "So . . . ?" She paused by the door.

"In that case," Vasiht'h said, "I think I'll have the biggest crepe they have."

"They have one they stuff with bananas and chocolate." Kuriel grinned and wiggled her blue fingers. "And then the chocolate melts, because the crepe is still hot, and it's gooey and gets all between the spaces and it's like having fondue wrapped in pastry."

"Sold," Vasiht'h said.

Jahir did in fact have gelato, at the insistence of the girls and his partner both: salted peanut, which went well with the cup of espresso. Once they were seated, though, he said, "You do know you should not be chasing the identities of your anonymous donors."

"I told them not to do it!" Meekie exclaimed.

"You did not!" Kuriel objected. "You said we *shouldn't* and then you asked, 'but no, really, do you think you know.'"

Meekie cleared her throat, ears flicking back. "All right, I did say that. But only because we all sort of knew. If we hadn't sort of known, we wouldn't have done it."

"That part's true," Persy said.

"And . . . you're not angry at us, are you?" Meekie asked, hesitant. "We just . . . we wanted to say thank you. Because you two . . . you were such a big part of our lives in the hospital. I guess it's not fair for us to say we're close to you because we don't . . . I mean, we're not technically . . . friends? Or . . . I'm saying this wrong." She covered her face with a hand.

Vasiht'h started to reach for her and paused when Jahir murmured, /Let me./

/Are you sure?/

/It has to be me, arii./ Jahir slipped his fingers around Meekie's wrist and tugged her hand gently until it lifted off her face, exposing her astonished eyes. With that touch he took in her surprise, her gratification, and her confusion and yes . . . her love. Did he need the touch to tell him? They had loved him with all the open-hearted innocence of children when they'd met in the hospital ward. Growing into their teens had only complicated those feelings, not erased them. "Meekie. We are friends. More, I think, for we spent a great deal of time together, and in difficult circumstances."

"Family," Vasiht'h said firmly.

"Even though we don't . . . really talk or see one another

much?" Meekie asked, but the hope in her belied the hesitance of her voice.

"Family can go long periods without seeing one another, and it changes what one feels not at all," Jahir said. "And there is no reason why you should not see us more often, when you are older and more likely to travel."

"You can visit us on Veta one day," Vasiht'h said, smiling. "Give an inspirational talk, or even start a chapter of your charity there. We've got a hospital."

"We do have plans to spread out," Persy said, subdued. "I mean . . . this is what we want to do with our lives. We want to help kids."

"Like us," Kuriel added, fingers nervously tapping the walls of her sundae glass. "Kids like us. Like we were. Still are, I guess, because sometimes I don't feel all that grown up."

"Having said that, though," Vasiht'h said. "This is me reminding you that just because you're close to someone, doesn't mean you get to trample their boundaries."

Persy blushed brightly, looking down at her cup of melting gelato.

"We didn't think of it that way," Meekie said, wilting.

"We just thought . . ." Persy stopped and turned her cup on the table. "I guess it doesn't matter what we thought. It was still wrong."

"I think it matters that we didn't intend to hurt anyone," Meekie said, looking pale. "We were thoughtless, not mean. So we apologize for being thoughtless, because it really does upset us that we hurt you, and that makes it all right. Right?"

"And family forgives mistakes," Kuriel added, "if we say 'sorry'? We are sorry."

"We are," Meekie agreed.

"We just wanted to say thank you," Persy said. "We didn't do it to make you feel hunted. We don't want that, ever."

Kuriel whispered, "You need to actually say the words."

"I know." Persy raised her head, meeting Jahir's eyes with a confidence he found astonishing in one her age. "I am sorry." She smiled, weakly. "Will it be okay if I promise to use my powers only for good from now on?"

"So long as you understand that knowing 'good' is not always simple," Jahir said, "and that you must be willing to reflect on your actions when you discover otherwise."

"That's . . . part of being grown-up, isn't it," Persy said. "Finding out that things are . . . complicated."

"By that standard we've been grown up a long time," Kuriel muttered.

"In some things," Meekie said. "But not in all of them. Which is how we trip up, I guess. Just because we know what it's like to be scared about things most people our age don't have to worry about doesn't mean we get it about everything. Like invading the privacy of someone really important to us."

"We are bad at normal relationship things," Kuriel agreed, glum.

"I think you're doing great," Vasiht'h said. "Plenty of adults don't think things through this much."

"Are we all right, then?" Kuriel asked, anxious, and the other two girls looked so worried the Eldritch couldn't help the tenderness that afflicted him at the sight.

Jahir offered his open hand to Kuriel and Persy, keeping Meekie's in the other. Persy set her hand in his palm, and Kuriel grasped his thumb, and he squeezed all three. So much good in them, and so much intensity: their youth was like a draft of strong wine on an empty stomach. "We are good, yes. Of course I forgive you—Meekie is correct, it matters that you didn't intend to hurt, and that it distresses you to have done so." He smiled. "I think you will do great things. And I hope you keep us informed about the course of your lives. And if time slips away in between your updates, it won't change anything. Not in us."

"Oh, thank Iley." Meekie exhaled gustily; he could feel her hand trembling still in his. "I was afraid we'd messed it up."

"Which would have been awful forever," Kuriel said.

"Amaranth would have killed us," Persy muttered.

Kuriel nodded. "So dead."

Vasiht'h laughed. "Somehow I didn't think the unicorn-lover would have been the dangerous one?"

"Oh, it's all the sad looks." Kuriel affected a stricken look with trembling lower lip, ears dipping. "Y-y-you. . . . you drove the princes *away* . . . ?? How *could* you!"

Vasiht'h covered his face, laughing.

"Really, it's awful," Kuriel said. "Disappointing her is so, so bad."

"Worse after Nieve," Persy said, quieter. "She takes things a lot harder now."

Jahir thought they all did . . . himself included. But he only squeezed their hands. "Well, you shall not have to distress her, then."

"All this talk about us and what we're going to do," Meekie said suddenly. "And we never ask about you and what your plans are! Do you have any?"

"Our plans," Vasiht'h said, "are to keep doing what we're doing, because we enjoy it and we're good at it."

Something about the way the Glaseah delivered this line felt . . . not glib, and not determined. Portentous. Jahir suppressed the urge to study his friend's face for clues, finding none in the mindline sufficient to explanation.

"How did you decide to work on a starbase anyway?" Persy asked. "That sounds like an interesting story?"

/Yours to tell,/ Jahir said.

/You know I know you're foisting all the storytelling off on me because you don't love to talk . . ./

/But you do?/ Jahir proffered an abashed feeling through the mindline, where it wouldn't touch his mouth and give the girls to wonder. /Consider it a gift?/

Vasiht'h laughed aloud. "It is. And actually, the story of how we had to fight to stay there is just as interesting."

"Oh good!" Meekie said. "I love a story. I'm going to get a refill, anyone else?"

They talked for another half hour, one Jahir found revelatory. In the past, Meekie's question about their plans would never have occasioned an answer: he and Vasiht'h didn't discuss their lives with the girls because the context in which they'd met them had made the girls the focus of all their time together. They came to please, to entertain, to comfort, and one did not comfort children with the quotidian details of adult lives they had no context to understand. But the children were no longer children, and if they were not yet adults they were in that tenuous space where every act was preparation for that adult life, or separation from the childish one they were leaving behind. Now they *could* speak to the girls about their decisions, and the challenges they'd met when first they'd settled on Veta, and it was both appropriate and . . . pleasant. It was pleasant.

Jahir had never contemplated this particular permutation of his longevity. He had focused so singularly on the tragedies of his companions growing old and dying that he had missed that he could watch children grow into new companions. There was a poignancy in that as well, but it felt hopeful, rather than despairing.

"I can't believe this guy is now your therapist!" Meekie was saying, stunned. "How does that even work?"

"That's near-magical levels of people skills right there." Kuriel shook her head, wide-eyed. "I want to be like that when I grow up."

Vasiht'h laughed. "The secret is in my . . . uh . . . aegis." He spread his hands. "Baked goods. Everyone agrees on them."

"So you just give people cookies until they like you?" Persy asked, amused.

"I can get behind that," Kuriel said. "Cookies for everyone!"

"And with that, it's time for us to go," Vasiht'h said. "We have a shuttle to catch."

"We'll walk you out!" Meekie said.

It remained a brilliant afternoon, warm with golden light dancing on every awning that rippled in the breeze. As Vasiht'h hugged Kuriel and Persy, Meekie hung back. Looking up at Jahir, she said, quietly, "I'm guessing the money's going to keep coming?"

He glanced down at her.

"Just . . . guessing."

Jahir smiled, wry. "Your guesses are rather unnerving, arii."

"I just . . ." She trailed off. "Persy's good with money and she's the one who's driving the ship. Which is great because none of the rest of us like that part or are as good at it. But she's human, and I think humans don't necessarily recognize some of the . . . um . . ." The Tam-illee tapped her lip nervously with a finger. "The realities of the Alliance."

"One of which is. . . ."

"That you Eldritch actually are as rich as the princes in fairy tales," Meekie said. "And what that means, materially, for us. Since you also live a long time."

Jahir considered this. "Arii? What is it you're asking me?"

"I just want you to know . . . that it's all right to stop giving us money. And all right to keep giving us money. It's not going to matter to us, because we love you. And discovering how rich you are isn't going to change anything. I mean . . . we love you because we love *you*, and I don't want you to think because . . . because we thought of you as some fairy tale prince that we expect you to be that way?" Meekie's ears fell. "I am *so* bad at this."

"On the contrary," Jahir said gently. "I think you are excellent at it. And only like to grow more so with time."

"All right." She blew out a breath, relaxing visibly. "I didn't mess that up, then. Yay!"

He laughed. "Not at all. And keep in touch, as it pleases you to do so. As you've observed, I will be . . . available . . . for a long time."

"Iley willing," the girl said firmly, and had her hug from him before joining the others. They waved, he waved back, and as he watched they melted into the riotously bright stream of people passing through the shopping district. Vasiht'h padded over to join him. "Did you ever think . . . ?"

That they would see the day that even one of the girls would be freed of their prison to be normal again? "No," he said. "I hoped, but I did not believe."

"Me neither, to be honest." Vasiht'h's sigh was a happy one. "But it's so good, isn't it."

"Little finer in this life, arii." At the Glaseah's glance, he clarified. "To see those one cares about healthy and about their lives, contented."

"Yes," Vasiht'h agreed. "And speaking of being about your lives . . ."

"We are due to be about ours, yes."

On the way to the nearest Pad station, Vasiht'h added, "You gave them a lot, I'm guessing?"

Jahir paused a heartbeat before replying, "Would it be an issue if I did?"

"No," Vasiht'h said, and his fierce satisfaction filled the mind-line with an anthem he would probably have been appalled to hear himself, given its martial tenor. "No, if I had money, I'd use it for just that sort of thing."

But not, Jahir thought, on himself, or his partner, or his 'normal life.' He suppressed his resignation, and not well enough. Before Vasiht'h could ask, he said, "I will miss them."

"I will too," Vasiht'h said. "They're going to be busy, growing up. But I bet once they settle down, they'll start sending us mail. Watch. Give them ten years, maybe."

"We'll see," Jahir murmured.

CHAPTER 7

"WHAT DO YOU MEAN YOU haven't talked to him about it yet?" Sehvi hissed.

"I haven't found the right time!" Vasiht'h answered.

"It's been two weeks!" Sehvi leaned into the camera, her face so close he could pick out the darker striations in her brown irises. "Do you even know if they've got slots left in the test? They only take a certain number of people per session!"

Vasiht'h winced. "I know. It's just . . . things have been busy!"

"Busy or something else?" She folded her arms and scowled at him.

"You were the one telling me to respect his autonomy!"

"And you've put this off so that you could do that?" Sehvi snorted, rolled her eyes. "I highly doubt that. Tell me the real reason you're stopped up on this, big brother, so I can tell you why you've got it wrong again."

"You love that, don't you," Vasiht'h said with a sigh.

"Only because you listen to me when I tell you to stop doing dumb things." She smiled a little. "It makes me feel useful. So. 'Fess up."

"Fine. I like our life the way it is?"

Sehvi sighed. "You're alone, I take it."

He nodded. "Jahir's out swimming."

"So, go bake something. I can see the kitchen from here. And make it something unusual, all right? No cookies, you can do those in your sleep. Something you have to think about, at least a little."

"I did just get a bag of local filberts . . . I wanted to try some kind of muffin with them?"

Sehvi wrinkled her nose. "Make them chocolate?"

"Isn't that too expected? Chocolate and hazelnut?"

"It's expected because it's *delicious*."

"Good point." He padded back toward the kitchen, leaving his sister's image projected on the wall of the den. He could see her from the island where he usually mixed his doughs, partially because her image was so large he could practically count the whiskers on her muzzle. "Look, it's complicated."

"Isn't everything." She leaned back with her cheek in a palm, watching him. "Go on. Tell me."

He eyed her as he took down the jar of filberts. "When you and Kovihs start having relationship issues . . ."

"I'll be the first one to listen patiently when you say you told me so," she answered. "So far you're out of luck there, though. Kovihs and I work things out because we, you know, communicate."

"It's how much we communicate that's the problem, though," Vasiht'h said. At her expression, he lifted his hands. "It's just . . . I can tell what he's feeling. Through the mindline. And it's . . ."

Complicated. Vasiht'h made a face at the bowl he'd brought down for the batter, seeing his reflection in it grimacing back at him. Not bad, no. But they'd gotten home and resumed seeing their clients and everything had seemed fine on the outside, but he knew the Eldritch was . . . busy . . . with something. That it troubled him a little. Not a great deal, but Vasiht'h hadn't liked the feel of it. Like . . . demission. "He's working through something."

"Isn't he always?"

Vasiht'h brought up the recipe and eyed it. Not really different from most of his muffin mixes. Putting chocolate in it still felt like cheating. What would work with filberts? He brought one to his nose and rubbed it, sniffing the oils. Setting it down, he went for the genie.

"You should at least put chocolate chips in that," Sehvi called.

"I'll put chocolate chips in *one* of them. On the top." Vasiht'h requested some espresso and inhaled the fragrance rising off it. Ah, yes. "I think he's . . ."

"Working through something."

"Yes."

"So why leave him stewing?" Sehvi asked. "Pull him out of his head before he drowns there."

Vasiht'h set the espresso cup down, startled.

"Right?" she said. "Two weeks is more than enough time to ruminate about something. Your job as his best friend is to help him work through it before he stops being functional. Also . . . what on the worlds are you doing?"

"Making coffee hazelnut muffins," Vasiht'h said. "They'll be amazing. You'll see."

"No, I won't," she said. "But I regret that. I could eat the one with chocolate chips on it."

"I'll eat that one for you in spirit."

"Meaning you'll just eat it."

"Mmm-hmm."

Sehvi laughed. "Will you talk to him?"

"Only if you promise to tell me about the first fight you have with Kovihs."

"You haven't had a fight yet with your Eldritch, you know." At his skeptical look, she laughed. "Seriously, you're a therapist. You know what real relationship fights look like."

"I guess I do," he said. "We just . . . we have the mindline. You know? It's hard to get to the point of complete dysfunction everyone else does."

Sehvi snorted. "Thinking like a mindblind race. You should know as well as I do that the things in our heads we don't say out loud are far more likely to start fights—really awful ones—than the things we share out loud. Or don't. No, you'll just have to face it. The two of you are as sappy a couple as anything written by one of my romance authors."

"Right. And you and Kovihs have two kits now and have had no enormous fights?"

"Unlike you, I have no problems owning my happiness." She leaned toward him. "So . . . you'll do something about this?"

"I guess I will." He smiled at her. "Thanks, ariishir."

"What I'm here for."

After she'd disconnected, Vasiht'h brought out a second bowl for the wet ingredients, ignoring the sound of her voice repeating in her head in time with his pulse. *No problems owning my happiness. Unlike you. Unlike you.*

Was that what it was? Was he waiting for some other shoe to drop? And what a horrible metaphor that was, since he had no less than three other shoes that could fall out of the sky and smack him on the head. Vasiht'h sighed. But maybe it wasn't fair. He would be happy if he thought Jahir was happy, but he had the nagging feeling that Jahir wasn't. Hopefully that wasn't him projecting.

The hand Vasiht'h wanted to smack his brow with he kept firmly on the spatula.

Jahir was not, in fact, concerned about his relationship at all. Returning to Veta had felt like coming home, and while he'd experienced a pang of guilt over how gladly he embraced it over the world he'd abandoned, it had not been sufficient to flagellate himself for it. Or at least, not much. He hadn't even spared much thought for KindlesFlame's suggestion about his potential license as he'd settled back into his routine with Vasiht'h.

No, it was a letter from his mother that had been occupying all his thoughts.

I have been mulling on my last visit to Ontine, during which I gave to the Queen our promises and allegiance, and all that went as expected.

What puzzles me were some of the interactions I had in the drawing rooms. Do you find it strange that I was approached by Lady Filiana on the matter of how I make do with neither husband nor sons at my side? She has lost yet another grandchild, alas, and her sole child is now once again without issue. She fears for the succession. Well and again, I hardly blame her in such a situation. What startles me is that I have become somehow a symbol of a woman alone! How ridiculous, do you not agree? I am the least alone of any woman I know on the world. I have no less than two sons to my name, and within the same generation! Such riches have not been often seen since Landing!

But we are not so fruitful as we were. Perhaps it is for the best, given our longevity. I am selfishly glad to have the both of you, however. You and your brother are the light of my life, and I do not fear to write it.

It was a completely routine sort of letter, and yet he was still deliberating on its contents away from the tablet, in the water. He'd gone to this swim in order to escape, because nothing soothed him like water. And yet, his feelings about his people, his duties to them, his eventual return . . . they distressed him with their knotted mingling of grief and guilt, regret and love, so much that even exercise did not soothe them. The tangle was enough to turn him from thoughts of the license, solely by association, for he knew he would one day return to be the doctor who prevented the death of Lady Filiana's grandchildren. Perhaps literally, for barring disease or accident, Lady Filiana and her grieving daughter would still be alive and almost certainly still be trying to bring forth the needful heir.

Who was he to decide that now was not that time? He could finish his education, return immediately, and go to that work, and yet he wasn't. Why? What made his comfortable life here a moral choice when weighed against the good he could be doing for those who were suffering far more?

And yet, he didn't want to give up this life.

He and Vasiht'h had resumed meeting with their existing clients and seeing new ones, and these people he knew they materially aided, which made him wonder what made their problems less important than his people's. Was the good he did here sufficient payment for the good he wasn't doing at home?

Jahir knew these questions to be imponderables. There were no right answers. But he had to be satisfied with himself, and he was afraid that he wasn't. That he was reneging on some point of honor to which he was irrevocably committed as part of his own self-definition. He could read the statements from his investment manager about the use of his money by all the charities to which he donated, and still it wouldn't pay for the loss of another Eldritch child, perished for want of medical care because he had decided to tarry here.

That KindlesFlame had made it clear there was a deadline should have clarified his decision. It didn't.

Packing from his swim, Jahir headed back to the apartment. The starbase had seasons wherein the temperature changed a few degrees. It was late summer by Veta's standards, so the breeze was freshening across his shoulders. Around him the Pelted wandered toward cafes and shops: the byway was broader than the ones in Seersana's shopping district, so it didn't feel as crowded while still being dense with the Alliance's staggering visual diversity. In the beginning, he'd been overwhelmed by the number of species . . . now, he thought his fascination was more basic even than that. The Eldritch were, to the last man, woman, or child, tall, elongated, and white. Their hair, at most, had a wave—otherwise it was uniformly straight, and only the most well-to-do of noblewomen had someone to curl a tress or two artistically around her face. His people grew to around the same height, and very close to the same density of muscle and fat. Even their faces had a certain homogeneity, since there were so few of them and breeding was necessarily close and tangled. A Galare would probably recognize another Galare, even before being introduced, and having one's mother's eyes meant, very probably, having one's cousin's, aunt's, grandmother's, and great-grandmother's.

Here even two Seersa might be wildly dissimilar. What must that be like, he wondered? And how could he give it up?

When he passed through the door into their home, he was arrested by an ambrosial scent. "What . . . is that?"

Vasiht'h, sipping kerinne at the breakfast table, looked up from his data tablet and smiled. "Filbert-coffee muffins. Dusted with cocoa. They're in stasis . . . have one?"

"I think I shall."

The muffins in question were not the only thing waiting in stasis. There was a cup there of coffee—the kind leavened with chicory perhaps, from the oily dark that clung to the ceramic when he tilted the cup. Staring down at this evidence of such care, he felt something in him trying to crumble and stiffen at the same time.

"You should take the licensing test, you know."

"I . . . I beg your pardon?" he exclaimed, so startled he almost questioned that Vasiht'h had spoken at all.

But he had, and at Jahir's utterance his partner twisted to look toward him. "The licensing test," Vasiht'h said. "The next one is on Tsera Nova? We could go together. I'll go drink purple things with umbrellas and get sand in my fur on the planet while you slave away at three days of tests. Then you join me and I make you drink the best purple things with umbrellas. I'll have figured out by then which ones are worth the time."

"You . . . would have me do this."

Vasiht'h set his cup down. "Arii? Come sit? Bring the coffee and the muffin."

Jahir did so, because it was easier than objecting that he had suddenly misplaced his appetite. Nor could he reject an offering made so obviously with love. "I did not know you knew."

"I figured it out with some help," Vasiht'h said. "But . . . that's less important than that you know I don't mind you doing it. And you really shouldn't waste the time you've put into it already. Before you say you have the time to waste . . . it's not about that. It's about respecting the time you've already put into it. You know? If you don't take it seriously when you're studying it, you can't expect yourself to start taking it seriously when it's real."

"If I do take the exam," Jahir said, grasping at anything to make sense of the conversation, "I will not have a full license until I accrue the necessary practical hours at the hospital. It will take away from the time we spend here."

"Not much, though," Vasiht'h said. "And you'll enjoy it." He chuckled. "Actually, having done therapy research in a hospital, I can tell you that you'll generate a lot of referrals."

Jahir stared at him. The mindline was quiescent . . . no, more than that. It was soft as a blanket, warm like sunlight. Quiet, the good quiet of a companionable silence. "You are taking this so very much more well than I anticipated."

Vasiht'h leaned over and cut the muffin into quarters. "And you're taking it a lot worse than I expected. Your accent's showing. Here. Try this, tell me if the flavor combination works? I like it, but you're more the coffee connoisseur than I am."

Jahir sampled the muffin, and there was something grounding about the familiar act of trying some new recipe. It was . . . "Sublime?" he said. "Unexpected, though. One grows resigned to chocolate and hazelnut."

"Chocolate and hazelnut is good. I wanted something different."

Jahir set the quarter down. "Why?"

"Did I want to do something different with the muffins? Do I want you to do it? Or why I'm not upset?"

"Yes?"

Vasiht'h settled back, warming his palms on his mug. His amusement sparkled in the mindline, just a touch, like sunlight on a pond shadowed by lily pads. "I'm guessing if I start with why I decided to change a recipe, you'll be . . . um . . . 'wroth'."

That startled Jahir into laughing. "No, never. That's rather too much passion to expend on what would only be a minor irritation."

"But it's related." Vasiht'h nodded toward the muffin. "The way you put it: 'one grows resigned' to things. You do that too much. Never about other people—you wouldn't let the girls 'become resigned' to not having enough money to accomplish their goals—but for yourself? All the time! And I hate that. You deserve good things too."

"Perhaps," Jahir said, quietly. And then drawing in a breath and forcing himself not to avoid discomfort, "No, certainly I do, the same as every other being does. But I question whether it's meet for me to give myself those things."

"It's not a gift to take care of yourself," Vasiht'h said sternly. "And you have to do that. The Goddess doesn't put us here to neglect ourselves to the point where we need to be carried by everyone around us. A little of that is okay, because we can't be strong all the time in everything, but not constantly. We have . . . ah . . . responsibilities." He smiled crookedly. "But wouldn't my sister howl through this whole conversation."

"Her words, I take it?"

Vasiht'h laughed. "She'd be pulling at my ears. 'So you were listening but do you ever show it.'" He shook his head, tapped the table near Jahir's plate. "But she's right. Self-care is not indulgence."

Jahir said, quiet, "Where I'm from, arii, two outworld educations certainly are."

Vasiht'h leaned forward. "So why are you doing it?" He lifted a hand. "And don't tell me 'because I wanted to' because one, you never do anything for only one reason, and two, you never do things for yourself unless people push you to."

"This," Jahir said, "is the moment where I eat more of your muffin to conceal my chagrin, isn't it."

"Probably," Vasiht'h agreed, his affection mingling in the mindline with his exasperation. "Jahir . . . you're here now. You can blame yourself for that, and miss the opportunities you could take advantage of . . . or you can make the most of it. Why would you do the former when you can do the latter?" The Glaseah paused, grimaced. "Honestly, if you're going to lean toward the former, why even be here at all? You can't be half a martyr. Or you could, but it's ridiculous."

Jahir stared at the coffee, made for him, and the muffin, submitted to him for his opinion. "It seems so unfair, that I might have so many opportunities, when other people have so few."

"It is unfair," Vasiht'h said. "But we can't make the universe fair. That's too big a job for any one person. All we can do is receive the gifts we're given with gratitude and use them wisely. And help people, where we can, when we're able. Which requires us to be healthy enough to do that first."

"Sometimes we make ourselves healthy by helping others," Jahir murmured.

Vasiht'h sat up and walked around the table. Before Jahir could ask, he found himself enveloped in his partner's furred arms, and the embrace was so surprising he yielded to it without hesitation. They touched so infrequently this way, and when they did it was almost invariably at Jahir's instigation.

/You are bound and determined to make things as hard on yourself as possible, aren't you,/ Vasiht'h said, in the mindline that proved—to his mind, and so to Jahir's—that the Goddess loved them. */But it's all right to have good things in your life, arii. And all right to say 'yes' to them. So say 'yes' to this one?/*

Jahir was silent a moment, resting in both the physical and mental embrace. Finally, he offered, of the hug, */I accepted this?/*

/You did,/ Vasiht'h agreed, drawing back to look at him. */And without a pause. I know this is harder for you because it's all about you, not just me. But it is a little bit about me, too, because it would make me happy to see you doing something that matters to you. And this matters./*

"What we do also makes me happy," Jahir said, voice roughened.

"I know," Vasiht'h said. "Or I would be a lot more scared about you apparently feeling the need to learn a completely different job. But this isn't about either-or. It's about both-and. Right? You can have both licenses, and it's not going to hurt us. Or you. Or some nebulous other people who don't have the same chances you have to do the things you get to do."

Jahir thought of the Eldritch dying of unnecessary causes on the homeworld and wasn't so certain about that. But . . . he also couldn't help them until he had the education. "I suppose it wouldn't take a great deal of time to sit the test."

"It wouldn't, no. We'd get to have a vacation, too. With purple drinks with umbrellas in them."

Jahir leaned back out of the embrace. "I don't know about the purple drinks. The ocean view sounds pleasing, though."

"After you take the test. Otherwise you might get distracted."

With a sigh, Jahir smiled at his best friend. "You're convinced about this course, then."

Vasiht'h snorted, resuming his place at the table and drinking the rest of the kerinne. "It's just a test, arii. What's the worst that could go wrong? You fail it and have to do it again? Then we reschedule for a different time, after you take a few more classes."

"And if I pass?"

"Then you get your provisional license and do some work at the hospital, and we move our schedule around to accommodate it," Vasiht'h said. "That's hardly the worst thing in the worlds, and the fact that you even think it might be is leading." He pointed. "Do I need to refer you to Allen?"

Jahir laughed. "No, please. I daresay one of us seeing him is enough."

"Exactly." Vasiht'h smiled at him, and through the mindline the love felt like a warm wave, enveloping. "So is this settled?"

"I . . . think so, yes."

"Good. Then finish your muffin and let's make plans."

CHAPTER 8

THE TRIP TO TSERA NOVA could take as long as five days and as short as a single day, depending on the number of flight connections and the speed of the individual vessels. Even having had experience booking such trips, Vasiht'h decided to leave the arrangements to Jahir. It was one thing, apparently, to buy passage to Core worlds, which supported a constant flow of traffic of nearly every kind. Planets primarily attracting tourists . . . Vasiht'h wondered if it they were hiking the prices up on purpose, and if that was legal. But maybe there simply weren't as many options to choose from, and the people with the money to go to entirely different planets just to recreate weren't going to bat their lashes at the amounts required by dedicated passenger liners. With some creative juggling, he could have traded time for savings by hopping to one of the Core worlds first, then taking a short leg from there, but . . . his head started aching. He got the feeling if he started scheduling such contortions, Jahir would ask him why, and then they would have another tiresome conversation where the Eldritch didn't actually say anything, just looked at him mournfully.

Vasiht'h hated those mournful looks. They worked far too well.

Vasiht'h didn't pick the hotel either, because there was no such thing as a cheap hotel on Tsera Nova. The only economical alternative for that was to stay on the station, and Jahir refused.

"We are not going to—" The Eldritch paused to lift the tablet and read from the marketing brochure, "—'the tropical jewel in the Alliance's Crown neighborhood' to sleep in orbit."

"We can sleep in orbit and go down every day!" Vasiht'h said. "That's what Pads are for!"

"Padding from orbit is itself not a minor expense," Jahir pointed out, setting the tablet down. "And the accommodations in orbit are not substantially less money."

"They are compared to those prices . . ."

Jahir shook his head, expression stern. "No, arii. You talked me into this . . . well and again, we shall do it. And I shan't go to excess. But I wish to do the thing in relative comfort. Or would you prefer us to wait until autumn? The licensing exam then is on Asanao, in some mountain retreat, I believe."

Vasiht'h had seen the photos of the 'mountain retreat'. It was so high on the peak you had to use a Pad to reach it, because any trail would have been too steep for mere vehicles. Its major attraction was the path around its perimeter . . . the invisible one created by a field-generator, which allowed you to enjoy the thousands-feet drop under your feet. It was alternately billed as having 'the most breathtaking views on the planet' and being 'the ultimate test of courage.' "Ugh, no. Absolutely not."

"Then I shall book us a hotel, and I will be the one Padding to the station for the exam," Jahir said. "After I finish, we can tarry a few days longer to enjoy the sights. Yes?"

The viseos on the tablet between them seemed to sparkle at him. Vasiht'h imagined his triumphantly successful friend picking through a light meal and then diving into an ocean. That ocean, the pellucid aquamarine one that gleamed in the perfectly photographed sun. "Yes."

The Glaseah didn't start feeling excitement until they were

packed and once again at Veta's docks.

"Rather more traveling than we usually indulge in," Jahir observed. "Two trips within a year."

"Maybe we should travel more?" Vasiht'h asked, but saying it he immediately knew they wouldn't. "Or, you know. When the mood strikes us."

"Or need does." The Eldritch was watching the crowds stream past, the mindline generating a warm wind that seemed to brush against the fur on Vasiht'h's sides. "I believe this might be better classified as . . . a business trip?"

Vasiht'h laughed. "Yes, I guess so! Who would have thought it."

"We could go to more conferences, I suppose."

"Or," Vasiht'h said, resettling the strap of his carry-on over his shoulder, "we could just stay home and be domestic."

"There is a great deal to be said for domesticity."

"One of the many reasons we get along so well." Vasiht'h grinned, catching the sparkle in his friend's eye.

"One of the many."

The liner Jahir booked for them made the trip in a leisurely day and a half, necessitating a sleepover in a surprisingly comfortable cabin, given its size. The ship was typical for its purpose, Vasiht'h guessed: big windows everywhere, great food, lots of entertainment, helpful associates. He and Jahir spent most of their waking hours in the passenger lounge, which had its window wall open to Wellspace, overlaid with a glittering projection of their location relative to their destination and popping up landmarks in normal space as the ship passed them, unseen. Jahir read medical journals, as was his habit; Vasiht'h caught up on his backlog of messages, writing all his relatives including the ones who preferred only sporadic correspondence.

After dinner, when they'd repaired to their cabin to sleep, Vasiht'h asked, */Are you nervous?/*

Jahir sat on the edge of his bunk, shaking his sleeves down over his hands. Staring up at the ceiling, he answered in the intimacy of the mindline. The associated emotions . . . like a clear sky, bright with sun and potential. */No? Not the way you would suggest, I think. I know the material. I do not fear the test./*

/The rest of it then? After?/

"Mayhap," Jahir murmured aloud. His sigh was subtle, more visual than audible: Vasiht'h could see it lift his shoulders, make his braid shift against his neck. */I am nervous like a horse ready for a run, waiting to be released to it./*

Which wasn't the whole story, Vasiht'h thought, and felt a flush of satisfaction. The puzzle of his partner's complex emotions never ceased to fascinate him . . . when he wasn't worried that it was his fault, anyway. Like now: would he learn what had made the Eldritch shift out of the mindspeech into words? What uncertainty had prompted it? The mindline wasn't giving any hints.

"It'll be done before you know it," was what he decided to say aloud, and plumped his pillows.

"Yes."

There was something in the endlessness of the Alliance that stole one's breath, at the contemplation of the concept, at the confrontation of the reality. Disembarking from the passenger liner onto the orbital station's dock, Jahir had to remind himself to keep walking lest he trip Vasiht'h behind him . . . for the dock's entire exterior wall was flexglass, and the planet spread in that vista, so enormous, so vibrant and dark a blue. . . .

"Goddess," Vasiht'h said, coming up alongside him, wide-eyed. "Can you imagine what it cost to put that up instead of something more sensible?"

"But oh, how good that they did!" Jahir said.

"It is a tourist destination, I guess." Vasiht'h came to a halt beside him while the traffic flowed around them out of the gate. "Those are some interesting cloud patterns, though."

The white swirls glossed the surface of the world like paint under the glass of a marble, so crisp they looked sharp to the touch. The impossible clarity of vacuum never ceased to delight

Jahir . . . that and the Alliance's ability to create a pane of material so clear he could see through it thus.

It was the outrageous size of it, and the breadth of the view, as if he could fall forward into it, that made him feel suddenly how fortunate he was, and how impoverished his people were.

"On the other hand," Vasiht'h said cheerily, "if this is what the dock looks like, the place you're doing the test should be gorgeous. I hope you'll be able to concentrate."

"God and Lady save me," Jahir answered, to the Glaseah's amusement. "Speaking of which, I must report into the proctor. Can you handle the hotel?"

"I'll take care of it," Vasiht'h said. "If we can check in, anyway. If it's too early, I'll get our baggage transferred to a locker and go get my feet wet."

Jahir smiled at him. "I'll send a message as soon as I'm free."

"Great," Vasiht'h said, beaming up at him. "I'm glad we made it."

"I am as well," Jahir replied, and was surprised and gratified to discover he meant it.

They parted ways, Vasiht'h back into the dock to use the ground-facing Pads, and Jahir further into the station in accordance with the instructions he'd been issued when he'd registered for the test. The walk proved illuminating. He had passed through many staging platforms since leaving the fringes of the Alliance for its Core. Living on Veta had accustomed him to the starbase's architecture, which served its specific imperatives, mostly commercial and military, but even the most basic of the Alliance's stations had an aesthetic focus possible only to a civilization with a powerful industrial base. The Pelted could afford to put windows on every wall and plants in every corner, because they already had the facilities that could create such things. Why not, then?

This though was the first station he'd visited built specifically to service a tourism industry, and it cast every other platform into the shade. He exited the docks via a floating bridge over a spreading terrace of shops and exquisite miniature parks, small

enough for a handful of people. Each of these terraces was floating over a transparent floor, so that the visitors seemed to be
visiting islands suspended in space over the planet. Many people
were tarrying on the broad bridges, translucent ones like his,
staring down at the world and exclaiming at its features.

It was not just beautiful, but whimsical as well. Fountains
on one level sent water soaring in thin colored arcs into bowls
further down. As he stopped to look, he discovered they weren't
on timers, but reacting to the people near them. Specifically the
children: different colored splashes would follow them from platform to platform, and then "run away" when noticed or chased.
Clouds of bubbles drifted past as well; as he watched, a school
of them drifted past his shoulders, and amid them he found
fish, streamlined into some artist's conception of creatures that
would be at home in the shoals of space. He reached toward one
and it darted under his fingers to be petted, its solidigraphic skin
warm and slick.

This was the Alliance at play. Not just the technology: it
showed in the people visiting, too, the slowed tenor of their
conversation, the frequent laughter, the shrieks of delighted
children. It seemed a pity to leave the area for the convention
center where he'd be sitting the exams. He would have to bring
Vasiht'h here later . . . it was just the sort of thing his partner
found delightful.

After the terraces, the convention center should have seemed
more mundane. But it had sculpted its halls around rock gardens
of staggering beauty, and all the rooms had more of the enormous windows: some looking inward at those gardens, others
outward at space. Jahir followed the paths to a door that opened
on what was thankfully a very normal sort of lecture hall. There
was a Hinichi wolfine standing at a desk, her hair pinned into
a golden swirl behind her cream-colored ears. At the sight of
him, she glanced at her tablet, then back up. "You would be Jahir
Galare, I presume? Welcome, alet."

"Thank you," he said.

"Do you mind filling out some paperwork?" she said. "Have a

seat, please. Can I get you something to drink?"

"Water would not go amiss, thank you." He seated himself at one of the desks and accepted the proffered tablet. It surprised him, how easily she'd handled him—he tended to create problems with paperwork, given the censors' habit of sweeping it up. As it was, it didn't surprise him that anything he'd filled out prior to arrival had vanished. The hacks his former client was developing for him did not yet reliably work on every type of data he wanted to remain permanent. He could wish the censor would allow him to make some choices rather than deciding for him what evidence of his existence he was permitted to leave behind.

"Thank you," she said, when he handed the tablet back to her. "We have an orientation session after lunch today, and then you're free until tomorrow morning. The exam starts promptly at mark-eight. We don't allow anyone in after we shut the doors, so I tell everyone to show up early." An impish smile. "That guarantees most of them show up on time."

He laughed softly. "I imagine so. Lunch then would be at . . ."

"Mark twelve, so Orientation begins at mark one. You might enjoy the terraces? There's a planet-facing set and a space-facing." Another smile. "They orbit the center of the station."

"Do they," he said, trying to imagine how that worked, or who had engineered it.

"Oh yes. It takes about two months. When you're walking around on them, you're actually being moved."

"Wonders never cease," he murmured.

"Not here, they don't," she agreed.

———∞∞∞———

Vasiht'h stared up at the sky, mouth agape.

"Gorgeous, isn't it?" the Harat-Shariin pantherine said as he checked the Glaseah's reservation. "I never get tired of it."

"It's unearthly," Vasiht'h said. "Like the clouds are sculpted."

The pantherine chuckled. "They are! We have brilliant weather control systems here. You'll never have a bad day on Tsera Nova."

Vasiht'h shook his head. "I wish that could be said of every place."

"I'd agree with you, but then I'd be out of a job here, and I'd hate to be out of a job here." The Harat-Shar grinned. "All right, you're set. Your room's twelve-seventy, and the path will light your way there. I encourage you to check out the amenities. We have an amazing spa. They'll do things to your muscles that will make you want to ooze into a pillow and never move."

"That . . . sounds good, actually." Vasiht'h hitched the bag more comfortably over his shoulder. "Thanks."

"My pleasure. And welcome to your home away from home, the jewel of the Alliance Crown!"

Vasiht'h eyed him, amused. "You deliver that line well."

"Would you say I did it with gusto?"

"Oh, definitely."

Another grin, so bright Vasiht'h almost imagined the sparkle tinging off the pantherine's eyetooth. "Then make sure you mention it on your service review."

Laughing, Vasiht'h left him behind and padded out from under the cabana where the hotel check-in service was handling those visitors who preferred to talk with someone in the flesh, rather than let a computer handle their arrangements. That the hotel offered that service struck Vasiht'h as only the first of its many signs of luxury: most hotels operated like the one in Seersana, with live employees handling concierge services but computers handling check-in and room assignments.

The Diamond Sands resort was in fact on the beach, a cluster of small buildings built onto decks, and the decks surrounded in verdant foliage. Each of those buildings had maybe twenty rooms, with a central courtyard for sunbathing or—checking the brochure on his tablet—bonfires at night, or cook-outs hosted, naturally, by the hotel and its five-star restaurant staff. Vasiht'h didn't have to look at the prices to know it was ridiculously expensive, and he didn't much care with the breeze off the ocean blowing through the fur on his flanks. People said the sound of waves on the shore was soothing? He found it exciting. Like his Eldritch, enigmatic and unknowable, and therefore an invitation to grapple with the Goddess's many mysteries.

The path had lit, true to the Harat-Shar's promise, the stones under his paws glowing a cerulean blue. When he moved forward, the glow moved just far enough to keep in front of his next step. Following the guide, he trotted to one of the small buildings and walked up the deck's stairs to the topmost platform, some seven feet off the ground. The room unlocked for him onto an airy suite that was mostly balcony. Peeking through the side door he found one bedroom, also rimmed with a balcony, if a shorter one. The view was utterly spectacular.

"I could be rich," Vasiht'h said aloud, "if being rich meant this sort of thing all the time."

And immediately thought better of it, because he couldn't imagine being rich, and the idea made him uncomfortable.

He also couldn't stop staring out the window wall. Shaking himself, Vasiht'h walked toward it and discovered it wasn't a wall at all, but a force field that went permeable when he stepped through it. Startled, he looked over his shoulder, then gave up calculating expenses and just enjoyed it. The balcony's golden planks were warm under his feet, and the sea was close enough that he could see the foam on the breakers of waves that were an unlikely aquamarine, clear as a gem. The heat would have been uncomfortable had it not been for the constant breeze. Had they engineered that as well with their weather control systems, or were they just lucky?

He jogged back inside and checked the time, then made a call. When Sehvi answered, he had the pick-up pointed at the view, and leaned into it to grin at her.

"Oh my Goddess," Sehvi breathed, and then flung a pillow at him. "I'd hate you so much if I didn't love you so much! I am so jealous!!"

"No, no, don't be jealous, see, I'm sharing!"

Sehvi laughed. "I wish." She shook her head. "You actually made it!"

"I know," Vasiht'h said. "I wasn't sure I would either."

"And you even let him buy!"

"That obvious, is it."

His sister snorted. "Um, yes? Look at it! You're all right?"

"I'm guessing it's going to be one of those 'I'm all right until we leave and then it'll hit me when the sea air isn't addling my wits' situations," Vasiht'h admitted.

"Oh good," she said. "At least you won't have a distempered freak while he's trying to pass a big exam."

"A . . . a *what*?" Vasiht'h said, laughing.

"A distempered freak." She put her nose in the air. "I'm reading Nouveau Regency romance now. I figured it would help me understand your partner better."

"What you mean to say is that you'll read anything with a romantic plotline and Jahir is just your latest excuse."

"Well, yes?"

Vasiht'h began to answer when an overhead image of the hotel appeared in front of them both, as if the suite had aimed it deliberately to be in view for both him and whomever he was talking to. Could it do that on purpose? A happy woman's voice: "Welcome . . . to the beautiful Diamond Sands Resort, Tsera Nova."

"Ooh, nice," Sehvi said.

"The Harat-Shar at the front desk had a better delivery." The overhead view swooped toward them as if they were flying closer, landing them in a central plaza Vasiht'h hadn't seen yet, bedecked in garlands of tropical flowers. A band was playing something islandy, Vasiht'h guessed, from the steel drums and the mellow beat, and visitors were milling in the center, eating, drinking from glasses with umbrellas, looking sun-burnished and happy with flowered crowns and leis. "Your seaside destination for *joy*."

"Seriously? Joy? I can't tell if they're overachieving or if I'm just bitter because I'm not there to experience it."

Vasiht'h rolled his eyes. "It's marketing, ariishir."

"They look joyous, though! Look at that bunch of kits dancing with their granddami." Sehvi sighed. "Why aren't I there."

"At least you know where to take your vacation next?"

"Oh, wait, it's still going. Let me get popcorn!" Sehvi vanished, leaving Vasiht'h to watch the hotel's projected 3deo spiral out from the plaza to visit the spa, where every kind of Pelted was having some brain-meltingly good procedure done to them, from the Phoenix whose feathers were being painted to the Ciracaana getting what must be a two hour massage, because Ciracaana had a lot of limbs to massage. It did give him to think, though, because if their massage therapists could handle one kind of centauroid, they could handle him, too. . . .

Sehvi returned. With actual popcorn. He stared at it and said, "I thought you'd have cookies."

"I found out that making caramel popcorn is easy," she said. "Have you tried it? And then you can melt chocolate on it . . ."

"See exotic sites!" the hotel exclaimed.

"Look at that!" Sehvi said, pointing with a hand full of glossy popcorn. There were nuts in there too. Vasiht'h wanted to hear more about this recipe, but he followed her gaze and:

"Oh, I have to do that."

"You have to do that," she agreed.

On the 3deo, a bridge was appearing over the water, leading to a nearby "island paradise," because no island here was just an island, and honestly Vasiht'h couldn't blame them for the superlatives. "Every night, the Bridge of Dreams extends to Serenity Palms. Made of rainbows . . ." The bridge, translucent against the dark water, suddenly lit in a gradient of brilliant colors, ". . . and songs . . ." Shot now of people crossing it, and every footstep causing a chime to sound. Which should have created a cacophony, but the 3deo showed more and more people crowding it and the bridge chose the notes somehow so that they sounded amazing together.

"Doesn't it strike you as crazy sometimes, the things we waste our time on?" Vasiht'h asked.

Munching popcorn, Sehvi said, "No bridge made out of dreams, rainbows, and songs is a waste of time."

Serenity Palms was a crescent-shaped island, curved around a lagoon so perfect it looked fake. The entire thing was shallow enough for the average adult to stand at its deepest point—under several glistening waterfalls—and the majority of it was shallow enough for children to chase the schools of iridescent fish. A handful of canopied booths sold refreshments that were looking more and more refreshing all the time. "And for those who prefer a little more greenery," the 3deo continued, "and breathtaking views . . ." The 3deo followed a winding path through more of the riotous flowers, pink and peach and yellow, up to the promontory from which the waterfalls issued. There was a balcony there, with a lookout over more of the island chain, and *that* was a lot more Vasiht'h's speed than the vistas offered by the courage-testing mountain retreat.

"You have got to do that."

"Pet the friendly indigenous wildlife!" the 3deo added, showing a delighted human tourist stroking the length of what looked like a happy furry snake. It had wings of translucent skin so delicate they looked like soap bubbles, if soap bubbles came in colors as bright as hibiscus flowers.

Sehvi started laughing. "The look on your face."

As the 3deo continued about the small skiffs that could be rented from Serenity Palms—cue image of beaming tourists on a sailboat, their fur scintillating with water from the ocean's splashes—Vasiht'h said, "All right, I admit. This is going to be glorious."

An hour and a half before orientation gave Jahir plenty of time to wander the terraces, choosing the planet-facing ones he'd already glimpsed. He had lunch on one of them, at a thin, tall restaurant that would have been ridiculously inefficient on his homeworld . . . the food would have been cold long before it arrived to the topmost floor. Here, dishes were popped from the kitchen up dumbwaiters and straight into the hands of the waitstaff who breezed from table to table in sarongs and colorful vests. Jahir looked out the window at the children chasing the colored water, and the planet below with its dazzling oceans, the swirls of clouds hanging over them like ornaments. He ordered the fish and it flaked onto the fork, steaming from the thin crust. Ground nuts, maybe? He hadn't asked. It had looked pretty.

Back at the convention center, he found himself confronting a group large enough to merit the lecture hall: at least sixty people, he judged, and more trailing in after him. He found a seat in the back corner and watched his fellow test-takers enter. Their ages ranged from youths he judged barely out of college to graying elders, and their races ran the usual gamut: high on the Core's races with a spattering of the more unusual Pelted, like the Aera and Phoenix. No Malarai with their feathered wings, he noted, disappointed.

That disappointment lasted until an Akubi ducked its crested head beneath the lintel and squeezed its feathered sides through the door, ruffling its wings when it cleared the posts. Jahir was not the only one to stare at the sight, for the Akubi were not usual and he'd never heard of one in a medical profession. They were true-aliens, the Akubi: reminiscent of the raptor-like dinosaurs, and usually hovering over nine feet tall, with dark feathers, hide, and scales and whiskered maws with serrated bone edges. Fortunately, their eyes were less inscrutable than those of the birds they resembled, for the skin around them folded and bunched to give them expressions. Usually amused.

Lifting its head, the Akubi said, "I see you've noticed me!" A rustle, several chuckles. "Which is the intent, because I am your proctor." A gaped mouth, with eyes almost entirely closed, was a grin in this species. "As you can see, I have a nice long neck to look over everyone's shoulders, and an aerial predator's keen eyesight to see all the way into the back, even to those who might want to hide." It pointed the claw at the apex of one of its wings at Jahir. "I see you."

"I see you also, alet," Jahir answered, smiling.

"Excellent. Now that we've settled that . . . I'm Song of Wine Skies at Sunset, healer-assist lead at Succor Most General Hospital on Karaka'Ana. Let's talk about how this exam is going to go."

The Akubi commenced a repeat of the information sent them

in the post-scheduling packets: the exam would require three days and consisted of twelve sections; each daily session would last six hours and cover two sections before breaking for a lunch hour, and then the remaining two sections; pass/fail information would be available immediately after the final exam. Jahir listened with only partial attention, as his thoughts were busy with his lack of discomfort at having been picked from a crowd and addressed. Such attention would have distressed him when he'd first started school. It had nothing to do with the reaction of the people around him either, for he was now garnering the same curious looks he'd received on Seersana.

No, he no longer feared the unknowns of the Alliance, and he'd become accustomed to being one of its few mysterious species. No doubt Song of Wine Skies at Sunset collected its share of stares as well.

An Akubi medic! How did that work? Jahir knew nothing about their homeworld's technology, and the only Akubi he'd known for long enough to evaluate had been employed as a star-base dockworker, where its strength was an asset and its size less inconvenient. Akubi did not have functional hands, and while they had two thumbs on their feet, those feet were also the size of most Pelted's entire chest cavities. Perhaps the Akubi only worked with larger species? Maybe he could ask later.

At the conclusion of Orientation, Jahir waited for the room to empty before taking his leave. His tablet had an outstanding message from Vasiht'h, so he tapped it: "Come on down, the water's fine," accompanied by an image he assumed to have been taken from their hotel room. Smiling, he checked the location of the nearest Pad and went in search of his friend.

"The Bridge of Dreams, is it?" Jahir asked, bemused. He had stepped on-planet only to find himself drawn into a luau in the hotel's central plaza, such as any collection of buildings this disparate could be said to have one: an enormous octagon of polished dark brown wooden planks, surrounded in deck chairs shaded by umbrellas, with scattered tables and benches. The sea breeze gamboled gaily among the throng in the center, where the guests were dancing or clustering around the large open grill. There, skewers of meat and vegetables were being basted with what looked like a sauce involving pineapples? It smelled delicious, anyway.

"I can't decide whether to try that tomorrow or the day after," Vasiht'h said. "I feel like I should at least wander aimlessly the first full day and look at the beach. Except how can you say no to a music-making bridge with colored lights leading to a paradisiacal island where you can rent boats to sail around a lagoon shallow enough for even me to fall into without drowning?"

Jahir laughed. "And is that what you're planning to do? Go sailing?"

Vasiht'h grinned at him. "At least once. But you need to come too. You like sailing."

"I do," Jahir said, finding the fact that he could say so surprising. It was one of his few good memories of Heliocentrus. In fact: "This is a great deal like Heliocentrus. Save not so dire."

"The gravity here is great," Vasiht'h agreed. "You know what they call planets like this?" At Jahir's quizzical look, the Glaseah said, "New Year worlds. Because so many people make resolutions at the start of the new year to lose that little bit of extra weight? And worlds with gravity like this, just a few shades off of Terran norm, but without being noticeably lighter, do that without the effort or the trips to the clinic for metabolic therapy."

"What a beautiful name!" Jahir exclaimed. And laughed. "Rather painful statement about our natures, however."

"A New Year world," Vasiht'h agreed. "Perfect, since you're doing something new too, that's going to start something for both of us."

"Not so great a change as all that," Jahir demurred.

"No, but still a change." Vasiht'h watched a handful of Pelted children chase one another past, giggling and squealing, and through the mindline Jahir felt his wistfulness, and that steadfast core the Eldritch had found so attractive from the very beginning. "But this is a good thing for us both. I'm glad we're here. And not just because I'm planning on drinking pink drinks on the beach of Serenity Palms while you're sweating through your test upstairs."

"Pink now is it?" Jahir asked.

"I tried the purple one, it wasn't anything to write home about."

A cloud of butterflies swept past, their wings a stunning electric blue. Jahir watched them, wondering if they were some contrivance like the fish on the station. "Are those real? I had no idea butterflies were typical near the coast."

"Don't they migrate?" Vasiht'h wrinkled his nose. "I seem to remember reading something like that?"

"They are the most unlikely colors. Like everything here, flowers inclusive."

"Oh no, the flowers I believe," Vasiht'h said easily. "The ones on Anseahla are as ridiculous. That color on the butterflies, along with the eye-punch yellow, though . . ."

"Engineered?"

"No," Vasiht'h said. "There are laws against genetic engineering these days. Tinkering to fix problems, yes. Aesthetic tampering or creation of new species . . . not so much." They watched a Tam-illee toddler catch one in her hands, squealing, and then release it. "That answers that. They're solidigraphic. There must be projectors somewhere. Under the deck, maybe?"

"Magic," Jahir murmured.

"Might as well be," Vasiht'h agreed, smiling at him easily. "So, do you have any idea what you'd like to do after the exams? They end pretty early, don't they?"

"Late afternoon daily, yes."

"You could go swimming?"

Jahir looked past the deck to the sea, rolling endlessly onto the shore, the roar of it, the softness of the spume. A tremor ran the length of his spine. "I think . . . I shall save that. As reward for completion of the task."

"As if you need motivation," Vasiht'h said affectionately. "But there's plenty to do at night that doesn't involve swimming. I looked the schedule up . . . there's live music all the time, and bonfires, and things like this. I can check out the more involved things by myself, see if they're worth doing."

"Like the bridge," Jahir said, amused.

"That's a definite yes! There's also a day-long cruise out to this . . . sandbar in the middle of nowhere? Where they've built a series of platforms for people to stand on. And then the local cetaceans come and do tricks." Vasiht'h grins. "I want to see that. Supposedly they showed up one day to play and someone got the bright idea of training them. Of course no one wanted to constrain them in pens or anything, so they did it on a lark. But then the animals kept coming back? So they brought in a bunch of foreign animals to play with the natives, and they do a show. By now it's not even the original animals, either . . . the whales brought their kits to play with the crazy land mammals too."

"That sounds . . . astonishing," Jahir said.

"I can't imagine it, so I'm going to have to see it," Vasiht'h agreed, satisfied. "If it's worth the trip, we can do it together when you're done. Maybe they'll let you swim with them!"

"In the sea," Jahir murmured.

"In the sea." Vasiht'h looked over at him, his love warmer than the sun gilding his fur. "So, do you want a pink drink? To inaugurate our enterprise."

Jahir considered. "Something yellow. And virginal. I suspect I will need my wits about me in the morning."

CHAPTER 9

T HE SELECTIVE PERMEABILITY of their wall admitted the warm evening breeze, redolent with the scent of brine and night-blooming flowers, and Vasiht'h couldn't remember the last time he'd slept so well. His dreams overflowed with memories of home, twined with sensory impressions: sand under his pawpads, the feel of sun-heated fur on his back, the taste of pink drinks: tropical fruit and sweetness. He woke refreshed, stretching in the nest of pillows he'd made beside Jahir's bed, and found his friend peeping at him from beneath his cocoon of blankets, because even in warm weather the Eldritch refused to sleep without several layers over him.

/Good?/ Jahir asked, the sending wreathed with laughter like champagne bubbles.

"All right, I could get used to this," Vasiht'h admitted. And grinned. "But just in case familiarity breeds contempt I'm glad we're only staying a week. I'd hate to lose my wonder over it." He slid out from amid the pillows and stretched, forelegs splayed before him and tail behind. "Breakfast?"

Jahir sat up, braid sliding over his shoulder. "If I must."

"You're taking a test, you need a good breakfast. Let's go see what the hotel has."

Acquiescence in the mindline in this case felt like blushing. Vasiht'h hid his amusement and went to freshen up.

The hotel had multiple breakfast options, as one might have expected from its expense. Vasiht'h decided against ordering into their room in favor of the buffet, which was set up in the open air plaza. He hovered while his partner made his choices, because he didn't want Jahir to undereat this week of all weeks, and then trotted alongside the Eldritch to the nearest Pad. The hotel had five public-facing ones, because of course it did. Why force its clients to come down by shuttle when they could walk?

"Good luck today," Vasiht'h told him. "You'll do great, I know."

"Thank you, arii," Jahir said. "You'll be . . . seeing cetaceans?"

"If I can schedule it," Vasiht'h said. "Otherwise, I'll keep busy." He grinned. "Shouldn't be hard."

Jahir laughed, quiet. "No, I imagine not. I will return."

Vasiht'h saw him off and sighed as the mindline went diffuse and tenuous. He'd spent time apart from Jahir, but the attenuation of the mindline never ceased to mystify and disturb him. Why should something mental be subject to laws that dictated physical behavior? How did it work, anyway? Something quantum? Vasiht'h thought of himself and Jahir as two objects vibrating in sympathy and found the imagery charming and amusing.

"Well, that's that," he said. "Time to do something with myself."

The whale show was apparently popular; when Vasiht'h tried to book it, the first available slot wasn't for another two days. He scheduled that and studied today's list of activities, decided tentatively on a walk along the beach, a massage at the spa, and then a show with air dancers. He couldn't not investigate the latter, because if he saw it first, he'd be able to anticipate Jahir's wonder at the sight when he took the Eldritch later.

This was, he thought, another situation like Jahir's arrival to Seersana U, where the Glaseah got the pleasure of re-experiencing the Alliance through his partner's eyes. Except by now he was so used to Jahir's reaction to novel experiences that Vasiht'h could plan his own adventures so that he could enjoy them *twice*: once because they were new to him, and again vicariously through Jahir. How lucky was he?

Grinning, he went to the day.

There was little exciting about a test, no matter how momentous. Jahir reported to the lecture hall and was assigned his desk—the one he'd chosen during Orientation, he noted—where he was then isolated by a privacy screen, which fascinated him. He'd observed during his tenure at the university that most every interface in the Alliance could tessellate into unreadability when a privacy screen was activated. He'd expected this test to use that technology to prevent cheating, as the university had. But to have the field on, muting the noises outside his immediate area as well, felt like a courtesy. It minimized distractions.

While he waited for the testing to begin, he evaluated his mental state. Was he worried? Not at all. Nervous? Not that either. Nor guilty. There was no choice now but to go through with his course, for to do otherwise would be to waste the money and time spent arranging this, and to disappoint his partner.

"Day one of three," Song of Wine Skies at Sunset intoned from the front of the room. "Commend your souls to your gods, aletsen. Commence."

Hiding his smile, Jahir turned his attention to the interface as the first question appeared.

"So a Glaseah!" the human said. "How does that work? I mean, so many limbs?"

The cream-colored tabby Asanii beside her covered her face with her hands. If she could have sunk into the bench in the spa's waiting room, Vasiht'h was certain she would have. "Don't mind her, please, she just blurts the first thing that comes to mind."

"Actually, it was the third thing that came to mind," the human said cheerfully before peering again at Vasiht'h. "The first two would probably have been even more annoying! Maybe?"

"Definitely?" Vasiht'h guessed, taking a chance on the woman's demeanor, and—

The human laughed. "Yes! You get it! Poor Gladdie, I don't know why she puts up with me." She offered her hand, then stopped mid-reach and turned it palm-up. "Oops, sorry. I keep forgetting. Hi! I'm Kristyl, and this is my best friend Gladiolus."

"I hate that name," the Asanii muttered.

They were a pretty pair, young women both, the Asanii's soft ivory fur only faintly darkened by gingery stripes and her long, pale hair tucked up into a chignon with wooden hairsticks. Her human friend had skin a few shades darker, and light brown hair that fell in glossy waves over her bare shoulders. They were both in swimsuits and sandals, the Asanii's more demure in color and cut than the human's.

"We're here for massages too," Kristyl said, ignoring what was probably her friend's recurring complaint. "This is my first time off-planet. Except I'm on a planet. I mean this is my first time out of the Sol system. I've never been this far into the Alliance. Except it's more like it's out of the Alliance, isn't it?"

Amused, Vasiht'h said, "It's not far from the Core, really. By our standards, it's still in the Alliance. You'd have to keep going into the colonies to hit the lawn."

"The lawn!" Kristyl said, delighted. "Like there's a house and if you're not in a house, you're on the lawn! I love it!" She leaned forward, green eyes sparkling. "Metaphors are fun."

"She likes to take things literally," the Asanii murmured.

"You don't have to keep apologizing for me." Kristyl patted her friend's arm. "I know I drive you crazy but that doesn't make you responsible for my behavior."

"It does if we're seen together," Gladiolus said, ears sagging, but she was smiling, and it was a helpless smile Vasiht'h had felt moving his features once too often. "Because people have expectations."

"Stupid ones, often," Kristyl said decisively. "But back to you! What's your name? And are you here alone or do you also have a long-suffering friend to ride herd on you and die inside at all your faux pas?"

"Oh my," Vasiht'h said, laughing. "Do you really think that about yourself?"

"No," the human replied, cheerful. "But I can see where other people might so I save them the trouble of thinking it and feeling uncomfortable about hiding it."

Vasiht'h grinned. "Well, I see why your friend likes you. You're irrepressible, and it's adorable."

"I assure you it gets tiresome after a while," Kristyl said. "That's why I dote on Gladdie. She never gets angry at me for long. Even when she's had to listen to me run on and on for hours."

"No one's so perfect that they don't have a few tiresome habits," Vasiht'h said. "I'm Vasiht'h, and yes, I'm with someone, but he's on the station for business. He'll be joining me in a couple of days. I'm taking in all the sights, see which ones I think would interest him most."

"You think he'd like a massage?" Kristyl asked, interested.

"No, that's for me," Vasiht'h told her. "Because to your original question, I have no idea how it's going to work with all the limbs, and I want to find out."

"An adventurer, like me!" the human crowed. She tugged on her friend's arm. "We should have lunch after. Are you busy?"

"Kris—"

"I'm asking," the human said. "He can say no!"

"You haven't given him a way to refuse without being rude!"

"Oh, mm. You're right." To Vasiht'h, "I'm sorry. That was abrupt, wasn't it."

Vasiht'h laughed. "I'd love to have lunch after. My unlikely massage needs an hour and a half. Maybe we can meet at the plaza and decide what to do from there?"

"Great! We'll see you there! Oh, hey, they're calling us up. Later!"

As the human vanished down the breezeway after the sarong-wrapped Harat-Shar attendant, her friend paused, ears bright red. "Ah . . . about all this . . . she . . . grows on you?"

"You don't have to explain her to me," Vasiht'h said. "I understand completely."

"You really can bow out if you have other plans. . . ."

"I don't," Vasiht'h said. "You should go, they're waiting for you!"

The Asanii exhaled, smiled. "All right. Thanks." And trotted off after the human. Vasiht'h watched her vanish around the corner and chuckled to himself. He had no doubt Gladiolus had suffered for her friend's ebullience more than once. For his part, he found Kristyl's attitude preferable to the one he often found in humans visiting the Alliance . . . which tended toward far less positive engagement with what they found.

An adventurer, though! He shook his head, bemused. That was the last way he would have chosen to characterize himself! And just because he was willing to get a massage? But that was hardly a risk worthy of an adventurous personality! A hedonist one, though . . . someone called his name and he rose. He supposed he was about to find out, and then he'd have the chance to tell Kristyl all about it.

"They did what!" Kristyl said, giggling. "No possible way."

"It's completely the truth." Vasiht'h rested his hand over his heart and bowed his head. "They brought in two more people."

"Three people!" Gladiolus sounded dazed. "That sounds decadent. How can they even afford it?"

"Oh, look at this place, would you?" Kristyl waved a hand at the view, the palms nodding in the breeze, the drinks, which this time had three separate colored layers: yellow, blue, and orange, with umbrella in green and a chunk of pineapple on the sugar-encrusted rim. "You think they don't charge enough to have a separate masseuse for every limb of a centauroid client?"

"Technically they had a separate therapist for every two of my functional limbs," Vasiht'h said. "But it was still . . ." He let the words die off, chuckled. "It was *definitely* decadent."

"Ours was good too," Kristyl said, cheerful. "We had them on an open deck, and you could hear the surf, and feel the sea breeze on your skin. And I think the Harat-Shar working on me would have had sex with me if I'd asked, which was kind of ridiculous? But flattering? Maybe? Except, don't they have sex with anyone?"

Gladiolus had her head in her hands again, but Vasiht'h could just see the smile her palms hid. "They don't want to have sex with *everyone*, arii. That's just . . ."

"An urban myth? I like those." Kristyl brightened as a waiter came by with their food: an enormous bowl of coconut-crusted prawns on a bed of something that looked like it involved diced mango, along with a mound of sweetly fragrant rice tossed with some kind of dark green leafy vegetable. "But I didn't think that was an urban myth. More like . . . a Pelted legend!"

"Just as long as you don't expect all Harat-Shar to have sex with you, you're fine," Vasiht'h said. "They're not all alike, you know."

Kristyl darted him a merry look, like she was sharing a secret. "I had no idea. I thought, you know, point of cultural pride! Besides, I'm human, don't I qualify as an exotic experience?"

Gladiolus moaned under her hands.

Vasiht'h said to Kristyl, "You try to make her do this, don't you."

The human ladled a healthy serving of the dish onto Vasiht'h's plate. "She's way too worried about what other people think of her. I'm just helping with that. You know."

"I do." Vasiht'h glanced at the Asanii. "So, how did the two of you meet?"

"On Terra—" Gladiolus paused, glancing at her friend with a soft, bemused smile. "I guess the whole 'never been off-planet' thing gave that away, though?"

"Possibly," Vasiht'h said, over a forkful of the dish, which was savory and tangy and sweet in ways he instantly wanted to deconstruct. The coconut milk was obvious. Was the peppery taste solely the mango, or had they added something to intensify it? "But I never let that kind of thing get in the way of a good story." He thought of Rexina Regina and all his sisters' endless commentary. "Anyway, I like spoilers."

Kristyl guffawed. "Me too."

Ignoring them, Gladiolus continued. "Right, so, I went to Terra, because my field of study was history and I wanted to really understand the Rapprochement." The Asanii stirred her drink absently until the colored layers broke and made whorls against the glass. "There was a Study Abroad program at my university on Asanao that would send you to live on Earth for a couple of years, and you'd tour the important sites there, and on Mars, and visit the Moon and all the places with historical significance both prior to our arrival and during the events of the Rapprochement. And it was really fascinating."

"That's how she met me," Kristyl agreed. "I was at the university that hosted the Study Abroad program and she got assigned to my dorm room." She beamed. "It was love at first sight."

Vasiht'h glanced at the Asanii curiously, found her blushing brightly at the ears.

"I'm allowed to say that, right?" Kristyl said. "Cross-species friends forever stuff isn't weird once you're out of the sticks? Besides, he's a Glaseah, they're supposed to get that sort of thing."

Gladiolus reached over and put her hand on the human's wrist, squeezed. "It's always all right to say that sort of thing, because it's true." She sighed, sheepish. "Although, yes, he's probably not going to misinterpret it. Sometimes I think you say things just to be outrageous."

"On purpose?" Kristyl gasped dramatically. "Would I do that?"

"Even I know you'd do that," Vasiht'h said, and made them both laugh.

"Anyway, ever since we've been doing things together," Gladiolus said. "And we just graduated, so I thought . . . why don't we do some outrageous thing to celebrate?"

"I'm rich," Kristyl said, unperturbed, reaching for the bowl to reload her plate.

"She is!" Gladiolus said. "She's paying for everything!"

"Paying for everything's fun." Kristyl licked her fingertips of some of the coconut sauce and resumed eating. "Also, I love the way she has to tell everyone that, because everyone thinks all humans are poor. Kind of like everyone thinks all Harat-Shar want to have sex with everything."

"Is this the part where I act shocked and say 'wait, not all humans are poor?'" Vasiht'h asked, bemused.

"Sure!" Kristyl said. "And then I say, 'nope, some of us are filthy rich! Like me!'" She laughed. "I admit, I really like people's reactions to that, because people really *do* think we're all poor. I bet you're thinking it too: 'wait, a rich human? That doesn't happen! How did that happen!'" She pointed her fork at Vasiht'h. "And I'll tell you how. Construction. My family's been in construction for generations. And Terra needed a lot of it." She sucked on her straw and ahhed. "Anyway. I'm a trust fund baby and that's okay, because I'm going to use my powers—my filthy rich powers—for good."

"Like taking your best friend to a ridiculously overpriced resort planet as a graduation gift," Gladiolus said fondly.

"Exactly. Exactly that."

"So, are you shocked, just shocked at the rich human?" Kristyl asked cheerfully.

"No," Vasiht'h admitted. "I was more wondering how Gladdie feels about being your plus one."

"I love it," Gladiolus said, laughing. "I would never have seen any place like this without Kristyl."

"See, I think that's fair, because I would never have seen any place off Earth without her," Kristyl said. "I had the money, but I would have felt weird without a friend to tour it with. And to apologize for me." She grinned at the Asanii, who grinned back.

"So tell us about you and your friend?" Gladiolus said.

"Oh," Vasiht'h said, guessing how this would go. "He's an Eldritch."

"WHAT!" Kristyl howled. "Oh my *amazing GOD*, I can't even imaaaaagine do we get to see him? Are they as unreal as they are in pictures? Do they have sex with anything because I'd love to!"

"Kristyl!"

"Sorry, not sorry," Kristyl pressed her hands to her cheeks. "But are you *serious*??"

Vasiht'h was trying hard not to laugh. "I am, yes. And yes, I'll tell you the story."

"Oh thank goodness." Kristyl waved the waiter over. "Thank you so much for delicious food please bring us more of these colored drinks!" She slurped the last of hers. "We're going to need it, so need it for this, I just know it."

———⊗⊗⊗———

"A human," Jahir repeated, bemused. "And an Asanii."

"Are dying to meet you," Vasiht'h answered, the mindline bubbling with mirth that tasted like . . . some kind of fruit-flavored cocktail? Jahir licked his teeth, trying to identify flavors he hadn't actually tasted. Apricot? Peach? Lime? "And I'm not sure that's hyperbole, either. If you'd rather not have them fawning over you I'll make sure we're conveniently unavailable when you're done with your test."

"You like them," Jahir guessed, from the effervescent pleasure washing through the mindline.

"Oh, they're fun." The Glaseah laughed, watching him change into something less stifling for their trip down the beach to the performance. "I've agreed to gad around with them while you're busy. It's better than doing everything by myself. There's only so many calls I can log to my sister before she throws a pillow across interstellar space at me."

Jahir glanced at him. "You are not lonely?"

"Not even!" Vasiht'h sat up. "Don't think that, not for a moment. If I don't like something about this situation, I can easily change it. Like I did, deciding to do things with these two. If I hadn't met them, it would have been someone else." He chuckled. "The way Kristyl accretes people, it might end up being several more someone elses, even."

"She has a way about her," Jahir guessed, finding the mindline cryptic when he sought impressions of the two.

"Ridiculously, yes." Vasiht'h squinted. "You sure you want even that much by way of clothes? It's hot out."

"I shall burn without it," Jahir said. "And when the sun goes down, the breeze will be cooler."

"I guess that's true." Vasiht'h rose to follow him out the door. "How did the testing go?"

"It was not difficult." After the grueling experiences on Seersana, pushing his degree through in as little time as possible, and then the gauntlet he'd run in Heliocentrus, Jahir's grasp on matters medical had become nigh instinctive. Learning additional material during his correspondence courses had been pleasure, not difficulty, and being tested on them felt like a leisurely ride under sunlight. Exertion, but satisfying. "I believe I will not waste our time."

"I never thought you would," Vasiht'h answered, fond. "Anyway, music now, and food. And colored drinks."

Jahir sampled the mindline again. "That taste of fruit."

"They make them in layers, so if you drink them with a straw you go through different flavors! If you stir them, though, it tastes like fruit punch. And doesn't turn brown, and I'd like to know how they manage that."

"I did not know you to love alcohol," Jahir said, bemused.

"I didn't either, until they put umbrellas in it." Vasiht'h laughed. "They all come in non-alcoholic versions, though. The ones without them are mostly sugar. A lot of sugar, granted, though without the crash, and that's another thing I wonder about. This place is apparently magical."

"Speaking of magic, we should spend some time on the station when we're done," Jahir said as they strolled down the path toward the beach, where the sun was staining the sky orange near the horizon. "There are marvels there you would appreciate."

"Oh?" Vasiht'h glanced up at him.

"Also, interesting food."

Vasiht'h laughed. "Then of course we'll have to make a point of stopping on the way out. But really, look at this." He stopped in front of the beach, spreading his arms. "Those colors. How do they even do that without clouds?"

"It is rather mysterious." Jahir paused alongside him, facing into the breeze, and lifted his head to feel it on his face. He felt his partner still and do the same, savoring the sensation not just on his own cheeks, but on Jahir's as well, so much more sensitive without the fur. "It is beautiful here."

"I love it," Vasiht'h said. "Obviously I should have lived by the ocean all my life. It's too bad the starbase doesn't have one."

"Not in the city-sphere, certainly. Perhaps one day we will live someplace like this."

"Maybe," Vasiht'h said. "Anyway, we're going that way."

That way involved a knot of people on the beach, and eventually resolved into a demonstration of firedancing while accompanied by a choir so tightly rehearsed they seemed to have a single voice. The sight of the dancers, silhouetted by the setting sun as they leaped with their flaring staves, was mesmerizing.

"How fortunate we are," Jahir said to Vasiht'h on the way back to their room.

"Aren't we just," Vasiht'h replied, contented.

CHAPTER 10

W HEN VASIHT'H FOUND Kristyl and Gladiolus the following morning, the human had in fact acquired more hang-
ers-on: an entire gaggle of them, in the form of six Harat-Shar,
milling around her, chattering.

"Look!" Kristyl exclaimed, arms raised. "New friends! I found
them last night by asking if they wanted to have sex with a rich
human."

"We said yes!" one of the Harat-Shar crowed, a golden-eyed
male with a grin Vasiht'h swore stretched from ear to ear.

"And then I said I was kidding," Kristyl continued, pushing
her sunglasses up. "And they were all disappointed and it was so
sweet that we danced all night. Even Gladdie danced!"

"There were so many of them, it seemed rude not to," Gladiolus muttered, but she was smiling too.

"We met at the blacklight rave," the human finished. "We
didn't see you there! Not your thing, I'm guessing, with an
Eldritch as a friend. Do they dance?"

"I don't know," Vasiht'h admitted. "But I admit a rave would
be one of the last places I'd take him."

"I bet!" She beamed. "Anyway, this is . . ." She pointed in turn.
"Tati, Misha, Nikita—those are both boys, by the way—Bassam,

Khadija, and Nasira!" As the human said their names, they
lined up and posed, leaning on one another, swooning, flexing
or spreading their arms in a 'ta-da'. Five of them were related,
Vasiht'h judged, sandy-coated lynxines with tufted ears and
bright eyes in either gold or green, but Nasira was a zaftig snow
pardine, gray-eyed and sleek. Also, hot, because she wasn't even
wearing the abbreviated things that passed for clothes on the
others, preferring to go in the fur except for an orange hibiscus
tucked in her mane. "They want to go with us over the bridge
today! You still want to come?"

Vasiht'h laughed. "I wouldn't miss it."

"Hooray!" Kristyl pointed. "Onward, everyone!"

The Harat-Shar hooted and spilled toward the beach, and
Kristyl jogged after them. Vasiht'h fell into step alongside Gladiolus. The Asanii also had a flower, a white lily behind her ear that
matched the breezy white gauze robe she was wearing over her
white bikini, which was more abbreviated than yesterday's swim-
suit but more modest still than Kristyl's "strings and triangles"
edition. Gladiolus's expression hadn't changed since yesterday:
bemused resignation. Vasiht'h wondered if it was permanent by
now and hid his smile. "I guess this is typical of her."

"It really is. I don't know how she does it. She just . . . explodes
into a place with the most outrageous comments and somehow
people don't get offended? Or at least, not as many people do as
I think really *should*." The Asanii shook her head. "I don't know
how she does it. It's like she distorts reality around her."

"It makes you wish you could get away with some of the same
things, doesn't it?"

The Asanii glanced at him, wide-eyed. And then she laughed,
hesitant. "Oh, Stars, is it obvious?"

"It's natural," Vasiht'h said. "And I think it's good. The alternative would be to hate her for it, or be jealous. Wanting to be
like her is far more positive."

"I guess so," Gladiolus said. "I certainly wouldn't want her to
change. She's crazy but she's perfect the way she is."

'And you love her,' is how that ended but Vasiht'h didn't feel the need to say it. He just smiled as they left the resort's boundaries for the path to the bridge. In front of them the Harat-Shar had started an impromptu skipping contest and were dancing in circles around Kristyl, who was blowing bubbles from a vial she wore as a necklace. "That," he said, "was a perfect thing just waiting to happen."

"Kristyl and Harat-Shar? Oh, Stars, yes," Gladiolus said, chuckling. "The only surprise is that it took so long to happen."

"And that there was no all-night orgy?" Vasiht'h wondered.

The Asanii shook her head. "She's not interested, I don't think. Or if she is, she's waiting for something."

Vasiht'h looked over at her surreptitiously, but Gladiolus was looking ahead, smiling at the raucous laughter.

He would have to ask Sehvi later just how oblivious he was most of the time. And wondered if Gladiolus liked romance novels.

The Bridge of Dreams was as fantastical as its literature. More, because it was a real thing that felt like something out of a story, an impression fixed in Vasiht'h's mind forever because his first sight of it was of six Harat-Shar and a human gamboling onto it and their footfalls beating out a glorious swirl of rising notes as rainbows broke around their bodies. He stopped short alongside Gladiolus as the seven of them gleefully noticed the results and started whirling one another around, Kristyl bouncing in the center blowing bubbles that reflected the colors.

"I am never going to forget this for the rest of my life!" Gladiolus breathed, wide-eyed.

"You and me both," Vasiht'h answered. "Come on, let's add us to the memory."

The bridge's planks floated just above the water. Vasiht'h thought it should have disturbed him given they were almost perfectly transparent, but when he stepped, a blot of colored light spread from around his paw, briefly illumining the edges of the bridge and each of its planks. It made him feel magical, as if he had the power to command energy just by walking. And music . . . what would his musician partner think of this place? Vasiht'h chuckled. Better to ask how long he would spend walking back and forth, trying to understand it!

As he followed the impromptu Harat-Shar dance party, he grew accustomed to the glow and could enjoy the sight of the fish darting beneath him more. The edge of the bridge was lined in a rim of lights, so he never worried about accidentally falling off. And the weather was sublime; halfway across the span, the bridge rose ten feet off the water, feeding into a pavilion built entirely of force fields and light, like something out of a fairy tale. There one could stand and see the island, the mainland, and the vast expanse of blue ocean, reflecting a cloudless sky so deep Vasiht'h felt like he could fall upward into it and swim until he left atmosphere.

He was still staring up when Kristyl joined him. He expected her to break the silence, so of course she didn't, because she seemed to enjoy playing with people's expectations. It made him smile and glance at her. "It's amazing."

"Isn't it? And to think we made all this!"

"We . . . did?"

"We did," she clarified, fisting a hand and pointing its thumb at her chest. "Humans, I mean. Oh, I don't mean this world in particular. But we made you Pelted, and you Pelted made this place, which means without humans this would never have happened."

Vasiht'h chuckled. "You're right. But I bet no one is comfortable with you when you say *that* kind of thing."

"Oh no, everyone hates it," she agrees. "Pelted because it implies that humans were right to make them—even though none of them would argue that they'd prefer to be alive right now than not alive at all!—and humans because half of them hate themselves for doing it badly and the other half hate themselves for doing it at all." She shook her head, tsked. "It's like no one ever learned to look at things as they are and say 'yeah, that. That's the thing, right there.'"

"And the thing right here is that Pelted exist because of humans," Vasiht'h said, amused.

"And this resort exists because of Pelted," Kristyl finished, and opened her arms to the sky. "Therefore, by the laws of syllogistic inference, which I've forgotten most of because that was first-year math, or maybe philosophy, this resort exists because of humans! And I get to take credit for it!"

"Ah, but you in particular weren't the one who made the Pelted?"

"True," Kristyl conceded. "I just paid them exorbitant sums to help keep this place running."

"Except by her twisted logic," Gladiolus said behind them, "she is a member of 'class: humans', and 'class: humans' are responsible for making the Pelted, therefore she gets some of the credit."

"I get the blame for it all the time," Kristyl said. "I might as well enjoy the credit. Myself, if no one else will give it to me."

Vasiht'h flinched, because he had no doubt that merely by being human and among the Pelted, Kristyl suffered some of the inevitable repercussions of the Pelted's discomfort with their creators. He'd thought that mythical once: human prejudice. But while like almost everything, the situation was more complicated than 'everyone has a problem with humans,' there were people, a lot more people than he would wish, who found the existential questions raised by their creation far too painful not to take it out on the 'class: humans' to which Kristyl belonged.

"It's all right." Kristyl patted him on his arm. "I can tell by your expression that you feel bad about it. I know you don't blame me for making you. Which is great, because you'd be wrong. The other Pelted made you, not me."

Vasiht'h pursed his lips and looked at the sky. "Except by the laws of syllogistic inference, which you've forgotten, I exist because the Pelted exist, who exist because of you, therefore . . ."

Kristyl slapped her forehead. "Oh right. Sorry. Humans have done so many *great* things that I keep forgetting them all!"

Vasiht'h laughed, and so did the human, and that brought the roving Harat-Shar over to demand to know the joke. He wondered what she would tell them, and found out a moment later when she said, "Did you know this cloudless sky was brought to you by human engineering? For once, I can say that without transivity of implication. Actual humans designed the technology that keeps the weather here gorgeous. I know, because we toured it."

"What she means is that she talked her way into the control center and got them to show us everything," Gladiolus said. "It's not a tourist attraction. She's just impossible to say 'no' to." The Asanii paused, then added, "But it was fascinating, actually. The way they handle it? It's so complicated. They don't actually stop the imperfect weather, just . . . soften it everywhere, and make sure the worst of it moves elsewhere. Anyway, it was astonishing. I'm glad we saw it."

"Astonishing, she says, like it's something rare." Kristyl sighed with feeling and put her hands on her hips. "I'll have you know humans are responsible for lots of great things. Glory in our marvelousness!"

"How can we when you're hiding so much of it under your clothes?" one of the lynxines crowed, and they all laughed as Kristyl mock-pounced her.

As they pretend-wrestled, Gladiolus said, "You see what I put up with."

"I do, and you're not fooling me," Vasiht'h answered, grinning. "You love it."

———— ∞ ————

Serenity Palms was everything promised by the brochure, which Vasiht'h accepted as the theme for his vacation. It seemed unlikely that anything could be as paradisiacal as Tsera Nova's legends, and yet, here he was under an umbrella on sun-warmed sands, in a heat that was just hot enough to enjoy the water but not hot enough to be sweltering under a pelt. The ocean breeze was just right, brisk without achieving "blow your sunhat off" speeds. The lagoon was, in fact, shallow enough to dash through while chasing the fishes visible through the clear waters, and the fish were so exuberantly colored that Vasiht'h felt compelled to join the Harat-Shar train when they went splashing through it. There were even freshening stations discreetly tucked behind fancy screens, where one could step through an abbreviated Pad and have the salt crust and sweat whisked off one's body.

Vasiht'h had done that an hour ago and was having a different paper umbrella drink. This version was yellow and tasted like mango. Maybe. And something else . . . maybe coconut? It was cold, whatever it was, and like the view, sublime. So when the bikini-clad attendant stopped by with a tray, he was smugly pleased to discover a data tablet on it, blinking on standby. "A call for you, alet. Your sister?"

"Oh, certainly." Vasiht'h took the tablet. "Thanks." And made much of slurping from his straw before saying, "Why hello, ariishir! I'm so glad to see you."

"I bet you are, you hedonist." Sehvi laughed. "That's what I get for calling you in the middle of your vacation, isn't it."

"I'll be nice and share. Look—" He turned the tablet so she could see the lagoon, the gently swaying palms, the uninterrupted cerulean blue of sky and sea. "Isn't it marvelous?"

"I am consumed with jealousy," she said dryly. And paused, sighed. "Actually, I *am* jealous. I can feel my fur settling just looking at that."

"Uh oh. Why is your fur sticking up?" He split the image so she could retain the beach view while he looked at her. She did seem . . . tired? Exasperated? "Who's been fighting?"

"Pes'shek and Dondi—"

"Wait, neither of them ever get into a fight," Vasiht'h said, startled. Of his brothers, only Bret was insufferable. The others were the most genial souls imaginable.

"—about Dondi not respecting Pes's job, or something—"

Pes'shek was a primary school teacher who dealt with kits all day, the ones young enough to still be singing their alphabet songs. "What??"

"And it became something about how Pes is using it as a substitute for having kits of his own?" Sehvi continued. "Then it got into Dondi having too many relationships . . ."

Vasiht'h covered his face.

"Which got our cousin Ditreht involved . . ."

"Not Ditreht," Vasiht'h groaned.

". . . because apparently Ditreht is just as wild, and the moment Pes pointed that out, Bret got involved and summarily forbade Dondi from going out anymore with Ditreht and now Aunt Sattri is upset and you know how I feel about Aunt Sattri." Sehvi leaned into the camera. "Vasiht'h, help meeeeee."

Aunt Sattri was Sehvi's favorite aunt, the one she'd modeled herself after: a tough, fair-minded mother with a big family and a solid career in biomedical research. "Are you sure this fight is about Pes and Dondi and not about something that's bothering them separately? And they just happened to take it out on one another because it was safer?"

"It wasn't safer," Sehvi pointed out. "Because now our cousin's in trouble and Dondi's not allowed to go anywhere with him. Or rather, he *is* going out with him anyway, which is infuriating Bret."

Goddess, their family. For the most part so tranquil, and then abruptly, these little nitpicking fights that erupted like a summer rainstorm out of an empty sky. Except, as Vasiht'h well knew from his profession, the sky was never really empty. "I'll send a couple of messages and see what's going on."

"Thank you," she said, fervent. "I don't want my calls with Aunt Sattri to be about my brothers being stupid."

"I wouldn't, either," Vasiht'h said, because their aunt was not afraid to express her forceful opinions.

"Everything there's all right?"

Vasiht'h chuckled. "What about the view you're seeing isn't all right?"

"Good point. Testing going well for Tall, Pale, and Beautiful?"

"He seems satisfied," Vasiht'h said. "I'll send him a message, though. Just to let him know I'm thinking of him."

"Awww. You two are so sweet." Sehvi beamed. Then shook a finger at him. "Go fix my problem!"

"I see. This is revenge for me being on this incredible vacation without you."

"Exactly." She grinned. "No, seriously. Thank you."

"No problem, ariishir. Give my nephews a hug for me."

One of the staff came back with another tray, this one to replace Vasiht'h's nearly empty glass with a new fruit drink, and ask if he wanted snacks. And who didn't want snacks? The Glaseah waffled between the choices while the nice young Tam-illee waited and occasionally made helpful comments, before finally deciding on, "One of everything." What he didn't eat, he was sure Kristyl and her band would.

With that taken care of, he set to writing separate messages to his brothers. A very basic amount of bickering came with a large family living together, but this sounded more serious. Dondi was at the age where he'd be wondering what to do with himself; like Vasiht'h, he'd never evinced any grand life plans that might have steered him onto a set course. And Pes . . . maybe Pes was avoiding kits? Maybe Pes was thinking about them? Dondi's observations must have touched something sensitive to set off a fight like this.

Between messages, Vasiht'h sat back and nibbled one of the bacon-wrapped dates that had arrived, licking the honey glaze off his fingers as he watched birds fly into the wind so that they just . . . hung there, stationary. Thinking back on his childhood, he realized just how often he'd been the one to ferret out and remove all these little emotional burrs. Maybe Dondi had a secret calling, and was unaware of it? Maybe Dondi, one day, would be taking an amazing vacation on a resort planet and some sibling would interrupt it to request his expertise. "Dondi! One of my kitchen experiments just exploded! What did I do wrong??"

Come to think of it, Dondi wasn't bad in the kitchen. In fact, he was excellent in it. Vasiht'h tapped his finger against his mouth, thoughtful, and went back to work, and the work was pleasure, and the setting, a lagniappe.

How's it going? read the message, and even too distant to hear the mindline's embellishments, Jahir could imagine them: the prickling citrus of friendly curiosity, the warm-blanket embrace of affection, maybe a touch of bubble-bright enthusiasm. He smiled at his tablet and typed a response.

Very good, I think. The morning section was on epidemiology.

He returned his attention to the meal he'd been brought. The midday break was a welcome one, less because the test was difficult and more because it was *intense.* There were a great many questions, and one remained exquisitely aware of the time limit per section as one went on. He was enjoying himself because the material was challenging yet within his powers, but he had seen the faces of his fellow students as they exited for the break, and he could sympathize with their concern or despondency or relief. The Alliance allowed many paths into the medical profession, but it demanded excellence and rigor. Nothing less would do for a civilization created by a medical process, with all the biological, scientific, and ethical issues that obtained.

To have an hour to oneself, thus, was not luxury but necessity. And for once, he was hungry enough not to need Vasiht'h's constant reminders to eat, though he heard the Glaseah's voice in his head anyway: *Don't forget that what you're doing is using up calories, arii.*

Today's meal he was taking on one of the grassy terraces, at an 'outdoor' café where his seating overlooked a vertiginous view of the planet below, as if he was floating on an island in orbit. Which he supposed he was. The food was a delight though, a savory crepe with mushrooms, some wilted green, and a pale, tangy cheese. With good coffee, iced, something he usually avoided but the weather—could this place have weather?—was warm enough to need it. How were they simulating sunlight? Were they even doing so, or was it actual sunlight, filtered somehow for safety?

His tablet had words on it again, when looked down. *That sounds fun! For you, anyway.* That certainly had been written with a grin. *Would you believe I'm under an umbrella in the sun, mediating my siblings' squabbles long-distance?*

Jahir did not even pause before answering, *Absolutely.*

I guess that wasn't a very hard question, was it. It's beautiful, though, look, fish:

An image now, that moved when he touched it, of a school of pale blue fish with a subtle rainbow streak in the scales down their sides. They pivoted and dashed away as perfectly as if choreographed, and the light danced off those scales, pricking the colors to vivid life.

You found the serene lagoon, Jahir wrote.

With less than serene company, admittedly. Another image, this one a still of a passel of Harat-Shar chasing a human out of frame. Even without sound, he could hear her squeals: they were written on her widely grinning face. *You'll have to see this, though. It's perfect. And this island has an entire separate menu of fruity drinks, so I am having every one of them they make. To compare them against the mainland's and find out which is the best.*

Naturally, Jahir replied, smiling. *Thus you can guide my choice when I arrive.*

Only the best for you, arii!

Jahir smiled at the tablet.

You're on your break, I am guessing? I'll let you go back to eating. You are eating right?

He laughed at that, quietly under his breath. *Yes. I promise. You see? Here is my meal.*

That looks good! But there's not much of it. At least tell me there's a side salad, or an appetizer you've already finished.

Jahir sighed a little, smiled. *I promise to eat dessert.*

Send me a viseo! And good luck on the rest of Day Two!

He shook his head as he set the tablet aside. His meal was well and again large enough, but he would come in for his share of badgering did he not at least make an attempt. Nor could he begrudge his partner the constant nagging; he had seen himself through Vasiht'h's eyes in the mindline, on Selnor, when he'd been radically undernourished by his fight against that world's heavier gravity. He had no doubt the sight had left scars in his partner. Perhaps if Jahir had been well enough to notice his own body, he would carry them as well. The fact that he didn't . . . well. He was grateful for someone to watch him, sometimes. Was that not one of the many kindnesses of love? That it saved you from your own weaknesses, now and then? He glanced down at the world turning beneath the terrace's edge, its surface so pristine with so few clouds attendant, and smiled at the thought of the Glaseah awaiting him there.

When the waitress returned, he said, "May I see your dessert menu? And pray tell me you have something on it that can be carried away."

⸺∙∘∙⸺

That evening, Jahir allowed himself to be plied with one of the fruit drinks—white and honey yellow—while Vasiht'h recounted the day's adventures across the Bridge of Dreams, as well as his attempts to reconcile his brothers. "That does sound like the work of a day," the Eldritch said of the latter.

"I know," Vasiht'h said, chagrined. "It's so rare for them to have a fight this vicious. I know some other issue is driving it, on both sides. It's just a matter of figuring out what." He put his cheek in his palm, looking out over the dark waters as they ran to shore and broke with a hushed noise. The remains of the dinner they'd ordered was scattered on the table on their balcony, where Jahir had requested they remain. The test had been wearying, and he had not wanted to go abroad, even to be part of a background crowd. The food had been delightful, though, and the experience of watching the distant sun set at an angle over their view, sublime. He had no complaints.

"It's funny," the Glaseah said after a while, thoughtfully, "how much easier it is to handle my worry about their fight here."

Jahir laughed, quiet. "Tell me not that you require this level of luxury to ameliorate your anxieties!"

Vasiht'h chuffed. "Wouldn't that be a mess!" He lifted his head, staring at the stars. "I think this would get old after a while. It's beautiful, but it's unrelentingly novel. You know?"

"Eventually it would become less novel, which would put paid to your problem with it."

Vasiht'h said, "Maybe. Or maybe it would become mundane, and I'd be disappointed. It makes me wonder about the people who work here, and if they enjoy it, or if it's become . . . just another job in a beautiful place they don't really see."

Jahir was silent then, listening to the rolling of the surf, the hiss of it as it crawled up the sand under their balcony. At last, he said, "Such things are more a matter of one's existing mental state, I think, rather than any reflection on the working conditions. Or, at very least, the two matters are intertwined."

"Isn't everything," Vasiht'h murmured, rueful. He sat up, stretched. "Why don't we walk along the beach? It's pretty out, and our stretch of it looks deserted."

"That sounds fine," Jahir answered. As they walked down the balcony steps, he added, "Do not allow your brothers' fight to distress you overmuch. Surely you are not the only one at work on the problem."

"I'm sure I'm not, just the same as I'm sure I'm the only one who'll have anything useful to add to the process of reconciliation." The Glaseah chuckled. "I guess there's only so much you can do from a distance, though. Maybe I am taking too much on myself."

"As usual," Jahir offered.

Vasiht'h snorted. "I thought that was my line. You're the heroic measures one."

Jahir smiled at that and said nothing, letting the mindline speak for him. And as he expected:

"You're humoring me, aren't you."

"I said not a word!"

"Your silences are very, very talky."

Jahir hid his smile this time, folding his arms behind his back and pacing alongside the Glaseah as they started down the beach.

"You could say more, you know," Vasiht'h said, cocking his head up at the Eldritch. "I wouldn't be offended."

But he was smiling, so Jahir answered. "I could. But then you would know things too easily, and that would take some of the joy out of the discovery."

"I guess it would, at that." Vasiht'h scuffed his paws on the sand, and the texture seeped through the mindline: silky and warm, tickling where it worked up between the toes. "I think that's one of the things I love best about relationships. The person on the other end is always unknowable . . . no matter how well you know them, there will still always be an element of mystery, because they're not you. And yet, despite that, we trust them, and that trust, if it's a good relationship, isn't broken. It's like our relationship with life, just . . . writ small enough that we can get our arms around it. We'll never understand why we're here, what we're supposed to do, if things will work out all right, if we're doing the right things at the right time . . . but we throw ourselves into it anyway. Because that's the only way to get anything back out of it." Vasiht'h paused, wrinkled his nose. "I feel like I've talked all the way around this and not gotten to the heart of it."

"No," Jahir said, soft. "No, I think you have done a very good job of it."

"Do you think we're doing all right?" Vasiht'h asked after they'd walked some distance. "Throwing ourselves into things. I don't want us to stagnate."

"Nothing about our lives permits stagnation," Jahir said. "Every client we receive requires our entire heart and all our powers. If we never do more than what we are doing now, we will have spent our lives well."

Vasiht'h accepted that, though Jahir could sense him gnawing at it. Not anxiety, or at least it didn't have the savor of anxiety, acrid and jittery. More like the busyness of a mind at work on a puzzle, not liking how the pieces were fitting. "I wonder at times," he added, judging now to be the right moment, "whether your fear over my dissatisfaction with our life is . . . transference."

The Glaseah stopped short. Then laughed. "Are you psycho-analyzing me?"

Jahir stopped and faced him, smiling, brows lifted. "Do I

seem like the sort who would do such a thing without a license?"

"But you do have a license, and you're teasing me." Vasiht'h grinned, sighed. "Oh, I don't know. Maybe you're right. Probably you are. Writing all these notes to my family today made me think of the fact that one day I want one, and if not quite as big as mine, at least half as big. Where are children going to fit into our lives? What will that entail? When will I be ready?" He sagged, chuckled. "Dami's not the only one who says no parent's ever ready. That it's the process of having kits that trains you for having them. Which makes sense to me because . . . some things you only learn, in your gut, by doing them and finding out you can."

Thinking of his flight to the Alliance, and his subsequent successes—and failures—on its multiple worlds, Jahir said, "Yes."

"This is the point where we stop and you go through the surf and find an imperfect shell and give it to me as a symbol." Vasiht'h put a hand on his hip and gestured toward the sky, which had turned a purple nigh unto black, and was pricked with so many stars, and so luminous, that Jahir could discern the colors of the brightest without effort. "And then you tell me, 'You can only be all right with things once you accept that you can't know the outcomes, and be at peace with your own imperfections.'"

Jahir considered him, then headed for the surf. Behind him, Vasiht'h started laughing. "No, wait, I didn't mean that seriously!"

"You have been reading too many of your sister's romance novels." The water rushed toward but did not touch his boots. The sands had turned a silvery gray with nightfall, but the moon reflected off them differently than they did the bits of shell studded here and there. He paced the damp patches, searching, until he found a fluted edge, and pried from it a broken scallop, mostly intact but with a chip.

"And . . . trying to find parallels in my life inappropriately?" Vasiht'h said as Jahir started back toward him.

"And taking the wrong messages from them." Jahir reached for and took his partner's wrist, turning it so Vasiht'h's hand was palm up, and there he set the broken shell. "Which is that they are unbelievable, and life is never grand nor full of intimacy and drama. But for every year of cookies baked in a kitchen and shared chores and quiet work done well and without fuss, there is an hour of breathless glory and wonder, and you no less than any other being under the stars is deserving of such hours." Jahir smiled. "Whether you feel worthy of them or not."

Vasiht'h's blush was so intense the mindline was making Jahir's skin uncomfortably hot under his layers.

"Also," Jahir finished, folding the Glaseah's furred fingers over the gift, "all the shells on this beach are broken. I believe the more difficult task would have been to fetch forth a whole one."

"Isn't *that* a symbol," Vasiht'h said, mouth quirking upward into a crooked smile.

"None of us go unchanged from this life, or we are doing it wrong."

Vasiht'h barked a laugh. "Doing it wrong! Yes. I guess we are."

Jahir nodded once. "And you can only be right with yourself when you accept your imperfections, and that you cannot know all outcomes, so you cannot choose the best one."

Vasiht'h grinned. "All right. So noted." He looked up, the starlight glowing off the white stripes leading to the bridge of his nose. "It is beautiful, isn't it."

"An uncanny sky," Jahir agreed. "To be so clear."

"You can see forever. . . ." Vasiht'h sighed. Smiled. "All the Goddess's thoughts, made manifest. Anything seems possible. Including," he turned back toward their room, "you acing that test and becoming a healer-assist who thinks chemical formulas at me in his sleep."

"Do I do such?" Jahir asked, startled.

"Sometimes," Vasiht'h said. "And it's all good. You're better when you're stretching yourself, so let's get you to sleep so you can do it again tomorrow."

They returned to their room by way of the balcony, where Jahir tarried to stare outward, for just a moment.

CHAPTER 11

JAHIR WOKE TO A GREAT SENSE of well-being. That he could breathe easily, and the air smelled of the sea's briny complexity, and blooming flowers, and of distant water. That he was warm enough, for once, and without needing an excessive number of blankets. That the light on his closed eyelids was kind, and the sounds: the cry of shore birds, the reassuring regularity of the surf's hiss and boom. The mindline brought him the hum of Vasiht'h's contentment . . . arranging breakfast for them both.

When he returned to the homeworld, would he want to live thus? By the sea? But the coast abutting the Galare holdings was a cold one, with rocky crags and water he would not be glad to swim in.

This one, though . . . he'd touched the waters with his fingertips, felt the silkiness of the water, the grit of the salt. It would be warm. And today he would have his celebratory swim, after he passed the test, because he knew he would not fail.

Rising, he went to his ablutions, and from there to join Vasiht'h for breakfast in the main room, with the field set permeable to allow the breeze ingress.

"Look how pretty it is," Vasiht'h said. "The waves are all frothy. It's like lace!"

"Silvery lace," Jahir agreed, sitting to the meal. It was lighter than the Glaseah usually set out: slices of orange melon, tangy white cheese and large triangular crackers, small cups of espresso with honey. "You are coddling me."

"You like to travel light," Vasiht'h said. "I figure today, you can go into it how you like, as long as you eat a real meal at lunch."

Jahir laughed. "If you would have seen the places I've been eating! When we are ready to depart, I will show them to you and you shall choose which to try. The views have been spectacular." He leaked some of it through the mindline: the enormous and vertiginous vista beneath his feet, world turning, pristine as a jeweled bead.

"Phew. As long as I don't have to look down while we're eating!" Vasiht'h grinned. "I'll arrange a party for when you get here this afternoon. And no, don't argue with me on this one. This deserves celebration, doesn't it?"

"I will not have a license until I finish the required hours at the hospital. . . ."

"A second party then." Vasiht'h smeared his cracker with cheese. "On that, I'm in total agreement with the Harat-Shar: any excuse for a party."

Jahir chuckled softly. "Very well. And I shall meet these friends you've made."

"They'll be thrilled." Vasiht'h grinned at him, tapped the Eldritch's plate with his cheese knife. "Now, eat what little you've got there and let's see the end of this day together."

Jahir set to, and finished the meal listening to the Glaseah discuss all the assorted personalities he'd met, smiling at the whimsy of it. Afterward, they walked together to the Pad, where Vasiht'h halted and said, hesitant, "Hug for luck?"

His partner, who was always so careful of his need for space. Jahir went to a knee to properly receive, because even though the event didn't seem worthy of such a display, perhaps he was wrong to believe so. Perhaps this test would see their lives move in completely fresh directions and he would recollect forever with fondness the turning point they'd reached on Tsera Nova.

The Glaseah's shoulder was warm under his cheek, and his body reassuringly solid. And the mindline sang his friend's joy at the intimacy.

"There," Vasiht'h said. "Now go crush that thing!"

/*Such violence,*/ Jahir teased in the mindline, where he could soften it with his affection, /*from the passionless Glaseah!*/

/*Oh, you. Just get! Before I start sniffling at you.*/

/*You're not . . . ?*/

"Teasing," Vasih'th said aloud, grinning. "See you soon."

Upstairs on the station, Jahir walked to the conference center, keeping the planet on his left and glancing at it now and then. His partner would be busy with his visit to the cetaceans; it was comforting to think of him busy under those clouds. And at the end of this day, the Eldritch would be done, and he would swim, and there would be the entire rest of the week to enjoy the splendors of Tsera Nova at the Glaseah's side . . . and to sample only the best of the colored fruity drinks.

Smiling, Jahir presented himself to the Hinichi, and passed into the test.

"ARE WE READY!" Kristyl bellowed from the shore beside the pier.

"WE ARE!" her Harat-Shar posse shouted back.

Vasiht'h stood alongside Gladiolus and stared at the group, which had grown by two tigraines and an elderly Seersa couple. "Who are they? No, let me guess. You met them dancing last night?"

"Actually it was a limbo contest," Gladiolus said. At Vasiht'h's blank look, she said, "There's a stick, and you have to squeeze under it by arching backwards. And wiggling."

"That sounds . . ." Vasiht'h stopped. "Impossible."

"For you it would be!" Gladiolus grinned, ears flicking forward. "It was fun."

"And you're admitting it?" Vasiht'h said.

"I . . . ah. Yes." The Asanii's ears sagged and then she chuckled.

"Yes, I admit it. It's hard not to have fun with Kristyl. That's one of the reasons I love her so much."

"We find the things we need in other people," Vasiht'h said. "And Kristyl has fun in job lots, doesn't she."

Gladiolus laughed. "She really does."

Watching the group line up behind Kristyl, Vasiht'h asked suddenly, "How did the Seersa manage that contest?"

"They didn't," Gladiolus said. "They sat on the sidelines and heckled."

Watching the Harat-Shar process past, Vasiht'h said, "And . . . they're all coming with us? I thought the tour was full?"

"You *thought* the tour was full," the Asanii said dryly. "But apparently the boats have the capacity for twenty more people. They just don't book twenty more because they like people to have room to move around. Therefore—"

"When Kristyl showed up and used the force of her personality on them, they said, 'absolutely, you can take an extra ten or twenty people?'" Vasiht'h guessed.

"See, you know everything you need to know about traveling with her already!"

Vasiht'h laughed. "Well, let's go see the whales. And hope there's room to move around."

"The Harat-Shar claim they prefer to sightsee in clumps anyway."

Vasiht'h jogged after Gladiolus, who was last in line, and glanced out over the ocean. The waves still bore that choppy froth he'd found so pretty earlier that morning, and the sky overhead was blazing bright, except for some distant clouds. Beautiful, as usual, and with a stiffer breeze than the previous two days. Just the thing for sitting in the middle of the ocean—that would be stifling, wouldn't it, without a brisk breeze?

"And . . . eleven! That's all of us," Kristyl declared.

"Were you counting?" Vasiht'h asked, amused.

"Someone's got to keep track of everyone," the human answered serenely. She retied the brightly colored scarf that kept her hat on her head and squinted. "Kind of a rough sea."

"Is it?" Vasiht'h looked at it, bemused.

"Compared to the past few days." Kristyl frowned, rolled her shoulders. "Variation is a thing, I guess. You ready, alet? I hear there are seals, too, I can't wait to see alien seals."

"Seals?"

"Pinnipeds," the human replied, grinning, all bright white teeth. "Seals. And whales. Alien whales! Maybe they'll fluoresce? Or have two heads? Four flippers!"

"Or talk?" Vasiht'h offered.

She tutted, patting her straw hat into place. "Now, now, alet. Jokes about talking animals are in poor taste."

"Talking whales would be wonderful, though," Vasiht'h said. "I wonder why you humans never made any."

Kristyl's eyes sparkled. "We thought we'd leave you something to do."

"Ah, ouch," Vasiht'h said, laughing.

She patted his arm. "They might not have made whales, but they made you, and firebirds, and centaur grasscats, so . . . I'd say it was time well-spent. Though not giving fire to the firebirds was a strange omission. Why name them phoenixes and not give them the power to immolate? It's like you all didn't read our mythology at all!"

Vasiht'h started down the pier alongside the human. "You really are irrepressible, aren't you."

"I'll tell you a secret, alet, and I learned it really young." Kristyl tipped the brim of her hat down until it was shading her face. For once, she looked serious. "There's no making everyone happy, and no making everyone like you. If you stand out in any way, even to be exceptional, a lot of people will smile, but just as many people will frown, and those people are far more motivated to cut you down than the nice people are to bear you up. For every compliment you get, you'll get fifty complaints. You know? The world is just *waiting* to repress you. If you let it, that's it. You're done for." She glanced at Vasiht'h. "Do you get what I mean or am I explaining it badly again? What I mean to say is . . . if I can't make everyone like me, there's no use wasting time on being sad about it."

Vasiht'h glanced at her.

"I like people," Kristyl said. "A lot. To some people, that means I need to be disappointed when some of them don't like me back. To me it just means that if they don't like me, then they get to not like me. That's their choice. Just like my choice is not to cry about it."

"Well, *I* like you," Vasiht'h said.

She beamed and patted his shoulder. "Great, because you're about to be stuck on this all-day tour with me."

Vasiht'h laughed and followed her up the gangplank to the boat, which to his inexperienced eyes looked impressive: its flanks a gleaming white, the railings polished to a bright silver shine, and all its crew and staff in impeccable uniforms. The boat's name was the *Friendly Mermaid*, and at its prow was a cheerful-looking chrome figure: the mermaid in question, whose bottom half was an extravagance of long, trailing fins and whose top half was . . . an Aera, complete with long ears, pointed muzzle, and seashells over her breasts.

"Welcome aboard," a Tam-illee chirped as he stepped onto the deck. "I'm Marea SeesToShore, the first mate of the *Friendly Mermaid*. We're glad to have you with us this morning!"

"Thank you," Vasiht'h said. "I'm looking forward to seeing the seals and whales."

The Tam-illee laughed. "You'll love them. And you'll also love the complimentary spread we have in the cabin, with our panoramic view of Tsera Nova's South Beach Sea."

"Ah," Kristyl said from the other side, "But are there colored drinks? Because that's all he seems to order."

The Tam-illee grinned. "We have every color imaginable."

"Sometimes I drink kerinne," Vasiht'h complained to Kristyl, who patted him on the shoulder.

"Of course you do. Because it's also heavy and sweet. Let's go see this spread."

The cabin was already mostly windows, and the parts of it that weren't had been filmed with a smart coating so that they continued the uninterrupted vista with exterior camera input. Vasiht'h assembled a small plate of fruits with a cinnamon yogurt dip, because he couldn't not try that, and a crusty flatbread with melted cheese and big slices of tomatoes and some fresh herbs. There were fruity drinks, and he almost ordered the one that was yellow on the outside, but had a red middle. How did that even work? But decided at the last moment on the mint lemonade, made with crushed ice and real torn mint leaves so the whole thing turned a beautiful herbaceous yellow-green with emerald flecks. Breakfast had been light, by his standards, so the second meal was welcome.

Was the boat packed? It might have been, he thought, if the Harat-Shar weren't content to sit in each other's laps, or snuggle together in corners. He chose a seat next to the Seersa couple and introduced himself, discovering they were retirees doing a self-designed "notable sites of the Alliance" tour.

"You can't not come here," said the female, Keridwyn, a delicate woman with limpid sky-blue eyes set in a face strikingly patterned like a lilac Siamese. The grayish-purple was especially noticeable on the long fox ears. "Everyone wants to come here!"

"So far it's been great," her husband agreed. "We've been here a week and this is our last day. After this . . . where are we going again, honeyfangs?"

"We're off to the flagship location of TKI&I." Keridwyn grinned at Vasiht'h. "I want to go shopping. Where else but one of the most famous boutiques in the Core?"

"Even I've heard of TKI&I," Vasiht'h said, dabbing one of his melon slices in the yogurt. "And I don't wear clothes usually." He glanced at the male, Bodken. "I have to ask, though. Honeyfangs?"

Bodken snickered and bumped his shoulder against his wife's. "Well. She's sweet as honey, but with a little bite."

"No good being too meek," Keridwyn said, sipping her chocolate-creamed-coffee. "I started out feisty, I'm going to go out feisty too."

The trip to the cetacean show was just over three hours, and involved at least two other boats that left the dock shortly after them. Vasiht'h spent most of the voyage chatting with Kristyl's gang, and noticing how quickly the few passengers who'd booked the trip before she took it over were assimilated. It fascinated him that she should be so magnetic, when she was also so unapologetic about herself. Maybe that was part of the charm? She apologized cheerfully for missteps but never let them stop her, and there was something appealing about that unrelenting enthusiasm. It amused him to see the glimmer of intelligence in her eyes, or in her occasional comment; he wondered how many people assumed she was daffy.

"Plenty of people," Gladiolus told him later, when he was finally having that fruity drink with the weird red core. He was trying to preserve the separation by drinking the center first. "Underestimate her, I mean." The Asanii put her chin in her palm, resting the elbow on the railing of the ship where they were standing near the prow. The chop was stronger now, and the wind refreshing. "That's one of the reasons I think I want to be like her."

"Hopefully most of the time you'd rather be like you," Vasiht'h said.

"Oh, sure." The Asanii laughed. "You have a . . . best friend? Partner? Do you ever wish you were more like him?"

Vasiht'h considered that. "If I was more like him, I wouldn't enjoy how much unlike me he was."

Gladiolus eyed him, brows up. "Deep."

"Not really. I just like the differences? I think . . . the magic happens when the little ways you aren't alike line up. Like the bumpy parts of a key and the empty spaces in a lock."

The Asanii pursed her lips. "Still, you don't want to be too unlike your friends. Otherwise, it's too hard to stay close."

Was it? Vasiht'h thought of his own friendships, and his many clients. "It's like everything in life. It depends."

She laughed. "Why do things have to be so complicated, right?"

"Yes," Vasiht'h said, rueful, and obliged the waiter who stopped by with a tray by plucking up a skewer of roasted fruits.

He wasn't sure how that worked, except that they'd been coated with some kind of glaze . . . honey, maybe? Pepper? And the glaze caramelized?

"How do they even come up with these things?" Gladiolus said, staring at her own skewer.

"I don't know, but I'm glad they do!"

They stood together at the rail, watching the waves jump and dance and the sunlight play off their surfaces. Vasiht'h thought it particularly lovely, the way the light was growing . . . sharper, somehow? More orange? Something. They spotted schools of fish darting beneath the boat, squinted ahead at the sky in search of their destination, played 'what shape does that cloud look like to you.' They were still at it when Kristyl arrived, sliding between them and looping an arm around the Asanii's shoulders and another over Vasiht'h's after shooting him a questioning look and accepting his nod.

"Where are your adoring fans?" Gladiolus asked, brushing her nose against the other woman's.

"Inside, playing Truth or Dare." Kristyl grinned. "Can you believe they didn't know that game? It's tailor-made for Harat-Shar."

The Asanii groaned. Laughed. "I bet they're all naked already."

"They promised to be good. Mostly. Besides, at least half of them were already nude. What are you two up to?"

"Enjoying the quiet," Gladiolus said, just as a sea bird swooped past, screeching. She giggled. "The relative quiet!"

"I get it," Kristyl said. "Sometimes you don't want a party. Sometimes even I don't want a party." She wrinkled her nose. "Actually, most of the time I don't want a party, but parties happen around me."

"You should have been born Harat-Shar," Vasiht'h said, amused.

Kristyl tugged her hat brim down, only to have the wind push it back again. "I'm glad I was born human! But I wouldn't mind living with Harat-Shar. For a while, anyway. Then I'd want to try something different." She grinned, but her eyes were distant, and even as she finished speaking her gaze moved away, toward the horizon.

"You see the platform?" Vasiht'h asked. "Gladdie and I have been trying to spot it for a while now. Maybe your eyes are better."

"No," Kristyl said. "I just wonder about the clouds." Her eyes dropped to the waves. "And that. That . . . I don't want to say 'shouldn't be happening', but it shouldn't be happening."

"It's just waves?" Gladiolus said, but her voice rose toward the end of the words.

"Mmm." Kristyl squeezed their shoulders. "You two keep an eye out. I've got a game to organize."

"Should we be participating?" Gladiolus asked, frowning.

Kristyl beamed at her. "Don't worry, you'll win automatically." To Vasiht'h, "You too. You'll see." Then she sailed off, leaving the two of them at the railing.

"What do you think that was about?" Vasiht'h asked.

"I don't know," Gladiolus admitted, looking down at the waves parting around the boat's hull. "But I wish I did."

------◇◇◇------

Kristyl's game involved how long everyone could keep their life vests on—"If you make it all the way back to the hotel pier, I'll buy you a night of drinks! And you Harat-Shar, maybe there will be sexytimes!"—and though Gladiolus and Vasiht'h were automatic winners, she still pressed the vests on them. "So that no one thinks you cheated your way to the prize. Gotta follow the rules."

The *Friendly Mermaid*'s crew watched the festivities with professional interest. Vasiht'h wondered if any of them were worried about the same mysterious things Kristyl was, but no one showed any signs of it. Except the captain, who wasn't on deck at all. The first mate assured him he was down below, "coordinating with the trainers at the platform." Which seemed reasonable. Vasiht'h squinted into the bright sky, wondering how a few puffy white clouds and some enthusiastic waves could be so troubling as to inspire Kristyl to talk everyone into safety equipment. He patted the top half of his vest. Not that he minded . . . the only other time he'd been sailing, on Heliocentrus, he'd been asked to don the safety vests the moment he stepped aboard, and had assumed that to be normal until the *Mermaid*.

Whatever the case, the Harat-Shar took to the game with enthusiasm, and much groaning, as they preferred fewer clothes over their sun-warmed pelts. Kristyl placated them with fruity drinks, which Vasiht'h helped himself to as well. He sat with the Seersa couple again to listen to their account of the Truth or Dare session, and since they were wickedly incisive raconteurs he laughed his way through the entire thing and counted it fantastic entertainment. That got them, at last, to the sandbar's docking platform, because the show's complex was large enough to have one. Despite the photos, Vasiht'h had been expecting the place to seem more . . . rickety. But it felt remarkably stable, and large besides. There was a set of covered bleachers on a large wooden stage—if you could call it a stage with a big hole in the middle leading into the ocean—and several satellite areas reached by boardwalks, selling food, drink, souvenirs, even "changes of clothing," which sounded alarming. "Oh, don't worry, alet," the vendor there assured him as he peered at the shirts emblazoned with cavorting cartoon whales and seals. "It's just that some-times the critters like to splash the audience."

Vasiht'h wandered back from exploring to find Kristyl waving her arms at her Harat-Shar posse. "No, no, the deal is that you have to keep them on *until we get to shore.* Otherwise you can't win!"

"No breaks!"

"No breaks," Kristyl said serenely. "If you'd wanted easy-mode, you should have partied with some other girl." She put a hand on her hip and waggled it. "You gotta work for the best things in life."

A chorus of groans and laughs. Vasiht'h padded up beside her as the Harat-Shar dispersed to shop or take their places on the bleachers. "Serious about the game, aren't you?"

"I am! So you're not going to quit, are you?"

Vasiht'h chuckled. "And miss out on the free drinks? I haven't tried every flavor they make yet."

"You really haven't! I saw a blue thing over here. Let's go get you one."

He and Kristyl were strolling back from that booth when a large sea lion thumped past them, another human following. "That's right, Romeo, round them all up and get them seated." The sea lion stopped in front of them, lifted a black flipper, and waved it. "Exactly, get those two moving."

"Oh, wow!" Kristyl said. "That's a real seal. Like a Terran seal!"

"And he likes the ocean here just fine," the trainer said with a grin. "Though we do have to give him vitamin supplements. The fish here aren't *quite* right for our animals. But he's a bona fide California quasi-sea lion." She leaned over to rub his side. "Pretty far from home, aren't you, Romeo?"

The sea lion bent his head almost backwards and arrrred at her.

"What's a quasi-sea lion?" Vasiht'h asked.

"It's what happens when you breed super smart sea lions together for generations and they escape into the wild and keep getting smarter," the trainer answered, offering the sea lion her palm and getting it smacked by a flipper. "Right, Romeo? You are smart as a very smart dog, aren't you!"

"Is it all right to say stuff like that?" Kristyl asked her with the appearance of guilelessness. By now, Vasiht'h wasn't sure whether it was an act or not. "Some of the more canid-looking Pelted might find it offensive?"

The trainer eyed her. "A dog is a dog. Pelted are people." She nodded to them both and said to the sea lion. "Let's get the rest of our guests in their seats and start the show."

"Well, that went well!" Kristyl said to Vasiht'h.

"Humans tend to find you abrasive, don't they."

Kristyl flashed him a grin. "Just the ones that haven't internalized how many amazing things we're responsible for."

Vasiht'h couldn't help it . . . he laughed and followed her to a seat.

The sea lion thumped to the center stage, where he leaped into the water, only to appear on the edge of one of the other platforms and bark at the people shopping there. Vasiht'h watched him shepherd all the visitors to the bleachers from his vantage at the end of the third row, close enough to see but out of the 'splash section' which had been cordoned off with signs with warning cartoons. When the trainer and her accomplice finished their labors, about a hundred people had taken their seats in the bleachers. Vasiht'h hadn't noticed so many arriving, but craning his neck he could see the boats that had been following the *Friendly Mermaid* bobbing at the dock.

"There we go," the trainer said, her voice projecting to the back of the bleachers. "Looks like we've got them all, Romeo."

The sea lion jumped up alongside her and barked.

"They really are a fine looking group, aren't they?"

Another bark.

"Let's get this show started, what do you say?"

The sea lion leaned backwards and smacked his flippers together, an act for which he received a tossed fish. "Exactly. We're all excited! Welcome to Tsera Nova's *best* sea critter show! It's also the only sea critter show, but sshhh, don't tell anyone. Right, Romeo? Our secret?"

"Arr arrrrrr!"

"Exactly."

Terry the trainer was joined by two others, a Tam-illee named Rod and an Asanii named Serrafina. The show started in earnest with six leaping cetaceans, and only got better from there: everything from humorous skits to demonstrations of skill, interspersed with educational segments where the trainer talked about the mammals. None of them were "kept" . . . they lived in Tsera Nova's ocean, and returned willingly to "play" with the bipeds and earn their treats. The imported animals had been carefully selected based on their impact on the local populations, and were tracked to ensure they didn't overpopulate or destroy native habitats.

It was all delightful . . . a kind of metaphor for the sort of

interactions common to the Alliance. Weren't they all constantly
meeting on alien shores and seeing what wonders they found in
the spaces between cultures, peoples? The fact that the sea lion
chasing Terry the trainer across the stage willingly showed up
to engage in the game with a creature so different from him was
frankly miraculous. Vasiht'h glanced at Kristyl, who was sitting
a few Harat-Shar down from him, cheering and waving her arms
enthusiastically.

Some people might have found Kristyl's feelings about
humanity creating the Pelted and deserving the credit for them
offensive . . . but in the end, humans *had* made something
amazing, for any number of complicated reasons, some noble,
others sordid. But had they not had the audacity, Vasiht'h
wouldn't be watching whales splashing two rows of howling
Harat-Shar and laughing. The Goddess moved in ways mysterious, and sometimes you caught glimpses of how She worked and
it made you glad to be alive.

"I want a plush whale!" Gladiolus said, when the show
concluded.

"That's my line, usually," Kristyl said, grinning.

"Today it can be both our lines, and maybe they'll give us a
two-for-one discount," the Asanii said, bouncing down the steps.
Vasiht'h followed more sedately, reaching the stage at the same
time a drop of water plunked against his nose. He thought at first
it had come from the awning, but when he looked up, the sky had
grown . . . strange. Not cloudy, completely, but the color and angle
of the sunlight felt . . . off? As if it was scattering differently.

But he didn't feel a second drop, so he shrugged and followed
the women back to the souvenir booth, where he begged off from
buying any plush sea lions, t-shirts, or viseo recordings. Since
he had no interest, he wandered outside, where he found the
trainers huddled together with some of the crew from the boats.
Curious, he edged closer, until he could hear their conversation.

". . . do they know there are supposed to be viseo
opportunities?"

"No one's lining up, at least. It's in the brochure, but maybe they're not paying attention? Where are the animals, anyway?"

"We're not sure, they usually stay for a few hours after the performance, just to play." One of the Pelted trainers. "It's strange."

Terry, the human, said, "It's almost as if they're scared." When they glanced at her, she shrugged. "Back home, they'd get skittish sometimes. It was usually the weather."

"It's certainly not the weather here," one of her colleagues replied with a snort.

"Though it is a little blustery. Well, if anyone asks about the animals . . ."

"Just tell them what we always say," Terry replied. "We don't force them to do anything. If they don't stay, they don't stay."

They dispersed to make nice with the guests, leaving Vasiht'h to frown and look for Kristyl. The woman was holding a stuffed whale the length of her torso under an arm and was gesticulating at her posse, some of whom had taken off their life vests. "Oh, I'll give you a second chance, but you really do have to keep it on all the way to shore."

Another drop bounced off Vasiht'h's back.

——⚬⚬⚬——

The break for lunch had never felt so welcome, for the final phase of the test had been grueling. Jahir escaped the lecture hall, where the tension of his fellows was so palpable it needed no psychic power out of legend to feel it, nor a touch either. He'd wondered if he'd been imagining that the questions were growing more difficult, but no, the talk outside the facility had corroborated his hypothesis. Or at least, proven that they were undergoing a group delusion . . . at this point, Jahir wouldn't rule out such a diagnosis.

He wanted to move more than he wanted to eat, so he spent his break doing just that, exploring the boundaries of the convention center. Wandering the path inward brought him to a terraced garden, themed austerely on narrow running streams, pebbles raked around stones, and trees, either groomed and pruned into miniatures, or narrow-limbed and blossoming. The garden's culmination was a set of benches carved from red wood, set in a circle. Sitting there, Jahir thought he had rarely seen so harmonious a space, and he would have liked to enjoy it in a more natural setting . . . for there was no mistaking it for anything else. No planet he could walk on would have such a profusion of stars in its sky, nor so unblinking.

Leaving the convention center in search of a small meal to sustain him through the test's final phase, Jahir found the energy on the multi-level plazas . . . strange. People were clustering in places that two days of observation led him to find nonsensical. Passing these groups, he heard them murmuring something about 'spectacular clouds.'

Halting on one of the higher bridges, he looked down at the planet and found them correct. The pellucid cobalt blue of the seas was now interrupted by spirals of white. It delighted him, that he could see the shadows of those clouds on the sea beneath.

When he began the trip back to the convention center, still holding a cone of roasted chestnuts, he thought the clouds looked denser . . . but that was surely impossible. Wasn't it? He paused again on one of the bridges, watching, but couldn't tell.

Five minutes to return, if he didn't want to be shut out of the final half-day of the exam. He made haste, but wondered at his lingering sense of unease.

———⊗⊗⊗———

"All aboard what's going to shore!" one of the crew of the *Mermaid* shouted from the plank to the boat. Vasiht'h joined the line, once again last. The two Seersa were chatting amiably in front of him—wearing their vests, he noticed—and on seeing him, Bodken grinned. "So, what color drink are you having on the way back, eh, alet?"

"Rainbow?" his wife guessed. "White?"

"Purple, maybe," Vasiht'h said. "Or green." He twitched as another raindrop hit him. "Is it just me or is it sprinkling?"

"Oh, there's a bit of a drop coming down, now and then,"

Bodken said. "Odd that. Thought they didn't let it rain where the tourists were staying."

One of the other boats churned past, its prow bumping on the waves which were, Vasiht'h was not happy to notice, even choppier than they were before. And darker. Could water get darker? He glanced up at the sky and wondered when those clouds had moved in.

"And here's the last one," the first mate said as Vasiht'h jogged aboard. She smiled. "Welcome aboard, alet. Why don't you check the refreshments in the cabin?"

Something about that didn't sound like a suggestion. When Vasiht'h glanced at her, there was tension around her eyes despite her smile.

"That sounds great, thanks." He padded that way, found Kristyl at the door into the cabin. "Has anyone lost your game yet?"

"No one's going to lose my game," she said casually. "Because I'm going to nag anyone who gives up on it into sticking with it." She looked from the vest on his upper body to the one clasped around his barrel. "Those good and snug?"

"They are."

"So if I yanked on them . . ."

"Would you?" Vasiht'h asked, bemused.

"She would," Gladiolus said, stepping out of the cabin with a cup in her hand. "She's been doing it to the rest of us. At random."

"The Harat-Shar think it's funny!" Kristyl chirped.

"The Harat-Shar would," Gladiolus said with a sigh.

"Is that alcohol?" Kristyl leaned over, sniffed it. Plucked it out of Gladiolus's hand. "It is. Well, you don't need this!" She marched to the rail and poured it over the side. "There. That's better. Now you can go put something else in the cup. Like pure, clean water!"

Gladiolus squinted at her friend. "All right. Get it off your chest. Right now."

"It's probably nothing." Kristyl took the Asanii by the shoulders, turned her in place and gave her a gentle push. "Back in the

cabin! Why not get some nice, juicy fruit, too? Something with a
high water content?"

"Why?" Gladiolus asked, "Do you think I might be dehy-
drated soon?" As she vanished into the cabin, she called, "We're
surrounded in water!"

"Saltwater," Kristyl said, folding her arms and looking over
the side. "And alien saltwater, at that."

Vasiht'h said, "What are you worried about?"

"I'll tell you a secret," the human said. "I worry about
everything."

Was that the truth? Vasiht'h wondered. But he went in the
cabin anyway.

⸺⸺ oᴓᴓ ⸺⸺

If there was anything wrong, Vasiht'h didn't sense it in the merriment inside. He begged off from drinking another fruity drink
and had water, but didn't say no to the lunch spread. Why he
didn't eat as heavily as he usually would have, he wasn't sure. He
blamed it on the boat's occasional lurching, which made holding
a plate a challenge.

When he'd listened to as many stories and had as many
conversations as he felt he could handle, he slipped back onto
the deck and stopped at a point midway along the railing. There
he stared toward their destination: blue skies, the waves edged
in slanting copper light, crisp and brassy. Then he looked back
toward the cetacean stage: gray skies, darker gray waves, froth a
dull silver. One of the other boats was forging through it, following them to the hotel.

Joining him, Gladiolus said, "Looks like we're heading out of
the rain, at least."

"I guess they have to let it rain somewhere," Vasiht'h said.
"I'm just surprised they let it form over one of the attractions."

"Maybe it was one of those 'lesser of two evils' things," Gladiolus said. "Letting off steam in the system, you know?"

"What are you two doing outside?" Kristyl asked from behind
them. "You should be in the cabin."

"But look." Gladiolus pointed. "We're sailing into better weather. We could probably even take these off." She plucked at her vest.

Kristyl squinted into the light. "You can't win if you take it off before shore!"

Vasiht'h, still staring behind them, said, "It's strange how dark it can look so suddenly. I think it started raining?" Because the sky had turned the same color as the sea. Usually that mean they were connected by rain.

The boat behind them surged toward them.

Kristyl grabbed them by the arms, *"Back inside back inside back inside right now!"*

Vasiht'h looked over his shoulder as she hustled them toward the door, and his heart jumped. The trailing boat was racing toward them, pushed by the crest of a wall of water. "Oh Goddess," he whispered. "Be with us now."

CHAPTER 12

KRISTYL FAILED TO PULL THEM inside in time, and that failure saved their lives . . . because the second boat came down on top of them and smashed the cabin, like, Vasiht'h thought in horror, a knife smearing butter across a cutting board. He was still staring at the wreckage when the *Friendly Mermaid* threw him off the deck. Far, far off the deck into the heaving violence of a storm-churned ocean.

Vasiht'h liked swimming.

Nothing in this sea permitted swimming.

The two life vests around his body kept bobbing him to the surface, where he gulped in great lungfuls of air before the wind and waves shoved him back under, and none of that mattered as much as his need to get *far far away* from the boat. He didn't know what instinct spurred him, nor did it matter how little progress he was making. It was imperative that he not be anywhere near the wreckage. Because if it sank . . . and if in sinking, it sucked the water around it after it, to fill in the space where it once was . . .

Vasiht'h padded, barely able to see through the wall of rain, and the Goddess's name was a constant litany in his head.

To come to Tsera Nova to die! Ridiculous! He hadn't solved

his brothers' problems yet! Hadn't called Sehvi back! Wouldn't be there on the shore to hear how Jahir's test had gone!

Vasiht'h groaned. Jahir.

He thrashed on, desperate and adrenalized, and behind him through the howl of the wind he heard a terrifying groan.

Don't look back don't look back don't look back

He looked over his shoulder, and watched the rain-smudged silhouette of the two boats capsizing.

How many people were going down with them?

Should he go back?

Lightning cracked, so close he yelled, swallowed water, vanished under the waves, popped back up again. *You can't do anything to save them. You can barely keep your own head up.*

Swim, something whispered, and he flailed on.

———— ∞ ————

It felt ridiculous that pummeled by waves and half-drowned, he could still be worrying about whether he was failing someone. Himself. The Goddess. The people who might still be alive. His family. Bret, for Her sake. But he was convinced he was going to die, so why wouldn't he review his own faults in his last moments? Think loving thoughts of his family? Wish badly he had loved them more?

Think of Jahir?

Oh, Jahir!

The next wave smashed him down so hard something gave in a wing, and a pain brighter than the sun glimpsed between clouds made him yelp. *Just a wing, I can get by without a wing, just paddle, keep paddling.*

The broken limb no longer folded, though, and the waves kept smacking it. He thought he lost a few moments of consciousness, maybe more than once, but kept forcing himself awake. If he passed out in this, and stayed that way . . .

Without the life vests, I would have already been dead.

If he lived through this, he would owe Kristyl his life.

If he lived through this.

He had to live through this.

If he could breathe without inhaling water.

If he could swim and make some progress. Any kind of progress.

If his broken wing wouldn't also *tear* along the wing vane, now that the waves had gotten hold of it, like some kind of creature worrying at a piece of meat. . . .

Oh Goddess but that *hurt*!

And now, of course, he was bleeding. Did marine predators hunt in this kind of storm? Wouldn't that be perfect . . . to survive drowning, only to be eaten?

Something nudged his lower leg. He retracted it instantly, but again, something bumped him. Front paw this time. Vasiht'h sprang his claws. He wasn't going to die without a fight.

In front of him . . . a familiar head, barely visible in the torrential rain. He almost couldn't believe his eyes.

"Romeo?" he asked, astonished, the words lost in the gale.

Another head rose alongside, a sleek gray streak. One of the dolphins from the show. Again, something brushed his side. This time, Vasiht'h grabbed for the fin and held tight. The dolphin seemed to wait for him to settle—as best he could in the churn—and then began towing him.

"This is great," Vasiht'h gasped against the dolphin's side. "I really appreciate the help, but it's not going to matter if we don't end up somewhere."

No answer but lightning and the terrifying crash of thunder nearby. "All right, so no longer going to die by shark, or drowning, or being sucked under by the boat. Electrocution, though. Haven't solved that."

The dolphin kept pulling him. Vasiht'h didn't know where the sea lion was, except that he couldn't see anything through the noise, the waves, the rain, the everything.

I thought Selnor was the worst day in my life. I wasn't asking for things to compare it to! Head ducked against the dolphin, Vasiht'h thought, *Oh Goddess, I'll never ask for another thing in my life but I don't want to die here!*

The dolphin bumped into something. Looking up, Vasiht'h found an inflatable life raft, its rain-dulled orange sides the brightest thing in sight. Someone looked over the side and called, "Hey, hey, the critters brought us someone else!" One of the Harat-Shar. Kristyl's Harat-Shar. The tigraine leaned over and bellowed over the wind, "Come on!"

"I don't know if I'll fit!" Vasiht'h answered.

"You'll fit, damn it! We're not leaving anyone behind! Heave!" This to someone in the drenched uniform of one of the *Mermaid*'s crew, who grabbed Vasiht'h's torso.

"Get your claws into it," she yelled. "It's tough enough to take it!"

How they grappled him onto the raft, Vasiht'h had no idea. But they managed, and the raft, rated for a third the boat's capacity, was large enough for him despite the number of people already on it. Far more than he'd expected . . . far fewer than he wanted to see. Had the rest died? Or were there other rafts like this? If the sea creatures were helping find the stragglers in the water . . .

"Just lie down," the *Mermaid*'s crewwoman shouted. "I'll bind up your wing."

"All right," Vasiht'h answered, and discovered he was sobbing. "All right. Yes. Thank you."

Sitting still for that was almost impossible. The raft's floor was stiff but not hard, and the waves kept tossing them around. He feared he'd be thrown off, in fact, until he realized someone had snapped a clip to his life vest. The woman at work on him kept yelling something over the noise: apologies, he thought. But the process took longer than he wanted, and hurt like nothing he'd ever felt, and he was sure he did pass out at least once.

When he woke, it was to the same nightmare, except they were helping someone else onto the boat, and it broke his heart because it was Keridwyn, Keridwyn without her elderly husband, and he had to watch her scan the boat's numbers for his face before crumpling. Unconsciousness seemed better than this, but:

"Here," the tigraine yelled into the wind, pushing him toward the back of the raft. "You watch that quarter. If you see a fin or a sea lion head, wave so they can see you!"

Saying that if the creatures couldn't see the bright orange raft, one person waving in this torrential downpour wouldn't make much difference . . . he couldn't do it. His real role was to help anyone the dolphins brought out of the water. He could do that, Goddess willing. *Please,* he thought to Her. *Bring us more people.*

And then there was a time interminable. Minutes? Hours? A day? Vasiht'h squinted into the dark, clinging to his corner of the raft, scanning for a bobbing head, a disturbance in the water, an arm, a fin, anything. The raft had caught a current and was traveling, but where, he had no idea; he'd lost all sense of direction. Maybe it was carrying them further out to sea? Did it matter? His life had narrowed to one breath, then another, to being drenched from pelt to skin, to the pounding pain in his side where his wing was bound. They rescued one more swimmer, then another. And the storm never seemed to cease.

It couldn't last forever. No storm did. If they could just hold on, it would pass. Things had to get better.

He was chanting that in his head when the raft hit something and flung them all off it, and he was airborne while thinking, numb, that they were all about to die.

. . . and then the clip jerked him back—

. . . and he hit the ground. The *ground.*

That was his first thought, before something ripped along his side, and his next thought was obliterated by an inner howl. He wanted to curl into a ball and die, but the rain kept lashing him and the wind pulling at his body, and then someone was shaking him. The crewmember from the *Mermaid.* ". . . walk, can you walk?"

"Yes," he said from between gritted teeth. "I think."

The woman stayed long enough to help him stumble upright before limping off in search of other survivors. Presumably. There had to be other survivors? He followed her progress, thought that if she could drag her probably-broken leg after her in search of other people, he could too. They'd been thrown onto what looked like a beach? But it was too dark for him to see anything except the bulk of some kind of promontory behind them. So he hobbled along the shoreline, toward the only vivid color in sight: the orange raft, which had been crushed against something hard enough to deflate. He didn't want to think about what that might have done to anybody trapped in it.

The first person he found he didn't recognize. An Asanii, maybe from another boat? He helped the man stand and directed him toward the raft before continuing along the beach, bending into the wind and wiping the water from his eyes, over and over. The second he found was Keridwen, and she was unconscious. He couldn't tell if she was hurt . . . he could, though, pick her up, because she weighed as little as a half-grown child. He ignored the pounding of his heart and the ache in his side as he carried her back, her sopping tail smacking against his forelegs with every lurching step.

"That's good," the crewmember shouted through the gale. "Don't go back out, I'll cover the rest." She pointed. "We're going that way."

He wanted to ask why, but it was too much effort. He had a direction, someone to help, and a group to follow, so he did, trudging along the ragged line of survivors.

Vasiht'h kept walking. And walking. Rearranged Keridwen when his arms started complaining. Rearranged her again, wondering how she'd gotten so heavy. Kept walking. Stared at the person in front of him. Kept walking . . .

Stopped.

"In, in, in," the crewmember chanted, and they obeyed, passing through a door set into a stone wall and . . .

Then there was light. And quiet. He was dripping, and no longer cold, and no longer battered by the wall of noise and pressure outside.

"You made it!" a voice cried, and then Kristyl descended on

him and hugged him.

"Here, let me take her," someone said, prying the unconscious Seersa from his arms. "There are some medical supplies here, we'll stabilize her."

"Are you hurt?" Kristyl added, looking past his shoulders. "What . . . that looks awful. But not serious?"

He looked past his torso at his barrel, found the poorly-splinted wing. But Kristyl was looking at the other side, where he'd lost the skin on his ribs. She was right, though. Maybe? It was starting to drip.

"We'd better get you sewn up. Come on."

'Here' was the control center for Serenity Palms island, a bunker tucked into the rock that tourists climbed to reach the lookout point. It was already full of refugees from the storm: not just those on the boats, Vasiht'h divined by listening, but visitors to the island who'd been taken by surprise by the weather. A good number of them had escaped down the bridge before the wind had made it impassable, though a handful of those were missing. Possibly. Communications was spotty.

"But what happened?" Vasiht'h asked Kristyl once he'd had his rips sealed and his wing properly bound. "What . . . where did it *come* from?"

The human was sitting beside him, staring at the satellite image of their location. "No one knows. They've been trying to contact the weather station, but no one's answering. And I mean *no one*, even the orbital station general. It looks like outbound traffic's stopped up, though we're still receiving some data." She nodded at the image: the cloud cover on it wasn't moving fluidly, the way Vasiht'h was used to, but in jumps and starts. What he saw there, though . . .

"What is that?" he breathed.

"That's a hurricane," Kristyl said, matter-of-factly. "And it's on its way here."

"Here?" Vasiht'h repeated, dumbly. "To the island?"

"And then past it to the coast, yes." Kristyl smiled a little. "I'm sure the buildings will be fine, but all the nice landscaping's going to get pulled up by the roots. Nothing with an eyewall that well-defined is weak."

"But . . . a hurricane? On Tsera Nova? They were supposed to have . . ." Vasiht'h waved a hand. "Things. To stop that."

"Yes, well." Kristyl's smile grew mordant. "I guess sometimes when humans try great things, they fail at them."

At the front of the room, an Asanii in a staff uniform had climbed onto a chair. "All right, everyone! Listen up! I've squeezed some messages in and out, and we've got a big storm heading our way. It'll roll right over us . . . we're safe in here. So don't worry about that." He drew in a deep breath. "Having said that, though . . . we have less than an hour to check the rest of this island for survivors. People who might have been beached on rafts, or gotten lost, or found a hiding spot good enough for what we're experiencing now. It's not going to be good enough for what's coming our way." He scanned the silent room. "Technically what I'm about to ask goes against our safety policies, and I shouldn't be doing it. And you should absolutely not feel obligated to volunteer. But if you'd like to help us canvas the island for stragglers and direct them here. . . ."

Kristyl slid off her chair. "Count me in!" she called over the heads of the others.

"It'll be dangerous," the staffer said.

"Really?" she answered, with a tired smile. "I would never have guessed."

"Ha, right. Not too obvious, is it." He smiled, wan. "Thank you for volunteering. I've got short-range telegems, so you'll know when you need to make it back, and be able to get directions if you get lost, or be able to report people who are too injured for you to carry." He paused. "But you'll need a partner. No one goes out alone in this. Teams, only."

"I'll go with her."

Was that his voice? It was. Vasiht'h finished, "I've got a long back. It's good for carrying people."

CHAPTER 13

THE PROTOCOL FOR BREAKS for the exam struck Jahir as old-fashioned, something that might have served his people rather than the technologically-advanced Alliance. All the test-takers were permitted as many as they liked, but they had to be accompanied by the Hinichi to the restroom. Jahir wondered why some less obtrusive method hadn't been utilized: tracking via cameras, perhaps? But he had found, with interest, that the Pelted were still motivated by tradition, if not as slavishly as the Eldritch were.

He wasn't sure how far along he was into the second half of the day when he decided to take that break. He wasn't sure why he wanted one, either, as he had no pressing need. Something about being on the homestretch made him want to pause, so he could truly be present for the ending. So he requested a break, and waited until the Hinichi woman appeared at his desk to stand and follow her from the lecture hall.

"Restroom?" she asked politely.

He began to agree, then thought better of it. "There are other choices?"

She laughed. "Some people just want to sit somewhere and breathe. Or they want to eat. They can't leave the convention center grounds, of course, so they have to order it delivered here, but there's no reason not to."

Did he want to eat? No. But to sit somewhere and breathe . . . "What would be a good location . . ."

"To decompress?" She smiled. "I usually take people some- place they can look at the long view. It helps. Perspective, you know?"

"I do," he said. "And I would like to spend my fifteen minutes thus."

"This way, then."

To Jahir's surprise, they walked toward the terraces. The Hinichi did not lead him to the bridge, though, but made an abrupt turn before it, following the railing along a walkway that formed a sort of connected balcony for the top floor rooms of the convention center. The glass doors leading into them were privacy-darkened, but he imagined the view from inside must be inspiring: the outrageous creativity of the terraces, floating against the Alliance's premiere resort world? Beautiful.

Their destination was a small platform with a few seats pointed outward, toward the planet. It was tucked behind the corner of the convention center, and the noise from the terraces fell away abruptly, leaving a bubble of calm amid the bustle that stole his breath. Jahir came to a halt at the railing, looking out toward the limitless void. How still it was. His breath felt loud in compare, his heart. How small he felt, and how magnified, for he was here, able to bear witness to the glories of creation. That his people were denied this vision, and for no reason . . . !

But he was here now. There was time. And what he was about now would be part of that future, because what he was learning, he would need. His shoulders lost their tension, his wrists. His fingers rested soft on the rail, as they might have on the keys of a piano, in the silence before music.

At last he turned away, and said to the Hinichi standing a respectful distance from him, "Thank you."

"My pleasure," she answered, quiet, and began to lead him back.

Refreshed, he followed, and as he did looked toward the terraces . . . and again, saw the pattern that made no sense, except this time it was so distinct that his hesitation caused the Hinichi to pause, and then stop abruptly. Had he not been following several paces behind, he might have bumped into her.

"What in God's name!" she whispered, her ears trembling and eyes wide. "That . . . that shouldn't exist!"

He followed her gaze past the knots of people pointing and talking excitedly, and found clouds on cloudless Tsera Nova. And not just scattered ones, but an enormous spiral monster.

Right on the ocean, closest to the resort.

"My partner is down there," he said, without realizing he was going to speak.

"Hopefully they've evacuated . . ."

Hopefully wasn't good enough. "I need to know." His tablet was still in the lecture hall with his bag, so he set off for the nearest public terminal. The woman hurried after him.

"Technically you're not allowed to use any external data sources while outside the testing room," she said. "But . . . I'm here, so it's not like I'm going to miss you looking up any answers."

He didn't dignify that with a response, because every screen was showing warning signs and severe weather headers. He ignored them to find a terminal he could query for real-time news. Listened with difficulty, because once again his breathing felt too loud, and his racing heart. 'Unexpected' and 'missing persons' and 'catastrophic weather station malfunction.'

He switched directions and headed for the port, walking briskly. His minder fell into step beside him, almost jogging to keep pace. "Where are you going?"

"Down to the surface."

"I doubt they'll let you do that!"

"They will have to stop me."

"The test!" the Hinichi exclaimed. "Is back the other way! If you leave before finishing it, you'll have to take it all over again!"

He stopped to face her on one of the bridges, where schools of solidigraphic rainbow fish hovered and a world in turmoil turned below. "You would have me abandon my dearest friend to direst peril merely to finish an exam I can retake at some other time."

She squared her shoulders, her face settling into a mask but her eyes entreating. "Alet, you can't do anything down there. It's debatable whether they'll even let you through. They'll have rescue personnel—trained people—already at work on the planet. If you go, you'll just make more work for them." She pointed. "If you're going to have to wait it out anyway, why not finish what you started?"

"Because," Jahir said, quiet, "what I've started is not worth finishing, without that piece of my heart whom I have left on that world."

He kept moving, abandoning her on the bridge.

The activity at the dock was frenzied. Passengers arriving in-system, clotting like arteries as they discovered they could not continue to their destination on the ground; tourists who'd just fled the planet, desperate to depart or angry and demanding refunds; knots of people straining to use the Pads, or wanting to know why they couldn't use the shuttles. Jahir ignored them all, sliding around the crowds or through them, taking the agitating touches when he received them with a composure he knew was possible only because of a link he'd made with an alien who was parted from him now, and should never be. There had been a time such touches would always have incapacitated him. Now, armored in purpose—and fear—he let them glide off him like the water he'd hoped to swim in this evening, at the celebration that should have been waiting for him on Tsera Nova.

A harried-looking Tam-illee foxine stopped him when he neared the Pads and addressed him in rote words of courtesy drawn taut by anxiety. "We're sorry, alet, no one is allowed to use the Pads except emergency services personnel."

"I am a healer-assist," Jahir said, and he drove every moment he'd spent in Heliocentrus into the words, "with experience in trauma wards and acute and critical care."

Her eyes widened. Would she believe him? He did not flinch from her gaze, but willed her to let him pass . . . and she did.

"The destination's preset," she said. "Ileyspeed, alet."

"Thank you," he replied, and strode on.

Was it a lie? It had wanted only paperwork to confer the healer-assist certification on him on Seersana, and if that certification had been for psychiatric care, not physical, still, it counted. As did, he presumed, the exam he had almost finished and left behind. He would have passed that too. None of it mattered, except that he could assist in triage, and Vasiht'h was on planet. And where his partner was, he must be too.

I am on my way, arii. Do you not despair . . . and I shall not either.

CHAPTER 14

This is crazy, I'm not a hero, what am I doing out here . . .
Oh right, I'm keeping Kristyl out of trouble . . .
Or company . . .
Or both . . .

Vasiht'h hunkered against the winds, his side bumping against Kristyl's hip as they slogged down the path toward the trees where, if their scanner was correct, at least one person was hidden.

Or maybe it's that I didn't want to be left alone in there, thinking about how wrong everything can still go, or looking at everyone else and thinking about everything they've lost . . . He glanced at the human, eyes almost completely closed thanks to the rain. He hadn't asked about Gladiolus. He hadn't had to. If the Asanii had been among the rescued, she would have been at Kristyl's side already.

Vasiht'h didn't have to ask to know why Kristyl was out here.

The human pulled on his arm and pointed, which was easier than shouting through the wind. Vasiht'h nodded and followed her.

Anseahla had storms. The world tended toward wet and tempestuous, and the band where most of the Glaseah lived was semi-tropical, with rainy and dry seasons and all the riotous growth inspired by the heat and humidity. No stations finessed the weather, though when dangerous storms spun up over the oceans, they were dispersed. Vasiht'h didn't know how that technology worked; it struck him as a terrible omission, that lack of comprehension of something so crucial. If he knew, then someone here would know, and would be doing it to the storm heading their way.

Magical thinking, but what was left to him? Faith, certainly. But faith was a form of magic, one that kept you going when hope was having a panic attack.

Vasiht'h had been caught out in storms, particularly as a child, pelt-drenched and chased home by thunder's warning whipcracks. He'd thought he'd known storms. Had patted himself on the back for it, even.

The Goddess had a way of teaching the hard-headed. Usually involving sledgehammers. Which is what this wind felt like, when it gusted . . . like a wall smashing against him. These were only the hurricane's warning blows, promises of the gales to come. They drove the water against his face and side until his skin was sore with it, and he wondered if he'd bruise under the fur.

His sole consolation was that as a short heavyworlder with four legs that ended in clawed toes, he had an easier time staying planted than Kristyl, which is why he kept himself between her and the winds.

They reached the questionable shelter of the trees, which were bending so far over Vasiht'h wondered why they hadn't snapped yet, and began their search for the blip on their scanner. They'd been scouring their quadrant for nearly half an hour now, because the resort staffer had warned them that some people might not show on the scans for any number of technical reasons; Vasiht'h had stopped listening the moment the first had been 'they might be unconscious.' He suspected the staffer had stopped himself from saying 'they might be dead.' But they'd found no one, and Vasiht'h desperately hoped it was because there'd been no one to find, and not that they'd missed someone.

But they didn't miss this person. Kristyl got onto her hands and knees and looked under a rock and found a small Hinichi toddler. She had to pull the boy out by herself, because Vasiht'h couldn't lower himself easily, and the child himself had passed out. Injury? Fear? Exhaustion? He didn't know, but the boy was a light burden.

Kristyl checked the scanner, then the timer. She pointed at the countdown and yelled, "Go on?"

Vasiht'h glanced at it. They had less than fifteen minutes, but they hadn't finished their search area. "Yes," he shouted back, and they continued on.

They found no one else. They also didn't complete their canvass before they were called back. As Vasiht'h hurried after Kristyl, he wondered if he would carry the guilt of that unfinished search all his life, or if it would fade with time, or perspective. Would he look back one day and realize he couldn't hold himself responsible for every person the storm claimed? That it was hubris to think there had to have been anyone left for him to find, just because he hadn't stayed to make sure? Or would he come to believe that he'd given up too soon, and a real hero would have sacrificed himself to be certain?

At the moment, he was too tired to care, which was itself a revelation. That exhaustion could pull the plug on unproductive negative emotions, as well as positive ones. And they had found one person. He stared down into the face of the boy he was still clutching, and hoped to Her Heaven that his parents were waiting for him.

As it was, he and Kristyl were among the last of the teams to return, and the wind was buffeting their backs when they entered, water sleeting off them to pool around their bodies. Vasiht'h handed over the child and accepted a towel, which he set around Kristyl's shoulders before propelling her toward the drier inner sanctuary. The second towel he used on himself before fetching a cup of hot tea for both of them. The genies weren't functional on emergency power, but kettles were, and tea bags needed no fancy technology.

"Thanks," Kristyl said. He hadn't missed her eager scanning of the crowd when they'd first arrived. She sipped, her enthusiasm drained.

Vasiht'h sat next to her, his wet tail flopped over his also wet paws. Now that they were no longer outside fighting the elements, he felt the ache of his side and the broken wing badly, and shifted several times seeking a more comfortable position.

"Did you take a painkiller?" Kristyl asked, rousing from her despondency.

"You know, I didn't think of it?"

Her smile was crooked. "I'll get you something."

Vasiht'h didn't know if he wanted something for the pain, but he let her go because he could tell she needed to do something to keep from coming apart. He knew the feeling, because he was right there with her, breathing around a chest too small and tight for all the feelings he wasn't examining. He waited for Kristyl, counting breaths, and swept his gaze over the group, which had grown larger but not large enough. Not to account for all the people who must be missing.

But at the back of the room, near the hall to the restrooms, he saw Keridwen in Bodken's arms.

When Kristyl returned she found him sniffling, and she left again to get tissues. Handing them over, she put an arm around his shoulders.

"Your Seersa couple found one another again," Vasiht'h told her.

"Just like we'll find our other halves," Kristyl said. "You'll see."

Vasiht'h wiped his eyes. He knew he'd see Jahir again, barring some fresh catastrophe: he'd found his way out of the sea and to shelter, and the storm would be bad but it would pass and this would be over. He would get off Tsera Nova, and Jahir would be waiting for him on the station, and years from now . . . no, they wouldn't laugh about it years from now. But they'd look back on

it and say, 'Well, that happened and it's over, aren't you glad.'
But Kristyl . . .

"Maybe we should organize a game to keep people's minds
off the storm."

The human looked away. "I don't think most of the people
here feel like playing."

"Maybe not. But is sitting here staring at the satellite feed
any better?" When she didn't answer, Vasiht'h said, "I knew
these girls. Know them. I know these girls." He paused. "Strange
to realize I still know them, when I've been so used to thinking of
them in the past tense."

Kristyl was staring at him now, one brow lifted. "All right.
You got me with that opening. You knew some girls that you
know and that confuses you? It confuses me too, so rock on?"

Vasiht'h managed a laugh. "You remember my partner the
Eldritch."

She smiled, a little. "Who could forget."

"I met him in a hospital parking lot, where I was letting six of
its residents teach me to jump rope. Girls. Children."

Kristyl grimaced. "So this is a story about how things could
be worse, and we have to buck up like the brave sick children and
focus on the good things in life."

Vasiht'h paused. "Yes? And no?"

She chuckled. "There you go again. Confusing yourself, and
me."

"But you want to hear about how they taught him to jump
rope too, and how that led to us being friends?"

Kristyl hugged her knees. "It's got an Eldritch in it, and cute
kids. All you need is a kitten or a puppy and you're golden."

"No kittens or puppies," Vasiht'h said. "But there is a dog,
much much later."

"I'm all ears."

So Vasiht'h talked. They had time, and very little to do, and
maybe there was a moral in the story but he didn't linger on it
because he honestly wasn't sure what it was. That he'd thought
of the girls because they would have faced this situation with

courage and more equanimity that most adults was obvious to him, but he didn't think using them to illustrate the importance of those things would work. Would ever work. People weren't always in the right place to hear what they needed to hear, and beating the message into them didn't change that. Everyone's instinctive reaction was to stiffen up, armoring themselves against the blows. In the hierarchy of importance, defending yourself came way before listening, and the kind of introspection that prompted change.

Vasiht'h didn't tell her about the girls to teach her anything. He told her because he needed to hear it himself.

"So these kids are teens now," Kristyl said. By now they'd moved to a quieter corner of the room, and the human had found them a bag of trail mix. "And one of them's still too sick to leave the hospital? That's rough. But they're starting a business!"

"A charity." Vasiht'h hunted through the nuts and seeds for more of the dried banana chips. "They're not trying to make a profit. Just help other people."

"I'm impressed," Kristyl said. "I wonder if they need backers. Nieve's Girls, you said. I'll remember that." She popped a few sunflower seeds in her mouth, chewed, contemplated. "And two of them are human."

"Humans do do great things," Vasiht'h pointed out.

"When they don't make mistakes." She smiled lopsidedly.

"This isn't your fault."

Kristyl sighed. "I know. It's just reflex to think 'yet another thing we got wrong.' Shows you how pervasive the narrative is. Besides, we might have gotten something disastrously wrong here, but . . ." She jerked her chin toward the projection of the storm. "We planned for the disaster. We've got power, feeds, and access because the same people who designed the climate control protocols insisted that everything on the ground be able to resist the planet's natural weather anyway. Even the fact that the Pads aren't working was a planned failsafe, because violent atmospheric changes can make Pads unstable."

"So they were planning for their own failure?"

"They were covering all the bases," Kristyl said. "Because sometimes . . . bad things happen, and you can't stop them from happening." She shuddered a moment, hand flexing. "Anyway. We haven't gotten to the dog yet. Tell me that part."

"Right. That's got a human in it too." Vasiht'h grinned. "Don't worry. He's got a redemption arc."

She snorted. "Oh does he."

"So do I," Vasiht'h said, which made her eye him speculatively. He grinned wearily and launched into the story of how he and Jahir won their practice on Starbase Veta. That took them into the evening, because she insisted on stopping him frequently with questions, and by the end of it she was lying on her back on the floor, one hand on her chest.

"That was ridiculous."

"Really?"

"And completely implausible," she continued. "That a mysterious Hinichi just happened to be ready to retire and she just happened to be a therapist and she just happened to meet you all and decide to put you through your fairy tale Three Challenges in order to prove yourselves worthy of her gift? Really?" She lifted her head to squint at him. "You're kidding about all of it."

"Not at all," Vasiht'h said, amused.

Kristyl sat up slowly and eyed him. "Did anything like this happen to you before you met your magical partner I've not yet seen with my eyes to make sure he's real?"

"No . . . ?" Vasiht'h drew the word out. "But it might not just be about him. It might be that . . . before him, I took fewer chances?" He stopped, struck by the rightness of it. "Oh. Before him, I took fewer chances."

"Gladdie used to say the same thing to me," Kristyl said, softly. "Now she's taken one chance too many."

Vasiht'h reached over and hugged her, and the human turned her face into his shoulder and rested against him, and didn't cry. But Vasiht'h could sense the tension in her that was her desire to do so, and her refusal. Which was fine, because everyone dealt with crises in their own way, and if she wanted to not cry, he wasn't going to prod her until she did.

"Well!" Kristyl said. "Looks like we've got most of a day to wait through. It's time to organize a game!"

CHAPTER 15

Ⴟ AHIR STEPPED OFF THE PAD and onto Tsera Nova, and the
mindline steadied in his breast, removing the queasy feeling
he hadn't realized he'd been nursing throughout their separation. He touched his palm to his heart, wishing he could reach
through that connection to wherever his partner was, wishing
that he found the mere persistence of the mindline reassuring,
for surely it revealed that Vasiht'h was still alive. Instead, he
found himself thinking of the many ways one could be alive but
about to die in a natural disaster of this magnitude. He glanced
at the windows, and the rain lashing them, and the wall of gray
past them so dense he could barely see the silhouettes of the
palms planted just outside the building's front door. Could one
call it a natural disaster when it had been created by man, even
accidentally?

But he was here now, and there would be no going out in this
to search for the Glaseah. The mindline's quiescence suggested
he would not find Vasiht'h among the patients in whatever triage
center they'd set up, but he could at least put himself to use, and
perhaps search among the new patients as they arrived.

He'd been directed not to the hotel, which is where he would
have liked to go, but to a larger facility: the Tsera Nova Welcome

Center, if the placard over the now abandoned front desk was to be believed. He followed the stream of people until one of them said, "Medical personnel?"

"Yes."

The harried Asanii thrust an identification card on a lanyard at him. "Finger on the card, card around your neck, down the hall to the hospital."

Surprised, Jahir did as directed. The card, when he pressed a finger to it, did not find any data to populate the display with . . . no surprise, given the censors. He put it around his neck anyway, and went in search of a place to work.

All the noise he'd been expecting on Pad-down he found in the hospital's intake area, where clusters of people were talking or sitting or pacing or asking directions, all of a harassed staff too small for the crowd. When he walked in, a discomposed male in hospital scrubs stepped in front of him and said, "Where are you coming from and what's wrong?"

"From Tsera Nova's station, and I have done psychiatric intake in an acute care setting." Jahir showed him the blank card. "The data does not seem to be showing. Perhaps a problem related to the storm?"

"Sun and stars alone know. Network's been up, down, up, down ever since this hit. At least the local network's fine." The felid nodded toward the desk. "Go see what you can do."

"I shall."

The staff behind the desk didn't even look at his card: that he had one on a hospital lanyard was sufficient for them, combined with his air of patient confidence. "Psychiatric healer-assist?" one of them said. "Oh, thank Iley. Maybe you can get the lot inside to calm down."

"Not here?" he asked, glancing at the waiting room's agitated occupants.

"This is cake." She pointed at a door. "Through there, grab a spare set of clothes, keep going." She squinted. "Use the cubbies at the top, that's where all the tall spares are."

Whatever awaited him, Jahir thought as he passed through

the door, it could not be as perilous as Heliocentrus. Few experiences could surpass a wet epidemic, surely. But he felt a frisson of unease anyway as he dressed in the bathroom and braided back his hair, as he had so many times before his shift at Mercy. Finishing, he met his solemn amber eyes in the mirror and beheld again the medical professional. Which . . . was what he'd come to Tsera Nova to become, wasn't it? To procure a license to be, once again, Jahir the healer, not just Jahir the therapist?

KindlesFlame had reminded him more than once that not all medical practices were hospital critical care rounds. And yet, had the Eldritch had such facilities, his father would still be alive, and any number of Eldritch children would not have died with their mothers in childbed, and the dueling ground would not kill its participants weeks after they left it on both feet, the victims of infections modern medicine could answer.

Could he truly be this again?

He was standing in a bathroom when he could be outside it, finding the answer, for weal or woe. Jahir exited, and as the woman at the front desk had directed, kept going.

Tsera Nova was no Heliocentrus during a fateful drug epidemic.

It was not much better, however. The hospital had been rated for a certain number of people, and this was not that number, which included not only the wounded but their families, from whom they refused to be parted with the storm still blowing. The critical care area was full, and had spilled its excesses into the rooms beyond it, crowding those halls with equipment carts. And there was a particular air of distress that Heliocentrus had lacked . . . perhaps because Mercy had been a city hospital, and cities were full of people going about the business of daily living which necessarily included dealing with illness and injury. No one came to Tsera Nova save to find pleasure and respite. Tourists did not expect to end up in hospitals during their vacations, much less in such numbers.

Jahir had expected the staff to put him to work on triage,

but the Hinichi in charge of the floor had one look at him and said, "Go distract the miserable ones. The nervous breakdowns spread."

So he found himself at the work for which he'd originally trained, and it wrenched his heart to be about it without Vasiht'h at his side. This was their clinical practice writ severe, all the small challenges fallen away before hearts stripped naked by panic and pain. How powerless he felt, listening gravely to the sobbing of a woman who'd seen her sister's ribcage smashed while she watched, or the exhausted self-recriminations of a father who didn't know where his wife and children were. The wordless wailing of the toddler, unable to understand why he hurt so badly, Jahir was at least able to assuage, with a touch and a whisper of the same magic he'd used for the girls in the hospital. All of it he shouldered without stutter . . . until he found the three young children sitting alone on a bench, their faces white and eyes staring, ears crumpled.

"Where are their parents?" he'd asked the first healer-assist he could hail.

"No one knows," she'd answered, before hurrying on.

He knelt before them and took their hands, and it touched them not at all.

Would it be better, Jahir wondered as the hours went on, if he was among the healers at work on the merely physical injuries? Would he find it easier if he could use the power of the Alliance's endless devices to whisk people from pain's embrace? If he could see their injuries seal shut and their bones knit with his physical eyes? Or would it make the inevitable times he failed to save them worse, for the contrast?

Could he find joy here, as he did in studying it? Or would it be better to reserve himself from the practice of medicine, in any form, given the pain it brought? Because in this life there were no guarantees, save the one waiting for them all at the end.

He thought of Vasiht'h, and thought it fruitless to ask the question, when he'd already answered it, over and over. To be wholly present was forever worth the suffering for the gifts that came, like flowers after rain. Jahir glanced out the windows at the silence of the thrashing storm, and reached for the Glaseah. Received the certitude that Vasiht'h yet lived, and prayed that he was safe somewhere, waiting out the hurricane.

------∞∞∞------

Once the storm's strongest winds reached them, there were no more new admissions. Jahir used the lull to stop in the break room, hearing the ghost of voices from Mercy urging him on. There was no buttered coffee, for which he was grateful, but the memory of Paige's impish expressions made him smile as he added cream to the normal, black variety available. The result might not approach the caloric load of the concoctions in Helio-centrus, but the taste reminded him powerfully of surviving his shifts there. He thought of Paga for the first time in far too long, and wondered if the Naysha's invitation to experience the waters through a mindtouch still stood. Once he and Vasiht'h left Tsera Nova, he would find out, and take the Naysha up on it if so. He and Vasiht'h would leave Tsera Nova. No other future was possible.

Tsera Nova's excellence in catering extended to the hospi-tal, for even the abbreviated spread available for the staff looked superb, and had stasis plates to maintain its freshness. He took a warm croissant in the hopes of plying the three speechless chil-dren with it but found them sleeping in a pile on the bench, all too-large ears and too-small tails and too, too serious faces. Even dreaming, they found no surcease.

"Still no sign of the parents," came a voice behind him. The same healer-assist . . . her low soprano with the softly furred timbre was unmistakable. He looked over his shoulder at her. "And they haven't budged. Haven't drunk or eaten either." Her eyes caught on the bread in his hand. "You might as well eat that yourself, they're not likely to be up anytime soon."

Jahir folded the croissant up in the napkin he'd been holding it in and set it alongside the largest child's hand. "Do we have their names?"

She nodded. "The database tagged them when they came in. They've got extended family back on Karaka'Ana. We'll contact them as soon as all this passes." She waved a hand. "Maybe a day or so."

"So little time, to be so long," Jahir murmured.

She nodded, studying him now. "Your name, though, I don't know. The computer doesn't recognize you."

He suppressed the need to glance at his blank tag. "An error caused by the storm?"

"Possible, but not probable." She sat on the bench beside the smallest of the children, leaned over and tucked some of the felid's hair behind his neck. "Am I going to find out, when all this is over, that you were never here?"

"Possible," he said. "Perhaps not probable."

She chuffed a tired laugh. "Like some healing fairy, sent through the ward to lift everyone's spirits? That sounds possible *and* probable, given how tired I am. An Eldritch healer-assist seems less likely."

"It does, doesn't it?"

"And yet." She sighed, smiled a little. "At least tell me you're licensed to practice."

He glanced at the ceiling. "I have done my time in hospitals."

"Just the kind of answer I expect from a visiting angel." She put her elbows on her knees, leaning forward on them.

"I assure you, no visiting angel has ever been vomited on by middle-aged Seersan women who were relieved to discover their chest pains were a stomach virus, not a cardiac issue."

The woman blinked, then barked a laugh. "I don't know. If the angel was actually *in* a hospital, I'm sure there would be plenty of them with vomit stories." She eyed him. "You haven't done any harm."

"That would be the beginning of our credo."

She smirked. "And you've made a lot of people more comfortable. So . . . nameless Eldritch . . . thank you." She started to offer her palm and drew it back. "Ah, sorry, I forget."

He reached for her wrist and caught it in gentle fingers,

tasting her fatigue, her worry, and her patient acceptance of all those things. Setting his other hand on her palm, he said, gently, "Jahir Seni Galare. Xenotherapist."

The woman smiled. "Gwenivir Murphy. Chief Nurse." She lifted her brows. "Now was that croissant your meal, selflessly donated to kits who aren't awake to eat it? Because if so, you should get some real food into you, while we have some time."

"You think things will get worse?" he asked, surprised. "Are we not now in the middle of the storm?"

"Sure," she said, rising. "But if you really have worked in a hospital, you should know—"

"One takes respite where one finds it," Jahir finished. Didn't sigh, smiled instead. "Truly we are all alike, are we not."

The nurse snorted. "In the medical profession? Close enough. That's what the training's for." She nodded her chin toward the break room. "Go fuel up."

As she was the Chief Nurse—"As you say, alet."

Murphy chuckled as she left. "Wish all my assists were as biddable as you."

The food remained beautiful in the break room. He chose another croissant for himself and found it buttery enough to need no condiment. By then, it was long after midnight, and he couldn't remember when the day had sped. This afternoon he had been taking a test on the station, and yet it seemed so long ago, and not long enough to account for his exhaustion. He found a corner and sat with his back to the wall, and there he drowsed until the tattoo of running feet jerked him from uneasy dreams.

Had the hurricane passed? But as he rose and followed the runners, he saw the behemoth over them. Off the sea at least, and perhaps now it would break itself to pieces on the shore— the meteorologists were of two minds over whether it would dissipate, or if Tsera Nova's land masses were too small for the task. Regardless, there should have been no more admissions, and yet when he arrived in triage there were dozens of new, very wet, very distraught patients. He glanced at the window and was shocked at the sunlight, wan and gray and strange.

"Storm's eye," someone said, in passing. "Can you check on that group there, they won't stop hyperventilating."

"Yes," Jahir replied, and went.

When next he looked up, the windows had gone dark again, rain-fogged, and the storm on the overhead screens had visibly moved. He rolled his aching shoulders, cold beneath the thin fabric of the medical uniform, and looked through the crowd. One sole patient remained, a bedraggled tabby Asanii sitting on a lone chair. He'd been aware of her going back into a room for treatment and being released to the waiting room again, but not why.

"Alet?" he said. "Would you like a blanket, or something warm to drink?"

She looked up. Her pupils dilated in her eyes, visibly. "You . . . ?"

Jahir hesitated. Did she recognize him? "Yes?"

"You're . . . Vasiht'h's Eldritch," the Asanii said, ears trembling.

"You know him?"

"I . . . yes . . . he . . ." Her shoulders tightened, and she bared her teeth in a grimace. Watching her pack her fear and grief back under her skin was painful, but he did not interrupt. He would not have wanted his own fragile attempts at control shattered in her situation. "Kristyl made friends with him, the way she makes friends with everyone."

"And you are Kristyl's friend."

She nodded, head lowered, and her voice was a hushed rasp. "She's my very best friend. And I don't know if I'll ever see her again."

"Would you like to talk about it?"

The Asanii glanced up, pushed her hair back from her eyes. "We were on a boat."

Jahir sat across from her, leaning forward with his hands clasped over his knees.

"I don't remember how I ended up in the water." She wrung her hands, noticed herself doing it, and wrapped her arms around herself instead. "I don't remember getting out either. I don't know how long I was in there, it was . . . I . . . they told me they found me hanging onto a piece of the hull." She laughed. "Unconscious, I guess. I used to call myself clingy until Kristyl told me that was wrong. That I just liked to hold tightly to things that mattered. I guess surviving mattered." She inhaled shakily. "It was a rescue ship. Coast guard. They were sweeping for survivors. We stayed out so long we weren't sure we'd get back, but they asked us . . . they asked all of us aboard if we were all right with staying out until the last moment and we all said yes!" She looked up, eyes fierce, rimmed in red. "We all said yes."

"I understand," Jahir said, quietly. "So I would have said as well."

She nodded once, a jerk of her head. "Then we came back, and it was scary. I asked once if we were going to make it back and the sailor told me 'yes' and I just . . . I decided to believe him because not believing him would have made my last moments worse, if I was going to die. Does . . . does that sound dramatic?"

"On the contrary," Jahir replied. "It sounds like a clear-eyed choice."

"Clear-eyed." She sighed, shuddered. "She used to tell me I was that, too." Wiping an eye with the side of her hand, she added, "I could use that drink now, please? Maybe . . . do they have hot chocolate?"

"I am certain they do. I shall fetch it for you."

When he returned, the Asanii was sitting straighter, dabbing at her eyes with a tissue from a box that had appeared at her side: someone else had checked on her, he thought, and handed her a cup. She said, "Thank you," and added, "I'm sorry. I feel like I already know you, because of Vasiht'h, so I didn't introduce myself. I'm Gladiolus Ardune."

"Jahir," he said.

She studied him, her smile tired. "It's strange to finally meet you. I half-believed you were . . ."

"Fictional?" he offered.

"Mythical?" She laughed. "No. I never thought he was lying. But I guess when I tried to imagine what it would look like, for a

Glaseah to have an Eldritch friend, I . . . kept coming up blank. He was always so happy when he mentioned you. I thought . . . I'm not sure what I thought. That you wouldn't be so real."

"I admit," he said, because he could find no way to engage with that save through humor, "that I was not entirely sure you and your human friend were more plausible."

"Kristyl is completely implausible. That's why I love her." Gladiolus swallowed. "I hope . . . I can't imagine that she's alive. For both of us to survive this?"

"And yet you survived," he reminded her. "Clinging unconscious to a shard of a hull."

"With a broken leg," Gladiolus said, ears sagging. "I guess that's ridiculous." She looked into her cup, huffed a little. "Knowing Kristyl, she rounded up an army of dolphins and rescued everyone else, and they're even now sailing back, covered in rainbows."

"Would that be typical?" Jahir asked.

"You have no idea." The Asanii smiled, pained. "I hope you get to find out." She glanced at the window. "Do you know how much longer we'll be stuck here?"

"The rumors in the breakroom suggest another twelve hours or so. Perhaps less."

The Asanii shuddered. "Is there something I can do to help? I can't just sit here and do nothing for twelve hours."

"You might attempt sleep?"

"No. There's no way I'll be able to sleep. I'll lie down and close my eyes and think about all the ways things could go wrong." She shook her head once, a twitch as if to toss the images out of it. "I'll pour coffee or fold bedsheets or mop floors, just give me something to do."

Jahir studied her, wondered. Went with his instincts. "Are you a good listener?"

"A good . . ." She trailed off and chuckled, wan. "All I do is listen, most of the time. I like listening."

"Then perhaps you might accompany me. My work is the work of a counselor, and many here are in need yet."

Gladiolus glanced at the room, then at him. "You and your partner are therapists, aren't you? Vasiht'h said so? But I don't have any special training . . ."

"You have something I don't," Jahir said. "You have survived the storm. That experience is something you share with those here that I cannot."

"Oh," she said softly. And then nodded, standing. "Yes. I can do that. Where do we start?"

"Where the injuries are worst." He paused. "If you can? If it is too difficult, there is no shame in saying no. To take on the burdens of others when you are yourself worried . . ."

"You're worried too, aren't you?" She met his eyes. "I want to do this." Softer. "I think it might help me too."

"This way, then."

CHAPTER 16

NOT ALL OF KRISTYL'S formidable skill could make any activity distracting enough from the news and uncertainties they suffered while waiting. But her efforts did help. Even the staff members found themselves participating in and adding to her schedule of events. One jokingly offered her a job; Vasiht'h watched them both laugh as if they meant it, observing the formalities. And everyone's eyes returned again and again to the screens. Someone had suggested turning them off, but that had lasted all of ten minutes before group consensus led them to renege on that vow and resume staring at the path of the hurricane.

Vasiht'h found the waiting interminable. The facility had a basic medical kit, one sufficient to sealing cuts and resolving minor contusions. Anything more complicated would have been whisked via Pad to the mainland hospital for diagnosis and treatment. His injuries, while not incapacitating, hurt like the Goddess's hell, particularly since the immobilizing wrap around his torso was someone's best take at it. No one here was a licensed healer or healer-assist, and while all the staff was trained in first aid, there was first aid and then there was professional-level care. The more critically wounded had been isolated in a room out of the way, and the staff members who exited that room did so with grim expressions.

How ridiculous it was not to be able to just step over a Pad and fix all this! Or call someone and have them walk someone through basic care! He didn't understand the explanations why their systems weren't working, only that it had something to do with the location of the transmitting end and its proximity to the storm and whatever disordering fields it was emitting. Vasiht'h sipped from a cup of calming tea and watched the white arms of the hurricane rotate on the screen, thinking of how powerless people were without their tools. Such tools they were, born of the thoughts of the Goddess's children, following Her precepts. And yet, tools did not make gods of men, and in the end, they all died.

"Something wrong?" he asked when the same staff member, a concerned-looking Tam-illee, had gone in and out of the back room one too many times.

He glanced at Vasiht'h and plastered a smile on his face. "Everything's under control, alet."

Vasiht'h canted his head. "Is that what you'd tell your therapist?"

That gave the todfox pause. "If I had one . . . ?"

"You can borrow one now, if you want." Vasiht'h smiled and tapped his chest. "I have a license to practice. And I could use the work."

Another pause, and then the Tam-illee laughed, wearily. "Couldn't we all. Still, I don't want to worry you. You're a guest."

"I think the distinctions between guests and staff melted away hours ago." Vasiht'h glanced at the main room, where the games had given way to people sleeping or talking very quietly. "We're all in this together."

"I guess so," the todfox said reluctantly, and ran a hand over his head, between his ears. "I guess a therapist isn't likely to panic, either."

"I'm a Glaseah as well as a therapist, too," Vasiht'h said. "Trust me, I don't fluster easily."

The Tam-illee chuckled. "I bet!" And looked back into the room before saying, "If we could get them to the hospital . . . but we can't. And I'm afraid. At least one of them looks really bad."

Vasiht'h didn't need to ask how bad. "The storm's already hit the coast, right? It won't be much longer."

"It might already have been too long." The todfox rubbed his eyes with the butts of his palms. "This sort of thing isn't supposed to happen here. I took this job because it's wonderful. People come to Tsera Nova happy and leave happier. I spend all day watching people laugh and play and relax. Even when they're upset and I need to fix their problems, they're already less upset than people doing normal things in other places. If that makes sense?"

"It does," Vasiht'h promised.

"It's just . . . so . . . positive. I love my job." He looked toward the room again. "And then this?"

"An accident," Vasiht'h said. "They happen." He rested a hand on the todfox's wrist, drawing him back from his agitation. "A terrible accident, in this case, but . . . have you ever had anything even remotely this bad happen here?"

"Never!"

"So . . . it's not likely to happen often, is it?"

"No," he said. "But . . . it wasn't supposed to happen at all."

Vasiht'h shook his head. "We do our best, alet. But to think we can control everything . . . that's not reasonable. Some might also call it arrogant."

The Tam-illee's ears drooped. "I know that." He tapped his temple. "Here. But here," finger on breastbone. "Here, I think . . . 'what's the point of everything we know how to do if we can't stop things like this from happening.'"

"Those people relaxing and laughing," Vasiht'h asked. "Can you picture them in your mind?"

Surprised, the todfox looked at him. "What?"

"Tell me about one of the laughing people," Vasiht'h asked.

"I can't . . . I don't . . ."

"Child or adult?" Vasiht'h asked.

"Child," he said automatically.

Vasiht'h nodded. "Girl or boy?"

"Both? There were . . ." He stopped, smiled. "There were six of them. Four girls, two boys. All Tam-illee. Two separate families, here to celebrate something. The kits weren't clear on it, but it had to do with money. A promotion, maybe? And the littlest girl had a shirt with a pegasus on it. A purple one."

"Were they chasing the fish?" Vasiht'h asked. "I chased the fish. It's hard not to."

"It is, isn't it?" The Tam-illee laughed a little. "But no, they asked me to take a viseo for them, and it was the funniest thing. They were all yelling and bouncing and jostling and not paying attention, but then the oldest boy gave me the tablet and I pointed it at them and they all just . . ." He made a gesture with his hands, pressing them together. "Came together instantly. Posed perfectly, smiled, were completely motionless. I took some stills and said, 'All right, done!' and they burst apart and ran in all sorts of directions . . ." He laughed and snapped his fingers. "Like that! How did they do that? How many pictures do you think they posed for, to have that instinct?"

"Probably hundreds," Vasiht'h answered, smiling. "I bet those two families have been friends since before the kits arrived."

"It has to be so," the todfox agreed. And grinned at him. "And then they chased the fish."

Vasiht'h nodded. "That must have been a pretty picture."

"Kits are wonderful," the todfox said with a sigh. And then frowned, and smiled crookedly. "You're about to say 'that's the point of everything', isn't it. Yes, disasters happen and they're awful and we can't stop them. But most days are about . . . children laughing, and the sun on your face, and your favorite meal on a hard day, just when you need it. . . ."

"Yes," Vasiht'h said. "You see? You already knew the answer."

The Tam-illee leaned back against the wall, sobering. "I guess I did. But why is it so hard?"

"Because it's so good the rest of the time," Vasiht'h said. "So when it's bad, it's awful."

That startled a chuckle out of the male. More quietly, he said, "I think one of them's going to die."

"Then it was their time to go home," Vasiht'h said, gentle. "And not all your grief or fear or worry will change that. All it'll do is deprive you of the strength to keep going for the people who will survive."

"And if I can't stop feeling those things anyway?"

"Then know you're not alone." Vasiht'h looked up at him. "Do you need a hug?"

"I . . ." The todfox stopped, a bemused look on his face. And then his ears dropped, and he said, sheepish, "I wouldn't say no?"

Vasiht'h offered his arms, and the Tam-illee bent for the embrace. And stayed there, trembling, for several long breaths, which Vasiht'h felt intimately against his ribcage: how the other male was trying to keep from shaking, or crying. Or maybe he was, just softly; Vasiht'h could smell salt, and thought of the ocean.

Backing away, the todfox said, "Thanks."

"You're welcome." Vasiht'h paused a few heartbeats. "So, what *is* your favorite meal?"

Surprised, the Tam-illee said, "Ah . . . I like sushi?"

"You're in the right place for that, I bet!"

"Oh yes, it's wonderful here. You should try it if you haven't."

"I'll make a note of it," Vasiht'h said.

The Tam-illee smiled a little. "I should . . . get back. But . . . thank you again."

"My pleasure," Vasiht'h said.

He remained in the hall after the todfox had gone on to the main room, wondering at the interaction. It didn't surprise him that he couldn't turn off the instincts that had led him to become a therapist; his sister's pithy observation about his wanting to take care of everyone had stung because of its accuracy, after all. What did puzzle him was that . . . he'd been right when he'd told his impromptu client that he didn't fluster easily. He didn't, when other people needed him. Or at least, he thought that was how that worked.

How could he be both an anxious mess and everyone's rock at the same time? Was that even possible?

He glanced at the storm on the nearest screen, and then at the sleepers. Tempting to go among them and try to rest, but he knew he'd fail. Instead, he crept into the room where the injured had been sequestered. There was a staff member dozing on a chair in the corner, her uniform wrinkled and the data tablet she'd been holding slumped onto her lap in her open hand. There were six people in the room, lying on blankets. It didn't take Vasiht'h specialized medical knowledge to identify the one that had frightened the Tam-illee: a middle-aged Asanii woman, her flesh already seeming to have shrunk away from her spirit. Sitting alongside her, Vasiht'h gathered up her limp hand. Maybe she would die . . . but maybe she would feel the heat against her fingers, and use it as an anchor.

Stay with us, he whispered. *Not just for yourself, but for all the people who would miss you . . . whoever they are. Including me, and the Tam-illee staffer whose name I don't even know. He doesn't know your name, either, but he doesn't have to, because we're all voyagers together, and in the end, we all go home to the same place. And that makes us kin.*

She didn't miraculously wake—that really would have been something out of the fairy tales Kristyl accused him of living in—but that was all right. He was doing good work, right here, and that was all he needed.

CHAPTER 17

".... SIHT'H, VASIHT'H, WAKE UP."

Wisps of dreams clung to him: lights on water, shimmering; orange eyes bent over him, alien but familiar; the knowledge that he wasn't alone. Vasiht'h blinked several times, found himself sitting next to the pallet with the Asanii. Who was . . . still breathing. He looked up and found Kristyl crouched next to him, her light brown hair tied back in a messy tail and hollows under her eyes. She looked awful, but: "It's over. It's time to go."

"Really?" he asked, unable to believe it, but people were walking into the room, people in medical uniforms, with real stretchers. "We can leave?"

"Pads are open again," Kristyl said. "First destination's the hospital and you need it for your wing, so let's go."

"I guess . . . but these people . . ."

"They'll go through too, and first," she said. "You're ambulatory so you'll have to wait on them." She glanced at him, lifted her brows. "You are ambulatory, right? Or are you stuck that way?"

"No, I can stand." To leave this place, Vasiht'h would pry his legs up with his hands if necessary. He rose, working the kinks from his back legs, and gently set the Asanii's hand on her breast before saying, "All right, lead the way." He paused. "You're coming with me?"

"I'm hoping . . ." She hesitated, then shrugged. "I know it's a long shot, but."

Of course. "I could use the company." He thought of Mercy and shuddered. "I don't like hospitals."

Kristyl glanced at him with a frown. And then shared a lopsided smile with him. "I'll protect you then. Come on."

Together they made their way back to the main room, where the staff members were corralling the guests into columns based on the urgency of their situations. Vasiht'h, with his injury, went into one of the lines waiting to move after the stretchers went. He was all too willing to let them go first, searching the pallets as they were carried past between jogging emergency medical assists for the Asanii whose hand he'd been holding. She was the second one through, and he exhaled, raising his gaze to search for the Tam-illee from last night. Had he noticed? And yes, the todfox was standing next to one of the columns, his eyes locked on the stream of evacuees with a look of profound relief.

"All right, your turn," someone said, and Vasiht'h's line started moving. "Go on through and register at the desk, they'll check you in."

'Register at the desk' turned out to be optimistic advice. Vasiht'h stepped over the Pad and into a chaotic tangle of reuniting families and agitated new admissions. Kristyl wrapped a hand around his upper arm and steered him out of the way of a crash embrace between two Tam-illee, and somehow they made it to someone in uniform, who was scribbling on a data tablet as fast as the people dictating information to him could speak. "Here!" Kristyl called. "Another one!"

"What's wrong?" the med tech asked him.

"Broken wing. Maybe ribs? I don't know about that part."

"Breathing all right? Can you inhale all the way? Any stabbing pains?"

"Yes, yes, no, but it aches."

"And a broken wing . . . that's a quick fix. As soon as we free up a bed for you, we'll have you back, alet. Name?"

"Vasiht'h."

"Thank you."

"Now we just have to find a place to sit. . . ." Kristyl trailed off and smiled. "At least this is a much better place to wait than we were before."

And . . . it was, despite it being a hospital, because the number of people finding one another was heartening. Vasiht'h watched two more reunions as the stream from Serenity Isle continued flowing, and he was so distracted by the relief of just being here, and the storm being over, that he didn't realize. . . .

. . . that he could taste coffee . . .

He licked his teeth and reached, tentatively for the mindline.
/Arii?/

/Vasiht'h!/

Vasiht'h sat upright so fast he pulled against his splint and hissed. */What are you doing so close! Aren't you in orbit?/*

Tension in the mindline now, an impending urgency. Sounds of people talking. Bootsteps snapping against tile. Vasiht'h frowned, processing the lurching of it, looked up . . . and found the Eldritch on the other side of the room. The Glaseah rose to his paws, stunned. What was he . . . why wasn't he on the . . .

Jahir strode across the room, and everyone around him flowed out of his way, such was his presence—Vasiht'h could only admire this sudden air of command—and then his Eldritch was in front of him, on one knee, and had taken one of his hands and pressed it against his chest where Vasiht'h could feel his heart racing under the thin medical uniform.

Was he blushing? He was. The Eldritch cupped Vasiht'h's cheek, those long fingers gentle against his fur. The skin under it was hot and he didn't even know why: gratification? Abashment? Pleasure?

. . . *Tsera Nova. Your seaside destination for joy*

Vasiht'h exhaled, eyes welling. Yes. That.

"You live," Jahir breathed, brushing his thumb against the Glaseah's cheek just under the eye. "Arii."

"A little beat up," Vasiht'h began, and when he felt the frantic searching in the mindline, "Not seriously! They even told me I had to wait for a bed. It's just a broken wing. I'm more scared and shaken than seriously hurt." He squared his shoulders and tried for sternness despite his watery tone. "But why are you here! You were supposed to be safe, out of the way, on the station!"

"Did you think I could tarry there when I heard this news?" Jahir's eyes widened. "To have the atmosphere between us was intolerable. I had to find you."

"Wow," Kristyl said from beside him. "And I wondered why you had all this fairy tale stuff happen to you. He *acts* like a fairy tale."

Startled, Jahir looked over at her.

"That's Kristyl," Vasiht'h said, smiling. "The human I've been telling you about."

"Not Gladiolus's Kristyl," Jahir said, astonished.

"Yes?" the human answered.

Jahir rose. "Come, now."

"Do you mean . . ."

But Jahir was already walking so Vasiht'h hurried after him. Even so, Kristyl beat him to the Eldritch's side. By the time Jahir was calling down the hallway, the human was in front of him and they both had a perfect vantage for the sight of the human and her Asanii friend rushing into one another's embrace.

/That's exactly what I needed,/ Vasiht'h said with a glad sigh.

Jahir eyed him. /You hurt when you breathe./

/It's probably nothing. Triaged already, remember?/

/Injuries to the chest cavity can be serious and subtle—/

Vasiht'h chuckled tiredly. /Then I'm in the right place for it to go terribly wrong, right?/ The mindline surged with horror, sour and edged with scalpels, and he held up his hands, wincing. "Sorry! Sorry, I spoke before I thought. Or, I thought before I could think better of it. I didn't mean to worry you."

The prickle in the mindline smoothed down again. Jahir glanced at him, his smile faint. "I know. None of this was supposed to have happened."

"And yet, life does. And accidents too." Vasiht'h shifted on his paws, grimacing. "I do ache, though. Sit with me until they call me back?"

"And after."

"Always after," Vasiht'h said.

CHAPTER 18

𝒯AHIR ACCOMPANIED VASIHT'H WHEN HE WAS called back for
formal diagnosis, which involved a broken wing and several
bruised ribs. A quick session under a bone-setter put paid to
both injuries, and the hospital released them, with thanks to the
Eldritch for his aid. He'd considered asking if they wanted him to
remain, but he himself didn't want to stay, so he refrained. What
he most wanted was to escape the planet entirely, and from the
exhausted tension in the mindline, his partner felt the same.

"We might as well pick up our things from the hotel," Vasiht'h
said as they headed for the doors out of the lobby. "There's no use
staying. I'm assuming they won't be having any parties on the
beach for a while."

When they stepped into the wan sunlight and confronted the
destruction, they both stopped short. The buildings remained
intact, unsurprisingly: the Alliance did not build flimsy struc-
tures. But entire trees had been pulled from the earth, leaving
muddy sockets, and the detritus that had been whipped from the
landscaping and the sea had been thrown against windows and
roofs and all over the ground.

"Unless they're 'let's clean up' parties," Vasiht'h finished, the
distress in the mindline twitchy and strange, tinged with the

taste of saltwater.

"They will be some time in the doing," Jahir said. "Even with the Alliance's many tools."

"Yes," Vasiht'h answered, perturbed. "Let's . . . go see if we can check out. Do you think we could catch a shuttle back to Veta today?"

"It is likely," Jahir said, thinking of the expense and deciding not to mention it. He no less than the Glaseah was eager to be gone. "And we can take our meal on the station while we wait. You will probably enjoy the station."

"I'm guaranteed to enjoy anything that doesn't involve being on the surface of Tsera Nova." The Glaseah smiled, wan. "Probably not the sort of thing they want to hear from departing guests."

"No," Jahir agreed. "But in this case, I doubt they will blame any of us." He watched the Glaseah trot ahead of him toward the public Pad station and allowed himself to exhale. He'd never allowed himself to seriously consider the possibility of Vasiht'h dying in the storm, despite knowing the mindline being active was no guarantee of continued existence. To see that familiar shape, feel it in his mind, sense and see no harm . . .

Vasiht'h paused and looked over his shoulder. "Coming?"

"Yes," Jahir said, and hastened after.

⸎

Their hotel was nearly empty, but the one person at the concierge station offered to escort them to their room, 'because some of the buildings are blocked by downed trees.' That was where most of the staff was: assessing the damage. Vasiht'h felt badly for them, though his foremost desire involved getting back home, where the most he had to worry about was whether one of their clients would be having a bad day. Having Jahir alongside helped, enough that Vasiht'h couldn't find it in his heart to upbraid his partner for heading for the epicenter of the disaster instead of staying out of harm's way.

Which would have been out of character, anyway. When had Jahir *not* flung himself into danger to save others? And to help Vasiht'h? *He'd probably go to the ends of the universe for me.* Vasiht'h snuck a glance at the Eldritch pacing him. *But then, I would too. I proved that already when I went to Selnor.*

"A fin for your thoughts?" Jahir asked, quiet.

Vasiht'h looked at the Asanii leading them back to the shore. "Just . . . glad you're here."

"I will be being glad you are here for quite some time."

Vasiht'h didn't comment on the fumbling of the language. That Jahir could lose some of his facility when overcome, and that he was overcome because of the Glaseah, was too gratifying.

When they reached their room, they found their door accessible, but the two doors beside them . . .

Jahir, staring with him at the crumpled stairs, murmured, "There but for the grace of God and Goddess."

"Amen," Vasiht'h said, fervent.

"Go ahead, aletsen," their guide said. "I'll take care of the paperwork on our end. And on behalf of Diamond Sands . . . our deepest apologies for your distress. You'll be contacted by a representative regarding a refund. We'll make this right."

"It wasn't your fault," Vasiht'h said. "But thanks. And good luck with the clean-up."

The look that got him . . . pained and exhausted and stricken all at once . . . he almost regretted saying it, though he'd been sincere. The stab of regret raised Jahir's head; glancing at the retreating back of their host, the Eldritch murmured, */Leave it be, arii. There is nothing for it but time./*

Which was the truth, so Vasiht'h didn't call the Asanii back. There was enough that needed repair without him wasting his efforts on something that only time could heal.

The view from their room couldn't have been more different from their experience that first day. Vasiht'h paused in front of the permeable wall after gathering his saddlebags, watching the gray waves smack against the shore beneath a sullen sky, part blue clarity, part torn-cloud smudges. When Jahir joined him with his messenger bag over his shoulder, Vasiht'h said ruefully, "You won't be swimming in that."

"I would prefer not to, no."

Vasiht'h folded his arms. "We'll have to find a different celebratory ocean to swim in."

"The starbase has them."

"Artificial, but at least not likely to involve hurricanes." Vasiht'h shook his head. "Let's go. I think we're both definitely done here."

"Yes."

On the way out, on the table by the door, was the shell Jahir had found for him on the beach. Vasiht'h paused, then palmed it as they walked out, rubbing his thumb along the smooth inside edge. How many shells had been washed up by the storm? How many of them had been broken by it? He was in possession of a shell that had been shielded from the disaster . . . did that make it better than the shells that had weathered the storm? Or was he reading too much into this? As usual? Was it reading romance novels that had made him start putting too much stock in symbols, or was it his association with an Eldritch, who loved such things? Or both?

"You are thinking very busily," Jahir observed.

"Too busily," Vasiht'h admitted. "We should go find someplace to eat."

<hr/>

Jahir did one better, and got them a temporary room on the station so they could drop their bags and take a quick shower, which Vasiht'h discovered he really, really wanted. Goddess alone knew how much salt was crusting his fur, and he hadn't even noticed in his eagerness to be gone. After that, the Eldritch escorted him to the terraces, and they really were everything he'd promised. They ate what was either a very late lunch or a very early dinner at a restaurant with a patio overlooking the world; Vasiht'h found Tsera Nova palatable from this distance, though his eyes kept returning to the torn-taffy clouds stretching over the ocean. How had the rest of the tourists fared? Had Kristyl and Gladiolus left yet? Were they checking on the Harat-Shar they'd gathered? Were Bodken and Keridwen on their way to TKI&I, or had this incident put them off worlds-traveling? Would he ever see any of them again? Did he want to?

"Food has not made your thoughts less busy," Jahir said.

Vasiht'h looked up. "I just . . . I'm processing, I guess."

"A very great deal."

"It was a lot to take in." Vasiht'h pushed at his dessert with a spoon . . . a delicate flan with a clear mango glaze.

"You could share," Jahir said, quiet.

And through the mindline, he really could, and in every particular: the terror of nearly drowning, the fear, the chaos of the storm, the shock and relief of being rescued, the panic that rescue might not matter, and then the painful hours waiting out the hurricane . . . shaking himself, Vasiht'h said, "I'm not sure if I'm ready to. Or even if I can? I could, but some part of me wants to know why I'd want to dredge it back up, when I survived and what I want to focus on is the fact that it's over."

"Is this what you would tell a client?" Jahir asked. Like Vasiht'h, he hadn't eaten much of his dessert.

The Glaseah wrinkled his nose. "I think I'd tell me that being confused about how to react was normal, and to be easy on myself for a few days."

A smile that Vasiht'h felt through the mindline more than saw, tender as a ripe pear. "That seems reasonable advice to me."

"I guess I should take it then."

Jahir nodded. "Our ship leaves in two hours. We might walk?"

"Walking sounds good." Walking wasn't drowning, or sitting, waiting for something. "Let's walk."

⚬⚬⚬

For once, physical activity proved a better distraction for his partner than food. Perhaps food bought and eaten did not have the same power to soothe as food prepared by hand. Jahir strolled alongside Vasiht'h and watched the Glaseah exclaim over the solidigraphic fish, and laugh at the children chasing the jumping water, and muse over the shops selling brightly colored sarongs.

"A lot like my sari, except in more shocking colors."

It was while Vasiht'h was in the restroom that Jahir's data tablet trembled against his hip. Since he had very few alarms, he dug it from the messenger bag and flicked it on, only to find his test results. He had passed every section except the last two, for which he had been absent . . . which meant he'd failed the exam in toto. Did he feel anything about it? He could sense nothing in himself beyond the overwhelming relief that Vasiht'h was with him. His statement to the Hinichi stood: he could not imagine the Alliance without the Glaseah.

Vasiht'h, however, might have different feelings on hearing that not only had their vacation been truncated in the worst possible way, but that Jahir hadn't succeeded in passing the exam that had been their primary motivation for the trip. The Eldritch tucked the tablet back in his bag and buttoned it closed, smoothing his palm down the leather before folding his arms and composing himself to wait. The test could be retaken. He would concern himself with it some other time. Some better time, because obviously God and Lady had other plans for him.

When Vasiht'h rejoined him, Jahir said, "We are about due at the port. Shall we pick up our baggage?"

"I can't wait."

Chapter 19

Vasiht'h had never been so glad to see their apartment. The first thing he did after he tossed his bag in their bedroom was head for the kitchen.

"You will bake now," Jahir guessed, his amusement a gentle caress through the mindline.

"All the things," Vasiht'h agreed firmly.

"Then I shall fetch us groceries. And perhaps our evening meal, so that you might concentrate on aught else."

"Perfect," Vasiht'h said, getting out a bowl.

"I shall return anon."

"And I will be right here." Vasiht'h pulled out a sack of flour and dropped it on the counter, satisfied by the thick thump it made. "Wrist-deep in dough."

Jahir chuckled softly and went for his walk. Which was good, because the mindline clearly communicated the Eldritch's restlessness. Despite the brevity of their return flight, the transit had made them both feel antsy. Addressing that for Jahir meant stretching his legs, and for Vasiht'h . . .

"Call Sehvi," he told the computer. "If it's a reasonable hour on Tam-ley. And see if Allen's got an open appointment this week."

A chirp, and then the sound of the call connecting. Vasiht'h didn't bother looking up a recipe. For a moment like this he wanted something simple and old, so well-known it was muscle memory. That meant cookies. When Sehvi's face appeared on the wallscreen, he said, "Frosted or chocolate chip?"

His sister pursed her lips. "Embrace the power of both?"

"So now, it's 'both' and not 'there's only so much stomach to go around'?"

"You are talking about chocolate chip cookies," Sehvi pointed out. "For some things, you can find room."

Vasiht'h mmmed. "Frosted chocolate chip cookies."

"How can you go wrong?" Sehvi limned a shape in the air with her hands, a circle the size of a serving platter. "Better make a big one. So you'll have room for all the frosting."

"A frosted cookie cake sounds deadly," Vasiht'h said. "Works for me. How are you, ariishir?"

"I'm good," she said. "Still grumpy about this thing with our brothers making our aunt unmanageable, but otherwise all right."

"Wait, Pes and Dondi *still* haven't figured things out?" Vasiht'h asked, incredulous.

"Still? It's only been a few days, ariihir."

A few days . . . had it really? He stared into the bowl at the sugar and the butter he'd just dumped into it. Grabbing the spatula, he started mashing. "I'll call them and give them an earful. A proper earful this time. I can't believe they're making a mess over something so stupid."

"Maybe it's not stupid to them?" Sehvi said. "Um . . . Vasiht'h? What's wrong? And . . . come to think of it, why are you home? Weren't you supposed to be on vacation for a few more days?"

"We came back early."

"Early?" Sehvi said. "What went wrong? Don't tell me Prince Perfect actually failed?"

Vasiht'h dropped the spatula, stunned. He hadn't even asked. "I don't know."

"Wait, what? How can you not know? Isn't that the reason

you went?"

Vasiht'h returned to creaming the butter into the sugar. Vigorously. "Maybe you should search for recent news from Tsera Nova."

Sehvi eyed him skeptically, then looked down, presumably at a data tablet. He started counting, hit sixteen when she exclaimed, "Oh my Goddess! Don't you tell me you were there for this!"

"Broke a wing and everything," Vasiht'h said, subdued. Hearing the sublimated panic in her voice made the whole thing feel real, in a way Jahir's relief hadn't. Jahir had been there, participating. Someone who'd been elsewhere during the whole affair, reacting to it . . .

"Oh my Goddess. Vasiht'h. You're seriously all right??"

"I'm fine." Vasiht'h exhaled. "A little unnerved by the whole thing, but I'm all right."

Sehvi said, "Yeah, I believe *that*." She leaned forward, so wide-eyed the whites were visible all the way around the irises. "Talk to me."

"I think that was the worst day in my life? Days?" Vasiht'h cracked the eggs, watching the yolks drop. His heart was pounding hard again. "I thought I was dead." He twitched a little, resumed mixing. "But I didn't die."

"Fourteen people did!"

Had they? He paled under his fur. People didn't die on resort planets. Even resort planets having emergencies. That's what Alliance technology was for. To save people. Who had it been? That Asanii whose hand he'd held? Someone from the *Friendly Mermaid*? Terry the trainer, whose quasi-sea lion had saved his life? "Well, I didn't. And Jahir's fine too. He was out of the way for most of it." Or Vasiht'h thought he had been. When had Jahir come down to the planet? Why hadn't he asked? "And the first few days were wonderful. Just . . . you don't remember the wonderful beginning when the ending ends like . . . well. Like that."

"I bet." She studied him, still shaken. "Ariihir, are you sure you're all right?"

"I'll be fine in a few days. I just need to remember I'm not there anymore." Vasiht'h smiled at her weakly. "So, to help with that, why don't you tell me about your day? And I'll make cookies, and then I'll eat them and remember that this is my life."

"All right," she said gamely. "Let me start with your nephews."

"In trouble again?"

"Depends on your definition of trouble . . ."

Vasiht'h smiled. "Go on. I want to hear what I'm in for when I finally decide to have mine." He started adding the flour while listening to Sehvi, and wondered if he really was all right or if this was just another form of avoidance. Maybe Tiber would know.

⎯⎯ ∞∞∞ ⎯⎯

Allen's first reaction wasn't encouraging, which was to clasp Vasiht'h's upper arms and have a good look at him. "You're in one piece, physically at least."

"Don't tell me you know?"

The human shook his head. "The last time I talked to you, you were heading to Tsera Nova for a vacation while Jahir sat his licensing exam. You come back half a week early and want an emergency appointment? I did some homework. Come in, sit. How bad was it?"

Vasiht'h bent to shake hands with Sarah the dog, remembering when she'd been a shy rescue more interested in hiding than greeting visitors. Five years had transformed her into a quietly confident helpmeet. "It was bad. I got thrown off a boat into the middle of it and almost drowned before they pulled me onto a rescue raft."

"Rhack," Allen said, staring at him. And then, "Pardon me, that was unprofessional. Make yourself comfortable. Would you like kerinne?"

"Yes, please?"

The passing years hadn't seen much change in Allen's office. Vasiht'h took the rake up and tried to rearrange the rocks in the little plot in the center of the coffee table, but it was hard to concentrate. He accepted the mug gratefully and sipped from it. This was the taste of his normal life. Not fruity purple drinks with umbrellas, but kerinne, and hot chocolate, and sometimes coffee or tea.

Allen sat on the couch across from him. "I assume Jahir's all right."

"Yes. We're both here." Vasiht'h exhaled. "So why do I still feel so twitchy? We're back, we're safe. It's over."

"The physical danger's over," Allen said. "Obviously the existential danger is lingering. What were you working on before you left?"

What had he been working on? He thought of the trip to Seersana. Seeing Palland, and the girls. His reaction to his brothers fighting. His interactions with Kristyl and Gladiolus. His feelings about the sight of Jahir in a hospital setting again, his hair braided back to reveal the severe jawline that usually hid beneath the softer fall.

"My major professor back at Seersana U said it was important that we know what our lives would look like if we were alone," he said. "To be able to imagine what we'd do with ourselves, and what we'd want just for ourselves."

"Good advice," Allen said tentatively. "Did it make you uncomfortable?"

Vasiht'h eyed him.

Smiling wryly, Allen said, "Let me do the therapist things without you noticing them, will you?"

"Of course it made me uncomfortable," Vasiht'h said. "I'm bonded to Jahir mentally. He's part of my life. I'm not planning for him ever to not be part of my life." He stared at the rock garden. "And I'm not sure 'think of your life ending' was how Professor Palland meant me to conceive of what life by myself would be like."

"I imagine if you wrote him to tell him 'we're all alone when we die', he would have words with you," Allen said dryly.

"He'd explode." Vasiht'h imagined it, chuckled. "He doesn't do written communication well . . . that might get me a realtime call. I don't think I'd blame him, either. It's morbid."

"It happened to you, though."

"Almost happened," Vasiht'h corrected, petting the dog, whose tail thumped against the carpet. "Obviously I didn't die."

Allen tilted a hand back and forth. "I meant the events that made you think of it happened to you."

"Yes," Vasiht'h said. "And they'll never not have happened to me." He thought of Nieve's Girls. "This is . . . a pivotal moment, isn't it. Something that makes you re-evaluate your life and decide things about it."

"It certainly would qualify, yes."

"Then . . . why don't I want to change anything?" Vasiht'h asked. "And why do I feel like I haven't changed?"

"I don't know, arii," Allen said, gently. "Because it sounds a lot like you have."

Vasiht'h rubbed his eyes. "I didn't even ask Jahir about his test. And I made friends on Tsera Nova. I didn't stop to ask if they were all right. I haven't sent them any messages. I haven't done anything normal."

"And you know that's reasonable, given what you went through."

"I do, but I don't believe it." Vasiht'h took up the rake but couldn't make himself prod at the rocks. "My sister says I have problems owning my happiness. Having problems owning my right to be miserable is new. Do you think Jahir's rubbing off on me?"

The human made a face. "Anything I say in response to that is going to sound . . ."

"Prejudicial?" Vasiht'h asked, smiling a little.

"Ridiculous," Allen said. "Because it's not a productive line of thought. We're not here to talk about Jahir, arii. And your Palland is right, in that you're not just the you who's in a relationship with an Eldritch. You're also the you who existed before him, and the you who exists when he's not around. The you who does have dreams and needs separate from his."

Vasiht'h lowered his head until his brow hit the edge of the table. And gently knocked his head against it several times.

"What is wrong with me? Why am I so confused? Why can't I just be relieved to be home?"

"Because home was already complicated by the things you were working on," Allen said. "And the fact that your near-death experience hasn't clarified anything is upsetting."

"Is that what's wrong?" Vasiht'h asked, startled.

"That's what it sounds like to me," Allen said. "Pet the dog."

Vasiht'h stroked Sarah's fur obediently, fighting the nonsensical urge to start crying. And then he was crying. "Oh, Allen. I'm alive and fourteen people died."

It wasn't at all professional for the human to hug him, but he did, and it was exactly what Vasiht'h needed. If anyone had asked him if the man most skeptical of their methodology would become a friend of this caliber, the kind of friend he could hide his face against while he wept without even knowing why, he would have scoffed. But the fact that he had, and that strange and wondrous things still happened, helped him get himself back under control. He accepted the tissues Allen passed him and wiped his face and nose. "And I know, I know we don't get to choose when we go, and we don't get to know why we do when we do. But it feels so senseless. And I feel so lucky. How can I be so lucky, and waste so much of my good fortune flailing like this? I'm not a kit out of college anymore. I should . . . I should know what I want and be content with what I'm doing. Or know that I'm *not* content with what I'm doing, and be making plans to change it."

"That's holding yourself to a higher standard than you'd hold any of your own clients to," Allen pointed out gently. "We're all allowed to be works in progress, arii."

"I know that too, it just feels like I'm wasting time. Our time. And I know we have time, but at the same time, we don't. I almost died . . ." Vasiht'h shuddered. "Why am I even alive?"

"Do you need an answer to that beyond 'Aksivaht'h wanted you here?'"

"Yes!" Vasiht'h managed a watery laugh. "Except I know it's my job to make meaning in my own life. That's why I'm so upset with myself. There are a handful of teenage girls on Seersana who are way ahead of me and they're barely old enough to date. How can they have figured it out so soon, when I'm still not sure? Even after a hurricane?"

Allen frowned, leaning back and folding his arms. Seeing it, Vasiht'h said, "Oh, that doesn't look good. Why are you disengaging?"

The human chuckled. "Just because you know what it means doesn't mean you know what inspired it."

"I know, so tell me?"

"Your major professor's advice," Allen said slowly. "I think I know why you need to do the exercise."

"Because . . . ? I need to know what my life would be like if I was alone?" Vasiht'h asked, cautious.

"No. Because I think if you were alone, you'd find your life meaningful enough." Allen reached for his own cup. "I think it's other people's expectations of your life that are causing the problem. Because you care about them, and want to live up to what you feel they want for you, even though it's not actually what you want."

Vasiht'h stared at him.

"That's either a 'you got it in one' look or a 'you're so off base I can't even understand what you just said' look." Allen sipped. "Which is it?"

"I . . ." Vasiht'h stopped. Would he be happy with his life if he wasn't worried about . . . whose expectations? His parents'? His family's? Jahir's? Everyone he thought might be judging him? Was that even fair? Because he was obviously ignoring the people who thought he was doing great, who even admired him for having his life so together. Even Sehvi kept reminding him the reason he wasn't grappling with her challenges was that he'd already surmounted them.

"I . . . might have to get back to you on that one," Vasiht'h said weakly.

"So, 'you got it in one.'"

"I'm afraid so." Vasiht'h scratched under the dog's chin, much to her delight. "Or at least, it's so close that I'm going to have to work with it for a while. It's clashing with something else in my head."

"That being?"

"That sometimes we need other people because they're the ones who know us when we don't know ourselves." Vasiht'h looked over at him. "What if these other people know something about me I don't know? Something I'm missing?"

"That's possible," Allen said. "I wouldn't be in this profession—with you, I'll point out—if I didn't think that external perspectives can help us recalibrate. Sometimes, we really do need other people's help. But I submit to you, arii, that if these other people's conceptions of what you actually want from your life were true, you wouldn't be chafing so hard. You'd accept them and be angsting about how to bring about those changes. Instead, you're upset because you know what you want. You just don't think other people value it."

"Oh," Vasiht'h said softly. The dog beside him perked her ears, stared up at him with her gentle, patient eyes. "It's so true, isn't it. The work we do isn't valued."

"It's misunderstood," Allen said. "And it's intangible. It's easier to grasp the value of concrete things. You can't walk on therapy like you can a bridge."

"But you can use therapy to move forward," Vasiht'h said. "And sometimes bridges fail." He straightened his shoulders. "This has been really helpful."

"Good," Allen said. "Because I hate seeing you question something this fundamental about yourself. You're a good therapist, Vasiht'h. You bring a great deal of good into the world. That matters."

Vasiht'h stared at him, agape.

The human chuckled. "And yes, I said that out loud. I hope, after how we started our relationship, that the words carry some weight."

"You have no idea," Vasiht'h answered, still stunned.

"I won't even charge extra for it," Allen said, amused.

Sarah walked Vasiht'h out of Tiber's office, leaving him

among the people outside the glass doors. He forced his paws to
start moving, and soon he was trotting down the street toward
the Commons, and his thoughts . . . they weren't busy. For once,
he felt emptied out. As if Allen's words had been a bomb, and left
nothing in their wake but a crater and the wind. It felt . . . good,
though. Like he could finally breathe. So he did, sliding into the
lunch crowd as they headed toward the restaurants and shops in
the city center. Overhead the sky was a bright and perfect blue,
with the starbase's spindle limned in white against the arch. As
he looked up at it, he thought that here was a place that would
never know a storm. But weather wasn't climate. He remembered that perfect moment on Seersana, when his worries had
fallen away and let him see himself as something greater than
his constant anxieties. His emotional weather had cleared, and
he could see.

"Storms pass," he murmured, and exhaled. And smiled at
his reflection in a bakery window before pausing, and frowning.
Except he still didn't know how his partner had fared, and what
he was doing with his license. And his brothers were still fighting. Vasiht'h stared inside the bakery, watching the Tam-illee
behind the counter hand a cookie down to a kit with bright blue
bows tied into her hair while her fond father looked on. His eyes
drifted from the child to the cookie, and then the attendant.

The memory of Jahir's voice, of the sight of him looking after
the girls as they waved. *Would you not help them if you could?*

His own voice, answering. *No, if I had money, I'd use it for just
that sort of thing.*

Sehvi's voice. *Maybe he wants to do this thing, maybe he doesn't.
But you don't get to decide what he does with his life.*

Palland, accompanied by the scent of strong black tea: *No
matter how useful it is to compare our perceptions to an external perspective, we still have to commit to trying to sort it out on our own.*

And Allen, finally. *Sometimes, we really do need other people's
help.*

Vasiht'h went into the bakery, bought himself a muffin—
blueberry topped with cinnamon and crystallized sugar—and

sat in the bright, windowed area set aside for patrons while he
checked the balance in his account. He knew how much he'd find.
Vasiht'h not only did their budgeting, he set aside money for
savings and economized when he felt they were overspending.
Which was almost never, because as he'd once told Jahir, he had
few material wants, other than soft pillows and food. Jahir . . .
well. The Eldritch was almost monklike in his tastes. Most of
his extravagances, when he indulged in them, involved experiences: concerts, art exhibits, tours. And wasn't that another sign
that they were where they should be? Neither of them spent like
people desperate to escape their lives.

As he expected, their trip to Tsera Nova hadn't changed the
numbers. He'd told Sehvi he would be upset about that when he
got back, but he found himself glad instead that there was no
evidence that they'd gone. How long would that be a sore spot?
He guessed he would be processing for a long time. Years, maybe,
given how often he still thought of the events in Heliocentrus.

No, what mattered was that he had money enough for an
extravagance. If he thought that indulging it wouldn't be making
someone's life choices for them. He tapped his finger on the
tablet, frowning, then reached over and pulled a piece of the
muffin off the top, trying it. The recipe was good. He thought it
had something unusual in it. Cardamom? He stared at it, smiled.
Giving someone an opportunity wasn't coercing them. Especially
if they wanted it and just didn't know it yet. But . . . if he bought
it in advance, that would apply undue pressure, wouldn't it? He
frowned, then nodded. There was a middle way.

He put away the bank info and started searching. An hour
later, he was ready, and selected one of his commtags. It took
a while for his brother to pick up, which was fine. Vasiht'h was
still savoring the muffin. When Dondi finally answered, he didn't
wait for his brother to greet him. "Would you put cardamom in a
blueberry muffin?"

Dondi, whose mouth was already open, closed it and looked
contemplative. "That sounds great, actually." Then he scowled
mulishly. "And if you're calling about my fight with Pes, I already

read your message and I don't care what you think this is about,
it's totally about—"

"Ariihir!" Vasiht'h held up a hand. "How do you feel about a
trip to Asanao?"

Dondi's flat-footed expression, complete with gaping mouth,
was painfully comical. "W-what? Asanao? Why do you want me
to go all the way out there?"

"'All the way out there' is the middle of the Core," Vasiht'h
pointed out. "It's not like I'm talking about the boondock
colonies."

"It might as well be! Why on the worlds did you think of it?
And me?" Dondi frowned at him. "What's this about?"

"It's just a thought," Vasiht'h began. "There's a cooking school
there that's having trials for scholarships in three months—"

Dondi squeaked. "You mean the Ward Culinary Academy?"

Vasiht'h's brows rose. "You know about it?"

Dondi looked away, ears flagging. "I . . . you know. Like to
watch cooking contests." He scowled and said, "You're not
serious. You want to send me to Asanao to compete for a scholarship? Do you know how hard it is to get into Ward?"

"I assume very hard," Vasiht'h said. "So if you decide to do it,
you're going to be very busy for the next three months."

Dondi stared at him. "You're serious about this."

"What I want to know is if *you're* serious about it," Vasiht'h
answered. "Ariihir, you're good in the kitchen. You always have
been. And you enjoy it. But you've never made any noise about
doing something with that talent, which is why Dami and Tapa
haven't pushed you. I think you could use a push, though, because
you're flailing. You love to cook, so why not be a chef?"

"I don't know if I'm good enough!" Dondi said, staring at him.
"Vasiht'h, this is . . . that's a real school. With an actual reputation. An Alliance-wide one!"

"And you're my brother," Vasiht'h answered. "Neither stupid,
nor useless, nor bad at what you do. You are, in fact, excellent
at it. The nights you did the evening meal were always the best.
Even when you were only ten or eleven."

Dondi was looking down, no doubt to hide the blush Vasiht'h couldn't see through his dark-furred cheeks. "You're just saying that."

Vasiht'h snorted. "No, I'm not, or I wouldn't be offering to pay your way to the contest. And your hotel while you're there. And if you win the partial scholarship, well . . . we'll talk. Right?"

"You mean that?" Dondi said, incredulous. "You . . . you really believe I can do it."

"Mmm-hmm."

"I can't let you pay for my entire schooling!" Dondi exclaimed. "If I get the partial, I'll work my way through. Or at least, as much of it as I can."

"We can talk about it when you win," Vasiht'h said. "But if I were you . . ."

"I'll get to work right away!" Dondi said, eyes still wide. "They have archives of past wins, I need to look those up, see what kinds of things the judges expect, and oh, Goddess, Vasiht'h, are you serious?"

"Go register," Vasiht'h said. "And send me the confirmation when you get it, all right?"

"Is that to keep me honest?"

"Yes," Vasiht'h said. "Because if you blink, I'm going to nag you until you follow through."

Dondi laughed a little, uncertain. "Awfully pushy, big brother."

"I know," Vasiht'h said. "And I wouldn't be leaning on you if I hadn't seen how excited you got at the idea. But you want to do it, ariihir. I don't want you to talk yourself out of it, that's all."

Dondi said, "I . . . yes. You're right. In fact . . . will you stay on the line with me? I'll fill it out now."

"I'm still eating this muffin in this really nice bakery, which smells like yeast and sugar," Vasiht'h said cheerfully. "Trust me, I don't need any other incentive to stay put." And he meant it, enjoying every moment of both the muffin and his brother's distracted mutterings as he searched for and completed the registration process. Vasiht'h even had time to order a second pastry,

and decided on something that looked like a croissant but turned
out to be filled with a light, tangy custard. Not strong enough to
be lemon . . .

His data tablet chimed as a copy of the registration confirmation arrived. Vasiht'h spread the message and grinned. "So how
does it feel to be committed, ariihir?"

"Terrifying," Dondi said, but he looked excited, not frightened. "What are you eating now?"

"I don't know, but it's good."

Dondi fidgeted. "Um. About Pes."

Vasiht'h held up his hand. "I don't care. I'm not here to yell
at you about treating your family better. I'm here to confront you
with your future."

"Ow, Goddess!" Dondi laughed. "That's far more scary!" His
ears sagged. "Ah . . . I probably should apologize to him, though,
shouldn't I."

"I don't know," Vasiht'h said. "I don't know what the two of
you were really fighting about, or what you said to each other.
But I will say this: if something happens on that shuttle, do you
want Pes's last memories of you to be from that fight?"

Dondi shuddered. "Ugh! No! Thank you for that awful image."

"Of if something were to happen to Pes," Vasiht'h continued. "Because accidents do happen, ariihir. If you knew he was
going to die tomorrow, would whatever you were fighting about
matter?"

"No!"

Vasiht'h shrugged, a gesture that would probably have been
more effective without the croissant in his hand. "There you go."

Dondi sighed. "You ever have that thing happen where you
start a fight and then you say things during it that are more awful
than the actual fight? And then what you're upset about is what
happened during the fight, not the thing that inspired it?"

"Not only have I had that thing happen, everyone's had that
thing happen," Vasiht'h said. "So practicing how to get out of
that loop before you crash is a good thing." He grinned, lopsidedly. "One of the many wonderful things about being a bonafide

grown-up."

"I *am* a bonafide grown-up! Just because . . ." Dondi stopped and put his head in his hand. "Oh, no, don't you start."

"So that's what it was about, mm?"

"That's what it became about," Dondi muttered. "Just because I haven't figured things out . . ."

Vasiht'h said, "You've got a confirmation message in your mail right now that says you have. That you probably always had. You just hadn't figured out how to act on it. But you've got work to do now, don't you?"

"I do!" He paused. "And an apology to make." Clearing his throat, he added, "Do you mind if I . . . keep you informed? Like I should make a plan and tell you what I'm doing to follow up? It'll help me stay on track. You know. Especially if Ditreht comes round and wants to know why I don't want to go clubbing."

"I'd be delighted to review your plans," Vasiht'h said. "Especially if they include recipes."

Dondi brightened. "Great! It's a deal." The realization seeped into his face, and his eyes shone. "Oh, Goddess, I'm really going to do this? I am! Thank you so much, ariihir! I won't let you down."

"I know you won't," Vasiht'h said. "More importantly, I don't think you'll let you down either."

"No," Dondi agreed. "I'm going to go review the archives right now! I'll talk to you later!"

The croissant was so good that after eating it, Vasiht'h ordered himself coffee to wash it down before checking Sehvi's timezone. Tam-ley was now in late evening, so he settled for leaving her a message. 'Solved your problem. You're welcome. Love you, V.'

Now all he had to do was tell his partner that they'd be funding the launch of Dondi's culinary career. Somehow, though, Vasiht'h didn't think that would be a problem. Setting the tablet down, the Glaseah drank the coffee and thought about lunch.

CHAPTER 20

FOR DAYS AFTER THEIR RETURN, Jahir went about their routine without question, because he was so accustomed to the rhythm of their days that falling into it was second nature. But he was also aware that when he came to rest, his eyes moved toward Vasiht'h. Even with the mindline's evidence, he could not quite take for granted that the Glaseah was here and alive, and not a victim of the storm. Jahir had checked the news after their departure. He knew about those who'd died. Most of them had been on the ocean when the storm hit, the way his partner had been.

Jahir had accepted that he would lose the Glaseah too soon, but he'd assumed that death would be dealt by old age, not untimely tragedy. The closeness of that brush with a world without Vasiht'h had harrowed him in a way he found unnerving. There were so many ways the Alliance could bring him joy and comfort—the discovery that children could age into companions had been one—that the ways it could serve him sorrow cut the more deeply.

That was also the reason he had not looked too closely at his failure. He knew, intellectually, that he should reschedule, or possibly contest the exam's results. But too much had attached to it for him to see it clearly. His guilt over having the opportunity, when so many didn't; his shame that he was not planning on returning to the homeworld, when so many needed what he could learn; his ambivalence about the hospital setting, and his dismay over discovering how much he yearned for it anyway; his fears that he would find the Alliance's technology so magical that when it failed, its failure would be unbearable. . . . and overwhelmingly, the feeling that he'd both failed Vasiht'h by not passing, and done the only possible thing in response to his partner's danger. . . .

Time would smooth out this tangle, as it did so many. But he was not ready yet.

He still wasn't ready when he received a message on his way back from his daily swim. From KindlesFlame. Almost he didn't open it, for explaining to his mentor why he wasn't on the rolls of those who'd passed was beyond him, but he could not countenance avoiding the Tam-illee after all KindlesFlame had done on Jahir's behalf. Spreading the message, he read the words, and re-read them for comprehension.

Meet me for coffee? Tell me where, I don't know anything about this place.

Jahir stepped out of the middle of the throughway to stand beneath the awning of a café and reply. *You're on Veta?*

A few moments later: For another day, yes. So, date?

Hastily, Jahir sent him the address for the café with the scones, and made his way there to procure a table.

Fifteen minutes later, KindlesFlame sauntered onto the patio, hands in his pockets and tail swinging lazily behind him. The sight of him on Starbase Veta was so out-of-context Jahir almost didn't recognize him, seeing only a middle-aged Tam-illee, confident and easy in his own skin, and the revelation drew his breath from him: that he had begun thinking of Pelted of a certain age as 'old' because by his standards they were only a hair's-breadth from dying. But they were *not* dying. Men and women like KindlesFlame were in the prime of their lives, and more wick in fact than many Eldritch ever were, trapped in ruts of their own making.

"So!" KindlesFlame said, pulling back a chair. "Do I see before me the newest provisionally licensed healer-assist in the Alliance, and possibly the only Eldritch who can make that claim?"

"In reverse order," Jahir said, "I do not know, and . . . no."

KindlesFlame's brows rose. "Don't tell me you failed."

"I'm afraid it was nothing so simple," Jahir said. "Will you sit? This café is famous for its scones, and I am eager to introduce them to someone who won't quail at the sight of them."

"Don't think you can distract me with food." The Tam-illee dropped into the chair opposite his. "Order me the scones, sure, but explain."

Jahir called the waitress over and asked for coffee and a plate of both of the scone specials before facing his academic advisor. "Let me tell you then, about Tsera Nova."

The telling took longer than he expected. Not because of the events, though those needed their fair share of the time. But because KindlesFlame quizzed him on the exam's subjects, and they found themselves wandering through the subject matter, speculating or discussing current research. The scones arrived, one set of triple strawberry served with a side of cream whipped with honey, and another based on chives and yogurt that Jahir actually enjoyed, though he had to break his off in small pieces to eat it slowly enough to last the conversation.

"So are you going to go back and tell them you want to retake the final sections?" KindlesFlame asked, having rescued Jahir from the necessity of consuming the strawberry scones. He was licking his spoon of the remaining cream.

"Would they permit it?"

"Probably not," KindlesFlame said. "But they might. You have a way of talking people around." He lifted a brow. "I'm surprised you haven't tried it already."

"It would perhaps be easier simply to take the test again."

"You could, yes, though it seems a waste of money and time." KindlesFlame canted his head. "You haven't scheduled it."

Jahir looked at his mug. "No."

"But you will, won't you?"

To answer when he didn't know the answer . . . would what he said be a lie? Or would it become a self-fulfilling prophecy?

KindlesFlame leaned forward. "Jahir."

"I . . . had not thought so far ahead."

"You are not doing this." Surprised at the heat in the Tamillee's voice, Jahir looked up and found his mentor glaring at him. "You're not going to talk yourself out of this after all the effort everyone around you has put into supporting you into this decision. A decision, I'll remind you, that you wanted to make anyway."

"Alet—"

"Don't," KindlesFlame said. "Don't put that barrier between us. Unless you're willing to bow to my authority?" He lifted a brow. "Well?"

"I . . ."

"When we finish this conversation, you're going to go home and discuss this with Vasiht'h," KindlesFlame said. "And you'll reschedule the damned exam. And take it. And become the first Eldritch healer-assist in the Alliance, because Iley curse it, it's what you want, and it would be a damned waste of your talents not to go through with it. *Especially* after Tsera Nova. Do you understand me?"

"I . . . you are . . . reprimanding me?" Jahir said, surprised.

"I'm pulling you up by your neck and pointing you back in the right direction," KindlesFlame said. "Because apparently your partner hasn't yet. Which means . . ." He paused, then scowled. "You haven't told him yet, have you!"

"It hasn't come up?"

KindlesFlame pointed a finger at him. "That's the first thing you're going to do when you get back from this meal. Do you understand me? And in case you're tempted to renege on that, you're going to invite me to breakfast tomorrow before I get on the shuttle to go back to Seersana."

"You . . . feel very strongly about this."

"I do, yes," KindlesFlame said. "You didn't come this far just to stop short of the goal." He sighed. "Arii. Look at me, will you?"

Startled, Jahir met his eyes. They were gray—he had never noticed. Intelligent eyes, incisive and compassionate, and right now, far, far too intense. It made him flush.

"As an educator, you hope you'll have students worth your time," KindlesFlame said, each word taut. "And if you're lucky, you'll meet a few who are that perfect combination of smart, driven, and a pleasure to work with. It's not just about them—it can't be. It has to be about the interaction between them, and you. A spark that makes you look forward to coming to work in the morning. Reminds you that what you're doing makes a difference. When you retire, those are the people you look back on and think 'yes. That's why I went into teaching.'"

"Alet," Jahir whispered.

"You're one of my sparks," KindlesFlame said. "And if you think I'm going to sit back and watch that complicated head of yours sabotage you before you're even started . . . you're wrong. Because you really are barely started, Jahir. You've got centuries to learn everything you want to, and more importantly, to synthesize medical disciplines in a way most people can't. Because you have the time to assimilate disparate principles and see how they interact." He shook his head. "You have the potential to see things in a way none of us do, because most of us can't specialize in more than one field. Can you imagine the kind of synergies you'll see because you can develop the expertise across those boundaries?"

Jahir stared at him, stunned. "Oh, alet . . ."

"Yes?" KindlesFlame said. "Do you see?"

Did he! Oh, but he did. The idea was staggering. He had been so concerned with fitting into the Alliance's mold, and the ways he couldn't, that he'd completely failed to imagine the ways he might exceed it. "But . . . I am not ready!"

"No," KindlesFlame agreed. "Not least because you keep tripping yourself this way. You're going to need some time to stop second-guessing yourself. But Iley willing, you have that time too. You'll be a therapist until being a therapist doesn't teach you enough anymore. Then you'll become a doctor, and everything you learned as a therapist, you'll bring to that practice. And after that . . . research? Something else?" KindlesFlame tilted his head. "I don't know how much of it I'll be around to see. But I plan to be there for as much of it as I can."

"I can't . . . I don't . . ." Jahir trailed off. "Alet."

"Lafeyette."

Jahir looked up sharply.

"Either I'm your mentor, and you're going to do what I tell you to because I know better than you how to walk the path you're walking," the Tam-illee said. "Or I'm your friend, and you're still going to do what I tell you because I can see the mistakes you're making and I don't want you to make them."

"Sometimes one has to make mistakes to learn," Jahir breathed.

"And sometimes, you can save yourself the grief because you already know the lesson." KindlesFlame's voice gentled. "Arii. You've bruised your brow on this particular wall enough times. Don't you think?"

"It does seem familiar," Jahir answered, voice low. He turned his coffee cup, thinking of his brother's habit of fidgeting with silverware and surprising himself with how natural it was to mimic him.

"So. You'll go home to Vasiht'h and have the talk you've been avoiding," KindlesFlame said. "And over breakfast I'll get to hear the triumphant and probably funny story of how he had to drag you to the tablet to re-register. Yes?"

How could his heart feel like breaking, and it be entirely because of love? "Yes." He glanced at his mentor and said, "This seems a good time to segue into why you are on Veta."

KindlesFlame grinned and refreshed his cup. "It does, doesn't it? You'll laugh. I was here for a job interview."

Jahir straightened. "Do not say it!"

"Your general hospital needed a new Chief of Staff," Kindles-Flame said. "But I turned it down. It's not the right fit, not right now anyway. I can see myself being in charge of a hospital, but

I'm not prepared to settle down. I'd like to travel a bit, do the conference circuit first." He grinned. "Then I can ask for more money, anyway."

"You were almost Veta's Chief Physician," Jahir said, unable to believe it.

"I did say I was following up on some leads."

"But not this one!" Jahir shook his head. "Oh, but it would have been good to work with you, arii."

"No reason why we can't in the future," KindlesFlame said. "Eventually I'll want to stay in one place, if only because you can't go deep while you're going wide. Sinking into a good challenge . . . I can see myself needing that in the future. But later." He chuckled. "I admit it was hard to say no, knowing you'd be here."

"Perhaps, then . . . another time?" Jahir said.

"I don't see why not. And in the meantime, I'll badger you in mail, the way I have been." KindlesFlame looked at their empty plates. "That was an excellent appetizer. Are their entrees any good?"

"God and Lady!" Jahir exclaimed. "You could eat more!"

KindlesFlame grinned. "Well, you did eat one of my scones. What do you expect?" He waved to one of the waitstaff. "Now, back to that thorny hypothetical they posed in the health administration segment . . ."

From there, Jahir went home. What else, with such a vow riding him? And the mindline told him that his partner was waiting there; there would be no putting the discussion off, thus. As he walked, he wondered how he would begin it. Sought and discarded any number of openings, found none of them adequate. He was here, confused, grateful, full of regret and joy both. Was that not what it was to be alive?

In the end, he entered their apartment and set his bag on the stand by the door, and said to the Glaseah sitting at the breakfast table, "It was a New Year's world, but there was no new beginning. I did not pass the test."

Vasiht'h looked up at him. "I figured."

So much fretting for nothing. Of course the Glaseah knew. "How did you divine . . ."

"You would have said something," Vasiht'h said. "Even though you hate them, you know I like fusses. When you didn't bring up the need for a party, or even celebratory ice cream, I knew something went wrong." He touched his breastbone with a thumb. "In my heart. But I was avoiding looking at it for my own reasons." He smiled a little, and the mindline softened with resignation and love both. The image that carried was of a much-adored plush rabbit with its stuffing showing from a broken limb.

"Was that . . ."

"Not mine," Vasiht'h said. "My sister's. But don't tell her I told you about it, she might kill me." He nodded. "We started this whole business with a talk at this table, we might as well finish it here. Though I don't have any fancy muffins this time."

"Bread, though," Jahir observed, drawing a chair back for himself.

"Just plain sourdough with butter," Vasiht'h agreed. "Toasted. Sometimes you want something simple."

"And . . ." Jahir glanced at the mug. "Kerinne?"

"Café au lait, actually. In keeping with the theme. I was in this amazing bakery and they talked me into all sorts of things you're going to groan at the sight of."

"I do not groan," Jahir said, but he was smiling now too.

"Want some?"

"I have just had scones. The thought of more food is distressing."

Vasiht'h huffed a laugh. "Yes, I bet it is. So . . . you failed. How is that even possible?"

"It was forfeited when I quit the premises to seek you."

Vasiht'h's hand halted on the way to his mug. "You threw the test to rush after me."

"I saw the storm," Jahir answered, his own anxiety tightening into a knot. "There was news . . . it was dire . . . I could not but go?"

Vasiht'h's head hung, but the mindline had grown dense with emotions, like blooming flowers, bright and fresh and perfumed with happiness. "You really ran after me like a hero in a romance novel."

"I ran after you like someone whose beloved was parted from him, and in mortal danger," Jahir answered firmly. "There was little romance involved, I assure you."

Vasiht'h was laughing now. "Oh, that's not what Sehvi would say. She's going to die when she hears this."

Jahir considered. "Best tell her about this first, so that you might be spared your own death when she hears about your indiscretion with the stuffed rabbit toy."

"And you made a joke too!" Vasiht'h shook his head. "Oh, arii. So, you failed. But you haven't talked about it at all. Why? Were you just going to . . . soldier on without sharing it? Let me guess. You didn't want to upset me by telling me about it, so you haven't even figured out how to salvage the situation."

"KindlesFlame did say you would say something of the sort," Jahir admitted, wishing now he'd requested something to eat or drink if only to have an excuse to look at the table. He folded his hands together on it instead, ignoring the blatant reminder of the responsibilities his House ring represented. Hiding from the sight of such things did not make them go away. He should have known better by now. And yet: "I love our life."

"I do too," Vasiht'h said. "And I have no leg to stand on here, getting upset about your mental gyrations when I was going through my own ridiculous contortions. Trying to reconcile the fact that I didn't *want* a 'new year' of my own because I liked what we had. But so afraid to admit to it because it might not *look* like enough to anyone else, and then I'd have to feel ashamed of being happy in my 'rut'."

Jahir looked up, startled. "Oh, arii. No!"

"Yes." Vasiht'h shook his head. "Like I said. Not my finest moment either." He sighed and smiled. "So where do we go from here? Other than you taking the test again? And no, this time I'm not going with you, so pick whatever place you want as long as it's soon. I don't want you wiggling out of it again."

"I don't want . . ."

"A different life," Vasiht'h finished. "Me neither. But that's all right." He inhaled and said, "I think . . . we're both operating under the fallacy that just because you *can* do something, you *have* to. You can get licensed as a healer-assist, but that doesn't mean you have to change jobs. It can be just a thing that you are, and maybe sometimes keep your hand in, but that's it. I can be . . ." He laughed. "I can be anything besides a therapist in a committed mindbonding with an alien, but just because I *could*, doesn't mean I *have to*. Because I'm happy with where I am."

"Are you truly?" Jahir asked carefully, knowing the answer was almost always more complicated than 'yes.'

But Vasiht'h did say, "Yes." And then chuckled. "That doesn't mean I won't fret over things. All the things! But yes, I am happy. I want to keep doing this until we're both tired of it. And if we never get tired of it, and we're still doing good with our lives . . . why do we have to do anything else?"

Jahir exhaled. "Then . . . I shall take the test. And we shall continue as we are. Until we must not." Which, he reflected, was perhaps too odd and therefore revealing a comment, but Vasiht'h answered.

"Yes." The Glaseah lifted his eyes. "Funny how we can be so lucky in so many ways and still have so many struggles."

"To live is to strive," Jahir said. "Even in the most idyllic of contexts, there is friction."

"And I guess it's a sign that we're growing." Vasiht'h tore off a piece of his toast and pushed it over. "If we were complacent, we'd be all right all the time. Wouldn't we? But we're not. We're asking questions."

"One must be satisfied with the answers, if the answers are in fact satisfactory," Jahir said, accepting the bread.

"We both have that problem," Vasiht'h said. "But that's fine. It just means we can figure it out together."

Jahir said, quiet, "We are well?"

"We are, yes. Both of us." Vasiht'h nodded. "Maybe not

perfect, but . . . we're well. As long as you actually take the test and I get to have that party!"

"I promise," Jahir said.

"And what's this about KindlesFlame putting words in my mouth? You told him about this before you told me!"

"He ambushed me," Jahir said ruefully. "In the flesh. I took him to the scone café."

"He's *here*?"

"Interviewing for a position at the hospital he turned down."

Vasiht'h's eyes widened. "Wouldn't that have been something. Huh. I'm almost tempted to go tell him to take it just so we can double-team you when you're being unnecessarily self-sacrificing."

Jahir sighed. "He is well and again capable of doing so across the sector, I pledge it."

Vasiht'h chuckled. "I bet. So are we feeding him?"

"Breakfast tomorrow. At which time I am to report I have already registered for the next exam."

"Good. Oh. Mm. Speaking of which." Vasiht'h tapped his fingertips on the walls of his mug. "I . . . would like to send my brother to school on our money, if his scholarship doesn't cover it."

"Ah?" Jahir looked up, surprised. "You wish to spend our money?"

"You don't mind, do you? He needed a quick jab in the rear to get his head straightened out." The mindline darkened with exasperation, like a short and grumpy rainstorm. "He's good in the kitchen, so I sponsored him into a culinary competition that leads to a scholarship opportunity."

"You think he has a chance?"

"I don't know," Vasiht'h admitted. "But I really hope so. And if he does . . ."

"Your family's welfare is ours to caretake," Jahir said gently, extending his sincerity through the mindline like a vow on the tongue. "I would never begrudge the funds."

Vasiht'h sighed out. "I knew you wouldn't." Tilting his head, he added, "Does that make your family's welfare ours to caretake, too?"

Jahir thought of the worlds and time between himself and duty. "Not yet." When he looked up from the bread, he found Vasiht'h's eyes waiting. He said again, more definitely, "Not yet."

The Glaseah was willing to leave it at that, and he was glad.

CHAPTER 21

"YOU REALLY DID FIX MY PROBLEM," Sehvi said.

"I've fixed a lot of problems last week," Vasiht'h answered, plopping on the pillows in front of the screen. He stretched his entire body out, including the wing that had broken and had its vane frayed. Seeing it whole out of the corner of his eye relieved him. Not in a bad way, either . . . more in a 'I'm grateful for things I've been taking for granted' way. "I assume in this case you're talking about Dondi."

"Said he was sorry to Pes and everything. Grandly. Not only that, he told our cousin to stop messing around and start paying attention to what they were going to spend the rest of their lives doing, because they were running out of time to make decisions."

Vasiht'h's ears rose. "Goddess! Did he really?"

"Aunt Sattri is delighted. Now she spends our calls cackling about how Ditreht is rushing around in circles, trying to get his grades up and sweating about his future. Because if Dondi's straightened out, then the sky is *obviously falling* and he has to plan for it immediately."

Vasiht'h laughed, a lazy, huffing laugh made more difficult by the pillows pressed into his ribcage. "That's rich. I can't even imagine!"

"Me neither." Sehvi grinned and loomed toward the camera. "You look comfortable. Got everything tidied up on your end finally?"

"I think so."

"And Prince Perfection?"

Vasiht'h smiled. "Prince Perfection is leaving tomorrow to go re-take his exam."

"Oohhhh. So he has to re-take it?"

The moment he'd been waiting for since his talk with Jahir had arrived. "He failed it the first time to chase after me when he found out I was trapped in the storm."

Sehvi's gasp was dramatic, and involved both her hands flying to her cheeks. "He did *not*. Just like one of my Nouveau Regency heroes!"

Vasiht'h started chortling. "Yes. Exactly like. If they're the type to go dashing after their lovers-in-distress."

"You have *no idea*. I am absolutely going to send you the one I just finished, about the Hinichi duke who falls in love with this rag-and-bone Harat-Shar guy and there's a crimelord and an unlikely rescue and lots of hot 'Oh, I must not for we are too far from one another in station, why you do not even have the same accent!' loving action . . ."

Vasiht'h pressed his hand to his eyes. "Can my bank balance take another binge-read of some author's backlist."

"It can apparently handle sending Dondi to the one of the most expensive culinary schools in the Core!"

"Goddess, is it really?" Vasiht'h's eyes widened. "I hope he wins!"

Sehvi snickered. "If he doesn't, just think of the golden opportunity you'll have to let your partner buy you extravagant things without objecting to it for once."

"I'm still waiting to hear about your first fight with Kovihs."

"You'll be waiting a long time."

By tacit mutual consent, neither of them made much of Jahir's leaving for the exam on his own. Vasiht'h accompanied him to the docks and waved him off, and the mindline held nothing but a hearty cheer Jahir thought a trifle forced, but less so than he'd expected. Neither of them wanted to be parted again so quickly; both of them wanted the task complete. All there was for it was the doing.

Fortunately, there was an option to sit the exams soon, and not far, nor in any location so exotic as Tsera Nova: Aren's welcome station was hosting, only a short hop from Starbase Veta. He would be there and back in the three days it took him to complete the test, plus two on either side for the flight. One week, alone. He hated the thought, but knew that he was leaving Vasiht'h in one of the safest places in the Alliance. There would be no more need for dashing rescues worthy of a romance novel. For now, at least. Given that Vasiht'h had committed one, fleeing Seersana for Selnor to deliver him from the consequences of his decision to leave, and now he had returned the favor on Tsera Nova. . . .

Surely they had used up their quota of harrowing adventures. The Alliance, of all places, did not lend itself to perils so grievous, nor tragedies so quotidian as the ones on his homeworld.

Jahir hadn't known what to expect of the nomadic Aera's solar system, but the amount of infrastructure littering every orbit from innermost planet to outermost debris field was staggering. And the constant movement! They practiced traveling, he divined, delighted by the revelation. Even the most conservative clans, who preferred to bide in their home system, could not resist jetting around it. As the passenger liner swept closer, awaiting its docking assignment at Aren's welcome station, Jahir queried the flexglass window for identification of as many of those distant winking platforms as he could see, and found that they were not only practical—mining platforms, power collection—but recreational as well. At least one proclaimed itself the best diner in-system, and as far as he could tell, it was the only establishment in that particular asteroid.

The room he'd procured for himself was in the same section

of the station as the testing facility, and he dropped his bag on its utilitarian bed before going for a walk, because on the way to the hotel he'd passed such colors and scents that he couldn't not investigate. Aren's station was less a network of grim catwalks and dark bulkheads and more a bazaar, and he lost several hours wandering it, astonished that anyone would decide that tents and awnings were properly at home on a station, and agreeing with their decision because it was appealing in every particular. He indulged in a little shopping as well, because the gifting seasons were never far away when one lived at the pace of the Pelted.

That evening, he committed himself to a desultory review of the material before attending to his mail. Vasiht'h had responded to his report that he had arrived safely with an adjuration that he do well, one Jahir imagined him delivering with an expression of mock sternness. Jahir smiled and moved on to the next, which was another missive from his mother. He sank into the familiar details of estate management as she related them, of this mare in foal or that orchard's yield, of the lives of their tenants, and the lives of their peers. Only near the end did his mother mention politics, and briefly.

Liolesa's enemies are again at her heels, though why I have not been able to divine. Something to do with the heir, if I can trust rumor. But Bethsaida is a young spitfire, and well able to handle any criticisms, I am certain. Anyone who can bear the brunt of our Queen's frequent attention, as she must in order to take instruction on her duties, will find Liolesa's foes beneath notice! And yet, I have not seen Bethsaida at court as often as I expected. I know you had little congress with her, so asking you after her mind . . . well. If you know anything, I would be glad to hear it. She used to speak more with your brother, but as you know, your brother is also gone away, out of reach. Poor woman, trammeled on the world while all around her the exciting and eligible are flying from it! Were I her, I'd be rebelling myself!

Jahir tried to imagine his mother as a young maiden, balking at her own cage, and thought it humorous, until he wondered if she'd ever felt that resentment and desperation. But no, she continued:

I look forward to the day that I might also sample the wonders of the outworld . . . but that day is not yet, and I have always known it. I had goals I wished to accomplish first, and while most of them I have achieved, I have yet to finish the work I have chosen here. One day, though, my dearest, I shall follow your lead and see the wonders you have described with my own eyes! I will have earned it. Until then, how I cherish the sight of the seasons changing the land we have taken as duty, and the way the years turn, patient and measured. I love our home, and am its glad steward until you return.

Strange to think that when he did, he would be steward of more than the Seni lands. Looking up from the tablet, he found his eyes resting on the view through his room's window. What *would* happen when he came home as the Eldritch's first modern healer? Would his Queen's foes set aside their animosity in order to take advantage of his skills? If he was the only person who could help them, what choice would they have? What would that do to their world's politics, did so much power rest on one side?

Did not all that power rest there now? Perhaps that was the true cause of the resentment that seethed beneath so much of their people's masks, and perennialized so many of their most divisive feuds.

He had focused so much on the practicalities of what he would be bringing with him. That the situation might be more compli- cated than 'arrive and set up a practice' was . . . he inhaled. Both odious, and . . . a relief. He'd been so focused on his duty to go home and make himself useful that he'd missed that there might be barriers to his doing so that he alone could not address. And if that was so . . . then rushing home might be the least optimal of his choices. He drew down a fresh page to answer his mother, and almost by rote he responded to each of her comments about the status of their estate, not even needing to reread them to recall them in every particular. But once he had done . . .

You know by now that I plan to return a healer . . . but an Alliance-trained healer cannot operate in a vacuum. To offer those skills to our people, who sorely need them, I will require infrastructure. Even something as modest as a clinic requires technology beyond what we can support; the power grid alone is not a minor installation. There are political considerations to those modifications to our way of life . . . and even more such ramifications to my ability to help those who previously had no hope of aid, no matter their allegiances.

The more I consider it, the more it feels a matter for our liegelady. I would not disrupt whatever plan she nurtures now, as she no doubt does; nor do I know enough about the current mood at court to understand how my arrival—when I do arrive—will change things.

It feels presumptuous of me to address her directly with my concerns when I am not ready to offer solutions. Indeed, I do not yet have a license! But if you could, perhaps, learn enough to advise me, I would be greatly obliged to you—again, as I have been to you for so many other reasons, and never so glad have I been to be so much beholden.

Once again, I beg your advice, and look forward to hearing it. In the mean, wish me luck in my endeavors.

Your loving son,
—J

Having sent the letter, he put his tablet aside and looked again through the window, where ships of all sizes passed in and out of view, their lights gleaming like those of the park on Seersana, fairy-glows and holiday-bright. Had not the girls discovered it themselves? Nothing was as simple as one's good intentions made it out to be. And in the end, he was grateful. To live in a world less complex would have afforded him fewer opportunities for wonder. Had he thought his homeworld lacking in those complications? And those opportunities? More fool he.

Confused, and at peace with his confusion, Jahir rested himself on his foreign bed, and slept.

If anything, the exam was easier, for his memory of it remained fresh despite the intervening weeks. He gave himself to it for the required six hours each day and spent the remainder wandering the station, or sitting in one of its cafes looking out over the traffic surrounding it. There were no rare alien proctors to intrigue him, nor did he speak much, save to request a service, or answer an occasional question. The silence felt good, surrounding him amid the bustle of the Aera's noise. As if he was passing through a ritual space.

Only the final section of the test was new to him, and not new, for it covered emergency care. He wrote his answers in concert with the voices from Mercy, whispering out of memory, and this raveling of the most difficult experience of his life with the life he was living now felt . . . wholesome. Needful. KindlesFlame would have been the first to tell him that not all healers worked in hospitals. Even if he one day found himself there again, he would not be alone. A hospital required infrastructure, staff, other healers. The notion made his heart tense in his chest, and he couldn't tell if it was joy or awe or something more bittersweet. Perhaps he would be the first Eldritch healer licensed in the Alliance. But he would certainly not be the last. Who would be his companions on that journey? Would he be home in time for Vasiht'h to be one of them? What shape would that future take? And oh, how he could find the anticipation of it so glorious, when he'd found it so fraught before!

He was packing to leave when the results hit his data tablet. He had passed, and was now provisionally licensed, so long as he completed his practicals within five years. He stopped packing and sat on the bed to forward the note to Veta's general hospital, which had been waiting to hear from him since he'd told the staffing assist his plans for Tsera Nova, and his desire to have his volunteer hours count toward the full license.

And then he resumed packing. His hands were shaking as he folded his clothes into his bag. So little fanfare for something that had accumulated so much unexpected drama.

Vasiht'h would want a cake. Jahir found he wanted one too.

On the flight home, Jahir received a very welcome, and very
unexpected note, from Meekie, and it began, rather charmingly,
with an apology:

*Dear—I . . . don't know what to call you? I want to say Prince Jahir
because that's what we used to call you, but that sounds juvenile,
doesn't it? And it's probably inaccurate. And insulting, possibly. Oh,
I'm doing this all wrong. How do I start my letters to you? Please tell
me so I know! Because I'd like to write letters to you.*

*No one **knows** that I'm writing to you, by the way. That's maybe
the best part. They're all already nose-deep in everything else. School.
Family stuff. Field trips. Our charity work. BOYS. I don't know if
any of them took you seriously when you said we should write you.
But I wanted to, and so here I am, and I haven't told **any** of them. I
hope you don't mind that I do want to write you. I mean, you could
have said it and not meant it, just to be polite. If you did, you can just
ignore this letter!*

*But I'm really writing for advice . . . because, like we said, we all
want to go into the medical profession, and I'd like to be a therapist.
And of course, you and Prince Manylegs have been therapists for
years now. But not hospital therapists. I want to help kits like us, of
course, but . . . I'm wondering what a general practice is like too. I hear
you have to choose pretty soon after you get to college, and we're not
that far from university now . . .*

Jahir let the data tablet sag to rest against his chest, and closed
his eyes, and smiled. If there was a suspicious wetness around
the lashes . . . surely he had earned the right, to find life wondrous, and beautiful, and so, so full of blessings.

CHAPTER 22

ASIHT'H'S PALLIATIVES FOR anxiety involved baking, work, and being around people, mostly Jahir. With the Eldritch gone, and his absence the reason for his anxiety, the Glaseah indulged in as many of the other strategies as possible. Baking was less fun without someone to eat the results, so he delivered a lot of care packages, or handed out cookies to his clients. Work he could do, though talking about why Jahir was gone to clients who expected to see them both kept calling attention to the fact that Jahir was off on some space station and not here. That left being around people, something he enjoyed anyway. He visited friends, ate out and struck up conversations with strangers, went to entertainments, and sat in the starbase's many parks.

He missed Jahir, though, with an ache like a missed heartbeat. He touched his chest now and then, feeling that skipped stroke. So he could not have asked for a better distraction than the one that landed on his doorstep two days into Jahir's trip.

"Kristyl?" Vasiht'h said, incredulous, having opened the door on her, and: "Gladdie? And . . ." A punch to the stomach, hard with memories. "Is that . . ."

"This is Brock," Kristyl said, scruffling the toddler's hair. "We just got back from adopting him."

"This is obviously a story I need to hear," Vasiht'h said, wide-eyed. "Can I interest you in scones?"

"Someplace with a playground would be best," Gladiolus said.

"Okay, then . . . French toast."

"I like French toast," Kristyl said. "We invented that, you know."

Vasiht'h laughed. "I do." And shut up the office for the morning.

———— ∞∞∞ ————

The diner with French toast did breakfast all day, and it was built around a central courtyard where kids could play while their parents ate. Vasiht'h watched the two women deliver the boy to the corner of the playground nearest them, fascinated by their interactions with each other, with the boy. Gladiolus seemed more carefree, excited; Kristyl, more serious, her gaze flicking here, there, with a hypervigilance Vasiht'h associated with new parents. When the two of them rejoined him, they did so holding hands.

Vasiht'h glanced at the hands, then at the boy. "Happy family?" he guessed.

"Completely unplanned one," Gladiolus said, ears splaying. "And if you'd asked me if I wanted to have a baby, I would have said I was far too young."

"People on Terra have babies far younger than either of us," Kristyl said, stirring cream into her coffee.

"It's not about when other people think they're ready," Gladiolus exclaimed. "It was about us being ready!"

"We were ready the moment someone needed us." Kristyl smiled at Vasiht'h. "You know how that goes."

"I do," Vasiht'h said. "But how did you know . . . what are you doing here? And how did that happen?"

"You did tell us several times that you worked on Starbase Veta," Gladiolus pointed out. "Where's your Eldritch anyway?"

"Retaking his licensing exam."

"Which he failed . . . because . . . he came after you?" Kristyl guessed, and laughed. "Of course. What else? Your story continues to be like some unbelievable fairy tale, arii."

Was he 'arii' to her? Hadn't they earned that from one another, after surviving the storm? "I won't deny it has its ridiculously dramatic moments."

Gladiolus grinned. "Ridiculously romantic-dramatic."

Vasiht'h laughed. "For people who are interested in seeing it that way, then . . . yes. I prefer to think of it as . . ." What did he think of it? "My very best friendship. My forever-friendship. Goddess-blessed."

"Amen," the Asanii murmured.

"So, your son . . . what happened to his family?" Vasiht'h said. "Hinichi are awfully clannish. I'm surprised he didn't end up with some aunt or uncle?"

"That's the thing," Kristyl said with a frown. "They *are* clannish, and these particular Hinichi had disowned Brock and his father. Can you believe that? I thought disinheriting was something out of Earth's ugly old past, but apparently some things are universal."

"You notice she doesn't take responsibility for disinheritage despite the laws of syllogistic inference."

Kristyl wrinkled her nose. "Being cruel is a personal choice. I can blame them completely for it. Anyway, Brock's father was one of the people who died in the storm, and when we found out that his family wasn't coming for him, Gladdie and I volunteered to take him back home."

"She volunteered," Gladiolus said, scanning the menu. "I just went along because I always do."

"And I especially wasn't going to let her wander off after Tsera Nova," Kristyl said. "We took Brock to his homeworld, which is a colony and not Hinichitii, and that's where we met his family and his family wanted nothing to do with him. So . . . we decided to rehome him. With us."

"And you're all right with that?" he said to the Asanii.

"He needed a family," Gladiolus said. She looked over the top of her menu. "You didn't see him, those first few weeks. He was so lost. And the longer he spent with us, the more he just . . . unfolded."

Vasiht'h looked from her to Kristyl. "I admit, I thought you two were young to be parents myself."

Gladiolus snorted. "That's not the half of it. Now she wants to open an orphanage."

"You do?"

"Why not?" Kristyl said easily. "I have more money than God. What's money for, if not to leave the world a better place?" She called, "Brock! Pancakes? Or bacon?"

The boy looked up and bared his teeth. "NOM."

"Right, bacon," Kristyl said. "Carnivores. No breadth in their diets." She shook her head sadly.

"Technically he's an omnivore like you," Gladiolus said. "Human DNA, you know."

"Still getting the blame for everything," Kristyl told Vasiht'h. "It's a crime against humanity."

Vasiht'h chuckled. "Don't worry, I'm sure you'll rise above it."

They spent an agreeable hour there, eating the diner's signature French toast, which was crusted in cocoa and sprinkled with cinnamon pecans. Brock had the bacon, messily but enthusiastically, before abandoning his plate to return to the playground where he was integrating well with the other kits. Vasiht'h hadn't specialized in child psychology, but the fact that the boy wasn't avoiding others was a good sign.

"So are the two—sorry three now—of you going to keep traveling?" Vasiht'h asked Gladiolus once they'd finished the last crumbs. Kristyl was on the playground, drifting after Brock. "I was never clear on what your plans were after your vacation."

"That would be because we weren't either," Gladiolus replied. "But for now I think we're going back to Earth. They could use the orphanage more than a Pelted world could. Or for all I know we'll start that there and then go on to do other things. Kristyl's mentioned those girls you told her about . . . maybe we'll stop over to see them and give them money too." She grinned. "I admit it's fun to be the plus-one of someone rich."

"Is it?" Vasiht'h asked, rueful.

"I love it!" Gladiolus chuckled. "I guess I could feel like I'm not contributing enough, but that assumes that money's the only thing people bring to relationships. But it's not. It's just one of many possible things, and all it accomplishes is making sure the two of you are all right, and can do things you want to do. Since Kristyl's got that covered, I figure my responsibilities are different."

"Oh?" Vasiht'h asked, interested. "And what do you think your responsibilities are?"

Gladiolus looked at the other woman for a long time, and her expression softened. "To love her," she said finally, "and forgive her for the things she feels like she's done, just by being born human. Because she does feel them. It's why she jokes about it so much." She glanced at Vasiht'h. "She's a lot more complicated than she looks on the outside."

"Aren't we all?"

"Oh no," Gladiolus said, laughing. "Some of us are complicated where everyone can see it. That's easy to handle. It's the ones who keep their complications squirreled away on the inside that are hard."

"Oh!" Vasiht'h exclaimed. And smiled, gentler. "Oh. Yes. I guess that's one way of looking at it."

Gladiolus nodded, twirling a lock of her hair between her fingers. "This thing with the storm hurt her, a lot. Me too. We'll be a long time figuring it out. When Brock's family didn't show up for him . . . and then when they wouldn't take him, it was like something imploded. She's a lot less exuberant now, which I miss. But she's also a lot more . . . focused, and that's . . . I can't decide if it's exciting or scary. Both. Because what couldn't she do, now that she's decided to do something?"

The thought of Kristyl on the loose in the Alliance with more money than a divinity and all her odd thought processes brought to bear on the task of making things better . . . "Yes. I can see that."

"Whatever she's going to do, I want to be there for the ride,"

Gladiolus said. "So that's what I'm going to do."

"Even if it means raising a toddler?"

Gladiolus laughed. "That's going to be the least of our adventures." Her expression softened. "But I admit, it's already better than I imagined it would be. And I wouldn't have tried it, had she not just . . . thrown herself into it, and asked me to go along."

"We need other people sometimes," Vasiht'h murmured.

Gladiolus shook her head. "We always need other people. Life would be hollow without them."

⬳⬱

That stayed with him in the days that followed, like a drifting rope of incense, and his anxiety quieted beneath the dense cloud of his thoughts. About needing people. About people being complicated. About knowing who you were without them, so you could understand what you had to offer when you were with them. About love, and adventures you would never have embarked on without someone to face them with you. About being happy with where you were, because you knew you were supposed to be there . . . even if other people would have been miserable had they been in your shoes. All four of them.

Vasiht'h cleaned, and baked, and savored his contentment, accepting it for what it was. And maybe this too would pass, like the emotional weather it was, but for now . . . for now it was perfect. Even more importantly, nothing he felt in the future would take away the fact that he'd felt this moment now; and this moment would become part of him forever. He was ready, then, when Jahir walked back into their apartment and set his bags down, and the mindline was suffused with the Eldritch's gladness to be home, and pleasure at the sight of him again, and yes . . . with the love that shaped their lives, the lives they'd willingly chosen, and the adventures it brought them, no matter how unexpected, or how difficult.

"Did it go well?" Vasiht'h asked, even though he knew the answer.

"It is done," the Eldritch replied.

Vasiht'h nodded, smiled up at him. "It's late, but I bet you haven't eaten. Should we have dinner?"

Jahir paused. "So long as it involves cake."

"Hah!" Vasiht'h laughed. "Now I know you love me."

"Was there ever any doubt, arii?"

"No," Vasiht'h said, satisfied. "Never."

CASE STUDIES

THESE VIGNETTES WERE originally serialized online after the first set of case studies (reproduced now in their entirety in the backmatter of *Dreamhearth*), and represent the later years of Vasiht'h and Jahir's practice. Readers with long memories will find references to the events in those studies in the final case study presented here.

ꟻINITE

NEITHER OF THEM BELIEVED their client could fit into their apartment, and yet at the scheduled time the door opened and nine feet of alien pressed between the jambs, feathers slowly popping out to frame the alien's body. And then, in a rush, the entire creature was in their common room, shaking out his wings and the vast train of his tail. At their disbelieving stare, he leaned toward them, showing them the gape of a toothed beak in what served his species for a smile, and said, "Narrow bones."

They did not force him to squeeze into their office.

Their client was an Akubi, one of the few true alien races of the Alliance, giant, bird-like creatures with horned heads and hints of saurian scale along the sides of their long, muscled necks and on their backs. Their particular visitor was male, the smaller and duller of the three sexes: the males were the hunters, and their feathers and hides came in camouflage colors of mahogany brown and dull gray with a faint gloss of iridescent purple. Their smaller bodies had evolved to navigate the cluttered canopies of their world's enormous trees, leaving the larger females to fly the skies and grow the spectacular plumage that attracted groups of males to feed their clutches.

While the Akubi in the Alliance were few, they made for

genial neighbors. They were amazing mimics—which meant their client spoke Universal better than Jahir had when he'd first gone to college on Seersana—and for all their true alien origin they were often less inscrutable than some of the stranger third generation engineered species, like the Phoenix. They had such stable temperaments that finding one on their appointment schedule had been unexpected. Once their visitor had settled on the floor, mantling wings so enormous Vasiht'h felt a breeze over his bare toes, they asked what had brought him by.

"It bothers me," the Akubi said, "that the sky is finite."

———∞∞∞———

Their client had just moved to the starbase, and to its central city, which had been built in a spherical bubble on the starbase's skin; half its globe faced the hollow interior and the other half faced outward, forming the commercial docks built, maintained and overseen by Fleet. The bubble was, of course, finite . . . but the "ceiling" of the bubble was very, very far away. The city-sphere itself was large enough not just for the existing habitations— and their attendant parks and water environments—but also for growth, expanding outward into broad flat fields of short grass. The city even had climate: not severe, of course, but enough variation in temperature to trick the fruiting trees in the greens-paces into giving evidence of seasons. Most days, a citizen of the starbase didn't even think that they were in an artificial environ-ment; the only external clue was the distant spindle that showed pale as a midday moon in the sky.

But it *was* finite. And for the Akubi, who'd freshly come from skies as broad as a true world, the knowledge that somewhere above him was a clear flexglass wall was enough to give rise to panic attacks. He'd heard that Jahir and Vasiht'h did work in dreams: since his subconscious was fueling his distress, he'd been hoping they could heal it directly.

———∞∞∞———

For two months, they trawled the dreams of a true-alien and

found them . . . astonishing. Not because they were unfathomable, but because they were: were fathomable, were real, were breathtaking in their immediacy. In dreams they flew alongside their client on vast dark wings, through pewter-colored clouds into forests shadowed in black and purple, through wet air smelling of something strange and yet familiar. They felt the tickle of their mustaches against their breasts as they hunted climbing prey, tucked wings close and dove. They tasted blood, and it was good, hot liquid on tongues, stinging the insides of their mouths to life. They felt the euphoria of breaching the canopy to the free air above and dancing there with the third sex, the waiting-sex that could be either male or female and spent much of their lives waiting for the environmental cues that caused the change.

It was not an idyllic life, but it was a real one, a primal one, and they heard it in their minds as a heartbeat as urgent and complex as a drum song.

But they could not heal their client of his fears.

"This is going nowhere," Jahir said, resting the side of his head against a hand. He was sitting at the end of their sofa and taking up even less space than usual on it, body language tightly constrained. "Not that the experience hasn't been intense, but I fear we're deriving more benefit from our sessions than our client is."

The mindline between them was sour as a underripe grapefruit. Vasiht'h loosened a mouth that had puckered in response, rubbed his cheek. "Maybe we're going at this all wrong. Maybe we should be trying exposure therapy."

"You want to make him fly at the barrier?" Jahir said.

Vasiht'h glanced up at his partner. "That might be a little extreme for a first try. But he's never actually seen the barrier. We could take him there. On the ground."

Jahir was silent, but the mindline hummed with the intensity of his concentration. It stopped abruptly and the Eldritch said, "So systematic desensitization, in vivo." He chuckled a little. "A bit straightforward for two espers who usually dream-walk to do their work."

Vasiht'h's mental shrug tasted like flat seltzer. "If a Med-image platform doesn't work, you might as well try a plain old scalpel."

— ⊗∞⊗ —

Teaching relaxation techniques to a giant alien bird proved more difficult than navigating his dreams, partially because Akubi were more naturally relaxed than any Pelted or humanoid species they'd worked with. Jahir brought a handful of sensors and used them to monitor their client's vitals, but they rarely fluctuated in response to the techniques they taught him. He learned them anyway, grinning at them with a turned face and an enormous yellow eye that seemed to glitter in amusement at their perplexity.

Once the client had control over the techniques, they brought him to the barrier. No one lived that far out from the center of the city and the starbase wall, so they were undisturbed: one bipedal humanoid, tall; one centauroid, squat; and one avian shape that dwarfed them both, standing together on a plain of short green grass where it ended at a thick clear wall. Through it, one could just see the exposed interior wall of the starbase, stretching away toward the limit of their vision.

The sensors reported no change in the client's heart-rate or breathing, no special excitation of the brain. The Akubi looked up at the wall and said simply, "I don't like it."

— ⊗∞⊗ —

They tried exposure therapy for several weeks, going so far as to send their client on a flight along the inside of the barrier. The Akubi navigated all these challenges with seeming equilibrium, but did not report a decrease in his anxiety. "The world should not have an edge," he said, to which Vasiht'h said privately to Jahir, "What can we say to that? He's right."

— ⊗∞⊗ —

Four months into their treatment of the alien, Jahir said, "This isn't working either."

"I've run out of ideas," Vasiht'h said, warming his hands on his mug of kerinne and trying not to look disgruntled. The mindline was littered with the detritus of his discontent, though. "What's left to try? How do you fix the unfixable alien? Of something that, in the end, is a reasonable anxiety? Artificial environments *are* untrustworthy."

"Natural ones are too," Jahir said, tired. "Frankly, Alliance engineering feels a great deal more solid to me than being on a planet without the benefit of high technology." He smiled a little. "Perhaps we should take him outside the starbase on an EVA tour. Allow him a respite from dealing with the finite. Give him back the natural world so he can breathe and enjoy himself for a while."

"A vacation," Vasiht'h said. "I could use one myself." At the tickle of amusement through the mindline, he finished, "But not EVA. That's a little too much reality for me."

"Should we make the suggestion?"

"Why not?" Vasiht'h said.

⌾⌾⌾

As was inevitable, the starbase's commercial docks had a space reserved for recreational EVA, far from the traffic routes of incoming and outgoing merchant vessels. There, for a reasonable fee, one could be fitted with a slimsuit, attached to a tether, and sent off to experience space in all its magnificence. Visitors could walk along the skin of the starbase or choose to float weightless, and several hours later return to the safety of their carefully maintained habitat. The Akubi thought their suggestion intriguing and agreed that being able to fly in any direction without fear of running out of space would be a relief. They offered to accompany him to the EVA area and wait for him to finish, and he agreed.

For an hour, they sat in the visitors' lounge, looking out the vast window at the stars and the people floating on the ends of their tethers. They did not see their client, and after some time decided to pass the time reading, the mindline warm between them with a patience that deepened when shared. When the hour was up, their client padded into the lounge and both of them stood. There was a stiffness in the alien's gait that they had not yet seen. The silence in the mindline was a held breath. And then the Akubi spoke.

"There is such a thing as too much space."

———— ∞ ————

They saw their client only one more time, several weeks later. The anxiety had ceased: confronted with the infinity outside the starbase, the city-sphere had begun to seem very agreeable to the Akubi—"Almost nestlike," he said. It was not how they'd expected to help him, but, as Vasiht'h observed a few days later, walking alongside Jahir on the way to their favorite café, "we rarely seem to know how to do what we do until it's done."

"Our clients usually have a better idea of what they need than we do," Jahir agreed. "It's often a matter of getting them to show us what it is."

"The Akubi, though . . . that's not really how it happened."

"No," Jahir said with a smile that tasted wry, like strong lemonade. "Sometimes none of us know what's going on until it's over."

———— ∞ ————

For weeks after, they had trouble drinking anything cold, and one or both of them would wake from dreams of flight through a sky neither too endless . . . nor too small. Just enough space, for life.

Piano

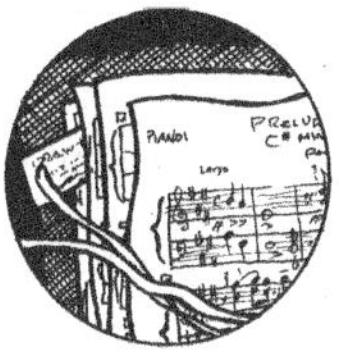

THEY HAD SEASON TICKETS for very nearly every cultural offering in the area—partly because of the mutual fascination that had driven them into xenopsychology, and partly because Jahir thought exposure to their clients' arts helped make sense of their dreams and the symbols they used to shape their personal narratives. It was a rare week that didn't see them making at least one outing to a concert, a play, an exhibit or festival; they were very well-educated on the many cultures they lived alongside.

But the famous concert pianist who was making an Alliance-wide tour was special even by their standards. Vasiht'h shook out his best sari, a shimmering red silk edged in gold, and pleated it over his lower body, carefully spreading its tails over his second back between the wings. Even Jahir, who normally did everything possible to efface himself in a crowd, dressed with such stark elegance that Vasiht'h was taken aback.

Drawing on white gloves, his partner said, "Shall we?"

They went to the concert hall, two among hundreds who'd been fortunate enough to procure tickets for the third and final performance the pianist was giving on Starbase Veta. At the proper time, the audience was seated, silent and attentive. There was a piano on stage, the high gloss finish of its upswept lid gleaming: a piano and nothing else. Vast screens hung above it, broadcasting close views of the stool, the beige and black keys, and the closed folder with the paper score on the stand.

The woman who entered was human, brown hair swept up and pinned in place with two black sticks. Her understated black gown made her seem kin to the instrument as she sat at it, tucking the stool closer and opening the folder.

And then she played, and for two hours held them all fast in their seats.

There was a reception afterward in one of the adjoining festival halls, as was typical for concerts. Sometimes the two of them attended to mingle, for they were fairly well known; sometimes they went home early. And sometimes they lingered if they'd been deeply affected by the performance, enough to need time to step back out of the world the art had created for them. So Vasiht'h was not surprised that they stayed for the pianist's reception.

He *was* surprised to find the artist approaching them. On her final night of a sold-out run, he hadn't expected to meet her in person amid the many fans waiting for her attention. But he thought that they were perhaps more noticeable than usual, particularly Jahir. His black coat might have been designed by an Alliance tailor, but he was the only Eldritch filling one, and his hair glimmered beneath the high lights like a polished pearl.

"Madam," Jahir said to her. "You have a deft touch. Your treatment of the dynamics in the final piece was particularly sublime."

Surprised, she said, "You flatter me, sir. Are you a musician then?"

"A hobbyist, merely," he said. "But educated enough to appreciate your talents. You play like an angel."

She flushed prettily. "I only wish," she said. "But as far as I've come I still have far to go."

Jahir introduced himself and Vasiht'h, who smiled at the pianist and complimented her skill, if with less erudition than his partner. And Vasiht'h watched and listened to the ensuing conversation. It was typical of them both and of Jahir in particular, his habit of asking questions that gave her an opportunity to talk about herself—while skillfully deflecting attention from himself.

But the woman only took that opportunity half the time. The other half, she made attempts at learning something about Jahir. At one point, talking about the second piece with its difficult key combinations, she laughed and said, "I'm sure you wouldn't have had any trouble at all . . . you have wonderful hands. No wonder you play."

Jahir demurred. The woman bade them stay and slipped off through the crowd. Watching her go, Vasiht'h said, "She's flirting with you."

"I know," Jahir answered, the mindline gray and low, like fog.

When she returned, she had the folder with the score. "If you'd like?" she asked. "A memento? I can sign it."

"We'd be honored," Jahir said.

She set the folder on a side table and put her name to it before handing it to him. He thanked her for the evening, she lowered glittering lashes and smiled, and then she returned to her public.

"She gave you her commtag," Vasiht'h observed. "Probably her private one."

"I know," Jahir said, "I was watching." He turned toward the door and began heading that way.

/You could call her,/ Vasiht'h said, reverting to the mindline for privacy.

/And why would I do that?/

Vasiht'h said nothing, though his suggestion took form between them, something warm and intimate that smelled of wine and was lit by dim candles. Jahir stopped and looked over his shoulder at him, then shook his head, a minute twitch of his chin.

"It would accomplish nothing," he said, quiet, and resumed walking.

They left the reception hall and found themselves in the

echoing silence of the antechamber. Vasiht'h said, "Is it because she's human?" Tinted in the mindline: *living too fast, dying too young.*

"No," Jahir said. "It's because what we both love would come between us."

That perplexed Vasiht'h enough that he stopped, frowning. Jahir did too, turning toward him.

"You play?" Vasiht'h said finally.

"I was taught," Jahir said at last. At Vasiht'h's frown, he said, "Arii? You know I love music."

"Of course I know," Vasiht'h said, for he'd observed his partner's devotion to it since they'd met in college. "But loving music doesn't necessarily mean you can play. Lots of people never learn, or they learn and never go anywhere with it. You play? Piano?"

Jahir inclined his head.

"Then why don't you? Ever play?" Vasiht'h asked, startled.

"I just don't," Jahir said, and resumed walking.

Vasiht'h hurried in front of him, blocking the way with the side of his body.

"What?" Jahir asked.

/*The concert hall is empty,*/ Vasiht'h said, where the mindline could put forth the strength of his suggestion.

Jahir hesitated, but Vasiht'h didn't move. And eventually, inevitably, Jahir turned toward the empty hall.

Together they advanced down the aisle, footfalls small in the vast space . . . climbed the stairs to the stage where the piano waited. Jahir stood alongside it, staring at it for so long Vasiht'h feared he would rethink the entire thing . . . and then the Eldritch sat on the stool and set the folder on the stand. He opened it to the second piece, calmly unbuttoned his gloves, and stripped them off his fingers.

"If you'll turn the pages when I nod?" he said formally.

"Of course," Vasiht'h said, mystified by this transformation of a man he'd known for years. He stepped up beside the piano and straightened.

"Thank you," Jahir said, eyes rising to the first line, growing intent.

And then he played a piece that Vasiht'h knew very well he'd never seen before. Jahir's mind was dense with it, with the novelty of it, with the excitement and concentration, and there was a quality to his thoughts like running water . . . as if the Eldritch had opened a channel between eyes and fingers, and nothing interrupted it. The first nod came so swiftly Vasiht'h almost missed it, but after that he turned each page with alacrity and growing astonishment. The Eldritch played the piece very differently from the pianist, but he played it flawlessly, and a song that had been wistful in human hands was elegiac in his.

When he finished, he stretched his fingers and rested them in his lap, then looked at his partner . . . waiting.

"How long?" Vasiht'h asked, low.

"I've had lessons since I was old enough to put my hands on an instrument," Jahir answered.

"So . . . several of that woman's lifetimes," Vasiht'h said.

"Very probably." Jahir rose. He pulled the gloves back on and closed the folder, tucking it beneath an arm.

"How can you enjoy it so much?" Vasiht'h asked as Jahir pushed the stool back under the piano. "Everyone must sound like an amateur."

Jahir chuckled. "She was no amateur, arii."

"You know what I mean."

Jahir smiled, one of the most Eldritch smiles Vasiht'h had seen on him, melancholic and distant. "I do, yet." He gestured for Vasiht'h to precede him to the stairs. "How can I not enjoy it? What she's done is frankly miraculous." At Vasiht'h's quizzical glance, he said, "I have had lifetimes of practice. She's had a third of one. And yet she sounds like that?"

"Oh," Vasiht'h said softly. Then he nodded. "Yes. I can see that."

Together they left the hall. Halfway home, Vasiht'h said, "You should play more often."

Jahir glanced down at him, then back at the path. "Maybe. Maybe I will."

Swimming

THEY BOTH HAD THEIR preferred form of exercise. Vasiht'h liked walking, one of the few activities his poorly-designed body was suited for. There was a park near their office that pleased them both, and when Vasiht'h wanted company Jahir paced him beneath the marble oaks, taking a single step for two of Vasiht'h's paws. When he didn't want company, his partner left him to wander, and that was good too: even parted, the mindline ensured they were never alone, not really.

The park also had a community pool linked to the water environment maintained for the city's aquatic residents, and while it was large it was also inevitably busy: not only did it attract families who came for recreation and training athletes, but also people who wanted a chance to talk in sign with their Naysha friends, or researchers studying the mysterious Platies.

Jahir preferred swimming despite the constant bustle. He wore a full-length bodysuit to prevent any accidental contact with other swimmers and their unguarded minds, and against the cold which he felt more strongly than both Pelted and humans. Usually when they arrived there was a free lane for his laps, but if they were all busy he would wait cliently for one to open and never begrudge the time. Vasiht'h would observe him from a distance while the Eldritch sat at the pool's edge, and his mind when he looked at the water was filled with the reflection of light off waves, with the Now of being immersed.

Strangely, given the utter uselessness of his body in water, Vasiht'h also liked swimming. He usually brought an inflatable for buoyancy and clung to it while his poorly balanced body paddled along under the surface. When Jahir was done with his laps he sometimes glided beneath the lane marker and reappeared nearby, sleek as a white otter, and together they'd float, sharing their enjoyment of the water through the mindline. Vasiht'h loved those times: his partner's mind, clear and clean and near, tickled through with air bubbles that felt like champagne and peace and pleasure. But they rarely had the opportunity to swim together, for Jahir avoided it unless he was sure they would have enough space.

One day when they'd had left the pool and were changing in the room provided for it, Vasiht'h asked him, "Is it so bad? You take more precautions not to touch people when you're swimming than you do otherwise."

"People don't have as much control over their movements in water as they do on land," Jahir said, stripping the bodysuit off. "They're more likely to pitch into you, and it's an environment where people come to play so telling them not to is unkind. The suit helps, so I wear it."

Remembering the taste of his partner's mind while contemplating the pool, Vasiht'h said, "But it's worse in the water somehow, being touched."

Jahir glanced at him over his shoulder, towel sagging in his hands. Then he resumed drying off. "Yes. Swimming clears my mind."

"And the clearer your mind, the louder the contact is when you're touched," Vasiht'h guessed.

Jahir said, quiet, "I value the calm." He wrung out his braided hair and dressed, and as he did Vasiht'h sampled the ripples that ran the length of the mindline. The acceptance of what was had a flavor, like the salt in ocean water . . . but he could feel a hint of wistfulness hidden behind it: the sunset seen from under constant waves.

———⊛———

They'd had a client from one of the other spheres studding the surface of the starbase, in this case one of the agriculture/aquaculture bubbles. Her need had been brief, a response to a trauma they'd helped her weather, but she remembered Vasiht'h and had been delighted to help him with his request. Two months later, then, when they had a weekend off, Vasiht'h led his partner onto one of the bullet trains that ran the girth of the starbase through its dense external wall and they whiled away a pleasant few hours eating in the highly-regarded dining car and then star-gazing through the clear tunnel the track ran through. They disembarked at the agriculture sphere's station, where Vasiht'h took a mystified Jahir over a Pad and to the facility recommended by their former client.

As was typical of Pelted engineering, the fish, seaweed and other aquacultural products used by the rest of the starbase were supplied by an artificially created, carefully maintained but otherwise entirely real ocean. Where the land used for crops met that ocean there were miles of beaches, and as was inevitable, someone had sectioned off part of the coastline and created a resort, including carefully sculpted grottos with ocean inlets.

These personal pools could be rented. It had bitten deeply into Vasiht'h's personal account, but he had booked what he could afford without any regret. He'd done so based on viseos of the prospective site . . . but he was not prepared for the reality of it, the brine and foliage smell, the distant roar of the surf, the utter calm of the water, so clear and bright a blue he could see straight through the surface to the sandy bottom.

Jahir stood at the edge of the water, staring. His absolute silence hissed through the mindline, wiping it clean.

"For me?" he said at last.

"No one else can use it for the next three hours," Vasiht'h said, deeply satisfied. "Unless you count the fish." He nodded toward the small building artfully hidden by climbing vines and lush tropical plants. "There are towels in there, shoes, that sort of thing, if you need them. I even brought your bodysuit, if you want it."

"I don't," Jahir said, still staring.

The mindline shivered with the vastness of the Eldritch's internal quiet. To Vasiht'h it tasted like incredulity and joy, and it washed down his back like sun-warmed water. The feeling was so powerful his back arched in response to it, wings mantling. A perfect gift, he thought. He smiled and turned to go.

"Vasiht'h?"

He paused, looked over his shoulder.

"If there's an inflatable in that shack you might come back in a couple of hours."

Vasiht'h hesitated. "I bought it so you could be alone, arii, because you can't be otherwise."

"I know," Jahir said, his smile like a sunrise on waves. "But come anyway, if you'll enjoy it."

"If you're sure—"

"I am. Two hours is long enough."

"All right," Vasiht'h said. "I'll be back then."

And he was. He spent a happy hour sunning himself on the rock in the middle of the pool, or paddling around his floating partner, and the mindline relaxed, expanded outward, lapping like the ocean at the strand. There was in fact an inflatable . . . but no bodysuit made an appearance, and if they brushed against one another, it mattered not at all.

WET

"THANK GOD YOU'VE COME," the healer-assist said. "They won't listen to me. I know what I'm seeing, but they're so sure nothing like this happens 'in civilized space'—" The human halted abruptly, hand at his ear.

Jahir and Vasiht'h stopped simultaneously, on the same foot even. The mindline had intensified when they'd stepped off the Pad into the bustle of the acute care facility at the hospital, so much that their bodies had synchronized in response. Their guide was listening to a telegem earbud and the moment its news accelerated his heart-rate they were both already moving to follow him. "Quick, he's seizing. This way!"

They ran, Vasiht'h's footfalls a quadruple drumbeat to Jahir's longer strides. They passed in a blur, pale tall Eldritch with hair a white flag, centauroid Glaseah, glossy black fur reflecting the bright hall lights. Vasiht'h's clearances for the hospital was over a year old but everyone recognized Jahir, and no alarm sounded when they sprinted after the man who'd summoned them and into a room where another human was flailing hard enough to have induced the halo-arch to withdraw to keep him from injuring himself against it. Jahir was already shouting over the chaos "DON'T SEDATE HIM, NO SEDATIVES!" when he crashed into

the side of the bed and reached for the body. Vasiht'h pulled back
to avoid touching the patient, friction burning his paw pads and
haunches almost grazing the floor.

"Who the hell—"

"What is he—"

"He's cleared, he's a specialist!"

"His vitals—"

All of it vanished as Jahir dropped into the man's mind like
a plummet. The mindline shot after him, his anchor to the real
world, and he trusted it and Vasiht'h to haul him out. If they
didn't, he'd die with the addict, because wet left no survivors.

⸙

"What the hell are you doing?" the attending physician said, hos-
tility defrayed by the sudden change in the statistics still being
reported by the halo-arch. "And how did you get here? I know
him, but who are you and what's he doing here and not over in
general admission?"

Vasiht'h flexed his toes, slowly, slowly. The sensations from
the mindline he shared with Jahir were distant flickers, too sick-
eningly quick for normalcy, and feeling them brought back terrible memories . . . but his task in this required him to be calm in
body and spirit, so he breathed deeply, concentrated on letting
his anxieties fade. Before he'd finished, the healer-assist who'd
summoned them spoke.

"I asked them in. They're xenotherapists, they've seen addic-
tion cases before."

"This is not—"

"This is a klaidopin case," Vasiht'h said before the physician
could barrel on.

"You mean we've got a wet addict?" one of the other assists
said, startled.

The physician scowled. "So HEA Rogers said, but there was
no specific evidence, and this is not a part of the Alliance known
for street drugs. If you hear hoofbeats in Texas, you don't assume
zebras."

"Wet gives a look," the healer-assist said stubbornly. "I've seen it before. This patient has it."

"A look," the physician repeated.

"And a feel," Vasiht'h said. "Which we could sense from across the room." Which was, Goddess save him, the absolute truth. He'd seen enough wet cases to know one after that benighted residency he'd insisted Jahir accept.

The physician frowned at the patient, whose body was limp under Jahir's hands. "What is he doing, then?"

"Bringing him out of the episode," Vasiht'h said, flexing his toes again. The claws pricked out. "We're linked espers. We work with people's dreams; it's given us a lot of practice dealing with the subconscious mind."

"And is that what's causing the seizure?"

"No," Vasiht'h said, suppressing his anxiety with difficulty. "This isn't a dream or a psychosis. It's a self-destructing brain. There's no negotiating with it. It's like a spinning gun emptying itself. The best you can hope for is to grab it without being shot."

Flashes of color. Light. Sound. Utterly nonsensical. Jahir fell into it, head tucked down and arms protecting it from the barrage. The battery was physical, as far as his consciousness was concerned. Worse than blows. Like being sideswiped with knives, some of them slicing, others bruising but promising worse. He drew in a deep breath and exploded outward, willing order onto chaos. The strain of it was winnowing. He never knew, throwing himself into a dying mind, if this one would be too far along for him to help—or make it out.

He pushed. The mind pushed back, trying to overwrite him, to make him undifferentiated from it, to make him as fast, as disordered, as frenzied and senseless as it was. He refused. He breathed out a white calm.

Be still.

NOISE

Be quieted.

LIGHT
Be calm.
EVERYWHERE EVERY WHICH WHERE GO THERE GO
HERE NOW EVERYTHING EVERY EVERY EVERY
It was always his hope that the first attempt would work.
When it didn't, he reversed . . . and drew the excess energy into
himself, and with it, the disease.

The patient's vitals abruptly stabilized.

"What the hell?" the physician murmured, but Vasiht'h was
already diving for the bed. He dragged Jahir off it bodily and
wrapped his arms and forepaws around his partner, tucking his
head against Jahir's in time to catch it as it fell limp. With a knife
made of anger and fear he cut the bond between the patient and
his partner and dove into the horrible reflection impressed on
Jahir's mind, into disorder and meaninglessness and fury. But
unlike Jahir he was fighting on familiar ground, and he had
his long history with the Eldritch to call on, years and years of
working with intertwined minds until some part of them reso-
nated with one another. When he reached, when he made himself
the center, the spinning slowly stopped, the colors softened, and
the noise fell away, until he could feel Jahir's arms around his
upper back, smell the sweat on the Eldritch's brow.

"All here?" he said, low.

"All here," Jahir answered, hoarse.

"We need a recovery room," Vasiht'h said, ignoring Jahir's
weak denial, a bare wash through the mindline.

Half an hour later, Jahir was holding a cup of hot tea in a quiet
room with a fish tank embedded in one wall. Vasiht'h was sitting
on the floor beside him, legs stretched and toes digging into the
floor. The physician had joined them, taking the chair across
from them.

"He seems to be stable for now. We didn't have to sedate

him."

"You can't sedate him," Jahir said. "Sedation kills them." He cleared his throat. "There is no stopping the process. The moment he overdosed, his fate was sealed."

"I don't know much about klaidopin," the physician admitted. "But it can't possibly be that cut and dried. Is this withdrawal? Can we address the symptoms?"

"That's what you were trying to do before we got here, isn't it?" Vasiht'h asked.

Jahir shook his head, hair shifting against his throat. His eyes were closed. "The withdrawal symptoms are irrelevant. By the time you have to worry about them, it's too late. The brain's compromised."

"No one's ever been able to mitigate the damage?"

"No," Jahir said, and opened his eyes. "He has three days, maybe two."

The physician studied him. "Whatever you did seems to have cost you a great deal."

"It does," Vasiht'h said before Jahir could say otherwise. "It always does. It's why we don't work acute cases."

"And you say he'll die?" the physician continued.

"Three days," Jahir murmured. "Maybe."

"Then why did you intervene?" the physician said. "If it was today or three days from now, why waste yourself on it?"

"To give you those three days," Jahir said, looking up at him without lifting his head. "No one's ever been able to mitigate the damage. But someone, someday, might find out how."

The physician sat back in his chair. None of them spoke for several long moments. Then he stood. "You can stay until you're ready to go. And thank you for your assistance." He paused. "I may ask for your help again. If that's all right."

"We'd be glad to help, anytime," Jahir said. "And you're welcome."

The two said nothing to one another after the physician left, but Jahir liberated a hand from the mug to rest it on the back of Vasiht'h's shoulder. Through it their sense of one another in the mindline intensified until the aura of the hospital receded.

———∞———

The healer-assist checked on them later. "Need more tea?"

"No," Jahir said, rousing himself with a sigh. "Thank you for calling us in."

"It was an act of courage to go around the doctor," Vasiht'h added.

The man snorted, sitting on the chair the physician had vacated. "If a doctor tells you a zebra's a horse, it's not courage to tell him he's wrong. Besides, he's not all bad. You gave him something to do, didn't you?"

Jahir started. "Did he tell you?"

The man guffawed. "No. But I haven't been going to the two of you for my problems for a year without knowing how you work. You always give me something to work on so I feel like I have some power over something, like I can do something productive, right? It helps me, so it'll help him. Us professional healers are all alike." He smiled. "So what did you give him?"

"The task of looking for a cure for wet-related brain damage," Jahir said dryly.

The healer-assist whistled. "Well, guess a guy's gotta have ambitions. You two need anything else?"

"No, we'll be leaving in a few minutes," Vasiht'h said firmly.

"Daley?" Jahir said. "Where did this patient come from?"

"No clue," the healer-assist said. "Someone dumped him on our doorstep and left without giving us his name. He had a standard jumpsuit on. No patches or names on it. I'm betting he came off one of the transients at the dock. Some independent freighter captain, maybe, getting rid of a problem. "

"That wouldn't surprise me," Jahir murmured. "If you would . . . be sure to inform Fleet. They'll want to know."

"I will."

"Thank you, Daley."

"See you in two weeks," Vasiht'h added.

The healer-assist paused at the door. "Want me to tell you

when he passes?"

Vasiht'h said "No" at the same time Jahir said, "Please." They looked at one another and Vasiht'h sighed, relenting. Jahir said, "I'd like to know."

──── ❧ ────

They saw their clients as normal for the following two days, but both were aware of the silence that lingered in the mindline, the awkwardness in their interactions. They no longer moved in lock-step; they were not even aware enough of one another's physical bodies to avoid occasionally bumping into one another. When the call from the hospital came Jahir intercepted it, accepted the news, and then disappeared into the kitchen. Ten minutes later he brought a single mug of steaming kerinne to the common room where Vasiht'h was reading a book on his data tablet.

"For me?" Vasiht'h said, taking it.

"I'm sorry," Jahir said.

Vasiht'h looked away. "I . . . I am too. Just the memory of that stint we did in Heliocentrus—"

"I know," Jahir said. "And I remain sorry to this day. Sorry that I didn't listen to you, and sorry that we went through it."

"But not sorry for the experience," Vasiht'h said.

"No," Jahir answered softly. "I learned too much about people. And about myself." He smiled. "And about you too, and where we both belong."

Vasiht'h sighed out, slowly, the steam blowing off the surface of the drink. "I guess the patient died."

"Just now," Jahir said, sitting on the floor beside him, knees up and arms resting on them. Their shoulders were just touching.

Vasiht'h swallowed. "Every time you did that, arii, back when it was new to us . . . all those dying people . . ." He flexed his fingers on the mug. "Every time you did it, I knew you weren't going to come back."

Jahir met his eyes, then leaned over and rested his brow against his partner's. /I can't make any promises/ became /I know/ became /I love you because you have to try/ and neither of them bothered to untangle it.

"Go get a cup of coffee," Vasiht'h said. "And let's do something normal for the night."

"Gladly," Jahir said.

THE CHRISTMAS TREE

T HERE IS A TREE ON OUR doorstep," Jahir observed.

"There *is* a tree on our doorstep," Vasiht'h agreed, coming to a halt. On the threshold of their combined office/living space was some kind of evergreen in a pot, chest-high . . . to Vasiht'h anyway, the shorter of the two.

"Why is there a tree on our doorstep?" Jahir asked after a moment.

"Your guess," Vasiht'h said, "is as good as mine."

They did not discover the provenance of their unexpected gift until after they'd brought it inside and settled down with warmed ceramic mugs . . . of kerinne for Vasiht'h, who liked the creamed cinnamon drink common to the Alliance, and of spiced cider for Jahir, who was feeling the cold of the season more than his Pelted companion, as always. It was not an unusual way for them to spend their free evenings together once the holiday season began . . . with the humanoid Eldritch casually seated on the couch, dressed in layers that did nothing to detract from the low-gravity length of his limbs, and his centauroid partner on the floor, forelegs stretched in front of him and paws crossed at the wrist.

"So this is from that Hinichi client we had that while back," Vasiht'h said, reading the information scanned off the tree's virtual tag on his data tablet. "The one with the adopted sister we helped."

"A tree," Jahir repeated.

"As a gift for the holidays," Vasiht'h said, reading off the tablet. "Hinichi have the custom of decorating trees for Christmas, which they evidently took with them during the Exodus when the Pelted originally fled Earth."

"So it's a human custom," Jahir said. His tone was peculiar, and through the psychic mindline they shared Vasiht'h could sense a taste he didn't recognize, smell something like their evergreen but mustier, like the duff of a forest floor.

"For some humans anyway," Vasiht'h said. "Not all of them celebrated Christmas even before the project that saw the Pelted engineered. Also, according to the database humans stopped decorating trees for Christmas not long after the Exodus. The custom died out everywhere except in small pockets, most notably among the Moon colonists. Humanity didn't resume the Christmas tree habit until after they met back up with us and saw the Hinichi doing it. Of course, the Hinichi decorate them with paper prayers . . . apparently humans used to use glass balls, or miniature toys, or food."

"Food?" Jahir asked, his bemusement in the mindline tasting like seltzer water, busy and curious.

"That's what it says," Vasiht'h said. "Popcorn or candy."

Together they looked at their unexpected tree.

"So what do we do with it?" Jahir asked at last.

"Decorate it?" Vasiht'h suggested.

"With what?" the Eldritch said. "We have neither glass balls nor miniature toys. And putting food on a tree doesn't strike me as . . . hygienic."

A considering silence. They nursed their drinks, studying the inscrutable fir.

"I guess we'll think of something," Vasiht'h said.

"Oh, you have a tree this year!" one of their regular clients exclaimed. She was a Harat-Shar who came to curl up on their couch and rest, and really it was all she needed . . . time away from work and the complexities of her many relationships. Vasiht'h usually tucked her in; she liked the room cold and two or three warm blankets tucked up over shoulders patterned with bold ocelot spots. "But it's naked!"

/Trust a Harat-Shar to put it that way,/ Vasiht'h muttered through the mindline, and Jahir answered with a wry amusement like underripe peaches.

"We aren't certain how to decorate it," Jahir said as she walked past, staring over her shoulder at it. "As we haven't yet had a tree."

"So you don't have any trimmings!" she exclaimed.

"I fear not," Jahir agreed as she stretched herself out on the couch.

"That's no good!" she said, and then firmly, "And it should be fixed."

The following day, they received another box on their doorstep. This one contained a little carved miniature of two Harat-Shariin children, fluffy toddlers mottled with ocelot and leopard spots, exclaiming over a tiny wooden horse.

"Oh," Vasiht'h whispered, surprise softening the word through the mindline until it became diffuse and gentle, like mist. "Beautiful!" He offered it to Jahir, who lifted it off his partner's palm by the hanger.

"This one," Jahir said, "goes at eye level." And feeling the amusement coloring the mist in the mindline, added, "Your eye level."

Their next client was a Hinichi wolfine, different from the one who'd left them the tree, who saw it in its pot in the corner and said, "By glory, a paw fir! A real one?" He leaned over and sniffed it and said, "Oh yes, a real paw fir. I hear they've been growing different kinds of evergreens over on the farms for the holidays, but I didn't know they'd gotten any from Hinichitii."

"A paw fir?" Vasiht'h asked, puzzled.

"Oh yes," their client said, sitting on the couch and resting his elbows on his knees. He chuckled. "Named because the fronds aren't prickly. They're soft, like the fur that grows between the toes of the digitigrade Hinichi. The name is a terrible pun, but it stuck. Paw fir. Paw fur. You see?"

"I wish I hadn't," Vasiht'h muttered while Jahir hid a laugh in the mindline that sounded like sleigh bells.

"I'll have to get you a book for it," the Hinichi said, grinning. "I haven't had a tree of my own since I left home as a stripling. But a paw fir should have a prayer book."

"You don't have to—" Jahir began.

"Nonsense," the Hinichi said. "You two keep me from living surly and sad. It's the least I can do."

A Hinichi prayer book was the size of Vasiht'h's palm with soft cream parchment pages, all blank. It had a loop for a hook, which their client had clipped on for them. Since Jahir hung the first, Vasiht'h hung this second . . . though he got a stepstool to do so. "Eye level," he said, much to Jahir's amusement. "For Eldritch."

One of the two, Harat-Shar or Hinichi, must have spread the word that the pair had a Hinichi Christmas tree—a naked Hinichi Christmas tree—because after that it was a rare day that they didn't find one package (or several) on their doorstep. An Asanii colleague sent them a sun-and-moon ornament, prompting them to consider the multiculturalism implied by an ornament themed on one world's religion meant for another's holiday. A former Phoenix client sent them a downy feather the length of Jahir's smallest finger beaded with a loop, accompanied by a note offering it in trade for the single Eldritch hair he'd found in the nest they'd made him. Gifts from the various Fleet officers they'd helped ranged from tiny solidigraphic star charts to Fleet sigils to genuine Terran carved fancies, all the way from Earth. Most of their gifts came from residents of the starbase . . . but they were startled to receive packages from former clients who'd left the starbase, either to take up residency elsewhere or to resume work with merchants or liners.

There was a day when Jahir came home first and Vasiht'h found him in their common room with a delicately painted ornament shaped like sheet music, a gift from a client who had come to them with an unresolvable sorrow, loving music and having no talent. The mindline tasted like tears and Vasiht'h left his partner alone with it. He would have liked similar treatment when he received a glass ball with dancing Glaseahn kits in it from the woman whose propositions he'd rejected, but gave in to the inevitable teasing about the persistence of his would-be suitor with good grace, because in all candor it was rather funny. In an embarrassing sort of way.

They did not think much of the decorating. They took turns hanging the gifts, and it was difficult to find a place at first because there were so many naked branches, and then it was difficult because there were so few. Neither of them realized how full the fir had become until one of their clients, leaving, said, "Now that's a proper-looking tree."

———— ∞∞∞ ————

"It is, you know," Vasiht'h said later that evening, sitting in front of it with his foreleg paws crossed and a warm mug in his hand . . . kerinne again, if spiced with a little nutmeg. "A proper tree. Maybe we should do this every year."

Looking at the ornaments, Jahir said, "I don't think we can't."

Even with the mindline for help Vasiht'h had to work through that one, but once he had he agreed with the sentiment. The gifts deserved display. "There is one problem," he said at last.

"And what is that?" Jahir said over his warmed wine.

"If this keeps up, we're going to need a much taller tree," Vasiht'h said.

"Arii," Jahir said dryly, "if this keeps up, we're going to need a taller ceiling."

———❧———

That night, after Jahir had gone to bed, Vasiht'h slipped from his sleeping couch and into the common room. He fetched the step-stool and set his forefeet on the topmost step and one hind leg on the bottom. At eye-level for Eldritch, he hung a slim mirrored icicle. Jahir spoke very little of his life before the Alliance, and of his upbringing as an Eldritch almost not at all. But years of sharing the mindline had taught Vasiht'h how to listen to the undercurrents in it, the symbols that his comments evoked on his partner's end of the line. And he had not been insensible to some of the glimpses he'd gotten of trees . . . alien trees, tall and stern and musty-scented, damp with snow and strung with mirrors like daggers to catch the light of the stars at midwinter.

"Happy holidays," Vasiht'h whispered, "my friend." And the words drifted down the mindline, and in a slumberous mind inspired gentle dreams of holidays on a world long abandoned, but never fully left.

Appendices

*C*ONTAINING A RECIPE, *information about the species of the Alliance, author sketches, acknowledgments, a rundown on other Pelted stories, and the author's biographical data.*

BRIEF GLOSSARY

Alet (ah LEHT): "friend," but formal, as one would address a stranger. Plural is *aletsen*.

Arii (ah REE): "friend," personal. An endearment. Used only for actual friends. Plural is *ariisen*. Additional forms include *ariihir* ("dear brother") and *ariishir* ("dear sister").

Dami (DAH mee): "mom," in Tam-leyan. Often used among other Pelted species.

Fin (FEEN): a unit of Alliance currency. Singular is deprecated *finca*, rarely used.

Hea (HEY ah): abbreviation for Healer-assist.

Kara (kah RAH): "child". Plural is *karasen*.

Tapa (TAH pah): "dad," in Tam-leyan. Often used among other Pelted species.

MANGO PINEAPPLE FRUITY DRINK

HOW COULD I NOT PUT IN a recipe for a tropical drink at the back of this book? Vasiht'h must have had dozens! Here then is a refreshing slushie for you to enjoy while reading (or since you've already made it to the back of the book, re-reading) *Dreamstorm.*

MANGO PINEAPPLE FRUITY DRINK
From the Jaguar Kitchen

- 1/3 cup frozen mango chunks
- 1/3 cup frozen pineapple chunks
- 1 small piece, fresh ginger
- mango juice or lemonade crushed ice

You will need a blender for this slushie! Throw the mango and pineapple chunks together in the blender cup, and a small (and I do mean small) knob of fresh ginger, peeled. If your tolerance for ginger is high, you can experiment, but fresh ginger is potent! Respect the ginger!

Once you've thrown in the solid ingredients, fill the blender cup to the fill line with either 1. mango juice; 2. lemonade; or 3. watered down versions of either if you want it less sweet.

Blend until smooth; sample to make sure all of it tastes good to you. Then either add ice and blend again if you want more of a smoothie feel, or crush the ice separately and shake them together for something a little more like a slushie.

If you are feeling virtuous, you could probably throw some kale or spinach in this, but honestly there is nothing healthy about this drink, it's solid sugar. Have your salad on the side and go for broke! You can also mess with the proportions; I love mango, so I tend to go mango-happy, but you might prefer the bite of the pineapple and want more of that. These days I don't measure it at all, I just eyeball it.

However you make it, I hope you enjoy!

The Species of
The Alliance

THE ALLIANCE IS MOSTLY composed of the Pelted, a group of races that segregated and colonized worlds based (more or less) on their visual characteristics. Having been engineered from a mélange of uplifted animals, it's not technically correct to refer to any of them as "cats" or "wolves," since any one individual might have as many as six or seven genetic contributors: thus the monikers like "foxine" and "tigraine" rather than "vulpine" or "tiger." However, even the Pelted think of themselves in groupings of general animal characteristics, so for the ease of imagining them, I've separated them that way.

The Pelted

The Quasi-Felids: The Karaka'An, Asanii, and Harat-Shar comprise the most cat-like of the Pelted, with the Karaka'An being the shortest and digitigrade, the Asanii being taller and plantigrade, and the Harat-Shar including either sort but being based on the great cats rather than the domesticated variants.

The Quasi-Canids: The Seersa, Tam-illee, and Hinichi are the most doggish of the Pelted, with the Seersa being short and digitigrade and foxish, the Tam-illee taller, plantigrade and also foxish, and the Hinichi being wolflike.

Others: Less easily categorized are the Aera, with long, hare-like ears, winged feet and foxish faces, the felid Malarai with their feathered wings, and the Phoenix, tall bipedal avians.

The Centauroids: Of the Pelted, two species are centauroid in configuration, the short Glaseah, furred and with lower bodies like lions but coloration like skunks and leathery wings on their lower backs, and the tall Ciracaana, who have foxish faces but long-legged cat-like bodies.

Aquatics: One Pelted race was engineered for aquatic environments: the Naysha, who look like mermaids would if mermaids had sleek, hairless, slightly rodent-like faces and the lower bodies of dolphins.

OTHER SPECIES

Humanoids: Humanity fills this niche, along with their estranged cousins, the esper-race Eldritch.

True Aliens: Of the true aliens, six are known: the shapeshifting Chatcaava, whose natural form is draconic (though they are mammals); the gentle heavyworlder Faulfenza, who are furred and generally regarded to be attractive; the Akubi, large dinosaur-like fliers with three sexes; the aquatic Platies, who look like colorful flatworms and can communicate reliably only with the Naysha, and the enigmatic Flitzbe, who are quasi-vegetative and resemble softly furred volleyballs that change color depending on their mood. New to the Alliance (and not pictured in the line-up) is the last race, the "Octopi" of *Either Side of the Strand*.

For a more detailed look into the species of the Alliance, a Peltedverse Guidebook is available through me; you can get it by signing up for my mailing list (from my website), by jumping on my Patreon, or by emailing me directly (haikujaguar at gmail).

THE SPECIES AND RACES OF THE PARADOX PELTED UNIVERSE

PLATIES

NAYSHA
1 2 3 4 5 6 7 8 9

HEIGHT IN FEET
10 9 8 7 6 5 4 3 2 1

HUMAN
ELDRITCH
CHATCAAVA
AKUBI
PHOENIX
FAULFENZA
CIRACAANA
GLASEAH
MALARAI
HARAT-SHAR
HINICHI
TAM-ILLEE
AERA
KARAKA'A
SEERSA
FLITZBE

Author Sketches

It's typical for me to do sketches while writing, a sort of mental doodling as I work out events and character arcs. These sketches are not intended to be the final word on what the characters look like! In fact, I usually have trouble pinning down people's looks. I just keep at it anyway.

Jahir and Vasiht'h are among some of my oldest characters in this setting. My original drawings of them . . . I think they date back to the early '90s! Needless to say there's a lot of *bad* art of them, by my standards, because there's a lot of art of them in general. Here are some of my favorites that pertain to *Dreamhearth*, or Jahir and Vasiht'h's years on Veta.

1. **Vasiht'h on Starbase Veta:** One of my favorite sketches of Vasiht'h, trotting past a bakery on the commons. I am amused that I took the trouble to tuck a doll into the arms of the sketchy child in the very back.
2. **Vasiht'h Baking!:** I couldn't not eventually do a picture of Vasiht'h in the kitchen of their apartment on Veta, making cookies. (Right? Right!)

3. **The Girls:** My first take on what all the kids look like in varying stages of adolescence. Top row, left to right: Kayla and Amaranth (before she trimmed her hair in this novel); then a much older Persy and Kuriel; and finally Meekie at the bottom (with a ghostly take at Nieve on the left there).

4. **Kristyl and Gladdie:** One of my favorite parts of writing pastoral novels is how vivid the supporting cast becomes. I loved writing Kristyl and Gladdie, so of course I had to draw them!

5. **Reunited:** How old was my knowledge of the events of this story? Apparently old enough for me to have drawn this reunion picture in 2002 . . . (the publication date on the first edition of the novel is 2018, just for context . . .)

6. **Vasiht'h with Scarf:** I couldn't not include this holiday picture, or . . .

7. **The Tree:** . . . this one, again, because this novel finally includes the case study it was drawn for, "The Christmas Tree."

8. **The Veta Apartment Floorplan:** Repeated in this book for people who want to refer to it!

9. **Rexina Regina:** And finally, because she's mentioned several times in this novel . . . here in all its eye-punching glory is Rexina Regina's author portrait. *beams*

Kayla

Cole

Amaranth

oli

Daisy

Kuri

Merkie

GLADDE

KRISTYL

mcahogarth.org

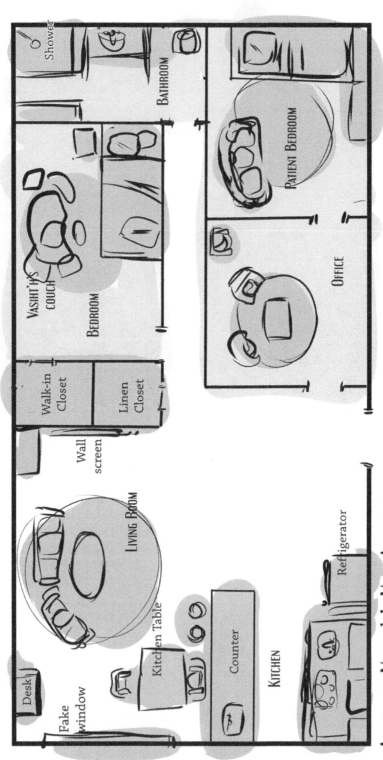

JAHIR AND VASIHT'H'S VETA APARTMENT
mcahogarth.org

ACKNOWLEDGMENTS

A S USUAL, BOOKS DON'T HAPPEN without a great deal of help. Here are my thank-yous this time around:

◆ **My copy-editors/first reader team:** Phil, Brooke, lunarennui, Lee, Ruth, Maigen, May, and Kelsey. You all are awesome. Many typos and adverbs were slain through your efforts, and many potential misunderstandings clarified. *bows*

◆ **Writerfriend L.Rowyn.** Who still listens to me whinge through every single manuscript I write. And who also checks my math. Particularly in regards to me finally quitting my day hobby. (Look, I listened!) (Also, read her books. They are awesome. I really, really love The Sun Etherium, but you can start with any of them and be happy. But if you like these books, you will love Sun Etherium particularly.)

◆ **Writerfriend Ursula Vernon,** with whom I can whinge about the painful realities of life as a full-time freelancer. Many sangrias have been drunk while we shake our heads sadly. (Look her up as author T. Kingfisher! I liked *Clockwork Boys,* start there!)

◈ **My Patreon subscribers,** particularly the ones who unlocked the Discord server chat and spend the day hanging out with me while I work. You're an amazing community. All the hearts.

◈ **And all my readers,** who keep my family fed and kept asking me for more Dreamhealers. This book concludes the five-book arc of their early life . . . I hope it brings you joy!

RETURN TO THE ALLIANCE

Dear Readers,

B Y NOW YOU'VE SEEN THIS section at least three other times, if you came into this series through the front door . . . and I hope you did, because by Book 4, you really need to know what happened in Books 1-3! And I also hope you're on your way to the final installment in the series, the novella Family, if you haven't already read it. Family is a "many years later" segment, and introduces characters and situations that are further developed in other series in the Peltedverse.

So let's shake this section up a little . . . with bullets! Here are your next stops, if you haven't already taken them:

◈ **The Her Instruments Series:** A four-book space opera adventure that starts with *Earthrise*. An irascible human merchant captain! A rescued Eldritch prince who turns out to be more things than he says he is! (You're so surprised!) Their furry crew, space pirates, slavers, and hijinks! We even get to see the Eldritch homeworld!

◆ **The Princes' Game Series:** A six-book series about the Chatcaa-van war, pitting an Eldritch ambassador against a court of draconic shapeshifters who are also torturers and sociopaths, and bringing in an enormous cast of Pelted and Eldritch characters . . . including some you already know, like Jahir and Vasiht'h. Note: many triggers! If you prefer not to engage with more difficult work, or like to go into it prepared by spoilers, a Reader's Guide is available via Patreon, the author's mailing list, or if you ask! Begins with novel *Even the Wingless.*

◆ **The Stardancer Series:** All done with Eldritch? You may want to move on to the Stardancer series, involving Alysha Forrest, captain of one of the Alliance's battlecruisers. Book 1, *Alysha's Fall,* is a dark prequel; you can check my website for keywords and warnings. But Book 2, *Second,* is more in keeping with the tone of the remainder of the series, which is sort of . . . original *Star Trek* meets furries in space.

◆ **Claws and Starships:** This is a standalone collection of shorts set in the Peltedverse, and contains one of my favorite novellas, *A Distant Sun* (sometimes titled *Broken Chains*), about a Pelted history teacher and the high schoolers he's educating about their origins.

If you have eaten the Peltedverse whole (so much chewing!), you might detour somewhere else in my backlist. I recommend trying my romance novels, which start with *Thief of Songs,* or visiting my aliens: the trigendered Jokka, with *The Worth of a Shell,* or the Ai-Naidar with *The Aphorisms of Kherishdar,* where conlangers will delight.

New books in the Peltedverse are coming! Patreon patrons get sneak peeks and frequent updates on those works-in-progress, or you can sign up for my newsletter to be alerted when new books are done and ready for purchase!

—M

About the Author

DAUGHTER OF TWO CUBAN political exiles, M.C.A. Hogarth was born a foreigner in the American melting pot and has had a fascination for the gaps in cultures and the bridges that span them ever since. She has been many things—web database architect, product manager, technical writer and massage therapist—but is currently a full-time parent, artist, writer and anthropologist to aliens, both human and otherwise. She is the author of over fifty titles in the genres of science fiction, fantasy, humor and romance.

The *Dreamhealers* series is only one of the many stories set in the Pelted universe; more information is available on the author's website. You can also sign up for the author's quarterly newsletter to be notified of new releases.

If you enjoyed this book, please consider leaving a review . . . or telling a friend! (Or both!)

mcahogarth.org
mcahogarth@patreon
mcahogarth@twitter